The Mists of Time

RUBICON

Linda Coleman

THE BOOKSMITH

The Booksmith
70 Derby Square
Douglas
Isle of Man
IM1 3LR
British Isles

ISBN: 978-1-909588-30-1

A CPI Catalogue for this title is available from the British Library

For James Purefoy.
My inspiration.

Prologue
January 49 B.C.

Julius Caesar stood on the banks of the river Rubicon, considering his options. He would soon have to make the most important decision of his life and he was, uncharacteristically, unsure what to do. As he walked along the banks, he said a silent prayer to the gods for guidance.

The Senate in Rome had given him an ultimatum: either he lay down his command of the province of Gaul and agree to return to Rome to answer the ridiculous charges made against him, or be declared an enemy of the state. If he chose the former it would mean the end of his career, but choosing the latter could lead to his death. It was an outrage. He was Caesar, tamer of all Gaul. The riches he had sent home to Rome had lined the Senate's pockets for years. He had given everything for them and in return they accused him of treachery. What more did he have to do to make them realise his worth and give him the reward he deserved? Ungrateful, pompous asses! His only defence would be to cross the Rubicon and force them to see reason. But were he to do this, he would effectively be declaring war on the Republic and unleashing his armies against his own people; how would history judge him for that action?

Some of Caesar's most trusted allies were in Rome lobbying on his behalf. One of them, the fearless Mark Antony, had been tasked with offering a compromise to the Senate's ultimatum. Caesar knew Antony's proposal would fall on deaf ears because the fools in the Senate had already made their decision and would not be swayed from it. His chances for a peaceful resolution were dwindling by the hour: the die had been cast and all he could do was wait to see how and where it would land.

As Caesar stared across the river, he noticed an unusual mist forming on the water. Hazy wisps danced in front of him, like ghostly fingers beckoning him forward. It felt as if the river was calling to him, telling him to seize his chance and march on. A part of him wanted to listen to the river's call, but his men had already done enough. To follow him any further would seal their fates as well as his. He could ask no more of them. He had to turn back and lay down his command. That was the logical option, but still the mist danced enticingly. It tempted him to believe he could succeed, if only he went forward.

Caesar closed his eyes and shook himself. He was being ridiculous; he did not believe in such omens. The river was not speaking to him; how could it be? He opened his eyes again searching for the mist, but it had vanished as quickly as it had first appeared. He wondered if it had all been in his imagination as he turned and strode back towards camp. Still, he had made his decision. He would not cross the Rubicon and start a war. To do so would be the act of a desperate and irrational man.

And if Mercury, winged herald of the gods, expected him to follow a different path, then he would have to send a more tangible messenger than a few wisps of tantalising mist.

Chapter 1
Present Day

Melissa Gordon possessed priceless pearls of wisdom that she shared with anyone who sought her advice: life is never fair; even when things appear to be going well they have a habit of turning bad; opportunities that look too good to be true usually turn out to be just that; and, finally, never trust anyone completely, because that is when they are most likely to stab you in the back! They were the only certainties in life as far as she was concerned, apart from dying, of course, but she had no intention of doing that just yet.

Melissa had not begun life as a pessimist. She had started out as every other young person had − looking forward to the future, optimistic about her prospects and believing she would do great things. That was all a long time ago. That was before she had met Anthony Marcus. And now, almost eight years later, here she was, sitting outside the Devonshire Arms waiting for him to show up.

She was angry with herself for ever agreeing to this meeting, but he had talked her into it. A chance to make up for the past was what he said. *Fat chance of that,* she thought as she sipped on her second glass of wine, all the while staring across the small village green that spread out in front of her. It was an unusually warm afternoon for late April and she had decided to sit outside to make the most of the sun. From her table close to the door she also had an excellent view of the green and the roads surrounding it, from the church in the far corner on her left to the village shop on the right hand side. She watched each car as it approached up the gently-sloping main road that separated the green from the shop, her anxiety rising and then falling as it passed on by. She did not want Anthony's arrival to come as a surprise to her. She wanted to see him coming. She needed to be prepared to meet him after all this time and to be in complete control, mainly to prevent her from slapping him round the face. This was her local and she had no intention of embarrassing herself on home ground. Maybe the wine was not such a good idea, but it was too late now. She tapped her nails on her teeth as her nerves began to get the better of her. *Maybe she should order a sandwich?*

The sound of a wooden chair being scraped across the flagstones to her left made her turn sharply to look in that direction, but it was only the old man she had watched a few minutes earlier crossing the green from the shop. Sitting down to enjoy a midday pint, he nodded to Melissa as he lit a cigarette and then settled back in his chair to read his newspaper.

Melissa glanced at her watch. Anthony was already over an hour late. *Fifteen more minutes,* she decided, *and then she would go.* Timekeeping had never been one of his strong points, but this was a new low even for him. It was not possible he had missed the place. It was the largest building on the green, except for the church. "I remember the one," he had said on the phone. "It's the grey building with the sandstone columns on either side of the door. I can't miss it."

As fewer cars came up the road, her concentration began to drift. She gazed at the tiny ferns that had seeded themselves into the cracks in the grey stone wall that marked the border of the pub garden. She became mesmerised by the delicacy of the ferns' fronds as they clung tightly to the stones beneath. While she was looking intently at the plants, the alcohol she had consumed began to numb her anxieties and her mind began to wander over the past.

Melissa had first met Anthony at university. They had both enrolled on the same archaeology course. She had paid him little attention to begin with. He was not really her type, or to be more precise, he was not the type of man who ever paid her any attention. Melissa had always tried hard not to be noticed; in fact, she was a loner. Her hair had been long and dark, lacking shape or definition, and had just hung around her face and shoulders, then down to her waist. Her best features were her large, dark-brown eyes, reminiscent of those of a deer, which were set into a pale, oval face. These she had kept hidden behind the most unattractive, thick-rimmed glasses imaginable. She was skinny, quiet and a deliberately dowdy dresser, usually wearing jeans and a jumper that was at least two sizes too big for her. She made every attempt to appear quite plain, all to hide the fact that she was painfully shy. What she lacked in looks, though, she more than made up for in brains. Blessed with a near-photographic memory, study came easily to her. Her books were the only friends she needed and, while others were out having fun, she would stick to the library reading anything and everything she could. She could speak three languages fluently in addition to her native English, and had an outstanding knowledge of Latin, which was particularly advantageous for her chosen career. Melissa was easily the top student in every class and great things were expected of her academically.

Anthony, on the other hand, excelled at getting noticed. He was not the tallest man, but his good looks more than made up for it, with his olive skin, dark hair and deep, dark-brown, nearly black, eyes. He enjoyed many sports, which meant he was very fit. In fact, he worked very hard to keep his muscular physique perfectly toned: apparently it went down well with 'the ladies'. Loud, brash and opinionated, he was always at the centre of whatever was going on and that usually meant trouble. He was not the student with the best results, but that was more to do with a lack of application than a lack of intelligence.

Anthony's Achilles heel was that he loved life: he was the first to buy a round at the bar even when strapped for cash and was always the last to leave it, often only with help from friends. When it came to women, he had the ambition to love every attractive one he met, as frequently as he could. More often than not, every last one of them loved him back for as long as they could hold his interest. It was more than just looks or physique that attracted so many people to him; it was his charm, his charisma, his confidence – just about everything, in fact. People swarmed round him like bees to honey. Whatever 'it' was that he had, he had 'it' in spades and the few who were not in the Anthony Marcus fan club were those who were either jealous of his popularity, or those who were so ordinary that they escaped the notice of most people – people just like Melissa.

And yet Anthony had noticed her, though admittedly not at first. It had all started as a bet. He had been getting drunk with friends one evening near the end of the first semester and the conversation had got round to the girls on their courses. Anthony had boasted that he could sleep with any one of them – just give him a name. Half the girls on campus were vying for his attentions, including those in his classes. Given that he had never failed to get any girl he wanted, he was fairly certain of his success. What he had failed to imagine was that anyone would have suggested Melissa. He had not even realised there was a girl called Melissa on his course, but he agreed anyway. In the cold, hard, light of day recognition dawned on him: it had to be the plain, geeky girl who was always getting top grades, but whom no one actually knew. At first, the mere thought of spending any time with her appalled him: he was the campus stud, she the queen nerd. They could not be more different, but a bet was a bet and Anthony had no intention of losing!

Finding out anything about Melissa from others was impossible. She was never seen in any of the usual hangouts and, as hard as he tried, he found no one who could call themselves her friend. She ignored him in the corridors and positively avoided him on field trips. Anthony was used to getting anything and anyone he wanted with little effort, but the more he tried to impress Melissa, the more she seemed indifferent to him, which both intrigued and annoyed him. This girl was not like the others: she was a challenge and he was always up for one of those. He became obsessed with the idea of taking this aloof girl down a peg or two. He needed to know what made her tick and get under her skin sufficiently to make her give in to him. One thing he did learn quickly was that they both shared the same vicious temper and could be provoked quite easily. This was the only emotion Melissa seemed willing to display in public.

Anthony knew Melissa always arrived at lectures early to sit at the front in the same seat, so he began arriving earlier to sit in the seat she favoured, forcing her to sit by his side. He tried to engage her in his favourite topics of conversation, but that failed dismally as she seemed to have no opinions on TV, sport, music or alcohol. She never laughed at his jokes, but he continued to crack them anyway. He started to follow her to the library whenever she was heading there, realising this was his way inside her head. He asked her advice on the best books to read and persuaded her to proofread his assignments. He made sure that he was in the library whenever she went there, usually every day.

It took months for him to get to her, but his dogged determination won through in the end and Melissa began to warm to his advances. She began to sit with him in the cafeteria for lunch and slowly he persuaded her to tell him about her life outside the university. They found they had a lot more in common than they had ever realised. It turned out they were both orphans. Melissa's parents had died in a car accident when she was seven and she had moved from the city to Long Sutton to be raised by her only living relative – her grandmother. Anthony had no memory of his real parents; his mother had died giving birth to him and he had never known who his father was. He was raised by his godfather, when he was four moving from the city to the Italian countryside, where his godfather had taken a job working on the estate of a widow. He vaguely remembered an aunt he had adored, but she disappeared from his life at around the same time that he and his godfather had moved. Anthony did not know what had happened to her, or why she had lost touch. Anthony and Melissa had reacted differently to the losses they had suffered and, whereas Anthony had rebelled and set about getting into as much trouble as he could, Melissa had become withdrawn and shy. They were as much the same as they were total opposites.

Melissa brought him back home to meet her grandmother at the end of their first year. He was only supposed to stay for a week before returning to Italy, but he fell in love with the Somerset countryside and stayed all summer. He was a different person away from university and Melissa had been surprised at how loving and patient he could be. They spent hours walking through the countryside and Melissa showed him all her favourite places and hideaways. He just seemed happy for them to be together and it was this new, relaxed Anthony that she allowed to make love to her in the fields beyond her house. After eight months Anthony had won his bet, but he could not have cared less. He was crazy about Melissa and nothing else mattered to him.

When they returned to university they rented a tiny flat where they remained for the next two years. To begin with, Melissa was unsure how long their relationship would last, fearing that Anthony would go back to his old ways, and to some extent he had. He would still go out with his friends and get drunk far more often than she liked, but the womanising stopped. He only had eyes for Melissa.

Anthony's grades were improving under Melissa's tutelage and she blossomed from his constant attentions. She cut her hair, acquired some more flattering glasses and even started to wear fashionable clothes, most of which she allowed him to choose. He introduced her to rock music, movies and cult TV shows. He even got her to attend a couple of football matches though, in all honesty, she would have preferred not to have gone. Her fears melted away and, over time, she let him in completely. He knew everything about her, what made her laugh or cry, how to make her angry and especially how to persuade her to forgive him after a row. Anthony, on the other hand, always remained a little guarded and she knew there were many secrets in his past he was not prepared to share. That hurt her to begin with, but she chose to ignore it. She had fallen completely and desperately in love with him, though she would never admit it to anyone but herself.

They both graduated with honours and continued on to the Master's course, specialising in the Classics. Things started to go wrong when one of their tutors died suddenly, just before the course commenced. He was replaced by Dr Victor Reyes, an unpleasant man in his late fifties, who had spent far too many years in northern Italy for Melissa's liking. His English was a little hard to follow at times, but his Latin and Ancient Greek were both perfect, as was his knowledge of all things relating to Rome and her Empire. In fact, he was the only person in the entire university whose Latin was better than Melissa's.

Melissa did not like the replacement in the slightest. He constantly picked holes in her work, which was a new experience for her, and put her firmly in the spotlight for all the wrong reasons. She became the butt of many jokes from her group. Over time, she found the attention difficult to cope with, and began to withdraw into herself once again. Initially, Anthony did his best to keep her going, but over time even he seemed not to notice, or to care, that she was slipping back into insignificance. He and *"Victor"* got on amazingly well. They both came from the same region of Italy and seemed to have a lot in common. Anthony could not understand what there was not to like. Yes, he would say, Victor was a hard taskmaster, but surely the subject was supposed to become more difficult, the further you progressed?

Dr Reyes lavished as much praise on Anthony as he did criticism on Melissa. He was always available to answer any of Anthony's questions and the two of them often stayed late after lectures, discussing topics that interested them both. Victor Reyes was opening Anthony's eyes to the possibilities of the future he could have, but seemed determined to make sure Melissa would play no part in it. Anthony looked up to Victor and hung on his every word. Once again Anthony was excelling at everything and this time he was leaving Melissa behind. If she made any comments about Victor, it would start a row. She was accused of not wanting Anthony to do well, and of trying to hold him back. He even told her that she just could not cope with him being better than her at something. The old Anthony was resurfacing and she was fading from his view.

And that was when he did it! He stabbed her in the back! Anthony took a piece of her work and plagiarised it to such an extent that it was easily recognisable as a copy. He simply put his assignment in first and she was the one accused of cheating. The affair coincided with her grandmother's death, and having to deal with the two events together nearly destroyed her. She could not believe that the man who meant so much to her could be so heartless. She fell apart and dropped out of the course. She never achieved her Master's degree, but, worse still, her world was in tatters and the little confidence she had gained vanished once again.

Anthony went on to his doctorate and joined Victor on a dig in Italy, where they uncovered an immense hoard of coins and jewellery from the time of Caesar. His charm and personality made him an instant success with the media and he became an overnight celebrity. He was so sought after for lectures and TV appearances that he became the rock-star equivalent of the archaeological world. No archaeologist had been so well-known since Howard Carter had discovered Tutankhamun's tomb, and job offers came by the bucket load. Working with Dr Marcus became the dream of many students and the honour of a select few, mostly attractive women who usually threw themselves at him. There had been rumours that he was willing to indulge more than their thirst for academic knowledge, but nothing had ever been proved. The old Anthony was fully resurgent, and getting quite a reputation.

Melissa, meanwhile, had no glittering success: her brilliant future was nothing more than a distant memory and she spent her life on minor digs or in junior positions. One even more disastrous relationship later, she now lived alone in the same house in which she had grown up. Deeply in debt, she worked in a local museum by day, and taught evening classes at an adult education college. The only positive thing she had done was to have laser eye surgery so she no longer needed her glasses. A great achievement indeed! Was she bitter and resentful? Probably, no, make that definitely. Did she hate Anthony? No. As much as she wanted to, she just could not bring herself to do so. He had hurt her badly and she was still mad at him for that, but even the years that had passed had not stopped her caring for him. Could she ever believe him again? Probably not! *So why was she even waiting for him?*

Melissa looked at her watch. Another fifty minutes had gone by and still no sign of him. She was annoyed at herself for not having left already. She downed the rest of her wine and bent under the table to retrieve her handbag. As she did so a familiar voice said, "I bought you another – I hope Pinot Grigio is OK?"

Melissa rose with a start and hit her head hard on the corner of the table on the way up. "Shit!" she exclaimed, closing her eyes as she winced. Her hand went instinctively to the source of the pain, only to find another hand already there. She took a deep breath and opened her eyes to look up at the man standing next to her. It was the first time she had seen Anthony up close in years, and his proximity made her resolve to be strong begin to crumble. He was older, yes, but he had hardly changed. He had the slightest hint of grey beginning at his temples and was well-tanned, emphasising the lines around his eyes that a life spent outdoors was causing to develop. These suited him and seemed to give him a certain gravitas, suitable for a man of his authority.

His hand moved tenderly through her hair and Melissa involuntarily closed her eyes again, this time at the softness of his touch. Memories of being with Anthony flooded back. Thoughts of what it felt like to be held by him overwhelmed her and she inadvertently turned her head towards his hand, desperate to make the moment last. He let out a half-laugh, half-sigh, obviously pleased with the reaction he had engendered. Annoyed with herself, she drew back from his hand, which had now removed a small splinter of wood that had lodged itself in her head. As he moved round the table to sit opposite her, his face transformed into one of his trademark, disarming smiles.

"No serious damage," he said, as he lowered himself onto the bench opposite. "I can't afford for you to put a dent in your most valuable asset. You're far too important to me for that."

She could not say whether it was his mildly patronising tone or her annoyance at herself for her moment of weakness that sparked the reaction, but the alcohol she had consumed with the intention of calming her down now had the opposite effect. Before she even consciously realised what she was doing she had extended her arm and slapped him hard across the cheek. The barman, who had been clearing the table vacated by the old man, looked across at them, but continued with his work half-watching the scene unfold. A woman walking her dog outside the pub stopped and stared at them. Anthony smiled and waved at the woman whilst rubbing his cheek, which was still stinging.

"Nice to see you too, Liss," he added in a low voice looking at her from the corner of his eye, still facing the woman with the dog, who seemed unsure whether to continue or wait to see what would happen next. Anthony had never called Melissa by her full name. It used to annoy her when they first met, and he knew it: this was a tactic to see if she would react again, but this time she did not rise to the bait. "Lovely day," he called out to the woman with the dog, who nodded in response and turned and walked on.

Once the woman had crossed the green and was out of earshot, Anthony turned back to Melissa. "That was a little harsh, wasn't it?" he said, in his most disarming tone. "I mean, I come all this way to see you and this is what I get!" His eyes seemed to be pleading with her for forgiveness, but his voice had a lack of sincerity that only annoyed her more. "Let's try that again, shall we?" he continued.

Melissa snapped. She picked up the wine glass from the table and threw its contents in his face. "Bastard!" she hissed at him, with a vehemence that betrayed her pent-up anger. She stood, her hands firmly planted on the table, and leaned across to him, her face only inches from his. "Two bloody hours waiting for you and your patronising crap! Why don't you crawl back into your latest twenty-something and treat her like a child, not me. I'm sure she'll get hours of fun from the role-play!" Her eyes flashed with rage.

Anthony still knew exactly how to press her buttons, and took a guess at what she would do next. He knew she would leave rather than show any emotion beyond the rage so prominently on display, and he needed her to stay. He knew there were years of stored-up anger to be vented, and that he deserved everything she had to throw at him. He had to make her let go of the pain so they could move on: too much was riding on the outcome of this meeting for him to let her leave.

The barman had crossed to their table "Towel?" he offered Anthony, in a hesitant tone, obviously unsure whether to get involved or to steer well clear of the situation.

"Thanks, but we're fine," Anthony replied. His eyes had not left Melissa's until that moment, but he now turned to the barman and rose from his seat, sighing as he did so. "This is totally my fault. I should have been on time." The disarming tone and smile were back. He stepped away from the table, placing his hand on the man's shoulder and began steering him back to the door of the bar. "I can easily change, but I really need to make amends before ..."

Anthony was gesturing in Melissa's direction, but she was no longer listening. She had grabbed her bag and was extricating herself from her chair. There was no point in being here. Anthony obviously got some kind of enjoyment out of making a fool out of her and she had no intention of staying around for more. She turned around far too quickly for a woman who had just consumed two large wines and no food, and immediately regretted it. The wall, road and village green before her began to blur into one single image and she felt giddy. She reached out to steady herself on the table, but missed as it moved in her view. She stumbled forwards and steeled herself for the fall she knew was coming, but was unable to prevent.

Yet, instead of the feeling of hard flagstones hitting her knees, all she felt was warmth around her waist and then that same warmth spreading up her back, down her right arm and enveloping her hand. Somehow Anthony had grabbed her as she fell. He had pulled her towards him, using his body to steady hers and was now holding her against him to stop her swaying. His right hand stroked hers comfortingly as he whispered, "You OK? You haven't hurt yourself?"

Melissa turned her head to look at him, leaning away slightly. His face was full of concern. She thought it was the first genuine emotion he had displayed since his arrival, but then her vision started to blur again and she was unsure if she had imagined it. She took a deep breath, mustering as much composure as she could manage. She looked roughly at where she thought his eyes would be if they were not moving so, and said in the most serene tone she could manage, "I … am fine … thank you … but I am going ... to leave now." She pulled away from him, but misplaced her footing and promptly fell again. Anthony pulled her back to him, and this time held her firmly. He slowly lowered her back into the chair, crouching in front of her and looked up at her face. *How much has she had?* he wondered, *I won't get any sense out of her like this!*

"Time to go!" Anthony said, decidedly. He rose again, lifting Melissa with one arm. He picked up her bag and half-steered, half-carried her to his car parked just along the green. She made a weak effort at protest, which Anthony ignored. The world was now reeling at such a phenomenal rate that she made no further objections. Guiding her into the passenger seat, he fastened her seat belt for her and closed the door, shaking his head as he walked around to the other side of the car.

Chapter 2

An hour and a whole pot of coffee later, Melissa and Anthony sat staring at anything except each other in the living room of her home. Anthony was noticing how tired the cottage was looking. It was exactly as he remembered, right down to the garish, flowery wallpaper in the living room, though it had not been so faded or peeling from the walls when he had last been there some eight years earlier. The paint on the door and the window surrounds was yellowing and needed refreshing.

He moved uncomfortably in his chair next to the fireplace. It sagged under his weight and creaked noisily as he shifted in it, making him suspect that he would fall through if he moved much more. His mind wandered back to the hall where he had noticed that the stair carpet was ripped and threadbare on the treads. It was a wonder Melissa had managed to avoid tripping on it and breaking her neck. It was as if she had allowed her interest in the house to die along with her grandmother; it was clean, but uncared for.

Melissa, meanwhile, was pressing a cold flannel to the lump on her forehead. She had hit it a lot harder than either of them had realised, but it had taken some time and sobriety to show through. Feeling sheepish and embarrassed by her earlier behaviour, small talk had run out some time before and she was beginning to wonder if Anthony was ever going to tell her why he contacted her after all these years. They were sitting silently and the afternoon was slowly ticking away. Although she was in no particular hurry to start the next round of the fight between them, evening was approaching and she wanted him to get on with it.

She knew she would have to take the initiative. "You said on the phone you had an offer for me?" she asked.

Anthony looked concerned as he replied. "Yes, but I don't know if now's the right time to discuss it, really. You should probably be resting. Perhaps I could stay over and ..."

"You won't get another chance," she cut him off coldly, appalled at the thought that he was angling for an invite to stay the night. "It's now or never, up to you." She put the wet flannel down on the coffee table and turned her full attention to him.

Anthony ran his hand over his chin. He was obviously thinking about where to start. He leant forward in the chair, resting his arms on his knees. He took a deep breath and began to explain his reason for coming. "I'm going on a dig this summer. It's going to be the last one for a while, maybe for good. I haven't made up my mind yet."

"Why's that?" Melissa asked purely to keep the conversation going. What he did, or why, was of no concern to her.

"I've just had enough. Need a break, bit of a change of pace."

"Really? That doesn't sound like you." Melissa tried, but failed to hide the sarcastic tone she had employed.

"People change, Liss. I've changed." Antony appeared sincere. He sighed and sat back in the chair and immediately regretted it as another spring prodded him painfully in the backside.

"So what do you want from me – a pat on the back?" she replied, with a little less sarcasm.

"No, I want you to join me on this dig. It's not going to be easy and I could really use the best minds I know on this. It'll be hard work and it could be a long slog, but I know you're not afraid of that."

Melissa laughed. "Sorry, but that sounded like you were offering me a job!"

"I am. I want you to be one of my Field Supervisors." Anthony rose from the chair and walked over to the window, staring out of it with his back towards her. "Do you remember how we used to joke that one day we were going to make the biggest discovery of the century? Well, I might just be about to do it and I want you to be a part of it. I know the location of one of Caesar's encampments. It's just north of the Rubicon. I intend to start excavations as soon as I get back and I want you to join me as soon as your commitments to your students are fulfilled for this year."

Melissa was not laughing anymore. She was sitting with her mouth open, staring at Anthony's back. He had not looked at her once since he had moved to the window and she had no idea whether he was being serious or not. She was completely thrown by everything he had just said. Her options began to whirl uncontrollably in her mind. This was a great opportunity for her. In one way it was the chance of a lifetime that she could never hope to achieve with her qualifications, but it was coming from a man who had used her to further his own career. There had to be a catch. She had to say no. It was the right thing to do, but, if she did, she would be stuck in her mundane little life forever. Of course, if she said yes, then she would probably end up abandoned somewhere in Italy, with no way home. And how could he be so certain of the location? No one was even sure where the Rubicon was.

Melissa's total silence was unnerving. "I'm guessing that's a no then?" Anthony finally said, sighing as he turned to look at her.

"What?" Anthony's question jolted Melissa into making a response. "Yes! I mean no! I mean, oh God what am I saying. I mean why? Why me? Why now? After all this time ..." her words faded as she finished the sentence.

"I'm not proud of all the things I've done, especially not to you." Anthony was being sincere. "When you first left me I hardly even noticed you were gone. My life was like a roller coaster after I hooked up with Victor, and I just didn't have time to think about it. I was doing so well. Money and opportunities ..."

"And girls," Melissa interjected.

"AND girls ..."Anthony nodded in agreement, "... came at me from every direction. It was like being a kid in a candy store. I had everything I could ever want, provided I was prepared to take the chances as they came up. And, believe me, they just kept coming. Victor made sure of that."

"And how is Victor? Well, I hope." Melissa made no attempt to hide the sarcasm this time. The mention of Victor's name twice in quick succession made her feel sick. If she hated anyone, it was him. He had taken everything from her a piece at a time, starting with her grades and ending with the man she loved. He was truly the one to blame for ruining her life, not Anthony.

"Victor's dying. He has bowel cancer. They've done all they can, but it's spreading to his other organs and now it's just a matter of time." Anthony stared at Melissa as if he was waiting for some form of acknowledgement of the statement he had just made. None came. Her initial thought was, *Good! He deserves it,* but she was not so heartless and she felt a pang of guilt. No one deserved to suffer like that, no matter what they had done. Melissa did not dare to react visibly either way to Anthony's statement. She simply stared back at him without displaying any emotion whatsoever.

He went on. "We found out three years ago. The treatment slowed him down for a while, but all the time he'd be planning what we'd be doing next. I've never known a man do so much research from a bed! He found the site I'm talking about. He found the Rubicon and then he tracked the location of the encampment. We start digging next month."

"So this is all for Victor, then?" Melissa still had no idea why her involvement was so important, but other pieces of the puzzle were starting to fall into place.

"In a way, yes, it is for Victor. It's lucky I already own the land because I knew we would have to do this over a long time, as and when he's up to working. Being good friends with the local authorities has made it easier to get the permissions I need to dig. I have negotiated a six-month permit so there are no pressing time constraints for this season. That's where this started, but now it's about you, too. Victor made some wrong choices in the past and he needs to put things right before it's too late."

Melissa shook her head in disbelief. "If you expect me to believe that Victor's dying wish is to give me a chance then you truly are an idiot. That man hates me!"

"That man is my godfather and I will do whatever it takes to help put his mind at rest!"

Anthony's words fell like a stone. Melissa felt a sinking feeling in her stomach as the full import of the words hit her. This explained so much of the past. The tell-tale signs had always been there, if she had only paid more attention. Anthony had been Victor's favourite from day one. She had always thought Victor was a lonely and bitter man who hated women, and that was how Anthony had described his godfather. Melissa assumed that Victor had never forgiven Anthony's aunt for leaving when Anthony was so small. He must have seen Melissa as a threat to the bond he had formed with his godson, and feared she would drive a wedge between them. He should have declared his relationship to a student when he was their tutor to ensure transparency, but that would obviously have interfered with his plans to help Anthony as much as he could.

"You never told me," Melissa spoke in a near-whisper as she digested his words.

"Victor wouldn't let me. He said you were too honest, you'd tell someone and he'd get in trouble for not having been open about his relationship to me."

"He'd have been right." Her words were tinged with the bitterness she felt.

"I couldn't take that chance. He's all the family I've ever had. You of all people know what that's like."

Melissa thought about her grandmother and how she had felt when she was dying. She remembered the pain that she had experienced after the old lady had passed away and the emptiness that had been left in her when the grief had finally subsided. She could not answer and simply nodded.

Anthony's gaze returned to the window. "He gave everything he had to give me a chance, Liss. He gave up so much to get me to university because he wanted a good future for me and I nearly pissed it all away. Then I met you and you got me back on track. But you know me. I never do anything by halves – all or nothing, me! The year we graduated, I told him I didn't care about a big career. I only enrolled on that Master's course to be with you. I was going to ask you to marry me."

Melissa grabbed the arm of her chair and gasped in shock. She put her other hand over her mouth to stop any further sounds escaping. She could not afford to interrupt him, not now. She had to hear what he was going to say next.

Anthony's hand had gone into his trouser pocket. He pulled out a small box. "I even bought you a ring." He was looking at the box, turning it over and over in his hands. "It's not much, I didn't have a lot to spend back then, but I knew you'd like it." He turned briefly, long enough to throw the box to her and then resumed staring out the window. He took a long, slow breath in before speaking again. "Victor told me we were too young to make such a rash decision. He said we should finish our education first because we had plenty of time for weddings later. I didn't know he was coming to be our lecturer at that point. I didn't know he'd hate you so much and I promise you I didn't know he stole your paper."

Melissa was still staring at the box she held in her trembling hands. It was well-worn, and she could imagine Anthony had spent many days over the years turning it over as he had done at the window. She found she could not bring herself to open it. Shock had overtaken every other emotion she had been feeling and she feared that the sight of an engagement ring she had never been given would mean a total loss of her faltering control. She could not move or speak. She shut her eyes tightly and felt the first tear fall onto her wrist. His last words had barely registered.

"I found out a year ago, when Victor finally had to give up his home and move in with me. I was clearing his house and ended up searching through some old boxes of junk he'd kept. I found copies of some of my old work. I suppose I got a bit nostalgic and so I kept digging through the box. I found some of your papers. I thought it was odd that he'd kept them and so I kept looking. I found tons of your stuff all with marker pen over it. Then I found more copies of my work that had been altered to include bits of yours. It got worse the more I looked. Then I found that final paper – the one we broke up over. He'd copied almost all of it into mine and changed the submission dates. I swear to you, I didn't know. I would never have done that to you – I loved you."

Melissa was still trying to fight back the tears which were now falling from rage, not pain. Her grip had tightened on the box in her hands so much that she could feel the corners digging into her palm. She was shaking too, torn between wanting

Anthony to stop and needing to hear it all. She looked up at his back. He had just delivered the two biggest bombshells in her life and still he was not looking at her. She was incensed.

"He ... did ... what?" The pitch of her voice rose with every word. She was fighting to hold back the torrent of abuse she wanted to throw at the man standing in front of her. Whether he knew what had happened in the past or not, he was the only one she could vent her anger on. "LOOK AT ME!" She shouted her demand at Anthony's back. After a moment he complied, his face full of shame.

"HOW DARE YOU COME HERE AND TELL ME YOU LOVED ME!" Melissa was still shouting. She rose to her feet, pausing long enough to slam the ring box on the table. "You knew Victor shouldn't be there without admitting to your relationship. You knew it was wrong. You could have stopped him any time you liked, but you chose not to. You and Victor used me to get you through that damned course. It's my work that made you famous. My work made you rich. And what did I get? A few years of lies and platitudes oh, and of course let's not forget the sex. I get to tell everyone I know about how I had the great Anthony Marcus! Well, lucky me!"

"Liss, you're being irrational," Anthony was trying to keep his temper, but her high- pitched ranting was grating on his nerves.

"Don't call me that. You no longer have the right to call me that." Melissa was bordering on hysteria. "Why are you really here, Anthony? Did Victor get such a kick out of destroying me last time that you thought another go might cheer him up? Send him off with something to remember? Or is it that you fancied a look at just how sad and uneventful your life would have been if you hadn't traded it in for mine? You come here making out that you are just as much a victim as I am, well, you can forget it. I have no sympathy for you whatsoever. I can't believe you would stoop so low."

Anthony tried again. "Liss, I ..." Melissa raised an eyebrow in contempt at his continued familiarity, making him pause. He began a second time "Melissa, if you would just calm down long enough for me to explain everything, you might find it easier to understand."

"Oh, there's more, is there? Oh, how lovely!" Melissa had walked to the door. She wrenched it open with such a force Anthony knew instantly that she had hurt herself. She stared at the opening, no longer wanting to look at him. Her voice went oddly calm and quiet. The change was quite frightening.

"I couldn't give a shit about what you have to say. I want you out of my house. Now!" She finally looked back across the room to where he stood. Anthony hesitated, preparing to stand his ground.

"OUT" she shouted, pointing at the opening until Anthony crossed the room to where she stood. He paused in front of her as if he intended to speak, then thought better of it and left. Melissa slammed the door behind him, shaking the pictures that hung on the wall. She leant against the door, sliding down it until she was sitting on the floor and finally gave into the tears that now fell in a flood from her eyes.

As soon as Anthony left the room, he knew he could not leave. For a start, his car keys were on the coffee table, but, more importantly, he had so far failed to achieve his objective of persuading Melissa to join him in Italy, and he was staying until he succeeded. He moved closer to the door, listening for any sounds from within. Hearing her crying made him angry with himself and he slammed his hand against the wall to release some of the tension he was feeling. His palm stung from the impact, but it took his mind off Melissa, briefly. What he wanted to do was to storm back into the room to comfort her, but he knew that any attempt to do so would probably result in the ornaments on the mantelpiece flying at his head. Experience told him he had to withdraw, allowing her to make the next move. He turned and headed for the kitchen. The evening was drawing in and he had not eaten since breakfast. He was pretty sure Melissa had not either. Logic dictated that where honesty had failed to have the desired impact, food might just get him a reprieve.

Anthony went straight to the fridge. He was pleased with what he found; plenty of fresh vegetables and salad. A quick rummage in the cupboards located dried pasta and a good selection of herbs and spices. Dinner would be basic, but quick – exactly the kind of meal they used to eat at university.

Anthony had always loved to cook for Melissa. She had never been good at looking after herself, and he had enjoyed coming up with new culinary delights to tempt her palate on their ever-precarious finances. Cooking had never been one of Victor's strengths and Anthony had learnt at an early age that, if he wanted to eat anything good, he would have to make it himself. As his career had taken off, he found he had less time to spend in the kitchen and his eating habits had gone downhill. That was only one of the standards that had slipped over the years.

His interest in archaeology had been sparked when he was nine: some Roman coins were found on their farmland and he had been fascinated that something so old and valuable had been left in the ground. He was hooked, and spent every spare minute looking for other potential finds around the farm. Despite rebelling at his English boarding school, he knuckled down to work for just long enough to achieve the grades he needed to get onto a degree course. He had been determined to obtain that degree, but had never thought he would achieve a first until he hooked up with Melissa. He was more than capable academically, but lacked the drive necessary to excel. She had given him his focus and he knew he had her to thank for the life he now had.

Being famous had opened up an entirely new world for Anthony, one that he had never dreamed possible. It had all come so fast that he struggled to keep control. It was like being on a never-ending roller coaster that had no brakes: he was offered book deals, TV and radio appearances and lecture tours at an alarming rate. It was demanding work and he spent months on end living out of a suitcase, but he loved every minute of it.

Being permanently on the move made lasting relationships difficult. Anthony had never had any difficulty getting women, but having a long-term relationship with one became almost impossible. Actresses, pop stars, and at least one heiress, threw themselves at him with such frequency that the choices became too hard to make. Even after he took a steady job at an Italian university, he continued to play the field. He enjoyed the attentions of the press and the number of beautiful women available to him only fed his desire to maintain his playboy status, despite the fact that his lifestyle was frowned upon by his colleagues in the academic world.

Anthony became obsessed with sex. The more he got, the more he craved and soon he needed to extend his gaze. His students proved the easiest target. He never ceased to be amazed at the levels of depravity to which some would stoop for the chance of a better grade. Had he been found out, he would have lost his position, but amazingly none of them ever said a word. He began to think he was untouchable.

That had all changed four years ago when a three-in-a-bed romp involving a pair of twenty-six year olds he had picked up in a bar in London made the English tabloids. It had earned him the nickname *Sindiana Jones*. There had been no point in denying the allegations: the pictures they printed made it quite clear it was him. He was lucky that these girls had not been younger, or students, or his career would have been finished rather than severely tarnished.

Victor had gone berserk at the revelations; he ordered Anthony to sort himself out and forced him to see a therapist for sex addiction. It took many months, but eventually Anthony came to realise that he used sex as a way to avoid confronting his inability to form lasting relationships. He had only ever loved two women in his entire life and both of them had, in his mind, deserted him. He needed to confront his demons. He could not resolve the issues with his aunt, as Victor would not give him any firm details about her, but he could try to work things through with Melissa.

He had had to put his plans on hold when Victor was diagnosed with bowel cancer. Victor was the only family Anthony had, and he chose to step back from the limelight to help his godfather through the treatment. It was humbling to watch a once great man reduced to a shadow of his former self. Victor had always been strong, never needing help from anyone for anything, but the combination of operations, chemotherapy and radiotherapy ravaged his body, leaving him frail. All through this experience Anthony had been there to help Victor cope with the simple daily tasks that could not be managed alone. Whenever life became too much to cope with, Anthony would find himself thinking about Melissa and how much he missed just talking to her. She had been the sensible one in their relationship, always knowing what to do when problems arose and never judging him for his stupidity. The more he reflected on their time together, the more he understood that she had never deserted him – he had been the one who had let her down. Worse still, he realised he was still desperately in love with her and he had to know if there was any chance to get her back.

And now he was here making dinner in her kitchen. She was so near and yet still out of reach. Being so close to her had not been easy for him. It had been nearly a year since he had last been with a woman, and he had paid for both her services and silence. Just having Melissa's body touching his when he stopped her falling had excited him, and his mind was now racing with thoughts of how much he wanted to feel her naked flesh pressing against him once more. He knew he could have forced himself on her as soon as they were in the house. She was far too inebriated to have resisted him, but, despite his many failings, Anthony could never bring himself to force any woman to sleep with him, let alone the one with whom he wanted to spend the rest of his life. He had to be patient and work his way slowly back into her confidence. He had done it once, and he could do it again.

His thoughts were interrupted by the sound of the living room door opening. Anthony stopped preparing the salad and took a couple of deep breaths, gaining control of his feelings and pushing them to the back of his mind. He resumed his dinner preparations as Melissa entered the kitchen.

"Dinner will be about ten minutes," he called over his shoulder as casually as he could manage. "Nothing too special, I admit. It's just the usual pasta, a fresh sauce and some salad. Hope that's OK with you?"

"I told you to go," Melissa replied, her voice cold.

"Couldn't," he replied, "I left my car keys in the lounge." He glanced over his shoulder at her. She looked terrible, with her face flushed and her eyes red and swollen from crying. The urge to take her in his arms was almost too much to bear. He resumed slicing the cucumber to distract his mind. "If you wouldn't mind giving me a hand, you could lay the table while I finish this salad."

They ate in near-silence. Melissa had not realised just how hungry she was. The last meal she had eaten was breakfast, since Anthony had not made it in time for their planned lunch. He was still an excellent cook who could make something out of next to nothing and she was grateful to him for having gone to the effort, though loath to admit it. She knew that he had other plans apart from just making dinner. He still wanted her to go on this blasted dig and she knew he was unlikely to give up too easily. *Best get it over with*, she decided.

She made more coffee and they returned to the living room, taking up positions on either end of the tired old sofa. It proved to be only marginally more comfortable than the chair that Anthony had avoided when he re-entered the room

"So, tell me more about this dig, then," she said. She tried to sound as disinterested as possible, but annoyingly, she was curious at his offer. It was why she had waited at the pub for so long, after all.

"I knew you'd come round. My cooking has never failed to work its magic yet." Anthony was grinning as he spoke. "Victor's been doing tons of research since he was diagnosed. The chemo made him so sick that for days he just lay in bed, but then he'd get a bit of life back and feel bored being stuck in the house all day waiting for the next lot of treatment. So, he spent hours with books and I finally introduced him to the internet. Can you believe he still thinks computers are evil?" He paused as he waited for a response, but Melissa merely looked at him with indifference. "Anyhow it's taken years of hard work, but he's found the Rubicon and the location of the camp."

"How can you be so sure?" Melissa's question was not unreasonable: scholars struggled to pinpoint the river to more than a rough area between the modern-day towns of Ravenna and Rimini, and to have located a temporary structure on the banks of an elusive river about which so little was known was beyond the realms of belief.

"He does know what he's doing." Anthony was blunt, almost rude in his retort. Melissa smiled to herself. He had no idea whether it was true or not. Victor had said jump and he had dutifully obeyed. It appeared that some things never changed.

After a moment's reflection, Melissa re-entered the debate. "OK. Let's assume Victor's right. Let's assume you have the river and camp locations. Why do you think there is anything there worth finding?"

"Caesar was there for months with the Thirteenth legion. That's five thousand men, give or take. There'll be tons of stuff in the rubbish pits alone."

"OK. So we strike lucky and find some broken pots, maybe some damaged armour or livery from the horses. What's so amazing that I should give up my jobs?"

Anthony was grinning again. "You don't need to give them up. That's why I was so late. I've taken the liberty of making some financial arrangements with both the curator at the museum and your college principal. Both will grant you extended sabbaticals in return for a donation and me doing some talks for them. I will be in charge as the Site Director and you and Victor will be my Field Supervisors. You may have to carry the bulk of the work, as I don't know how much Victor will be up to each day. I intend to give you complete credit for anything of value we find, and, if there's nothing there, then I'll take the blame for a wasted effort. I am offering you the opportunity to get your career right back to where it should have been, Liss …, sorry, Melissa. You can't lose. And on top of that, you get to spend a wonderful summer in Italy with me."

"And Victor will be there, of course. I don't know whether I consider that a big selling point." Melissa sighed and put her coffee cup down. "Anthony, it's not that I don't appreciate your offer, I do. I'm just not qualified to take the post you're offering me and you know it as well as I do. Anyway, I don't honestly know that I care much about a stunning career anymore. I'm quite happy where I am."

"You're not happy!" Anthony was spot on. "You hate your job, you hate the life you have and you hate me because it's my fault you're trapped here. I don't blame you for feeling like this, but I'm holding out an olive branch to you. Don't snap it off before you've really thought it through. As for your lack of qualifications, I say to hell with them. I know damned well you can do it because I now know I got my Master's out of your work. Anyway it's my dig, my rules. If I want to appoint a person who is under-qualified, on paper at least, then that's up to me."

Melissa shook her head, unsure if she could climb on the Anthony Marcus roller coaster without doing serious damage to her sanity. Anthony still had one last card up his sleeve. Melissa had no idea of it, but he had spent a very long time researching her life. He had done his homework well. He knew she was in debt and the state of the house had only confirmed his findings.

"Did I mention the salary?" Anthony asked calmly "I am prepared to pay twice what your combined salaries are now. All your travel and living costs will be covered for the duration and you can have full use of my personal assistant, if you can find a use for her, that is. Oh, and there will be a completion bonus of ten thousand if you stay right up to the last day I say I need you."

"That's insane!" Melissa blurted out. That was a lot of money to her and she desperately needed to clear some loans. "No one pays that kind of money for what you want! Is there something you're not telling me? What else do you expect me to do?"

"You can sleep with me if you want ..." Melissa started to open her mouth to protest, but Anthony raised his voice over hers "... but it is not a requirement of the contract." He was laughing at how appalled she looked at the suggestion. "I'm joking," he added.

Melissa threw a cushion at him in mock rage. She was still trying to look annoyed, but she was beginning to laugh, too. She composed herself and smiled at him. "I don't know what to say," she said finally.

"Say yes," he replied.

"I'll think about it. Give me a couple of days and I'll let you know." Melissa already knew the answer would be yes, but she still wanted to make him wait. There was no way she could turn down that amount of money.

"A couple of days, you say? I can do that." Anthony stood up. "I think this calls for a celebration! Why don't we head back to the pub and try that drink again?"

"I haven't said yes, so what is there to celebrate?" Melissa laughed.

"How about the fact you haven't said no!" Anthony was serious again. He reached down and took Melissa's hands, pulling her up off the sofa to stand in front of him. They were so close she could feel the heat radiating from his body. She looked up into his eyes and she felt the urge to kiss him welling up inside her.

"I've missed you, Liss," Anthony spoke so softly she could hardly hear him. "Do you think there could ever be a chance ..." he continued, but did not finish the sentence. Melissa had freed one hand from his and raised it to his lips to silence him. He closed his eyes and kissed her hand gently.

"You need to go," she replied. "If we're going to work together, we need to keep this professional. I'll call you tomorrow with my answer." Anthony opened his eyes again. She could see the desperation in them and she was beginning to feel old desires surfacing too, but she was not prepared to start a relationship with him again. Not now.

Anthony stared at Melissa, hoping for some glimmer that she was bluffing, but her face was unreadable. He nodded eventually and moved away. He collected his keys and jacket and they headed to the front door. Anthony paused on the threshold, turning back to face Melissa one last time. Then, with one last, longing stare, he turned again and walked to his car.

Melissa closed the door and leant against the back of it. She had survived seeing Anthony again. Could she survive spending a longer period of time with him? Life with Anthony was always exciting and he had already made her feel like a giddy schoolgirl again. As stupid as she knew she was being, she wanted to go to Italy. To hell with it, she *was* going!

Chapter 3

Melissa landed at Bologna airport in late June and immediately began looking for Anthony as she exited through customs. He said he would meet her, so she expected him to be waiting, but it appeared he was not. She checked the signs being held up by the multitude of taxi drivers standing in line in the arrivals lounge, but her name was not on any of them either. She turned on her mobile and waited for it to connect to the Italian network. Perhaps Anthony was running late and had sent her a message when she was on the flight. She hated the thought of having to pick it up from her voicemail – it would cost so much.

Whilst she stared at the phone, an exceptionally beautiful young woman in her early twenties approached her. Tall and slim, with movie star looks and flowing blonde hair that reached down to her waist, she was exactly the kind of woman Melissa envied. Her hour-glass figure and long legs were shown off beautifully by the designer dress and ludicrously high heels she was wearing. She was attracting looks from every man around them, which only helped to make Melissa feel more self-conscious in her old combat trousers and 'Springsteen' t-shirt.

Mobile phone in hand, the woman made a bee line for Melissa. She removed her sunglasses, revealing vivid blue eyes and looked between Melissa and the screen as if comparing her to an image on it. "Excuse me, are you Dr Gordon?" she finally asked.

"I'm Melissa Gordon, but I'm not Dr Gordon if that's who you're looking for," Melissa replied.

"Sorry. My mistake! Anthony was a little vague with the details. I assumed that as you'd been to university together and were on the same course, you had the same qualifications."

The woman was muttering, half to herself, as she tapped on the hand-held device, but Melissa realised she was there to collect her as soon as she mentioned Anthony. It figured: only he would send a beauty queen to get her.

"We were on the same course to begin with, but I didn't get as far as he did. And you are?" she replied calmly.

"Sorry. I'm Rebecca, Anthony's assistant. Well, I'm more than that really. Whatever he needs, I sort out for him. More like his right arm, I suppose. Can't do without me! Anyway, he's *far* too busy to come away at the moment and asked me to collect you." Rebecca was gushing with sheer enthusiasm about her boss like a teenager over a pop star. *Pretty and immature*, Melissa thought. *Just his type!*

"That's fine by me." Melissa picked up her hand luggage from the floor, grabbed the handle of her case and stood waiting, but Rebecca made no effort to move. She seemed too busy sizing Melissa up, or, to be more precise, she was too busy looking down her nose at her in a most dismissive way. "Shall we?" Melissa said, a little impatiently.

"Oh yes, sorry. Miles away! Jeep's this way." Rebecca turned and rushed off, heels clicking on the polished floor as she went, leaving Melissa to drag the luggage along in her wake.

The drive back to Anthony's house proved interesting. Rebecca kept repeating how important she was to Anthony, and that he told her everything, but then bombarded Melissa with questions about their relationship, which Melissa deliberately evaded. She found it amusing that a person who was supposedly so important to Anthony knew nothing about the woman she had been sent to collect. Rebecca obviously felt threatened by Melissa, who gave just enough information to answer some of Rebecca's questions, but not enough to put her mind at rest that Melissa was not planning to compete for the affections of the man they were both working for. The girl, and she was definitely behaving like a girl and not a woman, as evidenced by her intellectual immaturity, was obviously infatuated with Anthony. Rebecca's need to explain how important she was only demonstrated her own insecurities and Melissa wondered if Anthony was unaware how she felt. That was definitely odd.

Anthony was normally in tune with the raging hormones of any woman in his presence and usually exploited them to the hilt. Maybe he had changed after all.

There was one question Melissa was burning to ask, but it had nothing to do with Anthony. "How do you get on with Victor?" she said at a point when Rebecca paused to breathe. It was the only way she could get a word in to the conversation.

Rebecca went quiet and became tense as she tried to think of a tactful response. Melissa could have bet on Rebecca not liking him. That at least could be common ground and something they could agree on. She decided to help the girl out of her quandary. "If it makes you feel any easier, I can't stand him," she added.

Melissa watched Rebecca visibly relax as she finally answered, "I know he's really important to Anthony, but he creeps me out. He looks at me funny. Makes my skin crawl. Did he do that to you?"

Melissa laughed lightly "God, no!" she said "Victor never gave me a second glance. He hated me from day one. Probably still does. He's a rude, arrogant man and I'd be very happy never to see him again. I nearly refused this job because of him."

"Really? I thought he liked you. He seemed so keen for you to get here. Went on and on at Anthony for weeks about it. Kept asking when you'd arrive."

Rebecca continued to talk aimlessly about how wonderful Anthony was, but Melissa was no longer listening. This pretty young thing seemed incapable of constructing a proper sentence, which was becoming as annoying as the homage to her boss that she was reciting.

Melissa's thoughts turned to Victor. The news of his apparent change of heart unnerved her. Dying or not, she could not believe he would encourage Anthony to bring her there, unless he had an ulterior motive, and the thought that he could still be plotting against her sent shivers down her spine. Suddenly she found herself wishing she had never agreed to come.

Her thoughts were interrupted by the bumping of the jeep as it turned onto a dirt track between some trees. As the jeep cleared the wooded area beside the road, Melissa looked ahead and got her first glimpse of Anthony's home. What she saw nearly took her breath away. The house was a beautiful two storey villa, standing at the top of a gentle slope which ran down to a patchwork of fields on the plain, before gently rising again to another ridge. Far beyond the house, a thin area of ancient woodland snaked away into the distance as if it were following the banks of some long-vanished waterway.

The house was made from sandstone and reminded Melissa of the local Ham Stone quarried near her home in Somerset. The terracotta roof tiles and dark brown wooden shutters framing the windows gave the building warmth, welcoming its visitors. A veranda ran along the front and disappeared around the corner of the building, scattered with potted plants, chairs and abandoned coffee cups. The house looked lived in and well-loved, unlike the sad, tired cottage Melissa had allowed her own home to become.

Melissa climbed down from the jeep and went to grab her things from the boot. Rebecca was already disappearing into the house and she knew she would have to hurry to catch up with her. Melissa climbed onto the veranda, bumping the heavy case slowly up each step. An old rose twisted in and out of a trellis as it climbed up and over the threshold, almost hiding a little sign naming the property: 'Sub Rosa'. Melissa smiled to herself as she read it, translating it without difficulty into its English meaning of 'Beneath the Rose'. Since ancient times, the use of a rose hung over a meeting table meant that those present were sworn to secrecy. Melissa wondered what secrets this beautiful house had witnessed and now held in silence at the behest of its owner.

As she reached the screen door she could feel the cooler air inside the house wafting over her skin. It was a welcome relief from the blistering heat outside. She let go of the case and stood for a moment, enjoying the coolness.

The sound of a man's voice made her jump. "Why don't I take that for you?" Anthony said softly in her ear. He must have followed her up the steps, but she failed to hear him. He was standing so close to her that she collided with him as she tried to turn round, almost burying her face in his bronzed, bare chest. The muscular physique he had worked so hard on in his youth had further improved with age and was being emphasised by tiny beads of sweat that were forming on the skin stretched across his pectoral muscles. Melissa could not help but blush as she fought a sudden urge to run her hand across his bare flesh and wipe them away.

"Thanks for picking me up," she said, trying to sound as annoyed as she could to hide her embarrassment.

"Ah yes, sorry about that," Anthony replied. He shot her a knowing smile as if he had read her mind, making her blush more. "Victor fell out of bed and I had to wait here for the doctor. I hope Rebecca didn't drive you mad. She's a little intense, but very efficient. Anyway, come in and I'll show you around." Anthony was full of his usual charm as he picked up the suitcase and headed into the house, leaving Melissa to watch his equally well-proportioned back muscles disappearing through the door in front of her.

Inside, the house was as beautiful as its surroundings. Anthony was explaining how he had been forced to do a little remodelling. Originally there had been no hallway. The stairs, which climbed directly from just the other side of the door, opened into the first of three reception rooms. This room had now been partitioned to form the hall and a downstairs bedroom with a wet room for Victor because he was no longer able to climb the stairs.

Off the new hall, behind Victor's room, was a library. Anthony inherited this room and its contents when he took over the house. Every available piece of wall space was crammed with bookcases overflowing with books. The room was dark and cramped, and Anthony said he hardly spent any time in there because of that. In reality, it reminded him far too much of the old libraries and bookshops he'd frequented when he was trying to get Melissa to acknowledge his existence. For many years those memories had been too painful for him to bear, and he had avoided the room as much as possible. Melissa rather liked its oppressive feel, even more so as she ran her eyes along some of the titles adorning the shelves. There seemed to be copies of every book she knew on the subject of Ancient Rome, and a fair few of them were so rare that she had only ever dreamt of reading them. Some were very old, possibly first editions. She now had the same feeling of a child entering a sweetshop that Anthony had referred to when talking about his achievements in her lounge. To her, this was heaven and she was desperate to start digging through these wonderful old books, treating each one with reverential awe, but the tour was not yet over.

Running the full length of the house on the other side of the hall was the main living space. Along the outside wall were four large windows, each containing a set of French doors that opened onto the veranda where Anthony said he spent most of his time on hot summer evenings. With the doors open, the room took on an open feel and provided a great deal of air and light which reflected off the plain white walls, in stark contrast to the dark, musty library.

Upstairs were four bedrooms. The master bedroom had its own en suite and walk-in dressing room, whilst the two remaining furnished bedrooms shared the main bathroom. The last room was being used to store most of Victor's belongings.

Anthony walked into one of the spare bedrooms and threw Melissa's case on the king-sized bed that dominated the room, flopping down next to it while Melissa looked around her. The room was simply furnished, with only a wardrobe and dressing table on the wall opposite the bed, but the simplicity added to its beauty. Opposite the door were two open windows. Melissa crossed to one and looked out briefly across the fields below at the beautiful views across the gently-rolling landscape.

Above the bed hung a reproduction of the Monet painting 'The Red Boats at Argenteuil'. It was a picture Melissa adored and, when she and Anthony were together, it had hung in their flat above their bed. He used to joke that when he was rich he would buy a little red boat for her and sail her around the Mediterranean, leaving the rest of the world behind them. Seeing this picture brought back so many memories of happier times that Melissa felt herself becoming very emotional. She quickly turned back to the window and leant out of it, gathering her thoughts. She heard Anthony get up from the bed and walk up behind her. He placed each of his hands on either side of her so that his body was almost touching hers and spoke very softly to her.

"Well, what do you think of my home?"

Melissa gulped. She felt suddenly flushed, and her pulse raced in response to his close proximity. She gripped onto the windowsill tightly until her knuckles began to go white. "It's beautiful," she whispered, praying it would be enough and he would not expect her to say any more.

"I'm glad you like it," he replied brushing his body against hers as he leant round her and pointed out of the window. Melissa gasped a little, but he pretended not to have noticed, and carried on talking. "See those trees way down there?" He was pointing at the snaking woodland she had spotted earlier. "That's the start of the woods where you find the Rubicon. Don't get too excited. It's no more than a trickle these days. Never gets higher than your ankles, if that. I own the land down to it and up to the top of that ridge line beyond. Actually, I own just about everything you can see from this window. I could hardly believe it when Victor told me our home was built right on top of where Caesar's camp had been. How's that for luck? Come downstairs and I'll show you the site."

Anthony moved away swiftly and left the room, smiling to himself. He knew exactly what reaction he had deliberately provoked: it was all part of his plan to win Melissa back. He intended to stay professional, just as she asked, and never to make any attempts at reconciliation. His plan was to get Melissa to want him. She needed to make the first move if they were to ever have the chance of a real future together. Of course, he had no intention of playing fair and was determined to make it as difficult as possible for her to resist him.

Chapter 4

Over the next few weeks Melissa threw herself into her work. It felt good to be using her skills outside a classroom again. She forgot about her initial concerns and was beginning to enjoy herself, even though there were no real finds worth speaking of.

The site itself was huge, but there were surprisingly few people working on it. All of them, except for Melissa, Anthony and Victor were students who were working for extra credit. There were six of them living in a cottage a short distance from the main house that Anthony explained had been where he and Victor lived when he was small. Victor had continued to live there until his illness made it difficult for him to live alone and he reluctantly moved into the villa. Most surprising was the fact that none of the students were women. This hardly fitted with Anthony's infamous reputation, but as all six were crammed into the same small house, perhaps it was fortuitous that they were all male. A handful of other students who lived nearby came to the site on a daily basis, but their number barely doubled the complement of staff.

Attached to the cottage was a series of outbuildings. The largest of these was a barn that had been adapted to be the centre of operations. It was lavishly equipped with everything necessary for the dig, and Anthony had installed a water supply and a generator giving power, good lighting and a couple of computers. It meant there was no task that could not be performed from that building.

Rebecca was not an archaeologist and did no physical work on the dig. She was purely Anthony's PA and was responsible for administration and organisation, making sure everything ran smoothly. Annoyingly for Melissa, she was damned good at it. Rebecca kept immaculate records of their daily activities. Anthony worked with a Dictaphone for making notes which she would have typed up ready for him to review the next morning. She was also good with a digital camera and took pictures of the site and all the finds according to Anthony's directions.

Anthony was planning to put trenches into many of the smaller fields located to the side of the house over the entire period they would be working. He ran a very tight ship when it came to the dig. There were detailed schedules of work and site plans tacked to the boards in the barn. He called a meeting every day, making sure each person understood what had been achieved, what they were doing next and who they were to report to. They never opened more than three trenches at any one time, which was the maximum the small workforce could handle.

He insisted on the students referring to him as Dr Marcus and to Victor as Dr Reyes. It was a level of formality that Melissa found stuffy and old-fashioned and she flatly refused to go along with it, despite Anthony's opposition. She found it amusing to annoy him this way, as he had always been the first person to reject any sort of authority in his youth. They had effectively reversed their roles: Melissa was now the rebel and Anthony the stickler for the rules.

Every day she noticed she was spending a little more time with Anthony. At first she was suspicious that he was simply engineering reasons to be near her. There always seemed to be something he wanted her to consult on and he would send Rebecca to fetch her. When she arrived, it would always be something trivial that did not need both of them, but he insisted that she was an equal partner in this endeavour and had to be kept informed of every last detail. In the evenings, the two of them would share a private meal, before going for a walk, supposedly to discuss the next day's work plan, but mostly so that Anthony could show her around his estate. He would even join her if she was in the library, despite his supposed dislike of the room, not that Melissa particularly objected, because the more time she spent alone with Anthony, the less time she had to spend in the company of either Victor or Rebecca.

Her increasing closeness to Anthony had done nothing to improve her fractious relationship with Anthony's assistant. Almost as soon as she arrived, Melissa realised she was right about Rebecca's invented self-importance. As the only other woman on site, Rebecca lived in the villa with them, but beyond that Anthony treated her exactly the same as he did any of the students, insisting that she also should call him Dr Marcus. It turned out he was not oblivious to her attraction to him, but was trying everything he could to discourage her attentions by ignoring her and insisting on extreme levels of formality. He was often rude to her, but she was never deterred, being so totally smitten with him that she could not contemplate the possibility that he was not equally interested in her. In the house, she would wander around in her underwear, hoping that she would bump into him. On the occasions she came to the site, she would try to attract Anthony's attention by wearing skimpy t-shirts and shorts so tight that they left nothing to the imagination. Although he never paid her any attention, she completely distracted the students to the point where it was more productive to stop working when she was around. Melissa went as far as suggesting that it might be best to let Rebecca go, but, after an objection from Victor, Anthony refused to entertain the idea any further.

As for Victor, he had been surprisingly courteous towards Melissa on the few occasions they needed to speak. Generally Melissa did her best to keep out of his way and that seemed to suit them both fine. She could not fail to notice the way he behaved around Rebecca, who was not exaggerating when she said he looked at her strangely. If it had not been so ridiculous a thought, Melissa would have said Victor had a crush on the girl. He was old enough to be her grandfather and should know better than to chase such a young thing although her inappropriate dress made it as hard for him not to notice her as it did everyone else. Eventually Melissa plucked up the courage to confront him outright and his reaction again surprised her. Victor became tearful and simply said that Rebecca reminded him of someone he had loved in his youth. It was obvious that this mystery woman had been very special to him, but he would not be drawn into talking about her any further. Whether it was his age or his illness that had changed him, Melissa could not tell, but he was a different man to the one she knew from university. He complimented Melissa on her astuteness and advised her always to remain observant of the behaviour of others, telling her it was a skill that would serve her well in the years to come.

By the end of July, Melissa and Anthony were almost inseparable. Their relationship had reverted to the way it had been all those years before, each knowing what the other was thinking and finishing the other's sentences. The only thing missing was intimacy between them, but Anthony never pushed for anything more than friendship. Back in England, Melissa had insisted that they remained professional if they were going to work together, and it appeared Anthony was determined to do just that. He had grown up at last, which only made him more attractive. Now he represented the full package deal: looks, money, intelligence and a positive attitude.

Against her better judgement Melissa knew she was falling for him again. Every morning she would wake up determined to put a stop to their increasing closeness before it went too far. Every night she would go to sleep telling herself she would do it tomorrow, but tomorrow never came. Anthony was only a part of what she was falling in love with. She also adored his home, its surroundings and the relaxed life he had there. It was the most idyllic location, exactly the kind of place Melissa dreamed of living, and she found herself secretly hoping she would never have to leave.

Deep down, Melissa knew Anthony was her soulmate, even though he drove her mad at times. He was everything she wanted and the one thing it appeared she could no longer have. As much as it was her own fault, she was regretting her decision to keep him at arm's length. The more he stayed away, the more Melissa dreamed of him taking her in a passionate embrace and then living happily for the rest of their lives together.

Life was wonderful until the start of August when things went disastrously wrong. On the afternoon of the 3rd, Melissa made the exciting discovery of a drinking vessel that appeared to be intact. She called for Anthony and they worked together until the light faded in order to excavate it safely. Exhaustion and hunger caught up with them and they agreed to leave cleaning the compacted soil from the inside until the morning. Once the piece was safely stored in the barn with the other finds of the day they went back to the house to celebrate their spectacular discovery.

They sat up talking for most of the night and it was nearly dawn by the time they went to bed, which, combined with the wine she had drunk, caused Melissa to sleep late. She was eventually woken by the heat of the sun which had followed its celestial path to shine directly through the window and onto her bed, meaning it was already past midday. Melissa sat up suddenly, appalled at herself for having missed the alarm. Her head felt a little fuzzy, but she could not believe she had drunk so much as to have been comatose.

She dragged herself out of bed and over to the dressing table. As she opened the top drawer, she spotted a note addressed to her in Anthony's handwriting. He must have been in her room already and not woken her. She felt a sudden rush of excitement at the thought of his presence. She closed her eyes and imagined him bending to kiss her forehead as she slept. She could feel herself blushing as she gingerly opened the note.

> *Couldn't sleep – too excited. I came to get you, but you looked so peaceful I couldn't bring myself to wake you. Last night was a late one, so I turned your alarm off to let you rest. Please don't be mad at me, it was done with your welfare at heart. You know where to find me when you're ready – I'll be waiting for you. A xx.*

Melissa showered and dressed as quickly as she could and then ran down to the site. As she approached the barn, Rebecca stepped through the door and looked at her smugly.

"Oh dear," she said in a most condescending tone, "Don't think you should go in there right now. Not best pleased with you. Think you'll be getting a flight home sooner than you thought." She pushed past Melissa and flounced up the slope towards the house, leaving Melissa standing open-mouthed and confused.

Melissa entered the barn full of trepidation. She had no idea what was going on, but, if it made Rebecca happy, it had to be bad for her. Only Anthony and Victor were in the barn, sitting on the far side of a long table that was covered in trays containing the items that had been discovered. They were arguing, but stopped as Melissa entered. Anthony glanced at her as she approached them, before standing up and turning away, keeping his back to her.

"You're up then," he said gruffly.

"Yes," Melissa replied. "Sorry I slept in so late. Is there something wrong?" She could tell from his body language that there was. For some reason he would not look at her.

"I'm closing the site down," he said abruptly. "Rebecca will get you on a flight home as soon as she can. I'll pay you till the end of the month in lieu of notice and will give you the bonus as discussed."

Melissa was too shocked to respond initially. She sat down on a small stool opposite Victor, looking to the old man for some clue as to what had happened, but he just shook his head.

"Anthony, I don't care about the money. If this is over, then fine, but can I at least know why?" Melissa asked, once she recovered from the initial surprise.

Anthony finally turned around and shot her the blackest of looks. He folded his arms and continued to stare at her as if she already knew the answer to her question. Whatever had happened, he obviously believed Melissa played some part in it.

Finally he answered her. "We've found some intrusive material. There's evidence that someone has been deliberately tampering with yesterday's finds. Victor and I are in full agreement that we cannot continue. I've told Rebecca to make arrangements for the students to leave this afternoon, and for you to go as soon as possible."

Melissa was totally dumbstruck. There had to have been a mistake. She had no idea what was going on, but it felt as if she was the one being accused. "I'm sorry, I don't understand," she said. "What have you found and are you absolutely sure it was put there deliberately? Why don't you let me take a look and ..."

"Don't you think you've done enough already?" Anthony cut her off abruptly. "I gave you this opportunity and this is how you repay me? I was trying to put things right between us, Liss. I wanted to make up for the past. I trusted you would give me that chance." He turned away again, kicking his stool over in frustration as he did so. He was more than angry, he was hurting badly. Whatever it was that he had found he had taken it extremely personally.

Melissa was nearly in tears. The day before, she and Anthony had been so close she had begun to believe there was a chance they could get back together. Now he could hardly bear to look at her and she had no idea why. In desperation she turned to Victor again. He was looking at her sadly, almost as if he felt sorry for her. "What have I done?" she whispered to him.

Victor nodded at her, indicating he would do what he could to get her the answers she so desperately needed. "Show her," he said to Anthony, but Anthony never moved or spoke in response. He just stood where he was with his arms crossed, staring at the floor.

Victor stood up slowly and walked over to Anthony. He put his hand on his godson's arm and calmly repeated his request. "Show her, please. She deserves to know what you accuse her of. It is best that she know what it is she must do."

Anthony raised his head to look at the frail old man next to him, his face now full of concern. Victor was the last person Anthony thought would ever stand up for Melissa, and his confused use of tenses when he spoke only added to Anthony's fears that he had not been taking his painkillers as regularly as he should. He helped Victor back to his chair and picked up the stool, putting it back in position. He sat down and looked at Melissa again.

He put his hand on a tray on the table and slowly pushed it in front of her. "I cleaned the cup we found yesterday. This was inside, rammed in the very bottom."

Melissa looked down into the tray. She had honestly thought that this day could not get any worse, but what she saw made her heart sink further. She was looking at what appeared to be the broken parts of a watch and a small dress ring. Now she understood what was wrong. If Anthony had really found these inside the drinking cup, then the site had definitely been tampered with. She picked up the broken face and examined it. It was badly faded, but it looked oddly familiar. Such modern rubbish would call into question everything they had achieved and made further work pointless. He was right. She had helped him lift the damn thing and she knew that the soil was untouched. Whoever had done this had to be very skilled to have made the site appear so genuine.

Anthony continued talking. "It was cleverly done. That soil looked like it hadn't been touched for centuries. Maybe you can tell me how it got there, Melissa?"

Melissa looked up and stared into Anthony's cold eyes. He stared back at her blankly, as if all the emotion he had previously shown had drained from his body. This was not a good sign. She had watched him do this so many times before in the old days, usually when she had questioned him about Victor. It meant he was shutting down. He had made a decision and nothing would shift that thought from his mind, short of hard evidence to the contrary. She swallowed hard and asked the obvious question, even though she already knew the answer. "You think I did this?"

"Of course I do. Who else could put your watch down there? Look there's an inscription on the back. You can just make it out. It says – To Liss with love." Anthony was matter-of-fact in his tone as he carefully separated the watch back from the pile resting between her hands and turned it face up. He picked up the ring. As he did so, Melissa watched as all the pain and anguish from earlier flooded back into his face. "And this is the engagement ring I bought and finally gave to you in April. I should know, I've had it in my pocket for eight bloody years!" He tossed the ring back into the tray. "You must really hate me to do this." His last words tailed off and he sat in silence staring at the ring.

Melissa felt a sudden wave of relief surge through her. She was not guilty of what she was being accused of and now she could prove it. "They're not mine!" she said triumphantly.

"Both my watch and the ring are on the dressing table in my room. I'll show you." She stood up to leave. She was going to fix this and regain his trust.

"Are they really? I don't believe you." Anthony's voice was cold again. "Only two people knew what was written on the back of your watch, and that you had that ring – you and the person who gave them to you." He stood up suddenly and slammed his hands down on the table, making the finds jump in their little trays. "AND I KNOW DAMN WELL I DIDN'T DO IT!" he shouted the last words and then stormed out of the barn.

Melissa moved to go after him, but Victor called out, stopping her. "Sit down, Melissa. I need to tell you why you did this."

Melissa spun around. Victor's last words had incensed her and she was ready to retaliate. "How many more times must I say this? I didn't do it!" She ran her hand through her hair, trying to think clearly for a moment. Her mind whirled continually, but she kept coming back to an old fear that she had never quite shaken off. "Victor, I swear to you, if you are trying to set me up again, I will put you out of your misery right now."

Victor sighed and shook his head. "I am not trying to hurt you, Melissa. I tried to stop this many years ago, until I realised I could not. Now you must do what is necessary. You did put your things in that cup a long time ago, and you must do so again soon. Not today, but tomorrow or the next day perhaps. I do not remember exactly, too much has happened since then. You will ask a stranger to help you to do it, and he will. You have to send Anthony this message. You will both understand why when it is too late. I have done all I can to help you. You must face the rest alone."

Melissa stared at Victor. He was not making any sense whatsoever and she too was now worrying that his pain was intense enough to make him delirious, but she had no time to try to interpret his incoherent ravings. She left the barn and headed for the house as fast as she could, going straight to her room. She slipped on her watch and grabbed the ring box from the dressing table drawer, determined to take them and shove them under Anthony's nose to prove her innocence. As she headed back down the stairs, she heard the jeep starting. She ran to the front door in time to see Anthony leaving in it, throwing dust and grit in the air as he sped away up the drive.

In the silence that descended after the dust had settled, Melissa felt suddenly alone. She had never seen Anthony this angry and she was afraid she had lost him forever. Filled with the same overwhelming sense of desperation that she had felt the day her grandmother died, she sat on the steps of the veranda and stared down the drive into the emptiness left by his sudden exit.

As the afternoon dragged on, Melissa took a walk around the site. It felt like every one of the students was avoiding her or talking about her in whispers as they passed her by, carrying their bags to the waiting taxis. When she found she could not stand the accusing glances any longer, she headed off across the fields, through the trees and down to the tiny stream that Victor insisted was the Rubicon. She sat by the water's edge and watched the water trickling downstream as she mulled over the afternoon's events.

Someone had definitely set her up, but the question was who. Victor was her first thought, but he was too frail to have managed it alone. Rebecca was a more likely candidate, but she doubted the girl would ever put her hands in the dirt for any reason in case she broke a nail. That only left Anthony.

It occurred to her that Anthony had been in her room that morning and he had deliberately engineered it so she overslept when he turned off the alarm. He was the one who had given her both the ring and the watch, which had been a present for her twenty-first birthday. He could easily have obtained duplicates of both items and then put them in the site himself. She could not explain how the soil looked as if it had lain untouched for centuries, but what did that matter? Anthony had more years of field experience than she did, and was the most likely candidate for staging such an elaborate hoax. No matter how far-fetched it seemed, the only explanation she could think of was that Anthony was the one responsible.

Anger now began to replace her earlier feelings of grief. If Anthony had done this, he really was the total shit she had once believed him to be. She had done nothing wrong, but had been made to feel like the evil villain in a play. She was wounded by his actions once again, but had no idea what to do for the best.

She stared blankly down at the water beside her. For Caesar, the decision to cross the Rubicon had been a difficult one, but it proved to be a pivotal moment in his life. Now, as Melissa looked down into this pitiful little stream, she too was faced with an unenviable decision: stay and confront Anthony, or leave now with what little dignity she had left. Melissa was not the risk-taker Caesar had been and she had no more fight left in her. Giving Anthony a second chance had been a serious error of judgement on her part. Even though she doubted she could ever trust him, she had let him in again and dared to hope he was different. She had come here because she had wanted to be with him more than she cared to admit, but now her dream was over. Where Caesar had advanced, she would retreat. She decided it was time to leave her fantasies of an exciting future with Anthony Marcus behind, and try to return to her ordinary little life.

Melissa slipped her hand into her pocket and pulled out the ring box. She was determined to hurl it into the stream, but as she raised her arm above her head she stopped herself. All the time it had been in her possession, she had never given it more than a cursory glance. Now, having seen the grubby little ring in the tray, she felt an urge to examine it more closely. Slowly, she opened it and removed the ring. It was a gold band set with three stones: a dark sapphire in the middle, with a small diamond on either side. The diamonds had been set in white gold to make them appear larger. It could not have been very expensive, but they had only been poor students when it had been bought. Anthony had chosen well: it was exactly the sort of understated ring she would have chosen for herself.

She forced the ring over her finger with some difficulty. Her hands were fatter these days than they had been back then, but it went on eventually. She sat looking at it, thinking about how different their lives could have been had Victor not ruined everything when they were young. Melissa felt herself becoming emotional again and decided to put the ring back in its box. She pulled at it and instantly regretted forcing it onto her hand. No matter how hard she pulled, it would not budge. She dropped her hand into the cold water of the stream for a few minutes, but it made no difference. The ring was stuck fast. She would have to try and remove it back in the house.

Chapter 5

Melissa had not realised quite how late it was, or how bad the weather looked. She got up from the bank as the first drops of rain began to fall. As she walked back to the house, she noticed the large thunder clouds that had built in the sky. The air had become heavy and humid and she quickened her pace as the raindrops became larger. By the time she reached the barn, it was unusually dark and she was reliant on the light from the windows of the house to see her way back across the garden, until a massive lightning strike hit somewhere in the distance, illuminating the entire area. The rain came down so hard it stung her skin as it hit her bare arms, and she ran the final few yards back to the house and up the steps to the veranda. She was soaking wet and so distracted by the booming thunder, which followed close on the heels of the lightning, that she failed to notice the jeep was back.

Melissa opened the front door and walked into the hall, closing the door as quietly as she could behind her. She took off her muddy boots and tiptoed upstairs and into her room without being noticed. What she was not prepared for was another run in with Anthony who was sitting on the bed, his head in his hands. He looked up anxiously, though relief instantly spread across his face as he saw it was her. He stood up and reached for her, but she side-stepped his advance, making him pull back.

"Thank God you're OK," he said. "Where have you been?"

"Down at the Rubicon. I needed to think." Melissa hid her left hand in her pocket. She had no intention of letting Anthony see the ring stuck on her finger. She moved past him and pulled her case out of the corner, throwing it on the bed. "I need to pack, so if you will please leave, I can get on with it."

All of Anthony's intentions to hold back and wait for Melissa to come to him were gone. When he had returned to the house earlier and found her missing he had been beside himself with worry that he had driven her away through his own thoughtlessness. He knew he had overreacted, as always, and had searched the estate looking for her, including the riverbank, but he had not found her. Now she was here his relief overcame his intentions to hold back. He was desperate to hold her and to tell her how sorry he was. Moving around the bed he tried to slide his arms around her waist, but she pushed him away forcefully.

"Leave me alone!" Melissa said sharply. She was mortified that he could be so forward after the way he had treated her.

Anthony stood back a little, but would not leave. He reached past her and pulled the case back off the bed. "We have to talk," he said. "Please, I owe you an apology. I was being ridiculous earlier and I know that you didn't put those things in that cup. How could you? I've hardly left you alone for five minutes since you got here. Anyway, you're wearing the watch." He reached down for her wrist, but again she pulled away from him, making sure she kept her hand firmly in her pocket.

Melissa tried to reach for the case with her other arm, but Anthony stood in front of it. She glared at him, determined not to give in. "It's a little late for apologies, don't you think?" she said coldly. "You have made me the laughing stock of this dig. There's not a single person out there who doesn't know what happened earlier – thanks to your vacuous little helper!"

"I know, but I can fix it if you just give me a chance. Please, Liss, I have no idea how that stuff got there, any more than you, but you know as well as I do that it's pointless to continue with the dig." There was an air of desperation in Anthony's voice, but Melissa tried to ignore it. He had hurt her and she needed to get out of the room before her resolve faltered.

"Why should I give you any more chances? You've spent your life making a total fool of me and this dig is just another example. You've taken everything I had. My love, my future, my confidence and now it appears you want the only thing I have left: my dignity. There's nothing left after that." Her voice faltered and she looked away. She could feel her emotions building and the urge to run away became ever more desperate. She tried to move past him once more, but still he blocked her escape.

"Please let me go," she begged, choking back the tears as she spoke, pressing both her hands firmly against his chest as she tried to push him backwards, forgetting about trying to hide the ring.

"No," he said calmly, "not until you hear me out."

"I'll scream," her words were barely audible and she knew it was nothing more than an idle threat.

"Scream, shout, cry, hit me again if you like, but you will listen to me if it takes us all night."

Melissa took Anthony at his word. She raised her hand and went to slap him as she had so many months ago in the pub garden. This time he caught her wrist and held it fast.

"I want nothing more to do with you! I hate you!" Melissa spat the words at him as she struggled to free her arm from his vice-like grip. She glared at him, willing herself to mean what she had said.

Anthony simply stared at her for what seemed like an age as she continued to struggle, until he slipped his other arm around her waist and pulled her to him, releasing her wrist and using his newly-freed hand to hold her head against his chest.

"No, you don't." His words were gentle and soothing. "You should, but you don't. That's what makes this so hard for you."

Melissa tried for the briefest moment to pull away, but she no longer had the strength to fight him. She collapsed against him, her body convulsing in wave after wave of uncontrollable sobs.

Anthony was gently stroking her hair as he spoke. "You seem to think this was deliberate on my part, like I'm trying to wreck everything. Liss, don't you get it yet? I'm still in love with you. That's why it hurt so much to think you had betrayed me." He kissed the top of her head gently. "I know I'm a total arse at times, today proved that, but I swear I'd never do anything to hurt you deliberately. I was prepared to give up everything I had, just to get you here and I still am. Someone is trying to hurt us both. I don't know who yet, but

I'm not going to let them. Just because this dig is over doesn't mean my feelings for you will ever change. They never have, and they never will." He pushed her away just far enough to be able to turn her head towards him. Holding her chin with his fingertips, he took a deep breath before making an insane offer. "I'll go to the press and tell them I'm a fraud. I'll tell them I took your work and that you are the one with the real talent. Maybe someone will give you a better job. At the very least, you'll be able to sell your story and get even with me for all the pain I've caused you."

"You can't do that! I won't let you!" Melissa was horrified at what Anthony had said. At one time she had thought she would enjoy revenge, but just hearing him suggest it made her feel ill.

Anthony gently brushed a tear from Melissa's face. "Why not? What possible reason could you have for not wanting to see me ruined?"

"I love you!" Melissa blurted out the words without thinking.

Anthony stood staring at Melissa, his mouth wide open, not knowing quite what to do next. As determined as he had been to hear her say those words, he never expected her to do so after everything that had happened that day. Melissa went red. She dropped her eyes and began to pull away, finally jolting him into action. He pulled her back to his body forcefully, and kissed her passionately.

Melissa tried feebly to pull away for the briefest moment, but she could not bring herself to let go. Instead, she returned his kiss with as much passion as he had shown, wrapping her arms around his neck as she did so.

Anthony pulled his head away from Melissa and looked searchingly into her eyes. He wanted her more than anything, but he had to be sure she wanted him too. He needed a sign from her, something more than a single kiss. Sensing his doubt, she reached down and began fumbling with his belt buckle, finally undoing it and moving on to the button of his shorts. At the first touch of her hand against his flesh, all Anthony's uncertainties vanished. He swung Melissa off her feet and threw her onto the bed, dropping onto the sheets next to her. Now he had the permission he needed, he intended to make Melissa realise what she had been missing all these years.

Anthony had come a long way sexually since they had last been together. It had been his intention to use the skills he had learnt to ensure Melissa would never want anyone else ever again, but for a man who prided himself in his control, he was finding the sensations overwhelming him too much to bear. It had been a very long time since he had been with a woman and his desires became stronger as each item of clothing was struggled out of and tossed carelessly on the floor.

When there was nothing more between them, Anthony paused, taking a long look over the body of the woman next to him. Melissa blushed, suddenly aware of his intent stare. She shifted nervously and reached her hand up to the back of his neck, pulling his head towards hers, crushing their lips together even more passionately than before, until she felt his body slide over hers and begin its rhythmical dance.

Anthony knew how close Melissa was to giving herself to him. He pulled back slightly, lessening the pressure against her body, determined to make the moment last as long as he could manage. Despite his own sense of urgency, he wanted their reunion to be as tender as it had been the first time he had made love to her in those fields so long ago.

Melissa misunderstood his meaning. "Oh God, no," she gasped, fearing he was going to stop. She instinctively pulled her legs up over his hips. Her calves pressed down on his buttocks, determined to pull him ever deeper as she raised her body to meet each of his thrusts.

Anthony could no longer hold on to his own yearnings. He could sense what she wanted, and knew he wanted it too. Tenderness went out of the window as he rammed himself against her, making her scream his name out loud. Each thrust came as hard and deep as the last until Melissa gave in to the emotions flooding through her body. Her breath came in short pants as she quickened her movements against him. She sank her nails deep into the flesh of his shoulders as she arched her back one final time, before finally falling beneath him, quivering uncontrollably and allowing the tears of sheer joy to fall from her eyes.

Anthony felt his own desperation surge out of him. He collapsed on top of her, unable to lift so much as a finger of his own weight. He feared he was crushing her, but Melissa made no objection. If anything, she seemed to be holding him tighter than she had before. They lay together, limbs entwined, for the longest time before either had the energy to move.

Anthony finally slid his body off his lover's, and rolled onto his back, pulling her with him. As he wrapped his arms around her, Melissa raised her leg over his and ran her foot up his calf. He was so happy he could hardly bear to speak and ruin the moment, but there was still so much to say.

"I'm sorry, that was a bit quick," he said with a hint of embarrassment.

"Shhh," she murmured, her hand gently brushing through the hairs on his chest. "It's what we both needed. Just promise me we can do it again, a little slower," she added as she nuzzled her head against his shoulder.

"You give me a few minutes and we'll do a lot more," he replied. "I intend to give my future wife whatever she wants to keep her happy."

"Wife?" Melissa raised her head from his chest to look at him. "Is that your idea of a proposal?"

"Nope. I'd planned something far more romantic, but you're the one who jumped the gun and accepted me before I'd even asked. And with a ring that only cost me ninety quid at that!" As he had been speaking Anthony had run his hand over Melissa's. His fingers were gently rubbing her finger where the engagement ring was stuck firmly on her hand. "It feels a bit tight, actually. I think you should take it off."

Melisa put her head back on Anthony's shoulder as she groaned from embarrassment. "I hoped you wouldn't notice that. I only wanted to see what it would have looked like, but it's stuck and I can't shift it."

"Well you're going to need to, before it cuts off your circulation. Anyway, I intend to get you a much better ring. One that fits properly and costs considerably more than that one did."

They lay together in silence while Melissa pondered Anthony's proposal. She wanted to say yes more than anything, but she still had her doubts about the man lying beside her.

"Anthony, don't you think it's all a bit soon to be talking about marriage?" she finally asked.

"I'd hardly call it soon. We've known each other for twelve years," he replied.

"And we haven't spoken for eight of those." Melissa raised her head to look at him again. "Don't you think that, after everything that's happened, we should wait a little, until we're both sure this is what we want?"

Anthony shook his head. "Why is it everyone wants me to wait? First it was Victor, and now you. Waiting is how I lost you before and I can't bear the thought of ever losing you again." He rubbed her cheek gently with his hand. "Listen to me. There are things I never told you before, but I want you to know everything there is to know about me. I want to try to explain why I've done some of the stupid things I have. I want you to stay for the rest of my life, Liss, but first you have to forgive me for what I've done to you."

He looked up at her, desperate for her to back down and agree with him, but knowing she would not: Melissa was as cautious as he was reckless. He let out a long, deep sigh and stared at her in defeat. "I love you, Liss. I know that I always have, and I know I was a fool ever to let you go. It may have taken a long time and a lot of therapy for me to realise it, but you are all I've ever wanted and I'm already sure of that. I'd marry you tomorrow if you'd have me, but I'll wait. I've treated you badly and you need to learn to trust me again. I want you to be sure that I'm the one you want and when you are, maybe you'll just tell me. I'm not going to press you into anything that you're not ready for."

"Really?" Melissa asked playfully, trying to lighten the mood. "Because part of me thinks you have some very pressing ideas." All this time, she had been gently rubbing her leg against him, arousing him once more. "Tell you what, why don't you put that silver tongue of yours to a better use? I am most definitely ready for that."

"Willingly, Ma'am!" Anthony grinned and touched his finger to his forehead in a mock salute. He rolled Melissa onto her back, pausing briefly to look at her again before sliding down her body very slowly, intent on building up her anticipation. He was determined to make her say yes to his proposal, but for now he decided he would have to make do with making her beg him not to stop what he was about to do. There was more than one weapon of persuasion in Anthony's arsenal, and he would use all of them, if necessary, to get what he wanted.

In her room, Rebecca pulled her pillow over her head, trying to blot out the sounds coming from next door. It was so unfair. She adored Anthony, spending months doing whatever he asked in the hope of making a connection. When he had invited her to spend the summer with him she knew they would be working, but she had assumed that there would be something more between them, despite his denials of her. His reputation had led her to believe that all she had to do was wait and he would find his own way to her bed.

But then this woman from his past had turned up and stolen him from under her nose. Melissa Gordon was bright and talented and Anthony only had eyes for her. Rebecca hated Melissa for so many reasons already. Now this horrible woman was screwing the man she loved, and in the very next room. Rebecca vowed to get her revenge if it was the last thing she ever did.

In his room below them, Victor too was trying to blot out the sounds of Anthony and Melissa's lovemaking. He had dreaded this day for so long and tried so hard to prevent it from ever happening, but he had been unsuccessful.

Victor carried a dark secret. He was not the man that he pretended to be. For years Victor had suffered the misfortune of knowing both the past and the future.

From the moment Anthony first mentioned Melissa all those years earlier, Victor knew the lovers were destined to come to this day. He tried to separate them, but his intervention steered Anthony onto a course of self-inflicted destruction. Melissa was the best thing that had ever happened to his godson and Anthony only regained his focus when he decided to get Melissa back in his life. Anthony had never coped well by himself and needed a steadying hand to help steer him through the minefields that life put in his way.

Over the past few weeks, Victor had watched the former lovers becoming close again. Anthony was so happy it broke

Victor's heart to think about what was going to happen, but even he had no idea what the eventual outcome would be. All he knew for certain was that in the morning Melissa would be gone, and Anthony would be inconsolable once more.

Chapter 6

The storm blew itself out at some point in the night, leaving the air cooler and fresher. Melissa was woken early by the sounds of birds singing outside the open window. She felt invigorated, despite having hardly slept. Rolling over, she looked at Anthony sleeping peacefully next to her. She considered waking him and resuming where they had left off just a few hours earlier, but decided against it. After being so active for most of the night, he needed his rest – at least for another hour or so. That gave her enough time to shower and make some coffee.

Melissa slipped out of bed, grabbing her shorts from the floor and a clean vest-style t-shirt, underwear and socks from the dresser. She tiptoed out of the room, deciding to use Anthony's shower rather than the one in the main bathroom. She knew only too well how Rebecca felt about Anthony and suspected that the girl must have heard at least some of the night's activities. Melissa was not ready for a confrontation, so avoiding any accidental meeting seemed the most sensible option. She headed into Anthony's room, threw her clothes on the bed and went straight into the bathroom.

The hot jets of water hit her body like tiny pinpricks, washing away the last vestiges of sleep from her limbs. She began to think about the man sleeping in her bed again and wondered whether she should have invited him to join her in this large walk-in shower. *No*, she thought, *plenty of time for that sort of thing later*. They had the rest of their lives after all, if they so desired. She finished showering and dried herself on Anthony's towel before looking in the mirror, but it had steamed up from the heat and dampness caused by the shower. Smiling to herself, she wrote a message in the steam, knowing that it would be invisible until the next time the shower was used, before heading back into the bedroom to dress.

There was an unseasonably cold breeze blowing in through the open window. Melissa shuddered and grabbed one of Anthony's shirts from his closet to put over her t-shirt for extra warmth and headed down to the kitchen.

As she crossed the living room, something caught her eye through the French doors. She could have sworn she saw people in the lower field near the trees, but that made no sense. They were miles from anywhere and this was all Anthony's private land.

Melissa went to the nearest set of windows and opened them, stepping out onto the veranda beyond. The morning was bright and crisp at the house, but farther away towards the woodland, an unusual mist was hanging across the fields. Melissa supposed that it must have been this mist wafting in the breeze that had made her think she had seen people.

That really should have been the end of the matter, but for reasons unknown to her, Melissa had a sudden urge to investigate. She went into the hall and slipped her feet into her walking boots, then returned to the French doors and walked back outside and down into the fields.

The air definitely had a chill to it. It reminded her more of an autumn morning at home in Somerset than it did an August day in Italy. She supposed that had something to do with the mist, but she was no meteorologist, so what did she know? She continued on to the lower fields, enjoying the freshness of the air, breathing in deeply to make the most of the morning.

By the time she had arrived at the tree line the mist had thickened considerably. The way it hung seemed unnatural to Melissa, moving out of her way as she walked towards it. It was more like the fake mist in a horror movie, blown around by a fan, than a natural mist. There was an odd smell about it too, damp and earthy. It reminded her more of freshly-dug potatoes than a misty wood. The trees appeared as ghostly shapes in front of her. Her every footstep sounded much louder than it should as she crunched over fallen leaves and twigs. It was the only sound she could hear; no birds were singing and she was not disturbing any of the wildlife living in the undergrowth which usually dived out of the way when people passed by. She felt a little unnerved and paused, considering whether to return to the house to fetch Anthony to join her.

At that moment she heard the footsteps of another person in the woods. The mist had completely disoriented her and she could not tell whether they came from in front or behind. She could feel herself beginning to panic. She wanted to run, but had no idea which way to go. She wanted to call out, but her mouth was suddenly dry and she could not find the words. She was frozen to the spot.

Suddenly, the other person collided with her from behind. Melissa stumbled forwards, tripping over the root of a tree and falling onto her hands and knees. "Oh, it's you," a female voice said from behind her and Melissa recognised it as Rebecca's. She was relieved to hear a familiar voice, even if it sounded less than pleased to see her. "Sorry," the girl added with heavy sarcasm before continuing onwards. For once Rebecca was wearing a pair of jeans, probably due to the change in temperature, though the t-shirt emblazoned with the words 'Bite Me!' was as tight as ever.

Melissa got up and brushed herself off. This girl's attitude annoyed her more every day. Rebecca's complete lack of respect had been gnawing at her for weeks and this was probably the best chance she would ever get to confront her. She forgot about her uneasy feelings and followed Rebecca though the remaining trees to the stream.

The downpour from the night before had raised the water levels significantly, turning the babbling stream into a far deeper river. *It must have rained a lot harder than I realised,* Melissa thought casually. She hardly paid it any more attention as she quickened her pace to catch up to Rebecca.

"What are you doing down here?" Melissa asked as they drew level.

"Not that it's any of your business, but I saw someone in the woods. Probably press hoping for some dirty exclusive. This is private land so I intend to tell them to get lost. I have to think of Anthony's interests, you know." Rebecca was trying to sound important once again.

"How brave of you," Melissa replied sarcastically. "I'd have thought you would have gone to him first. Who knows what could happen to you out here alone with strangers around."

"And risk having to explain myself to you – no thanks. Still I've had to do that anyway, haven't I?" Rebecca muttered as she trudged on, whilst Melissa stopped dead. She was surprised at the comment that had just been made.

"What exactly is your problem with me?" Melissa called out even though she already knew the answer.

Rebecca stopped and turned to face Melissa. Her voice filled with hatred as she answered the question. "Oh don't give me the innocent act. You know perfectly well what it is. It's you being here, distracting him! I've worked at this for nearly a year, doing anything he asked and letting him treat me like crap just for a chance he'd notice me, but he never did. When he asked me here for the summer, I honestly thought it was his way of making his move. I didn't expect him to be bringing you!"

"I see. Look, I appreciate that you're infatuated with Anthony, but he doesn't see you that way," Melissa said calmly.

Infatuated proved not to be the best choice of words. Rebecca was immediately incensed. She stormed back towards Melissa and stood nose-to-nose with her.

"INFATUATED? I LOVE HIM, YOU STUPID COW!" Rebecca screamed the words so loudly they deafened Melissa. After a brief pause, Rebecca continued her rant. "You had your chance and you didn't want him. Why come back now? Because he's rich and famous? Or do you just want to hurt him again?"

"How dare you! You know nothing about me. I've loved Anthony all my life, but for your information he was the one who left me!" Melissa snapped back.

"Oh yes, I know all about how you're the supposed love of Anthony's life – Victor told me the other day – but you are nothing compared to him. I've seen the way you treat him. From the second you arrived you've deliberately annoyed and defied him at every turn. And I'm not fooled by all that stuff you pulled last night either."

"What?" Melissa was genuinely confused. Rebecca seemed to think her love for Anthony was all an act. "Of course I've been cautious. I needed to know whether I could trust him."

"That's right. Poor little heart-broken Melissa! You tricked him into your bed last night and now he's shagged you he thinks everything's fine. Well, he'll have to learn the hard way, I suppose! Bitch!"

Calling her a bitch was an insult too far for Melissa. She reached out, slapped Rebecca around the face and then retaliated. "You stupid little girl! You have no idea what's gone on between us. I've seen what he's done with his life and it's great, but he's made a lot of stupid mistakes with a lot of silly little things like you. And that's just what you would be, my dear, another stupid mistake. If the press are here looking for an exclusive it's because they've heard how you parade around in next to nothing, trying to make him slip. Are you sure you're not a plant? Hoping to cash in on a little kiss-and-tell number, are we? No? Well I'll tell you this for nothing, if you really think my fiancé will ditch me for a slip of a thing like you, then you are sorely mistaken!"

The shock of Melissa's final statement was immediate on Rebecca's face. Emotion overtook the younger woman and she sat down on the bank, her head in her hands. Rebecca began crying and sobbed so violently that her whole body shook. Melissa felt a pang of guilt for her slip of the tongue. She knew she was going to marry Anthony, but this was not the way to have told Rebecca. When they had been at university, Melissa had witnessed so many girls fall for Anthony, only to be destroyed by his cutting rejection of them, that she had thought it would no longer affect her. Now she knew it still did, only this time she was the one causing the pain. This poor girl had done nothing wrong and if she had been around just a couple of years earlier she probably would have got what she wanted so badly. Anthony had a knack of causing mayhem and destruction for those around him, whether intentionally or by accident. Rebecca was just an employee to him and nothing more, but Melissa knew there were no words she could use in consolation. Only time could heal the hurt that Anthony had inadvertently carved in Rebecca's heart.

Melissa stood in silence, looking around her. Despite the noise Rebecca was making, she was still aware of the uneasy silence by the river. The hairs on the back of her neck were standing on end and she had the distinct feeling they were being watched, most likely from the other bank. She could hear something other than Rebecca's sobs, but could not make it out. She squatted down and put her hand on Rebecca's shoulder, but the girl immediately tried to shrug it away.

"Get off me," she mumbled through her hands as she twisted her body sideways.

Melissa held on tight. Quietly, she said, "I think you're right. There's someone out there."

Rebecca looked up, shocked. She spun her head round to look behind her "Anthony?" she said hopefully.

"No" Melissa replied. She was looking in the other direction. "Over on the other bank. It's not Anthony, but I don't think he's from the press either. " She raised her arm and pointed across the water.

Rebecca followed Melissa's outstretched arm and saw a man emerging from the trees on horseback. He seemed to have come along a track that Melissa did not remember having seen before. The rider appeared to be there one second and then gone the next, fading in and out of view as if he was not really there at all.

"Is that a g-ghost?" Rebecca asked, not really wanting to hear an answer. "Victor said these woods were haunted, but I didn't believe him."

The man continued to the water's edge where he stopped, allowing his horse to drink from the river. He appeared not to notice the women on the other bank, because he was looking over his shoulder, as if waiting for another rider. Melissa studied his clothes. He wore a heavy cloak that was old and threadbare in places. He pulled it tightly around him to protect him from the cooling air. His lower legs were bare and he wore old-fashioned leather boots that looked Roman in design.

Melissa could not explain why, but something about the whole situation felt wrong. She was increasingly aware of how cold it was becoming, so cold in fact that she could see her breath forming into a wispy haze as she exhaled. She shivered suddenly, partly from the cold and partly from the sensation of fear growing inside her. "Let's not wait to find out," she replied and rose slowly, trying not to draw too much attention to Rebecca and herself.

Rebecca scrambled to her feet, slipping on the damp grass as she did so. Across the water the horse lifted its head. It had seen them, even if its rider had not. It seemed to Melissa that the animal was as nervous as she was as it started backing away from the bank, whinnying as it moved. The rider leant forward, patting its neck in an attempt to calm it. Melissa grabbed Rebecca's wrist and whispered, "Move slowly and try not to make too much noise. I don't think he's seen us yet."

Rebecca pulled her wrist free of Melissa's grasp. "Don't you dare tell me what to do!" she snapped back, a little too loudly for Melissa's liking.

If the rider had not seen them before, he had now. He dug his heels into the flanks of the horse and urged it forwards slowly. As he entered the water two more riders came out of the trees at a gallop and caught up to him. He had been waiting for them and now all three were heading straight for the two women on the opposite bank.

"Run!" Melissa shouted. She turned and headed for the trees on her side of the river, running as fast as she could, but she was no match for a horse. She heard the hoof beats behind her, chasing her down. She felt something punch her in hard in the back and she was sent sprawling to the floor. As she fell, she hit her head on a tree root, slipping into unconsciousness, but not before she heard the sound of a man's voice shouting something in Latin.

Anthony woke from the most sensual dream he had had in years. He had an enormous erection, but for the first time in many, many months he knew exactly what to do with it. He rolled onto his back and reached for Melissa, but she was not there. He sat up confused, wondering if the entire night before had been a part of his dream. His eyes scoured the room looking for evidence that he had not imagined it. He knew he was in Melissa's room, not his. He surveyed the strewn clothing – his shorts, his shirt, Melissa's bra. That was all the proof he needed that he had not been dreaming. He fell back onto the pillows, laughing. He had planned this outcome for so long and now, finally, he had her. Nothing could stop him now. He knew he was going to spend the rest of his life happy and contented with the woman of his dreams. They would marry. It was just a matter of time until she eventually gave in and said yes.

The smell of fresh coffee reached his nostrils and he reasoned that Melissa must be in the kitchen. He was tempted to wait for her to come to wake him, but that could be a while and his urge to be near her was too great. He began to imagine sneaking up behind her and pinning her body between his and the kitchen units. As he thought about all the ways he could entice her back to bed, he only excited himself further. He got up, pulling on his shorts with some difficulty and followed the smell down the stairs and into the hall.

When Anthony entered the living room he was surprised to find the French windows wide open. A chill breeze was blowing through them and cooling the room so much it made him shiver. He was heading across to close them when he heard Victor's walking stick tapping on the floor behind him. He turned to greet him with reluctance as the old man's presence would ruin his plans, but stopped when he saw the look of sorrow on Victor's face.

"I am so, so sorry," Victor spoke with total sincerity. "They have already gone."

Anthony was confused. "What do you mean – gone?" he asked.

Victor sighed and leant against the door frame for extra stability "There is much I need to tell you. Lissa and Rebecca went to the river earlier this morning. They will not be coming back, at least not for some time, if they ever can."

Anthony felt sick. He could not believe Melissa would leave, not after the night they had just spent together. He repeated his question slowly, pausing between each word to emphasise it. "What ... do ... you ... mean?"

"Lissa went to the river. Rebecca followed her. They were taken. You cannot help them."

Panic overtook Anthony. He had no idea what Victor was talking about, but it sounded like the women were in trouble. There was no river nearby, only the stream that was what remained of the Rubicon. He had no idea what would make the women go there so early in the morning, or why Victor had failed to call him sooner. And why did Victor keep saying Lissa? He had never heard anyone call Melissa that before, but there was no time to ask. All he could think about was getting to her. He threw on a pair of trainers and sprinted out of the house and across the fields towards the stream. Somewhere in the back of his head, a voice was telling him he was already too late.

At the stream, there was no sign of anyone having been there that morning. Anthony searched the near side and then paddled through the shallow water to the other bank. The only footprints he could see were his own, where his wet feet had touched the gravel at the water's edge, but in the growing warmth of the morning they too were fading fast. As forensic techniques were not dissimilar to archaeology, he knew he dare not contaminate the site any further than he already had by trampling to and fro across it and destroying any clues there might be to trace the women. He had to get help, and fast.

As Anthony turned to cross the stream again, a chill went through him, making the hairs on the back of his neck stand on end. He had never really believed in déjà vu, but he had the distinct feeling that he had been there before in that very spot and feeling a similar sensation of fear. He shook the feeling off, continued into the water and then began to sprint back to the house. He had to call the police and get them to come out as quickly as possible, praying there was still a chance to find Melissa before she was too far away.

By the time he reached the house he was exhausted. His heart was pounding in his chest and every muscle in his legs stung from the exertion he had forced from his body. Climbing the front steps was the final straw and he collapsed onto his knees at the top, gasping for breath. Victor was standing at the door, so Anthony tried to make hand signals to get him to call for help.

The old man shook his head, sighing and muttering to himself. Anger drove Anthony to pull himself to his feet. As he staggered towards the door, Victor finally spoke. "Do not waste your time. The police cannot help them. They have been gone too long – two thousand years too long!"

He leaned on the door frame and extended his walking stick across the gap to prevent Anthony from going inside. Tears were welling in his eyes as he continued, "I tried to stop this so many years ago, but you would not listen. I tried to save them by making her hate you, but you wanted Lissa back and now it is too late. I can do nothing more. She has to find her own way home, if she ever can."

Anthony stopped, completely confused. The build-up of lactic acid was causing agonising pains in his muscles, and he could no longer go on. Collapsing on the bench by the door, he gasped one word in total desperation.

"What???"

Chapter 7
49 B.C.

Melissa's head pounded as she regained consciousness. She opened her eyes and stared upwards. She seemed to be in a tent, lying on a camp bed, and she was freezing. As she tried to sit up, her head began to spin and, groaning from the sensation, she lay back down.

From out of nowhere a face appeared above her. It was Rebecca, and the young girl looked terrified. "Thank God!" she exclaimed, "I thought he'd killed you."

"Who?" Melissa pressed her hand to her temple and closed her eyes, trying desperately to remember what it was Rebecca was talking about.

"Anthony!" Rebecca wailed.

Melissa could not believe what Rebecca was saying. She tried to think about what had happened since she got up. She had left Anthony in bed and gone to the stream where she had met Rebecca. The two of them had argued and someone else had turned up. That was all she could remember, so something else must have happened. She knew Anthony would never physically hurt her, but she also knew Rebecca worshipped him and so was unlikely to make up such a farcical story. Melissa needed her to explain.

"What are you talking about?" she said.

Rebecca took a deep breath and began. "The men at the river. One of them is Anthony. They were all in fancy dress when they caught up with us. Or actually it was un-fancy dress. They looked like those butch fighters from that Russell Crowe movie. Anyway, Anthony kicked you in the back from his horse and you fell and hit your head. Then they dragged us here. It's like a really big campsite and it's full of men. Hundreds of them. Anyway, Anthony's behaving really weird, it's like he doesn't know me. Oh, and he won't speak English. Do you think it's a movie set or maybe some kind of themed role play? I didn't know he was into that sort of thing."

"He's not," Melissa said impatiently. She sensed she was hearing only half the story. There were so many questions still unanswered, but she guessed there was little more useful information retained in Rebecca's vacuum of a brain. She contemplated getting up again when the door flap of the tent opened. A man she did not recognise entered. He was tall, with a muscular frame and boyish good looks that belied his real age. He was dressed in the full military uniform of an officer in the Roman army. That would certainly qualify as fancy dress, but that was not what Rebecca had said the men had been wearing. It amazed Melissa how Rebecca could have ever worked for Anthony when she knew so little about the period of history in which he specialised. If this man was dressed as a Roman then Melissa surmised Anthony must have been speaking in Latin to Rebecca earlier.

"Good," the officer said. "You are awake. Your friend is unwilling to talk, but perhaps I can loosen your tongue."

One question was answered. He was speaking Latin, and very well. Whatever game was being played, Melissa was not going along with it. She sat up slowly and responded in English. "I don't know who the hell you think you are, but I want to speak to Anthony now."

The officer looked at her quizzically as if he had no idea what she had said. She tried again. "I want to speak to Anthony Marcus."

Still the man looked confused, but he had understood one thing she had said even if he changed the order of the words. "Marcus Antonius?" he asked "You wish to speak with Mark Antony? Are you acquainted with him? How do you know him? I know all of his friends and I have never seen you before. Where did you meet him?"

"Oh, for Chrissakes!" Melissa exclaimed. "Fine. Have it your way." She switched to Latin. "I will answer when I know who you are and where you have brought me." She made sure she was deliberately rude and short in her manner.

The officer was taken aback at her abruptness, but answered nonetheless. "My name is Caius Scribonius Curio and you are in the camp of Caius Julius Caesar. Now I ask you again, how do you know Mark Antony?" Curio crossed the tent and stood in front of Melissa. "Your attire is strange. You are not from any of the local villages. Tell me where you are from and why are you here, and I may be lenient with you."

Melissa was now the one who was confused. Either she had hit her head harder than she realised or there was more going on here than she knew. She had no idea where they were, but it all felt horribly wrong. She looked back at the man who had identified himself as Curio. She took a deep breath and prayed she was not about to make a huge mistake as she followed his lead in the conversation. "We are not from any land you have knowledge of. I will not answer any more of your questions. I will only speak with Anthony," she said calmly.

Curio was annoyed. He stepped towards her and slapped Melissa with the back of his hand, turning her head sideways and doing nothing to improve her headache. Rebecca gasped in shock and Melissa glared at her before turning her head back to face Curio. "I will not answer to you. I will speak only with Anthony," she repeated.

He hit her again, a little harder. Her face stung from the impact, but she was not backing down yet. She turned to face him again "You can do that as much as you like. I will not answer to you. I will only speak with Anthony."

Curio looked as if he wanted to kill her, but instead threw his arms up in the air in disgust. "INSOLENT WOMAN!" he shouted, "YOU WILL REGRET THIS!" And with that he stormed out of the tent.

Melissa put her hand on her cheek. "Damn, that smarts," she said. It was a weak attempt at a joke.

Rebecca looked horrified. "What's going on?" she wailed. "Where are we and why are they being so mean?"

Melissa sighed. "I don't know," she began. "From what he said it would appear they want us to think we are in a replica Roman military camp, but I doubt that very much." She stood up and looked around the tent. All of the contents were Roman in design: a camp bed, a folding chair and table, a portable altar with household gods, a comb, some other personal items. Melissa picked up the items from the table one by one. They had to be replicas, but they were very good ones. She had to get more information, and turned back to Rebecca. "OK, he said we were in an army camp. Tell me exactly what you saw."

"Tents, horses, men. Ooh, thousands of those. Oh and it's really, really cold. It's like winter out there or like we're in Siberia or something, but it only took us a few minutes to get here. I think we should still be on Anthony's estate, but we can't be because it's so cold. What's going on?"

The only answer Melissa had was a crazy one. Common sense told her this was not real. Logically, she had to be dreaming, but could not wake herself up. Maybe she just had to play along and this would work itself out. If it were a dream, nothing bad could happen to either of them: it would only be in her mind, after all.

Despite this, a tiny voice in the back of her head kept telling her she was in the same Roman camp that she had been trying to excavate for the past month and she had just met Curio, one of Caesar's officers and a good friend to Mark Antony. She thought about the facts as she believed they had happened. It had been summer this morning when she got up. She and Rebecca had gone to the stream that Victor insisted was the Rubicon, although the stream had become a fast-flowing river overnight. They had met three men on horseback who had brought them here. It was cold in the tent; every time the flap opened an icy chill blew in, which made it feel more like January than August. In the January of 49 B.C. Mark Antony held the office of tribune of the plebs. He, Curio and another of the tribunes had fled from Rome, fearing for their lives, and reached Caesar's camp, dressed as slaves. That fitted with Rebecca's initial description and what she could vaguely remember from the tatty cloak worn by the man at the river. Rebecca said they had been taken to a camp not far from the river and thought they were still on Anthony's land. The man calling himself Curio had said this camp was under the command of Julius Caesar. Everything Melissa was seeing and hearing led her to believe that, unbelievably, they had gone back in time to a pivotal moment in history. They were witnessing the days just before Caesar crossed the Rubicon and marched on Rome. But that was ridiculous. It was not possible.

Melissa kept thinking about something she had once read, which implied that when you had exhausted all of the impossible answers, whatever you were left with had to be the truth, no matter how improbable it seemed. She knew it was a quote from fiction, a Sherlock Holmes novel, if she remembered correctly, but it kept shooting back into her mind. She also remembered the odd behaviour of Victor the day before. It was as if he had known something like this was going to happen, although he had said he remembered it in the past tense. If they were really in the past, they were in big trouble, but they could not possibly be. She had to be dreaming. *So why could she not convince herself of it?*

Curio returned after a short while and when he did, he seemed smugly pleased. "You have been granted an audience after all," he barked. "It appears you have roused Antony's curiosity, amongst other things. I would advise you to think carefully before you speak, woman. Despite the lies Cicero spreads, Antony is no fool and your charms alone will not save you."

He took each woman by the arm, leading them to the entrance of the tent. His grip was firm and designed to control, but not to deliberately hurt, them. He pushed Melissa through the flap first and as her eyes surveyed the scene in front of her she began to realise the true scale of the situation. For once, Rebecca had not been exaggerating in the slightest: in front of them for as far as she could see were rows of tents all aligned with perfect military precision. Men swarmed between them like ants, all of them in Roman dress. There were piles of weapons and armour, all being sharpened, polished and repaired: it was an army in the midst of preparations for war.

"Holy shit!" Melissa exclaimed. Her mouth was wide open in total awe of the spectacle she was witnessing. She knew instantly that this was not a dream and it was not a re-creation. This was a real camp, it was freezing and now she knew they were in real trouble.

Curio yanked on her arm, pulling her in front of the tents and up a wider path. As he moved forward, the swarming bodies parted, allowing him clear passage. From the layout, Melissa assumed they were being taken along the Via Principalis to the centre of the camp. All Roman encampments were laid out on a grid and this would have been the main thoroughfare running through the centre. On her left were the tents for the men and, to the right, larger tents for officers' quarters and administration. One of these would hold the legionary standards and eagle. Melissa would have loved to have taken just a quick peek inside them, but now was not the time. About halfway along the Via Principalis there would be an open area to replicate the Roman Forum, or meeting-place, with the largest structure next to it for the Commander-in-Chief. Curio had to be taking them to one of the tents nearby.

Many of the men just stared at the women as they passed by; both of them were oddly dressed for the century in which they apparently found themselves and they were attracting a great deal of attention. Melissa began to regret asking to speak to Anthony. She had done so when she believed this was merely some horrible joke, but now she knew it was not. That meant they were going to see Mark Antony, not Anthony Marcus and she did not fancy making his acquaintance one bit. Some of the men made coarse remarks about both Melissa and Rebecca, mostly requests for Curio to share his 'spoils'. One particularly unpleasant remark made Melissa raise her hand to her mouth in a reflex action to cover her shock and for a moment Melissa wished she did not understand Latin so well. This seemed to draw Curio's attention briefly and she immediately dropped her hand to her side, hoping he had not seen it.

Curio made no comment and continued onwards towards the entrance of a much grander structure just ahead. It more closely resembled a marquee in sheer terms of its size and appeared to be at the very heart of the encampment. An odd feeling of relief began to rise in Melissa. It was highly unlikely this was Antony's tent. That would have been the same size as Curio's. This had to be Caesar's tent and centre of command. If they were going in there then they were most likely being taken to meet Caesar himself, if that was who he really was.

Melissa's thoughts spun wildly in her head. There might be an opportunity for negotiation, though she would have to be extremely careful. There was no chance of freedom, but perhaps she could save both herself and Rebecca from a fate far worse than death at the hands of some of the men they had passed. In her mind she rapidly formulated a scheme to offer Caesar something of great value in return for their continued safety.

Curio halted before the guards and spoke to one of them to request entry. The guard disappeared into the tent and Melissa heard him announcing Curio and his prisoners. A moment later he returned and Curio again pushed Melissa through the opening in front of him.

It took Melissa a moment to adjust her eyes to the change in light. It was much darker in the tent than it had been outside. She looked round as quickly as she could, surveying the scene in front of her. Four men stood around a long table at the far side of the tent, all in military dress. They were studying a range of papers spread across the table. One of them was much older than the others, with greying hair and a well-developed bald patch, and Melissa decided he had to be Caesar. The other three had to be his most senior officers, Antony, Pollio and Labienus, though which was which she had no idea.

The man closest had his back to them as they entered, but now as he turned to face them Melissa got the shock of her life. The man standing in front of her was her Anthony, or was similar enough to him to be his double. This explained why Rebecca thought he was here. In the dim light of the tent, the resemblance was uncanny.

Curio spoke. "Hail, Caesar! These are the women we intercepted at the river. This is the one who says she must speak with Antony." He pushed Melissa forward and released his grip on her arm. She stood motionless on the spot where he had left her. "She says they are from a land beyond our known world and I will admit their language is foreign to me, though some words do seem to bear a similarity to ours. I believe her Latin is excellent because she understands far more than she admits to." Curio had spotted Melissa's earlier reaction. She was annoyed at herself for letting slip that fact so soon and resolved to be more careful.

Curio continued talking, his attentions now on Rebecca whom he had pushed to stand next to Melissa. She stood shaking, staring at the floor. "This younger one does not seem to speak any Latin and appears to annoy her companion." *Damn him,* Melissa thought, *he really is too observant.* "She does have some redeeming attributes, though." As Curio made his last statement he reached forward and raised Rebecca's chin, allowing the other men to see her face.

Rebecca began to look around her and as her eyes found Mark Antony, she relaxed. "Anthony! Thank God," she gasped and hurriedly stepped forward. Curio reached out to stop her and found another hand already on Rebecca's wrist. Melissa had beaten him to it. She glared at Rebecca as she pulled her backwards. "Stay still and keep quiet, you stupid fool," Melissa hissed. "That's not who you think it is! That is the real Mark Antony and he'll more likely rape you than help us."

At the first mention of his name, Antony had moved towards them. He now stood in front of Rebecca, looking at her. The girl was close to tears, and Melissa pulled on her arm viciously to stop her collapsing against him. The last thing she needed was for Rebecca to give this Antony any hint that she would welcome any advances he might make. Antony's hand rose to Rebecca's cheek and stroked it gently before raising her chin again to look at her. The girl closed her eyes at his touch, making him smile. His hand moved down to her throat and then onto her t-shirt which fascinated him. He had never seen a garment like it before. The material was soft and felt unlike anything he had ever touched. Rebecca gasped slightly as his hand moved across her breasts and Melissa rolled her eyes in disgust. She had to stop this before it got out of hand.

Melissa turned to face Rebecca and pushed the girl forcefully backwards into Curio. He reacted spontaneously, gripping her arms and holding her fast against him. Melissa glared at Rebecca and then turned her eyes on Curio, who looked a little bewildered at this unexpected turn of events.

Melissa took a deep breath and spoke in perfect Latin with an air of authority she certainly did not feel. "There are private matters of great importance that I must discuss with General Caesar. We have travelled many years to meet him here at this important crossroads in his career, but it appears my companion is somewhat awed by the sheer presence of his handsome officer. I fear she will only be an unnecessary distraction to the proceedings. I would appreciate your assistance, either to restrain her, or, preferably, to remove her from his presence entirely until the negotiations are complete."

Curio glanced towards Antony, who had turned his full attention to Melissa. Both men had met a number of strong-willed Roman women, Curio's wife Fulvia for one, but Antony was intrigued that a foreign prisoner would be so bold in her manner. He walked round behind Melissa, surveying her closely. He had definitely never seen such clothing before and from the earlier display of anger from this woman, he concurred with Curio's assessment that they had never heard such a language. These women had to be from a land they had no knowledge of.

He moved closer to Melissa so that she could feel his breath on her ear. He spoke softly, but with a hint of menace. "You have no authority here, woman – I decide who comes and goes."

Melissa turned her head to face Antony. They were only inches apart and his proximity was unnerving her, making her feel very vulnerable. She did her very best to continue the act. "I beg to differ, sir. You may give the order, but the decision belongs to Caesar." She stared into Antony's eyes, determined not to blink first. Close up she realised that he indeed bore an eerie resemblance to her Anthony, particularly around the eyes which, despite the seriousness of his demeanour, seemed to be twinkling with mischief. As close as she was, she could see his face was more weather-beaten than her Anthony's, most likely from years of hard campaigning at Caesar's side. She could see two small scars – one on his cheek and one on his chin, both partially hidden by the stubble on his face. They seemed fairly recent, but had begun to heal. Her Anthony had no such marks. Antony lifted his hand to Melissa's face and repeated the same actions as he had with Rebecca. He was expecting some reaction from her, but Melissa was not going to provide one either way.

Rebecca had been struggling against Curio. She screamed at Melissa, "What are you saying to him? Stop trying to steal him away again."

Melissa reluctantly turned her head, breaking her eye contact with Antony. Rebecca was becoming a liability and even though the men could not understand what was being said, she had to be silenced. In one move, Melissa pushed Antony's hand away and then proceeded to slap Rebecca around the face for the second time that day.

"SHUT UP!" she shouted in English at Rebecca, who was so shocked to have been struck again that she complied. Melissa continued speaking in a more normal voice, but was still determined to shock Rebecca into submission. "If you want me to let him rip your clothes off you right here then just keep going. Otherwise put a sock in it! Believe me, it won't just be him you get, it'll be all of them – one after the other." Rebecca looked around Melissa at Caesar and the other two men at the table. The thought of them touching her repulsed her and she looked at the ground, quivering in fear.

Melissa spun round to face Antony again, regaining as much of her composure as possible whilst doing so. Antony was smiling smugly, pleased that he had triumphed in their mini battle of wills: she had looked away first.

"A fiery little thing," he observed glancing briefly at Rebecca. "Tell me, what did you say to her?"

Melissa needed to regain some air of authority and the upper hand. She decided to play it safe. "Please accept my apologies for the behaviour of my companion. She is young and frightened because she cannot understand our conversation. I have told her that you will not harm her, but that her behaviour has disrespected the very man we were sent to honour. I have punished her for her insolence and she will cause no more trouble, but I advise her removal – if it pleases you, of course."

Antony turned to face Caesar who gave the slightest nod. He looked back at Melissa. "It does not please me, but I agree that she is a distraction. Curio, take her back to your tent for now. We can deal with her later, together." Antony winked at Curio and casually waved towards the tent entrance. Curio released one of Rebecca's arms in order to salute Caesar and then left, dragging Rebecca behind him.

Antony's attention returned to Melissa. "Now, woman, tell me what it is you want from me."

"Sir, I beg your forgiveness, but it is Caesar I wish to see." Melissa was not wasting time with Mark Antony if Julius Caesar was there. "I knew I would not be granted an audience directly, but equally I knew you would be with him and so used your name to achieve my objective, as your reputation for welcoming a pretty face goes before you. I have important news for Caesar. I apologise to you in advance for my apparent rudeness, but do tell me, why should I deal with the staff when the master himself is present?"

Antony looked at Caesar and laughed. "Can you believe the nerve of this one?" he said to his senior officer. "I shall beat her for her sheer arrogance!" Antony turned round looking for something with which to subdue Melissa, but, as he did so, Caesar spoke for the first time.

"No, Antony. Her guile has got her this far. I may as well hear her words directly, rather than have you re-tell her story later."

Antony motioned to Melissa to accompany him towards the table. She did so, remaining one step behind him and stopped short so as to appear subservient. He seemed content that she at least knew her place in the room. Melissa asked politely, "Please, may I now speak?" Antony nodded and she drew breath to begin, addressing Caesar directly.

"Gracious Caesar, I am honoured to be granted an audience. My name is Melissa and I have come to you from a land far beyond the reach of the arms of Rome. My people have witnessed your many deeds and wish to be friends with the conquerors of the known world. I have been sent to offer terms for trade between our people." She paused. Caesar did not reply, but motioned for her to continue with his hand.

"Many of the women of my race are blessed with foresight. I am one of these women. I have seen a day in the future when all will fall to the might of Rome. The elders have sent me as a gift to you in good faith to demonstrate our commitment to a relationship as allies."

Caesar sighed. "Do you have any idea how many soothsayers line the streets of Rome? If I wish to hear wild stories I can get them for free any day I walk through the Forum. You offer nothing of interest to me." He looked down at the papers on the table.

"I do not speak of vague mumblings that are designed to confuse, or of wailings delivered in a semi-catatonic state. I speak of direct facts, given freely and willingly. For example, when your lieutenant here intercepted me at the river he was returning with unfortunate news." Melissa raised her hand slightly indicating she was referring to Antony. "He has been ejected from the Senate for using his tribune's veto. He, Curio and their companion had to leave dressed as slaves, as their lives may well have been in danger. The actions of the Senate leave you with little choice but to cross the Rubicon, march on Rome and wage war. The die is cast, Caesar." Caesar looked up. Melissa had gambled that he had already formulated the famous phrase she had read in so many books and it appeared she was right.

She continued quickly. "Pompey has no desire to face you in open conflict. He has only two legions, neither of which has seen action for many years. He knows that to face you and the battle-ready troops of the Thirteenth would be suicide when your reinforcements are so close at hand in Gaul." Caesar had more legions only a few days' march away. "He will still honour the wishes of the Senate to take up arms against you, but is making plans for a tactical withdrawal to the south as we speak. You will be able to take Rome and most of the towns in between with little or no bloodshed."

"So far you have told me nothing that I could not have bought from a good spy in Pompey's camp. You will have to do better than that to convince me," Caesar said, glancing again at the map on the table.

Fine, Melissa thought. She muttered under her breath in English, "Let's see how you like this!" She stepped forward to the table and took a look at the map. She pointed at it and reverted back to Latin. "You intend to split your forces, sending Antony here to Arretium. You will send more men here, here and here ..." she pointed at more towns "... whilst you remain in Ariminum to coordinate your operations. Iguvium will hold for a time, but not for long once news of Curio's advance reaches them, since only the commander supports the Senate and the town favours you. You will then move down the coast, turning inland to regroup with Antony and Curio at Corfinium. It will be the first town to give you any real resistance. Ahenobarbus will make a stand there and you know that he will not lay down his command to you willingly. He is a stubborn fool and will ignore Pompey's pleas to leave with his troops before your arrival."

Caesar eyed Melissa with suspicion, but her specific mention of Corfinium had registered an interest in his mind. The news that the town was held under the control of a man who had been his opponent for many years was new information to Caesar. Stranger still, it was odd for a foreign woman to be so aware of Roman politics and, more importantly, of his battle plans. Every move she had suggested was already in the plans that he had been considering long before her arrival, but had dismissed once he had decided against open war. She could not have known any of this from his officers, as he had not yet discussed his ideas with them. He thought back to his walk beside the Rubicon just a few days earlier. *Had the gods sent him a messenger after all?*

Melissa looked around the group assembled at the table. Antony had moved away again and she had lost sight of him, but she could not afford to worry about his whereabouts just yet. Her next move was risky, but it was her last shot at convincing Caesar she was worth listening to. "If Caesar will dismiss his officers I will speak to him of a matter that will prove my ability beyond doubt. I speak of a specific issue close to Caesar. A certain condition that gives him cause for concern ..." Melissa left the words hanging in the air as Caesar stared at her in disbelief. For a moment he seemed truly shocked, but then his expression began to change to one of rage.

"OUT!" Caesar barked the order so fiercely it took Melissa by surprise. She jumped, stepping backwards and collided with Antony, who had been standing behind her. He gripped her around the waist, tightly pulling her against his body. As she tried to pull away he whispered in her ear. "Not you, he means them. You are a clever girl, but I believe you may have gone too far. I can but hope!" Melissa did not like his tone. She could feel his excitement growing as she struggled against him and she had the most horrible feeling she had misjudged the situation. Victor had told her that her observation of the behaviour of others would help her, but she seriously doubted it at that moment.

Caesar sat down in a chair positioned on Melissa's side of the table. Antony held her still until the other officers had left, then threw her to the floor so that she landed on her hands and knees at Caesar's feet. She did not rise, deciding to remain where she was until given permission to do otherwise. Perhaps if she showed some humility, Caesar might be forgiving.

Caesar waited for some time before speaking. "What do you know of my condition?" he asked, finally.

Melissa pushed herself up to a kneeling position, sitting back on her heels. She kept her eyes focused on Caesar's feet as she replied. "I know that you suffer from spasms that require you to bite down on a strap to prevent you biting through your own tongue. You are unable to communicate and suffer disorientation and drooling. These events are followed by periods of great fatigue, when you are forced to rest. The spasms weaken you when they occur and they come more frequently as you age. These spasms are associated by some people with madness, but I assure Caesar that he is not mad. You fear they will be seen as a weakness and so only the members of your household and your most trusted officer are aware of them, and now I, too."

Caesar bent low in his chair and tried to gauge the expression on Melissa's half-hidden face, with little luck. He spoke quietly. "I could have you killed for simply knowing of this. You realise it and yet you still speak of it so freely?"

"Yes, Caesar," Melissa replied. "I am aware of the danger, but I have little choice. I need you to have faith in me and my ability to see your future."

"Then enlighten me. What will I do with you?" Caesar's tone was heavy with sarcasm. He sat back on the chair, examining his fingernails, as if totally disinterested.

Melissa took a deep breath. "You doubt me and are wise to do so, but your secret is safe. I offer my knowledge freely, but it will be withdrawn if I am not treated well. The potential of having such knowledge is tempting and I sincerely hope you will not harm me until you are certain I am of no value. Caesar, I can offer you so much more information: Pompey's escape routes, where you will face him, who will be victorious, even information on your own death when the time approaches."

"What do you mean when the time approaches?" Caesar had noted her last remark, despite his apparent disinterest.

Melissa raised her head to look at Caesar and smiled coyly. "I cannot see that far ahead, Caesar. No one can."

Caesar could not help but smile at this attempt to flatter him, but he quickly composed himself. "And what of the other girl?" Caesar was now openly interrogating Melissa.

Melissa looked thoughtful for a moment. She could say what she wanted as Rebecca could not contradict her, but it had to be believable. If she were clever, she might be able to keep both herself and Rebecca away from Antony, which would be a good thing: she doubted he would need to try very hard to persuade Rebecca to succumb to his advances. "She is my apprentice. Her abilities are not fully developed, but they will come to her soon if she can resist all temptations put in her way." Melissa moved her head slightly towards Antony as she said the last few words. Even though the move was subtle, Caesar caught sight of it and nodded briefly in acknowledgment.

Melissa pressed on. "I must warn Caesar, my ability is not subject to his whims. Visions come when they choose and they may not always be favourable. I am sure Caesar is wise enough to appreciate that a man should only open Pandora's Box if he is prepared to allow all that is inside to escape, whether it be good or bad."

"Indeed I do. Tell me, how many of your people are blessed with this gift?" Caesar had pulled one of his papers off the table, feigning further disinterest, but Melissa was recognising his tactics to make her drop her guard. She was starting to run thin on ideas, but she had no intention of being caught out that easily.

"All of the women are so blessed, whilst they remain untouched. My gifts are lost along with my virtue, which should happen at a time of my choosing, but I am prepared to surrender this decision to Caesar also if he so wishes it. I will agree to serve you faithfully until you decide I have outlived my usefulness or I am taken by force." Melissa deliberately moved her head to stare at Antony, and then looked back at

Caesar. "However the event should happen, the outcome will be the same."

Antony grunted in disgust. "I knew this was too good to be true! She only says this because she knows Curio and I have plans for her and her whiny friend and she thinks she can prevent the inevitable."

"Perhaps, Antony, but for that sound judgement alone I should applaud her." Caesar was trying hard to hide another smile. "Lissa you say your name is?" *Close enough,* Melissa thought and nodded, encouraging Caesar to continue. "Lissa, I will consider your proposal and send word to you of my decision in due course. If nothing else you have bought yourself at least a short reprieve from Antony's bed. I want your word that you will not try to escape, though, or I will ensure you are made available to the entire camp when he and Curio are done with you."

"I give you my word, Caesar, there will be no attempt at escape. My fate is in your hands and I obediently wait on your decision." Melissa bowed her head in respect to the mighty general.

Antony slid his hand under Melissa's armpit and pulled her roughly to her feet. He pushed her out of the tent, instructing one of the guards to take her back to Curio. Just before he let her go he pulled Melissa against him so closely that their bodies touched completely and said in a quiet voice, "Mark my words, if you are lying to him I will make you wish you had not been born. I will enjoy every hour that I take with you and, rest assured, I will continue to use you for my pleasure for many days before I am done." He kissed her so forcefully that she could not prevent his tongue entering her mouth and hungrily searching its interior. Then he turned and re-entered the tent, without giving her another glance.

Chapter 8

Mark Antony was not a stupid man. He had been reckless in his past and done a great many stupid things, but that could be put down to the innocence of youth. Antony had always lived his life to the full, including loving as many women as he could. Generally, he liked to treat them well, having found his liaisons to be more enjoyable that way, but there was something about the way this foreigner stood up to him that infuriated him. She should have been scared of him, but she showed no such fear. Her apparent arrogance was a challenge to his authority and it could not go unanswered.

Antony was used to strong women. He preferred them to have a mind of their own rather than merely being pretty decorations. His mother, Julia, was strong. She needed to be. His father died in disgrace when Antony was ten, leaving him a bankrupt before he was even a man. She had remarried another man called Lentulus who had been a good step-father to the young Antony and his two younger brothers. When Cicero was consul, he had Lentulus put to death for his alleged part in Catalina's conspiracy against the Senate, and a combination of grief for Lentulus and hatred for Cicero had driven Antony off the rails. He had moved into Curio's circle of acquaintants and the wild parties and dubious sexual encounters had begun in earnest. He ran up huge debts and eventually joined the army to escape his creditors.

He had grown up a great deal since then. His army career began in the Eastern Mediterranean provinces under another former consul called Gabinius, before serving under Caesar. He made the most of every opportunity that presented itself to demonstrate his capabilities to both generals and had quickly progressed through the ranks as a result. Being related to Caesar, albeit distantly, had not done him any harm either, though neither man ever mentioned that fact. Now he had become one of Caesar's most trusted officers.

Antony was far from convinced by Melissa's performance. Despite her knowledge of Caesar's epilepsy, he doubted every word she said. He believed her to be a con artist, though admittedly a good one. Perhaps the reason he had such a strong desire to take her on and prove her a fraud was to increase his standing still further.

Returning to Caesar, Antony felt it prudent to ask for his general's opinion before making any statement of his own. "What do you believe? Does she tell the truth?" he asked without committing any emotion that could betray his own opinion.

Caesar was shaking his head. "You know my scepticism on the subject of seers. I doubt any person can accurately predict future events. That said, this woman does seem more plausible than many and she certainly has guts to come here before me, and to engage you so openly. She has detailed knowledge of recent events that you were party to, yet there is no possibility she was in Rome at the time. If she had been she could not possibly have arrived at the Rubicon on foot before your party on horseback and yet it appears she did. And explain to me if you can how it is she knows of my sickness? None except those closest to me have knowledge of that. I trust each of those people to keep that secret, including you, Antony. She has made no wild predictions and needs no trance or ritual to 'see' the future; on the contrary she has remained lucid at all times and appears to be very intelligent. These two women are definitely foreign and I do not believe we have come across their kind before. You only need look at their odd form of dress to know this. And if her people truly have gifts of foresight then they would offer us a distinct advantage in the future. The benefits of such an alliance speak for themselves. The question is whether or not our visitor is trustworthy."

"And how do we find that out?" Antony could tell Caesar was going to go along with Melissa's suggestion, but he knew better than to challenge his general outright at such an early stage.

"Lissa is obviously concerned for her own safety and for that of the other woman. She is no fool and most probably is under no illusion about the desires of an army that has been away for many years; she certainly knows what you want to do to her, my friend! It is interesting that she seems less certain in regard to her own future than mine. She seems unsure whether we will hurt her or not. This leads me to suspect that she may be elaborating her usefulness to save herself. For this I can only commend her efforts; were I in her place and bargaining for my life, I would do the same." Caesar paused as he recalled a time when he had been taken hostage by pirates. He had convinced their leader that his worth was far greater than the ransom that had been demanded in order to buy time and to save his own life. He wondered if Melissa was aware of that incident also and had used the same tactics to impress him. He found he believed so and smiled to himself before continuing.

"The question we must ask ourselves is, do we give her the benefit of the doubt? It is my belief that we should for now. We have nothing to lose from having patience. I must say her proposed tactics for our advance were exceptionally well-thought out – for a woman! If she is proved correct, then I believe I can come to an agreement that is in the interest of us both, but there can be no visible links to me. It would not look well with the people for Caesar to have a woman for an advisor."

"And how do you intend to avoid any such stain on your reputation?" Antony asked.

Caesar thought for a moment. "I will place both of them into your care, Antony, as you have no reputation to protect. Assign them a bodyguard, a man you can trust to not defile them. Treat them well and do nothing to make them fear or distrust you. That may be difficult, I know, but we do not have long to wait until we reach the towns Lissa mentioned. We can review her worth to us at that point."

"And if she proves to be of no value?" Antony was fishing. He only needed the hint of ambiguity to dispose of the women in the most debauched way imaginable, and Antony had a very vivid imagination.

Caesar shrugged. "They are your responsibility. What happens to them will be for you to decide."

"Gladly!" Antony replied, relishing the wicked thoughts that were forming in his mind. "I am sure I can devise a fitting way to dispose of them."

"Do not get ahead of yourself, my friend," Caesar chastised Antony like a child. "There is still the possibility that they will prove useful. If this is to be the case, I will need you to utilise that famous charm of yours to best effect." Caesar paused, staring into space. He was again thinking back to his walk beside the Rubicon. *Had Mercury heard his thoughts? Was this woman the answer to his prayers?*

He returned his gaze to Antony, and smiled. Caesar was fully aware of his lieutenant's reputation with women and knew he needed to be very clear with his instructions to prevent any misunderstandings. "Something about this woman intrigues me. Lissa may yet prove to be one of the most intelligent women you or I will ever meet. I would advise you not to underestimate her, as she is easily your equal. Appeal to her with your mind, Antony, not your baser instincts. I have little interest in the younger one. I find her immaturity distracting. She may prove to be of little value in her own right, other than as leverage with Lissa. Take her if you must in time, but do not touch Lissa without my prior consent. No one is to do so. Do we understand each other?"

"As you wish," Antony replied. He was far from happy, but he knew he had to go along with Caesar's request, for now. Proving Melissa to be a fraud would only increase his standing, and the enjoyment he knew he would get from making her slip up definitely made it a task worth pursuing. The more he thought about it, the more interesting the prospect became. First he would play her game, luring her into her own web of lies until he could catch her out. Then he would make her beg for his mercy and for him to save her from Caesar's wrath.

The more Antony thought about it, the more he realised he was going to enjoy this game after all.

Meanwhile, Rebecca was sitting on the floor in Curio's tent. She was hugging her knees and rocking to and fro, trying to comfort herself. She had never liked Melissa, and the way the older woman had treated her was appalling, but sitting here alone made her realise just how frightened she was. Melissa had been gone for ages and right now, the sight of a familiar face was something she desperately wanted to see, no matter how much she might despise the person it belonged to.

After they left Caesar's tent, she had been dragged forcibly by Curio to the other tent. He had handled her quite roughly and her arm still stung from his firm grip. On their arrival, he tried to talk to her again and although she had no idea what he was saying, she knew precisely what was on his mind. He tried to force her onto the camp bed, but she managed to push him away. Then he grabbed her tightly and kissed her, so she bit his lip to make him stop. At that point he had slapped her round the face so hard that she had fallen at his feet. She was sure he would have gone much further if he had not been called away by another soldier.

Rebecca was baffled as to why every person she had come into contact with today seemed to want to slap her. Melissa had done it twice and then this horrible man. His ring had come in direct contact with her cheekbone and it had split the skin. Occasionally she put her fingers up to feel it to see if it was still bleeding, but the more she touched it the more it bled. She was confused, frightened, and all she really wanted to do was go back to Anthony's villa.

The tent flap opened and Melissa was shoved through it. Rebecca got to her feet and rushed over to her, hugging her tightly. To her surprise, Melissa hugged her back. After a moment they separated. Melissa looked at Rebecca's face and immediately felt guilty. "Did I do that?" she asked turning Rebecca's face to get a better look.

"No," Rebecca replied, "the man who brought me here did."

Melissa spotted a jug on the table and went over to it. She fished in her pocket, retrieving a tissue, and tipped just enough water onto the material to make it damp and cold. "Here, put this over it," she said, handing the tissue to Rebecca. "Don't worry, it's not too bad, but it'll be worse in the morning."

The two women sat down on the small camp bed and Melissa pulled the blanket up around them. It was freezing and they needed to keep warm. She had no idea what to say to the young girl next to her, so she started with an apology.

"I'm sorry for shouting at you and for hitting you in the other tent. Rebecca, we're in a lot of trouble here and I really need you to trust me and not fight me. Can you do that?"

Rebecca nodded warily. "I'll try, but I want to know what's going on," she replied.

Melissa was unsure just how much information Rebecca would be able to absorb, but she had to be honest. She took a deep breath and began.

"OK, I don't know quite how this has happened, but we are not looking for evidence of Caesar's camp anymore – we've found it. The real thing, I mean. This is 49 B.C. and we've just seen Julius Caesar in his Praetorium, which is what they call his command tent. That's why they are all talking in Latin. I've tried to convince Caesar that we could be of use to him, by saying we can see the future all the while we are virgins. We're going to have to wait and see whether he believes me or not, but, if he does, it should stop him from handing us over to the men."

"Where did you get that idea from, because I'm not, and no one would believe you were after last night!" Rebecca exclaimed. She seemed to have missed the point yet again.

"It's not my idea − it's been around for centuries. The priestesses at Delphi in Greece were supposedly virgins and even Ian Fleming used the same premise in one of his novels, but this is all irrelevant. What's more important than anything is that we don't do or say anything to change the course of history. That could be bad for us in so many ways."

Melissa looked at Rebecca for some sign that she had understood what Melissa had said, but Rebecca looked just as confused. Melissa tried again. "Look, whether you are a virgin or not doesn't matter. All that matters is that they *think* we are both still virgins to make sure they keep away from us. Got it?"

Rebecca nodded finally. "What about Anthony? He's here. Why is he being so off with us?" Rebecca still did not seem to understand he was not the man she thought he was.

Melissa sighed. "That man isn't Anthony. I know he looks like him and I don't understand why that is, but I assure you it isn't him. Next time you see him, take a good look. This man's a little shorter than our Anthony and he has a number of scars on his face that ours doesn't have. He is Mark Antony, as in Antony and Cleopatra. He has a reputation for being a bit of a ladies' man, just like our Anthony does, but there the similarities end. He will try to charm you and he will more than likely try to sleep with you, but you cannot trust him and he will hurt you if it suits him to do so. And remember, wherever he is, Curio will not be far behind, if you get my drift."

Rebecca shook her head. Melissa sighed again. She could not believe how dim this girl could be at times. She would have to spell it out for her. "It's like a supermarket offer; buy one, get one free. You let this Antony anywhere near you, and his best friend will expect the same. I'm guessing he's already had a go. Curio didn't just hit you for fun, did he?"

Rebecca looked down and shook her head again. "No. He kissed me and I bit him. That's when he hit me." She leant against Melissa and put her head on Melissa's shoulder. "I don't think I want to let him to touch me again unless I have to." Her voice tailed off to a whisper.

Melissa put her arm around Rebecca and hugged her again. "Listen, I've tried everything I can think of to stop that happening, but I can't promise you it won't. What happens to us is up to Caesar now. If he believes me, Curio won't dare to come near you again, nor will anyone else for that matter. If not ..." Melissa stopped as the words stuck in her throat. She found she was unable bring herself to tell Rebecca what was likely to happen to them if Caesar decided to hand them over to the five thousand lecherous men waiting outside.

Neither woman had been paying any attention to the doorway, where Mark Antony now stood watching them. He could not understand what they were saying beyond the mention of his name or that of his colleagues, but the behaviour of these two women intrigued him more by the second. In public, the older woman had treated the young one like a slave. In private, she was showing concern for her. Their odd behaviour warranted further study. *Know your enemy*, Antony thought.

He cleared his throat, making Melissa and Rebecca both look in his direction in fear. Melissa turned her body towards him, pushing Rebecca behind her for protection and for once, Rebecca did not resist.

"Well, well," he said. "This is a sight to excite a man! I would be happy to see just how close you intend to get, but I do not have the time and so must make do with my own imagination of where this could lead us." He crossed the tent and stood in front of Melissa. "Caesar has considered your request and I regret to inform you ..." Antony left the words hanging as he allowed his eyes to wander down to Melissa's breasts. Fearing the worst, she instinctively pulled the gaping shirt together to cover herself.

Antony looked back into Melissa's defiant eyes. He shook his head and made a gesture with his finger that inferred she was to let go of the material, which she unwillingly did. He nodded and smiled smugly, obviously pleased that he had forced her to obey him. He admired her heaving chest for some time, watching its rise and fall, the only visible sign of her growing fear as she awaited his words.

When he felt he had tormented her long enough he continued, "... I regret to inform you that Caesar has granted your wish. You are to travel under my protection from this day forward. I have assigned you a guard who is outside. You will remain here tonight, whilst Curio will move into my quarters. More permanent arrangements will be made tomorrow, but then you already knew that, surely?" Antony's last words were laced with heavy sarcasm. He could tell Melissa had no idea what he was going to say and that only raised his suspicions further.

Melissa closed her eyes as the relief spread across her face. She squeezed Rebecca's hand and whispered to her, "It's OK." Then she opened her eyes and addressed Antony again, ignoring his sarcastic tone. "Thank you. I am most grateful to Caesar for his generosity. I hope we can be of service to him for many years to come."

Antony laughed. "Oh I am sure you will make certain of that!" He had walked back to the entrance as he spoke, but now turned again to face them. "But when he is done with you, I wonder, will you both be so willing to service me?" he asked, re-emphasising the plans he had already intimated to Melissa outside Caesar's tent. She blushed and looked away as he laughed again and left, shouting something to the guard outside.

Chapter 9

Quintus Vitruvius was a loyal soldier. He had served under Mark Antony throughout the Gallic campaigns, distinguishing himself on many occasions. He was a little shorter than Antony and a fraction less well-built, but he was tough. In a fight, he was more than capable of taking down a man twice his size.

Despite his success in the legions, Vitruvius was a disappointment to his family, who came from the very region in which they were now encamped. His father was a smallholder, and he had always intended Vitruvius to work the land with him to help provide for Vitruvius' mother and younger twin sisters. He wanted his only son to have a good education and had scraped every sesterce to pay for a tutor, thinking that improving his son's knowledge of alternative farming methods would help them to improve the farm's output. Unfortunately, the tutor opened the eyes of a humble farm boy to far more than crop varieties and harvesting techniques. As soon as he was old enough to wear his first toga, Vitruvius ran away and joined the army.

His education gave Vitruvius an advantage over many of his colleagues in the legion: Vitruvius had a mind of his own and was not afraid to use it. At Alesia in Gaul, during Caesar's Gallic campaigns, he had saved the life of his superior officer, Gaius Trebonius, who was one of Mark Antony's friends. Caesar's army had encircled a hilltop fortress, trapping inside the chieftain Vercingetorix, who had become a thorn in Caesar's side by uniting the region's many tribes against the Romans. Other chiefs sent forces to relieve the siege and their men had surrounded Caesar's army, thus trapping them in front and from the rear. Antony and Trebonius were in charge of the defences of one section of the line which came under attack from both sides. The fighting was intense, with many Gauls succeeding in climbing the ramparts, forcing them to fight hand-to-hand with their attackers. As Trebonius fought one Gaul, another came at him from behind, intent on running him through. Vitruvius saw the Gaul before anyone else. He defied his orders to stay in formation and abandoned his place, leaping past two of his fellow-soldiers to save his officer, parrying the assailant's blow when the blade was only a fraction from Trebonius' back. He then engaged the attacker in a bitter fight to the death, even though he was injured himself and now had a long scar running the length of his right thigh as a constant reminder of the day. Antony witnessed the entire event, but had been blocked from going to his friend's aid by the sea of bodies fighting between them.

Vitruvius should have been flogged for defying his orders, but Antony intervened on his behalf. Antony encouraged freethinkers and rewarded Vitruvius' valiant defence of Trebonius by transferring the brave soldier into his personal command with the promise of increased responsibilities and promotion opportunities. Vitruvius had always hoped for promotion to centurion, when a post became available, and, as he walked into Caesar's tent on that cold January day, he honestly believed this was what was going to happen. Needless to say, he was more than a little dismayed to discover he had been chosen to guard two foreign dignitaries.

Caesar complimented Vitruvius on his prowess as a legionary soldier and insisted that he was the only man to be trusted with a mission as vital to the security of the Republic as this. Caesar promised the mission would be difficult and would tax Vitruvius to the limit of his experience. Vitruvius felt honoured to be regarded so highly and was pleased that he would be given such a chance to prove himself. His initial thoughts of dismay left him and he had willingly accepted the task.

It was only after he had been dismissed and was walking to Curio's tent with Antony that he learnt the full truth. Vitruvius had been chosen to play nursemaid to the two women that

Antony and Curio found on the way back to camp. It turned out Caesar had taken a liking to them and they were to remain off-limits to the rest of the men. As Vitruvius saw it, he was being assigned to guard Caesar's whores! He would be the laughing stock of the legion when the rest of the men found out.

At least one thing Caesar had said was true. It was a task that would be far from easy. Trying to keep hundreds of men away from these women would keep him on his toes day and night, but that was only one problem he had to overcome. The biggest threat was not necessarily from the men, but from Antony and Curio, who both had terrible reputations when it came to enjoying themselves. He only hoped that the thought of disobeying Caesar's orders might keep the pair in check, at least for a while. He would find it especially difficult to refuse his commander access to the women if he was ordered to do so. Antony was a man Vitruvius admired and looked up to more than any other for his military prowess, despite Antony's less reputable behaviour in his social life.

The night passed without incident. As Vitruvius remained at his station outside Curio's quarters, he was asked by a couple of the other men what he was doing, but he simply shrugged his shoulders and said he had been told to stand there by Antony and so that was what he was doing. He knew that to play dumb would keep most of the men disinterested. Luckily none of the others seemed to realise Curio was not in his tent, which had no doubt helped to keep them away. No one would dare to try anything all the while they believed a well-respected officer was entertaining the ladies.

The following morning Antony arrived early with a basket containing food and a flask of water. Vitruvius saluted his senior officer, but did not step aside. Antony looked at him quizzically as he waited for an explanation.

"Forgive me sir, but you said no one was allowed inside. These women have Caesar's patronage and so I cannot allow you to enter them. I mean enter there, sir." Vitruvius stared straight ahead as he made his statement explaining his actions.

Antony grinned at Vitruvius' unintentional slip. "That is exactly why you were chosen. You were the only man in this rabble that I knew would take my orders literally. You have done well, but they must eat and I must speak with them, so you had best join us inside. That way you can be sure nothing is entered that is not meant to be. And knowing the truth of what is going on will help you to keep a better eye on your charges."

Vitruvius nodded and stepped aside to allow Antony to enter before him. Antony stepped forward and then stopped suddenly. "Have you seen them yet?" he asked.

"No sir," Vitruvius answered. "You told me to remain outside the tent and that is what I have done."

"Only the older one understands us. She is tricky and not to be underestimated. The younger one does not speak any Latin, but is …" Anthony paused as he thought about Rebecca, then continued, "… Well, you will see for yourself. Come!" Antony placed his hand on Vitruvius' shoulder. "I am afraid this task is about to become a great deal harder for you, my friend," he added and then entered the tent.

It took Vitruvius a moment for his eyes to adjust to the dullness inside Curio's tent, compared to the brightness of the clear morning outside. He saw two figures sitting together on the camp bed. The first woman was reasonably attractive and appeared quite confident, or perhaps it was defiant, he was not sure. The second was younger and had a bad bruise on her face. It was very swollen on the line of the cheekbone, so much so that her eye was partially closed. As she turned her head to whisper to her companion, Vitruvius saw the undamaged side of her face and gasped involuntarily. Antony looked at him and smiled knowingly. He had expected a reaction of some sort. Vitruvius may have been the most honourable man Antony knew, but he was still a man and the blonde was stunning.

Antony put the basket down in front of Melissa and Rebecca and pulled the cover off. They seemed reluctant to accept his hospitality at first until he picked up a piece of bread and bit into it himself. *Sensible*, Vitruvius thought. If the situation was reversed he too would wonder if food provided by his captors was safe to eat.

The older woman spoke as she passed some bread to her companion, who ate it hungrily. "Thank you. We appreciate your kindness. Can you tell me what is to happen to us today?"

Antony laughed and pulled a chair over to sit on. "I find it most interesting that you see Caesar's future so clearly, yet you are unsure of your own." He watched Melissa for a response, but got none and so continued to speak without attempting to hide his sarcasm. "First some introductions and a little history for your guard here," Antony waved at Vitruvius, who stopped staring at the blonde and turned his attentions to his superior officer. "Vitruvius, this is Lissa and ..." Antony paused, realising he did not know the second woman's name.

"Rebecca," Melissa prompted politely. Antony nodded slightly in appreciation. *Re-be-kah.* Vitruvius was repeating the name over and over again in his head. That was a Jewish name, but this woman did not look Jewish. Her skin was too pale and delicate and her hair was the colour of gold, not the darker browns of most women from the Eastern Mediterranean region.

"This is Lissa and Rebecca," Antony repeated, bringing Vitruvius back to reality. These two say they are seers, allegedly sent here from a far distant land to assist Caesar in his endeavours. They are to be his guests until they have proved their worth, or he decides he no longer needs them. Apparently they can only see the future whilst their virtue remains intact and that is why you have been assigned to watch them. You are the one man in this entire army I can trust to keep them whole, regardless of who you have to kill to do so, provided it is not me, that is."

Antony turned his attention back to Melissa. "Deciding what to do with you has not been easy for me. Caesar has ordered that you must remain untouched, unless he decides otherwise, and I must ensure that his orders are carried out. There are many men in this camp and news travels fast. Because you are not unattractive, it will put you in greater danger though that swollen eye your friend has may help her for a time as damaged goods are always less desirable. We are to break camp this morning and as men on the move have no time to act on their desires, you will be reasonably safe until tonight. Vitruvius will be guarding you at all times. It is the best I can do."

Melissa was far from convinced. This was nothing more than a token gesture to appease Caesar, and it left her and

Rebecca considerably exposed. She was hoping for more and decided to see whether this was all Antony was offering or whether he intended to negotiate.

She decided to start with a tact she did not think he would anticipate. "I thank you, sir, for your generosity, but I must express my concern for this soldier. He cannot be expected to remain on duty both day and night. He must be allowed to rest."

Antony was surprised at Melissa's concern for Vitruvius. He had fully expected Melissa to attempt to negotiate, but not on the behalf of one of his men. His curiosity was roused, so he decided to play along and see where it would lead.

"How touching of you to show such concern. What do you suggest I do to solve that problem?" he asked casually.

"Perhaps you should assign another guard to help him in his task," was Melissa's response.

"I can put another man outside the tent, but Vitruvius is the only man Caesar will trust with you, other than me. You would not thank me for relieving him."

Melissa thought for a moment. "What if he sleeps in here with us? This is a large tent. We could find a way to divide it so that he has his own area near the door. That way any person entering the tent would disturb him before they could get to us. You could put any other soldier outside. We would feel secure and he would be able to get his rest."

"An interesting suggestion, but it is impractical for two reasons. Firstly, you have made the assumption that you are to remain in these quarters, but Curio is not prepared to give up his accommodation for another night. Unless you are willing to share his bed, you will need to be accommodated elsewhere. Secondly, for you to share a tent with Vitruvius under the circumstances you suggest would only make your predicament worse. Not all the men are stupid and many would try their luck, assuming you were common prostitutes and so fair game." Antony waited for a minute to let Melissa consider his words. "Of course, there is another option I can think of, but I doubt you would be willing to entertain it." He shook his head as if dismissing his own idea.

Melissa could tell she was being manoeuvred into a corner, but she had started these negotiations and now she had little choice but to continue. "Please continue, I would like to hear it," she said, trying to appear keen and not suspicious.

A smug smile spread across Antony's face. He could tell she did not trust him, but had little option other than to listen to his proposal. "The most logical solution is to tell the men that you are my property, gifted to me by Caesar. That will aid Vitruvius in his task as most of the men would not dare to take something of mine, and the ones who would are not worthy of my concern and I would willingly flog them as an example to the others."

Antony rubbed his hand across his chin as he considered the finer details of his plan. "The two of you would need to move to my tent for this ruse to be believed and, of course, I will also need to continue to sleep in it to keep up the pretence. We may still separate the tent as you have suggested saving you any embarrassment, though it is of little concern to me either way. When I am present, Vitruvius can rest. If I am away, I will order him to remain with you at all times to protect my property, thus allowing him to stay inside the tent without arousing too much suspicion."

Melissa was far from impressed. Despite her earlier misgivings, she knew that having Antony so close could be an advantage in terms of their safety, but it would present its own problems. Rebecca would struggle to separate this Mark Antony from the Anthony Marcus she adored, and she might willingly go to the former's bed if the temptation became too great.

"The question is whether I can trust you to exercise the same restraint as your men?" Melissa asked coldly.

Antony smiled at her with the same smug air of satisfaction. He wanted Melissa within reach of him at all times, in the hope that she would let her guard drop and be more easily caught out. He was surprised at how willing she was to consider his suggestion, but was eager to press his advantage rather than quiz her further at this stage. "I give you my word that all the while Caesar wishes it so, I will not touch you. Should the situation change he will give you to me and so it is sensible for you to be within easy reach. Do we have an agreement?" Antony extended his hand towards Melissa in a businesslike fashion to seal the deal. He had no intention of letting her think too long.

Melissa hesitated. They would be safer with Antony than apart from him, that was certain, but there was still her worry over Rebecca. She looked at the girl who had sat quietly eating throughout the conversation, and tried to decide whether it was worth taking the chance. Rebecca did not notice Melissa was looking at her. She was too busy staring at Antony.

Antony moved his hand backwards slightly as if to withdraw the offer, forcing Melissa to choose. She stood and grabbed his forearm in the typical Roman way, allowing him to do the same to her. "Yes, we have an agreement," she replied, but could not hide the nervousness she felt at her decision. Melissa knew he was going to make the situation almost impossible for her to control.

"Good! I will tell Caesar it is so." Antony's eyes twinkled wickedly as he relished how easily he had won. "Get them ready to leave, Vitruvius. I do not want them to hold us up." He stood up and left without another word.

Vitruvius too was concerned at the thought of Antony being so close to the women every night. He was loyal to Antony and would give his life for him if he was asked to do so, but he still regarded him as one of the biggest threats he would have to face to keep these women from harm. He had a feeling that the older one could put up a good fight and would be too much trouble for Antony or Curio to bother with, but Rebecca looked so delicate either one of them could crush her like an ant.

Vitruvius shifted his attention to Melissa. "You need to eat as your friend has done. It will be late before we stop again. I have sworn an oath to Caesar to protect you and I will do so, but you will need to do exactly as I say at all times. Do you understand me?" Melissa nodded.

Vitruvius crouched down in front of Rebecca. He reached forward towards her face, but she pulled back in terror. "Tell her I do not intend to hurt her, but I wish to look at her wound."

Melissa spoke quietly to Rebecca and put her arm around her comfortingly. "It's OK; he just wants to look at your face. He wants to help us."

Rebecca moved forward slightly, allowing Vitruvius to examine her face. His hands were rough, but he was surprisingly gentle with her as he pressed along her jaw line and up onto her cheek to gauge the extent of the damage. Rebecca flinched as he got closer to the cut.

He spoke to Melissa without taking his eyes off Rebecca. "Tell her I do not believe the bone is broken, but it will take time to heal." Melissa translated for him as he spoke. He ran his hand into Rebecca's hair and gently pulled it down from behind her ear to cover the good side of her face. "Tell her to keep her hair like so. Display the bruise prominently, not the undamaged side. Antony is correct; it will put some of the men off. The others will most likely think he gave it to her for resisting him. It will help to mark her as his property." He turned his head to Melissa. "Perhaps I should hit you also?"

"No, thank you. I will take my chances. Some of the men saw Antony kiss me outside Caesar's tent. That will be good enough to mark me as his." Melissa was appalled at the suggestion Vitruvius had made, but she appreciated he meant it with the best intentions.

Vitruvius nodded thoughtfully. "Most probably, it is a start at least. I would suggest that you do not encourage him to kiss you again, he will most likely take it as an invitation and I will not intervene to save your life if you encourage him. I will get you cloaks so you can cover yourselves. Now hurry up and eat, for all our sakes." He stood up and left, pausing at the door to look at Rebecca one last time.

After Vitruvius had gone, Melissa told Rebecca what was going on. She ate quickly and thought about what had happened. She was still surprised that they were not dead and wished there were some way to let Anthony Marcus know they were alive and well, knowing he would be beside himself with worry by now. Her thoughts turned to the confused conversation she had with Victor. *Did he know what had happened? Was that what he was trying to tell her after she and Anthony had argued the day before?* She sat spinning the engagement ring around on her finger, thinking how loose it had become in the cold January air, when the realisation hit her. *The ring!* It all came flooding back to her as if she could hear Victor saying the words there and then. She needed to send Anthony a message he would understand only when it was too late.

She turned to Rebecca "Find me something to dig with," she said.

"Are we escaping?" Rebecca replied.

Again, Rebecca's stupidity amazed Melissa, but there was no time to get into a discussion. "No, but we are leaving a clue that our Anthony will understand," she said and picked up one of the cups from the basket. She removed her watch and ring, placing them in the bottom. Rebecca handed her the other cup. It was the only other item of use. Melissa smashed it and began to use the pieces to scrape at the hard ground just as Vitruvius came back in the tent. He looked down at the two of them in horror.

"What do you think you are doing?" he said.

Melissa looked up at him in desperation. No doubt he would tell Mark Antony, whether she explained her actions or not. She had no idea whether he could be trusted, but she needed his help.

"I promise you I am not trying to escape. I will never try to run from you so long as we are in your charge," she said pleadingly, "but I promised my people I would leave them a sign that we were safe. Look. I only want to leave these worthless items in this cup and bury it for them to find. I need to show them we are alive and in charge of our own destinies. They must know we have not been taken as slaves."

"How can you be sure they will find it if you bury it here?" Vitruvius did not understand how burying a cup would be seen as an indication of safety.

"Antony told you, I can see the future and so can others in my tribe. They will know to find this cup on the third day of a month called August. It is not a month in your calendar, but it is in ours. Please help us. If not for me then do it for her." Melissa had noticed the way Vitruvius looked at Rebecca. She put her hand gently on his arm and pointed at the other woman.

Vitruvius was unsure what to do. Antony had told him not to trust these women, but he sensed no deception from them. It seemed a harmless enough request, and there was no time to check with Antony, who would be busy with his other duties.

The younger woman smiled at him. She was so beautiful, even with a bruised face. It felt as if Venus herself was asking for his help. He could not deny such a beauty anything, and he made a decision that he knew he would most probably live to regret.

"Give it to me. You will take too long if you do it yourself," he said, pulling a dagger from his belt. He dropped to his knees and began to dig a hole. As he did, Melissa rammed as much of the loose dirt into the cup as she could until it was full. Then she placed the cup in the hole and watched it disappear as Vitruvius covered it with dirt.

Chapter 10
Present Day

Anthony Marcus sat on the end of his bed. He was shattered both physically from the exertions of the morning and emotionally from the unbelievable tale Victor had subsequently recounted. It seemed Melissa had gone to the river that morning, become lost in the mist and ended up in Caesar's encampment two thousand years ago.

It was a ridiculous idea. Anthony's head was telling him that either Victor had lost his mind, or he was hallucinating as a result of the drugs he was taking. That was the more logical explanation, and yet Anthony had not rung the police. For some reason a part of him *did* believe Victor. As absurd as the old man's words were, something was telling Anthony that it did make sense. For a start there was the odd chill he had experienced at the river, giving him that feeling of déjà vu. The more he sat and thought about it, the more he knew he had seen a woman being taken into the mist from that very place once before. He was very small at the time, but he felt certain the woman was someone important to him, possibly his aunt, and that a man had come and dragged her away into the mist. She had never been found, although Anthony had no recollection of Victor making too much of an effort. Perhaps it had happened before, or perhaps he too was losing his mind.

If it were true it also explained how Melissa's wristwatch and ring could get into an undisturbed layer of soil. Victor insisted that Melissa was the one who put them there as a message to Anthony that she was alive and safe, at least to begin with. He felt so guilty for ever having doubted her and wished that Victor had explained things properly the day before, because then perhaps he could have prevented this from happening. Of course he knew that if Victor had tried to explain, he would probably have thought the old man had gone completely mad.

It was all too much for Anthony to cope with. His muscles still ached and he needed to relax them. He headed into the shower, turning the heat up and letting the jets of water massage the pain away. Tears filled his eyes and ran down his face, mixing with the water running over his head. No one could see him cry in there, not that he cared if anyone could. All he cared about was Melissa and whether she was truly safe. Victor said she would be fine, but seemed unwilling to give any more details than that. Anthony was less sure. Ancient Rome was a far more violent place than the worst parts of any modern city and no matter how extensive her historical knowledge was, he could not see how Melissa could avoid becoming the victim of a couple of thousand soldiers and their rampant sexual urges. He closed his eyes, trying to suppress his terrible thoughts of what torments she could be going through. He told himself that whatever did happen was not her fault, and that he could deal with any trauma that she had suffered if she could only find her way back home. Wherever Melissa was, Anthony could do nothing to help her. He could only wait, and pray that she would survive.

Getting out of the shower, he experienced a sudden pang of guilt. All this time he had never once thought of Rebecca. She was there too, and in far more danger, as she had neither Melissa's language skills nor her historical knowledge of the period. The fact that she was younger would make her a more desirable target for the sex-starved legionaries in Caesar's army. If the women were still together perhaps Melissa could keep them both safe, but if they had been separated, Rebecca stood little chance. She was as good as dead if she was on her own. The thought upset Anthony, but not in the same way that Melissa's loss was affecting him. He was disgusted at himself for putting one person's life above that of another, but that did not change the pain he felt.

Anthony wrapped a towel around his waist and turned to the sink. As he looked above it, his eyes fell on a word written on the mirror. As the realisation of its meaning hit him, he began to shake and had to grip the edge of the sink to stop his legs from giving way. He was totally overwhelmed by the sudden onset of grief that overtook him at the sight of that solitary word. Tears flooded freely from his eyes once again. He lowered himself to the floor and sat howling in agony at the painful thoughts that were again filling his mind.

The writing on the glass began to fade as the steam in the room dissipated. It was the simplest answer to the question Anthony had inadvertently put to Melissa in the midst of their passions. He had asked her to marry him and he knew that this was her answer.

It was the word 'Yes'.

Chapter 11
49 B.C.

Mark Antony broke camp with three cohorts of soldiers and moved towards Arretium, taking Melissa and Rebecca with him. The town was surrounded quickly and Melissa fully expected Antony to send envoys to discuss terms, but he did not. Antony led from the front in battle and, it appeared, in negotiations. He walked through the town gates alone and unarmed to sue for peace. He gave a speech to the townspeople with no rehearsal, explaining Caesar's motivation for entering Italy under arms and laying out his peaceful intentions to restore order. Soon the townsfolk were welcoming Antony as their liberator. It made Melissa remember another time when she knew Antony would walk alone into a hostile army camp and convince the soldiers to abandon their general and come across to his side. His courage was outstanding and Melissa could not help but admire the conviction he had in his own abilities. Once Arretium was taken, Antony headed south to rendezvous with the main army at Corfinium.

In the first few days, Vitruvius' skills were frequently tested. Some of the men were prepared to chance their luck regardless of who they were up against. He had to forcibly remove two men who had undone the pegs at the rear of the tent and slipped in. Initially, Antony seemed amused by the goings on, but even he was tested one night and was forced to come to Rebecca's aid. True to his word, he had the man flogged in front of the other soldiers as a warning of what they would all suffer if any man were to try anything further. The attacks quickly stopped.

Despite her initial concerns about his proximity, Antony managed to surprise Melissa on a daily basis. The first few days were difficult: Antony was not used to sharing his quarters with two women, let alone two women who were not there purely for his amusement. He slept naked and would wander into the women's side of the tent in the mornings without dressing. Rebecca would stare at his muscular body, which was even more toned than Anthony Marcus', her wishes evident from the look on her face. Even Melissa found it hard not to be impressed by his naked form, though she would do her best to look away. It took a while to set some ground rules around what was appropriate in terms of both conversation and behaviour, but as the days rolled into weeks the situation gradually improved.

Antony got into the habit of eating with Melissa and Rebecca every evening, before going out to fraternise with his men. This had nothing to do with him wishing to play the consummate host, but gave him his best opportunity to interrogate Melissa. He would ask her variations of the same questions day after day, trying to catch her out. Melissa was always very careful in her responses. She had decided at the very start to keep as close to the truth about her real life as was possible. That way, it was easier to keep to the same story and not have to worry about any lies that she may have previously told. The major exception was Anthony Marcus, whom she was careful to never mention.

Over time, Antony seemed to tire of the interrogations and instead began to engage her in debates about philosophy and politics. Melissa would ask him to tell her about his past escapades. After all, she was stuck in what she considered to be one of the most interesting periods of Roman history, so why not find out as much as she could from someone who actually lived through it?

The more Melissa flattered him, the more Antony was willing to talk and she began to see a different side to the man on whom her safety depended. He was not the mindless drunk that Cicero would later portray. He was intelligent, charming, witty and considerate, even generous when the occasion suited him to be. He was a man who demanded loyalty, but won it with ease. His men loved him and Melissa honestly believed they would follow him into the depths of hell if he asked them to. It made her wonder why his life would fall apart so spectacularly in the years that followed Caesar's death. Still, she knew she might yet find out, if she was lucky enough to live that long.

Antony was far from perfect. He displayed a vicious temper that frightened Melissa. He drank far too much and gambled excessively whenever the chance arose. In many ways Melissa found she could draw far more similarities than just looks between the man she was now living with and the man she loved and had left behind in her own time. It made it harder not to like this Antony, faults and all, but, as she kept reminding herself, he would kill her without question if it served his purpose to do so.

Vitruvius was a harder nut to crack. He appeared the type of man who liked to follow orders and tried hard to avoid speaking to Melissa at all, but he did have one weakness and that was Rebecca. Despite his attempts to appear non-committal in his attitude towards either woman, he would do anything for the girl. Melissa spotted this and used it from the very first day. After they made camp on the first night, he had brought a poultice for Rebecca's cheek and an extra blanket to keep her warm. From that moment, Melissa encouraged Rebecca to use his feelings for her to get them things they needed like extra water rations and some more appropriate winter clothing. Despite the language barrier, Rebecca knew exactly how to use her natural talents to best advantage. It appeared she had a use after all.

Melissa tried to teach Rebecca as much Latin as she thought was needed to get by. She could not guarantee to be around every minute and Rebecca would have to start learning to help herself. Unsurprisingly, Rebecca turned out to be hopeless at learning anything more than the basics of the language and Melissa soon found it was easier to leave her to point at things and let Vitruvius work it out for himself. He seemed more than happy to oblige, as it meant he could spend even more time with Rebecca.

Even though she was busy keeping Vitruvius' focus on her, Rebecca still harboured a wish for Antony to notice her. No matter how hard Melissa tried to persuade her to be careful around him, Rebecca either did not believe her or was deliberately ignoring her. Rebecca would adopt the same seductive poses in Antony's presence as she did to impress Vitruvius and would deliberately leave gaps in between the curtains that divided the tent to allow Antony to watch her undress. There were times Melissa wanted to scream at her to stop, but she knew it would not do any good. Antony was a man with a famously strong libido and it was only a matter of time before he would give in to his own needs, regardless of Caesar's orders. Melissa also feared that any relationship between Antony and Rebecca would hurt Vitruvius' feelings. As he was the only person in the whole camp that she felt completely safe to be near, Melissa did not want anything to damage the fragile relationship she was trying to foster with him through Rebecca.

What Melissa had failed to notice was that Antony was not particularly interested in Rebecca; he was more interested in her. She should have seen the pattern, but it had completely passed her by. All the women from history that Mark Antony had ever been involved with were strong-minded, wilful individuals who stood up to him. Rebecca did not fit that description in the slightest, but she did.

It was late February when they reached Corfinium and reunited with Caesar's army as it laid siege to the town. Melissa knew Caesar would expect more information and had already decided to tell him just enough to keep his interest.

Caesar sent for Antony as soon as they arrived. He returned a short while later with the news that Caesar was sending him to Sulmo. As he was confident he would not be gone more than a few days, it had been decided the women would remain in the main camp with Vitruvius.

It was a further six days before Curio came to the tent in search of Melissa. It was the first time they had seen him since their meeting at the Rubicon, as he had taken a different route to Corfinium. His interest in Rebecca appeared to be as strong as ever and he never took his eyes off her for a second.

"Caesar wants to see you," he barked at Melissa curtly. "Vitruvius, take this one to him immediately."

Vitruvius hesitated. "No, sir, Antony said I was not to leave either of them alone under any circumstance. I cannot take only one without the other."

Curio rubbed his chin as if he were considering the problem. "Caesar was insistent you were to take only her, but I can understand your concern for Antony's property with so many men outside." Curio looked Rebecca up and down hungrily as he delivered his solution. "I am as a brother to Antony. He trusts me like no other. I will wait here with the other one until you return, to keep her safe. You have your orders man, go!"

Vitruvius did not move. He had seen the look of terror on Rebecca's face when Curio had first walked in, guessing from her reaction that it was Curio who had given her the black eye. He saw the look in Curio's eye and knew what the man was hoping for. Vitruvius had no intention of leaving Rebecca alone with Curio again, so he motioned to her to come to him. She did so nervously and he pushed her behind him. Then he spoke to Curio again. "With all due respect, sir, they both come with me or none of us will go. That was Antony's first order to me and only he can rescind it."

Curio's expression changed immediately to somewhere between frustration and defeat, but he knew it was a waste of time to argue further as Vitruvius would never back down. He raised his hand and waved them all away, letting them leave without another word. Melissa knew he would never give up the way the rest of the men had, but was content in the knowledge that Vitruvius was smart enough to see through the attempted ruse. She had thought he was nothing more than the average soldier, but this action gave her reason to hope there was an intelligent person under his hardened soldier's shell.

When they arrived at Caesar's tent they were kept waiting. Once they were granted an audience, Vitruvius remained by the door with Rebecca and told Melissa to approach Caesar alone.

Caesar smiled at her as she approached. "Well, Lissa, it appears you have been correct in every detail save one. I have just received word that the town is prepared to surrender to me, as you predicted, but that Ahenobarbus has taken his own life." Caesar was in good mood and seemed genuinely pleased to see her. Antony was present too, having just returned from Sulmo, but he paid Melissa little attention as he stood on the far side of the tent.

Melissa shook her head, knowing Caesar's statement to be incorrect. "He has not. The poison he obtained was not strong enough to kill him. He is sick, but will recover and be forced to throw himself on your mercy."

Caesar looked at Antony and cocked his head slightly, as if they were sharing a private joke. "I know, as I had one of my spies deliver it in secret to his physician," Caesar replied, smiling again as he did so. "Only he and I knew of its limited potency. No one could have informed you. It appears you really do see both present and future events."

He raised his hands in a mock gesture of submission and laughed. "Forgive my crude test of your abilities, but I had to be certain you were not receiving intelligence from another source. I could not take up your offer of assistance if it were not so, and that is exactly what I intend to do. You will continue to provide me with information on my future and I will provide you with a home in Rome and an allowance to live on, administered through Mark Antony. You will remain in his care. I understand he has been treating you well and will have no objection in continuing with the arrangement." Caesar looked up at Antony who merely shrugged his shoulders without comment. Melissa could tell he was less than pleased. He may have been playing the willing host, but he still had another agenda.

Caesar's attentions switched to Vitruvius. "What say you, Vitruvius? Will you continue to protect your charges and keep them safe from harm? I will raise your pay by one half if you agree."

"Yes sir," Vitruvius answered without hesitation. It was not such hard work and he would be stupid to refuse more money. It also meant he could remain close to Rebecca, even though he knew she felt nothing for him. She was attracted to Antony, any fool could see that, but Vitruvius did not care. He was falling in love with her a little more every day and would do anything to stay by her side.

"Thank you, Caesar. I appreciate your kindness towards me and my companion," Melissa said with relief. She had kept them alive this far and it was about to become a lot easier.

It was time to offer up more information. "Caesar, you do realise that the delays here have allowed Pompey to retreat further south and have given him a chance of escape?" Melissa ventured.

Caesar nodded. "I had thought as much, but I have no wish to fight him. I would rather negotiate for a peaceful end to this stupidity. I imagine he has gone to Brundisium as it has the best harbour from which to embark for Greece. I have sent envoys to the town to negotiate his surrender. Tell me – will they will succeed?"

Melissa shook her head. "Pompey is in Brundisium, as you suspect, but he has gone too far to back down. Men like Cato harass him daily to attack you, yet he is wiser than they are. He knows he cannot engage you and win. He has already evacuated most of his men and now awaits the return of his ships to port to leave with the rest. He intends to regroup in Greece, just as you thought, before launching a counter attack. You are already too late to stop his escape."

Caesar sighed. He was genuinely saddened to hear he would have to fight Pompey to resolve the crisis, as he knew only one of them could win and the other would be destroyed. "You say I am too late to stop him, but I say I can still try. We must discuss my next move before I give the orders to pursue Pompey. Vitruvius, take that one back to their quarters. Lissa is perfectly safe here with us. Antony will return her to you in due course."

Caesar turned to Antony who began to lay out the planned advance to Melissa, just as history had taught her it had happened. Melissa explained that Pompey's fleet would be ready to leave as soon as Caesar's forces arrived at Brundisium, but Caesar knew Pompey would have to wait for the wind to be in his favour. He had to find a way to delay his former colleague from getting his ships out of the harbour long enough to take the town. Melissa suggested Trebonius might have the best solution, though even this was unlikely to work. She gave information that the town was covered in traps designed to prevent Caesar's advance and he immediately ordered Antony to send out spies to infiltrate the settlement and find a local Caesarean sympathiser to help steer them through.

As they discussed the battle plans, Antony watched Melissa closely. She was not afraid to speak her mind and appeared to be as good a tactician as Caesar when it came to warfare. He smiled to himself. This woman truly was his equal in intellect, and that only made him want to tame her all the more.

On arrival at Brundisium, Caesar made camp outside the walls of the city, blocking the main approach to the town. He sent men to the headlands on both shores of the harbour to encircle Pompey's fleet, which was waiting patiently in the harbour for a favourable wind to carry it safely away before the bombardment began. It was the first real battle Melissa had witnessed, even from a safe distance, and she certainly hoped it would be her last.

Caesar attacked the gates directly and with such ferocity that it briefly distracted the defenders from the activities of his troops on the headlands, where Trebonius was in charge of an ambitious scheme to build pontoons across the harbour entrance. It had been his idea to blockade the harbour, thus preventing the fleet from leaving its moorings, and, as Melissa informed Caesar, it was their only chance to trap them, albeit an extremely slim one. Trebonius' men did not have long before Pompey finally understood the danger they represented, at which they immediately came under fire from Pompey's troops who were intent on burning the floating structures in order to break out.

Even though they were well away from the fighting, the acrid smell of the burning pontoons was as terrifying as the unnatural orange glow that loomed on the skyline. Rebecca whined constantly about the inconvenience the battle was causing to her sleep, while Vitruvius paced up and down like a caged animal in a zoo. Not being a part of the fighting was driving him mad with frustration and his behaviour added to the tension Melissa was already feeling. This was the first real test of Melissa's memory of how events were meant to unfold and her anxiety grew by the minute at the thought that she may have given Caesar information that could change the outcome of the battle. They all needed a distraction.

Men moved to and fro constantly, with orders being shouted non-stop. Fresh troops would move to the front as the injured were brought back to the camp. Melissa knew that although a Roman surgeon's skills were good for the time, they were limited in comparison with modern medical techniques. Most of the badly injured would die on the battlefield. Those who made it back to camp would need their wounds treated and there were not enough people available to do the job effectively. Melissa talked Vitruvius into taking them to the injured men to provide whatever assistance they could. Rebecca was far from impressed by the idea, which she felt was beneath her, but Melissa insisted she came, hoping the experience might teach Rebecca some humility.

They cleaned wounds and bandaged arms and heads each day, collapsing on their beds from sheer exhaustion each night. One young man who had been working on the pontoons was brought in with horrifying burns to one side of his body. He screamed as the surgeon tried to pull the buckled armour away from his charred flesh. There was absolutely no chance he would survive, but the sight of Rebecca seemed to comfort him. Melissa told her to sit and hold his good hand until he finally slipped into unconsciousness and died. It was a horrible thing to make the girl experience and she retched every time she looked down at the boy writhing in agony beside her, but it silenced her incessant whining for a time. Despite her apparent shallowness, Rebecca came to appreciate that there were men in real physical pain, as opposed to the minor discomfort she was suffering.

When the news of Pompey's escape finally came, Melissa breathed a sigh of relief. She was tired, ached all over and was covered in dirt and the blood of many men. She could hardly wait to get back to the tent and take off her ruined clothing, which she fully intended to burn at the first opportunity. What Melissa really wanted was a long soak in a hot bath, but she knew there was no chance of that.

As she collected a pail of clean water, Melissa was startled by a familiar voice speaking to her. "I did not expect to find you here. I understand you have helped many of my men over the past few days and I am thankful for it. I wonder if you would be so kind as to grant me the same service."

She spun round to face Antony, ready to rebuff him for yet another inappropriate remark, but instead simply stared at him in horror. His right arm was covered in blood that had run down from a gash below his shoulder. It looked deep, almost to the bone, and would need to be stitched, but it was not life-threatening.

Antony spoke again. "I should learn to duck on occasion, but knowing when to has never been one of my better skills." He reached down and took the pail from Melissa's hand with his good arm. "Shall we go, in or is it your hope that I will bleed to death here?" he asked with a smile. Without thinking she reached out and took his bloody hand in hers and pulled him into the tent, shouting at Vitruvius to get the surgeon as she went.

Inside Melissa sat Antony down on a stool away from the door. She was concerned that he had been wounded, but she had no memory of such an event occurring, although admittedly it was not a wound worthy of mention by any historian. It made her wonder whether their sheer presence in the past was altering events, fearful that even the tiniest of changes could be significant to the future, but in reality it did not matter. What was most important at that moment was cleaning the wound to minimise the risk of infection before the surgeon began to stitch. The last thing she needed was for Antony to die from a septic wound because she did a bad job. That would definitely change history as she knew it.

Melissa searched for a clean cloth, but could not find one that was not already soaked in someone else's blood. In desperation she stared down at her tunic and spotted a reasonably clean section near the hem. Reaching down, she ripped the material away, exposing most of her thigh.

Antony smiled in appreciation. "Had I known the sight of a little blood would have you undressing for me, I would have stabbed myself on the first day!"

Melissa ignored him and began to wash his wound gently, making sure she removed every speck of dirt she could see. Antony never took his eyes off her for one moment. He was mesmerised by the care she was taking over him, despite his having never done anything to merit such attention. He had been deliberately antagonistic and nothing less than rude to her, but still she treated him as tenderly as a mother would her child. What force drove this woman on was a complete mystery to Antony, but, as he watched her tend his injury, he resolved to be more considerate of both her and her companion, hoping it might help him to understand them better.

The surgeon came over and confirmed Melissa's suspicions that the wound had to be stitched. There was no anaesthetic, meaning it was going to be extremely painful. Melissa handed Antony a flask of wine which he downed in one go. Vitruvius moved around behind his commander, to hold him still while the surgeon worked. As Melissa moved out of the surgeon's way, Antony reached out and grabbed her arm.

"Stay. Talk to me, please." He spoke the words with so much sincerity that Melissa found she could not bear the thought of leaving him. She had forgotten momentarily which Anthony she was with and her only thought was to help the man in front of her through the next few minutes.

Melissa sat down on the other side of Antony, took his left hand in hers and stared into his dark brown eyes. He stared back at her, holding her gaze. She had no idea what to say and so she began telling him about her garden. The sensation of the needle tugging at his flesh made Antony's grip tighten on Melissa's hand, making her regret her decision to let him hold it. She could hear popping noises from her finger joints as he squeezed, and the sensation of her own bones grinding together sickened her, but she kept talking. All the time Antony stared at her, listening intently. She continued to talk even when the pain from her own hand became so unbearable it made her cry. She watched his face redden as he struggled to hold onto what little control he had left, but still he stared into her eyes, never once blinking.

When the surgeon finished, Antony smiled weakly. "I believe that was the most honest you have been since your arrival," he said. "It is a pity I did not understand a word of it." He slumped forward as he passed out from the pain and it dawned on Melissa that she had been speaking English the whole time, although Antony had not corrected her. She realised that what she had been saying was unimportant – he only cared that she was there to help distract him.

Chapter 12

The journey to Rome was far more pleasant than the journey to Brundisium. Extra items kept appearing in Antony's tent: blankets, more food, clean clothes and even wine, which was a luxury they had previously been denied. When Melissa asked Vitruvius to explain where the items came from, he told her to accept them and to never mention them again.

Antony never spoke of the incident in the surgeon's tent and so Melissa assumed that the extra rations were his way of thanking her for her care and dropped the matter. Curio also ceased his attempts to be left alone with Rebecca. He had continually tried to separate her from Vitruvius' protection on the journey between Corfinium and Brundisium, but he too appeared to have lost all interest and Melissa assumed Antony had something to do with this as well.

Melissa knew Caesar could not remain in Rome for long. He would journey to Spain within weeks of their arrival, leaving Antony behind to maintain order in Italy. Melissa began to wonder whether she could give Caesar enough information to be allowed to remain behind. Ever since the incident at Brundisium, she felt safer in Antony's presence than apart from him, even though she expected to have little ongoing contact once they arrived in the city. It was not that Melissa felt Vitruvius could not protect them. She knew he was more than capable of taking any attacker down, but the sheer mention of a connection to Antony meant there would be little need for violence on his part, which would only help to make their lives easier.

True to his word, Caesar made arrangements for a home to be provided for Melissa and Rebecca. He arranged for a house to be rented in a backstreet on the Esquiline hill, placing the tenancy in Antony's name to limit any possible connection to him. He also provided a small allowance for Melissa and Rebecca to live on, again via Antony. Vitruvius was to live with them, and received his wage increase as promised.

The house Caesar provided was not the grand villa Rebecca had imagined. It was of a typical Roman design, approached via a door nestling between two shop fronts. It was small and a little shabby, but more than ample for their needs. The front door opened into a small hall leading through to a covered walkway running along the side of a small courtyard, open to the sky. Melissa was grateful for an open space, no matter how small, because she hated the thought of being trapped indoors all day, believing she would not be allowed too many trips into the city. The main living space consisted of a good-sized dining room and three other rooms suitable for using as bedrooms. A kitchen, store rooms and quarters for one slave completed the accommodation. As cages went, it was reasonably pleasant, or at least it would be once it had been thoroughly cleaned.

Melissa had asked for a slave to do the shopping and the cooking, which was not a skill she herself possessed. She was completely hopeless in the kitchen, living off ready meals and salads back home, and had no idea where to start with preparing Roman food. Antony put a stop to this saying it was an unnecessary drain on Caesar's generosity. As a result of Antony's interference, she and Rebecca would need to go out more frequently in order to buy provisions for themselves in the markets, but never alone. Vitruvius would remain with them at all times for their supposed protection, although Melissa knew his instructions were somewhat different. Vitruvius was under orders to ensure neither woman escaped. Despite assurances to the contrary, Melissa knew only too well that they were Caesar's prisoners. What Caesar failed to appreciate was that escape for them was not an option as they had no way to return home and nowhere else to go, but at least he was trying to make their internment as tolerable as possible.

Caesar granted Melissa and Rebecca one more honour. He granted them permission to wear stolas. These were the garments of Roman women, and it was not permitted for foreigners to wear them. The stola clearly marked a Roman matron, conferring status and a form of protection from unwanted male attention. However, Caesar believed that the unique abilities Melissa had demonstrated warranted her receiving every protection he was able to provide. This also meant Vitruvius' constant presence would be less conspicuous, as it would appear that he was guarding a high-born Roman lady. It was a bold move by Caesar, but no one was ever likely to question him about it and Melissa was extremely grateful for the ability to blend in.

Adjusting to Roman life was not easy for either of the women. Melissa was used to roughing it to an extent, having spent many occasions under canvas or in hostels, but for Rebecca the novelty had already worn off. She had coped reasonably well on the journey, but Melissa soon realised that it had more to do with Antony's proximity. Once he was gone, Rebecca became intolerable, refusing to lift a finger to help in any way. She refused to do any housework beyond cleaning her own room and hated going out into the streets where she felt in constant danger, even though Vitruvius was never far from her side.

The fact that there was no bath in the house was also gave Rebecca cause to complain. She was disgusted at the idea that she had to go to a public facility, but after a week without running hot water, she soon agreed. All Rebecca really wanted to do was lounge around in the courtyard, making the most of the warm spring air, whilst she blamed Melissa for everything that happened to them.

Melissa and Vitruvius went out daily on their shopping trips. They would go out early in the mornings to buy fresh provisions at the markets before the best of the produce was gone. To begin with, Vitruvius never let Melissa out of his sight and would insist on returning to the house as soon as possible, but over time he began to trust Melissa and allow her more freedom. On odd occasions he would leave her to browse in the bookshop, paying the owner a few sesterces to keep an eye on her, while he went to less salubrious taverns to drink and be entertained by prostitutes. Melissa had no objections to his behaviour. Vitruvius was a man after all, and he had needs of his own. A mutual trust was developing between them that

Melissa was intent on fostering at any cost, and she would always make sure she was exactly where she was meant to be when it was time for them to meet. She would buy him presents when she could save enough money, usually a honey cake from the baker's shop outside their house, or a book, on the rare occasions she could find one she could afford, which she would then borrow and read. Vitruvius was becoming her friend as much as her jailor and she enjoyed pleasing him and the liberties he granted her in return.

Vitruvius was just as happy with the arrangement. Despite Antony's warnings to the contrary, he found Melissa to be completely trustworthy. With Rebecca safely tucked away in the house where no harm could come to her, this meant he was free to do as he pleased whenever the mood took him. He had never imagined working for a living could be so easy and so rewarding at the same time.

Caesar summoned Melissa frequently over the few weeks he remained in the city. Antony would often be at the house by the time she and Vitruvius returned from their shopping trips, but he never once grumbled about being kept waiting. He and Melissa would leave for Caesar's villa across the Tiber and return after a few hours, leaving Vitruvius and Rebecca alone. Vitruvius would spend every moment of this time with Rebecca, sitting in the courtyard, teaching her Latin. Unlike Melissa, he found her to be a quick learner and it was not long before they could have limited conversations. However, as soon as Melissa returned home, Rebecca would feign ignorance again, pretending not to understand. She said it was to be their secret and Vitruvius was too besotted to betray Rebecca's trust.

Vitruvius had noticed that Rebecca was a different person when Melissa was away. She was always cheerful and willing to help him to do things like preparing meals for them, for which he was grateful, since he was also a terrible cook. Melissa's presence brought out the worst in Rebecca, and the younger woman would deliberately go out of her way to antagonise her fellow captive. It was as if Rebecca was rebelling against everything Melissa stood for, reminding Vitruvius of his relationship with his father, which served to deepen the feelings he had for her. He admired Melissa in so many ways for her ability to remain strong and to cope with her unfortunate situation, but he fell more hopelessly in love with Rebecca each day.

Caesar left for Spain alone. Melissa convinced him that he would be far too busy to drag two women, supposedly the property of Mark Antony, across the countryside, and he agreed that the women should remain in Rome. Antony was left in charge of maintaining order in the country in his absence, but would still keep a watchful eye over them. If they needed anything on the occasions when Antony was away, Melissa was to ask to see Marcus Lepidus. Lepidus was in charge of order in the city. He was a good man and a loyal and competent soldier. Calm and thoughtful, Lepidus provided Caesar's administration with a steadying alternative to Antony's act first, ask questions later approach.

Antony, meanwhile, went about his business, speaking with the troops stationed in the countryside, listening to their concerns and generally keeping up their morale. Antony's own morale was kept up by the constant attentions of his mistress, an actress called Cytheris who accompanied him everywhere he went. As Caesar's representative, Antony carried out the duties he had been assigned efficiently, if in a most unorthodox fashion.

He had been given one other task to perform beyond maintaining order, which was to persuade Cicero to stay in Italy. Marcus Tullius Cicero was a great orator and former consul of Rome. He was not a member of the Roman elite and had fought tooth and nail for everything he had achieved. So far, Cicero had remained neutral in the conflict between Caesar and Pompey, having retreated to his villa outside Rome before the fighting began. Many of the senators who had not yet decided which side to take were waiting to see what Cicero intended to do.

Antony had no love for the man he believed had murdered his step-father, but he did his utmost to persuade Cicero to come over to Caesar's side. He wrote countless letters that he discussed with Melissa, utilising both flattery and veiled threats to achieve his objective. Melissa felt privileged to be taken into his confidence in such a way, and never found a reason to criticise any of the beautifully constructed prose. The letters only helped to cement the view in Melissa's mind that Antony had been misjudged by so many people because of the wicked lies spread about him by his successors. He was a thoughtful and eloquent man, who was proving to be so much more than she had ever hoped he could be. Against her better judgement, Melissa was beginning to have feelings for the man she was indebted to.

In showing the letters to Melissa, Antony had found an excuse to spend time with her. Her intelligence and interest in the complex Roman political system still fascinated him. Having a woman to talk to as a complete equal was a new experience. He already had a wife to give him legitimate children, as well as a great deal of aggravation, and a beautiful mistress to entertain him sexually. But to find a woman who could stimulate his mind as well as his loins was a rarity that he had only ever found once before: unfortunately, she had married his friend Curio and was now beyond his reach.

Despite his intentions to get to know Melissa purely to be able to undermine her, Antony found he enjoyed her company and even longed for it. If only he could develop a closer relationship with this foreigner, he felt his life would be complete and he would have no need for either of the other women who currently shared it. He knew this was no more than an idle fantasy, as convincing Melissa to give up the life and benefits she had as Caesar's seer in return for a life as his consort would be impossible.

It was such a pity when Cicero finally decided to join Pompey. Even though he was a friend to Caesar, Cicero owed a great deal to Pompey, who had also risen from the lower classes and had given his support to Cicero's bid for the consulship many years before. Eventually, the pressures of loyalty made Cicero's decision for him. Antony took it badly and blamed himself for his failure, but it had nothing to do with his inability to express himself or argue his case. It was simply never meant to be. Melissa tried to console him with her words, but words were not what Antony wanted and his visits became less frequent. For him, the temptation of showing Melissa his true feelings for her was becoming too great and he needed to distance himself before making a mistake he would later regret.

Chapter 13

L ife continued reasonably happily in the little household until the heat of the Roman summer became unbearable. Antony had not visited since Cicero's departure for Greece. Melissa and Vitruvius continued to go out early in the mornings, but came back as soon as they had shopped for necessities to avoid being out in the blistering sun.

The heat seemed to affect Rebecca more than the others. She took to staying in bed for most of the morning and was unable to keep anything down if she tried to eat. All she could drink was warmed water with a little ginger root that Vitruvius gave her, a recipe his mother used to give him as a child when he felt nauseous. In the evenings when it became cooler she would eat like a horse, desperate to make up for her earlier self-imposed starvation. It was a pattern that worried Vitruvius and it was not long before he began to leave the house alone, so that Melissa could stay with Rebecca in case her health deteriorated further.

One morning, after Vitruvius had gone out, Rebecca surprised Melissa by getting up early. She seemed to be in better sorts, wandering into the dining room in the same casual way as she had before her illness. She sat on the couch opposite Melissa, who was reading one of the scrolls she had purchased for Vitruvius.

"Is Vitruvius out?" Rebecca asked quickly before Melissa had a chance to speak.

"Yes, he's gone to get more ginger for you and will collect water from the public fountain on the way back. You seem to be feeling better this morning." Melissa was suspicious. Rebecca seemed nervous, edgy even. She had failed to make eye contact and Melissa knew she was being evasive.

"Good," Rebecca said and looked at Melissa for the first time. "I have to tell you something and I don't want him to hear it just yet, although he'll find out soon enough. I'm pregnant. I'm expecting Antony's child."

"What?" Melissa said. She sat up, allowing Vitruvius' treasured scroll to fall to the floor. "How far gone are you? Did he rape you?"

"Nearly three months, and no he didn't rape me. *I* seduced *him*," Rebecca said smugly.

"When did you get the chance to do that? You can't leave here without Vitruvius and I know he wouldn't be party to this, not that you ever go out anyway. When exactly have you had sex with Antony?" Melissa was totally astounded by what she was hearing.

"That town where you made me sit by the dying guy. That was the first time and I admit he was a bit out of it. I'd gone to check on his wound, the way you'd been doing. He'd thrown all the covers off and I was going to put them back, but he was just lying there on his bed, naked, and I couldn't resist. I think he thought it was you to start with, but he soon realised his mistake. We did it whenever we could after that." Rebecca spoke as if it was an everyday occurrence.

"What? How the hell did you do that without my knowing? I was sleeping right next to you." Melissa knew she was not the lightest sleeper, but even so, she should have heard something.

"I wasn't putting so much water in your wine so that you would sleep heavier than usual. Anyway, we weren't always in our tent."

"Then where were you?" Melissa was dreading the next answer. She feared she already knew what Rebecca would say.

"In Curio's. You were right about them being close. Antony would loosen the pegs by his bed. I could slip under the canvas while he went out the front so Vitruvius didn't suspect. I didn't want to do it to begin with and I cried the first time that Curio touched me, but Antony sat and held my hands all the time he was with me."

"Held you down more like," Melissa interjected in disgust.

Rebecca poked her tongue out childishly before ploughing on, ignoring Melissa. "The sex with Antony afterwards was amazing. It seemed to turn him on to watch his friend screw me first, so I did it to please him."

"Oh this just gets better and better. I told you this would happen and you did it anyway. You stupid, stupid girl!" Melissa was appalled at the lack of judgement Rebecca had shown. This news also left Melissa with a new question to be answered. "If you've been with both of them, how can you be so sure it's Antony's?"

"I had a period when we got here. I haven't seen Curio since then because he went back to his wife, so it has to be Antony's."

"And when exactly have you seen Antony?" This had to be a joke. Rebecca never left the house. When Antony came by, they were all present. There had been no opportunity for them to be together. Melissa began to wonder if Rebecca was making it all up.

"He comes when he knows you and Vitruvius are out. That's the real reason we couldn't have a slave to cook and clean for us. It was the best way he could think of to get you out of the house so we could be alone. Have you never wondered why he's always here when you come back from the town, but never cares that you've kept him waiting?" Rebecca laughed callously. "And you think I'm dim! Well, who's the dim one now?"

Melissa sat back on the couch in shock. Now Rebecca's behaviour made perfect sense. It was not that she was frightened to leave the house – she was frightened of missing Antony. Every day that Vitruvius took Melissa to the markets, Rebecca was waiting at home just in case her lover dropped by. And yet still something failed to add up. Rebecca had too much detail for the few words of Latin Melissa had taught her. "Hang on. How do you know all this? Your Latin isn't that good."

"I know more than you think I do. Vitruvius has been teaching me when you're not here in the afternoons and you'd be surprised at how good Antony is at explaining things so I understand. He's very clever, you know. I've even thought about teaching him some English, especially now he's going to be a daddy." Rebecca lay back on the other couch as she spoke, dreaming of a perfect future with Antony.

"Absolutely not! You teach him one word and I will throw you out of here myself. The more Antony knows about us, the more dangerous he becomes, and you have no concept of when to speak and when to shut up. Don't you realise what you've done has already altered history? Who knows what we will go back to, that is, if we can ever go back. Don't make it any worse, please, I'm begging you." Melissa was distraught. She had risen from the couch and was pacing up and down. She put her hand up to her forehead as she tried to think. She felt suddenly tired and wanted to run away and hide. All her efforts to protect the future they knew had been for nothing because of Rebecca's stupidity.

Rebecca was speaking again. "I haven't had the chance to tell him yet because he's gone off to see some woman who is ill. I think he said she has syphilis. He sees her a lot because he cares about her."

Melissa looked confused. Syphilis was a term unknown to the Romans as far as she knew, so Rebecca must have misunderstood. Once she had wracked her brain for the answer, Melissa's initial confusion quickly subsided as the truth dawned. She burst into laughter. "It's Cytheris, not syphilis, you fool. Her name is Cytheris and she's not sick. She's another of Antony's many lovers. You didn't think you were the only one did you? You do know he has a wife as well? Her name is Antonia and they have a daughter." She sat down on the couch again and took control of her laughter.

Rebecca looked appalled, but Melissa had no idea whether it was because of her reaction to Rebecca's news, or whether the truth was finally beginning to dawn on the girl. Melissa went on calmly, hoping to get the point across. "Morals here may seem loose to you, Rebecca, but not in the way you hope. It is perfectly acceptable for a Roman male to have many mistresses, but his recognised children will all be from his Roman wife. When you tell him you're in the club, he'll drop you like a stone. Antony will never acknowledge that your child has anything to do with him and I can't ask Caesar for help because he won't give a damn about the situation, beyond the inconvenience it will cause him. Even if Caesar was prepared to intercede, the fact that you slept with Curio even once just makes it easier for Antony to deny responsibility and paint you as the camp bike!"

Rebecca stood up suddenly. "HE WILL NOT DO ANY OF THAT. HE LOVES ME! I KNOW IT! YOU ARE ONLY SAYING THIS BECAUSE YOU'RE JEALOUS THAT HE CHOSE ME THIS TIME, NOT YOU." She was screaming and stamping her foot like a petulant child. It only helped to reaffirm for Melissa just how immature she was. Of all the people she could have been stuck in the past with, Rebecca was the worst.

Melissa stared at Rebecca as the depth of the girl's hatred finally hit her. Rebecca wanted Mark Antony to love her, because Anthony Marcus did not. It was her way to get back at Melissa, by fostering a relationship with a man so similar to the one they both loved. Rebecca wanted to hurt Melissa by stealing this Antony away. The poor girl did not understand what a fool she had been.

At that moment Vitruvius stormed in, looking breathless. "What are you shouting about? I could hear you in the street," he gasped before calming himself and catching his breath. "Whatever the problem is, you will have to deal with it later. Antony has returned from his travels and is on his way here now. I had to run to beat him to the door."

Rebecca looked triumphant. "See. He has come to see me, not you. You'd normally be out at this time and we'd be alone. He won't be pleased to find you in, but that doesn't matter. Now I can tell him our news, and you'll have to eat your words."

Vitruvius looked like he was about to say something else, when a knock at the door interrupted him. He shook his head and mumbled to himself as he left to open it.

Rebecca was glaring at Melissa. "At least give us some privacy," she said with utter contempt, but Melissa had no intention of leaving and was about to say so when Vitruvius re-entered and announced their guest.

When Antony entered, the expression on his face indicated his surprise at the presence of both Vitruvius and Melissa, but he made no comment about it. He was caught off-guard and began with a simple greeting to give him time to think of a reason to be there so early in the day.

"I have returned from my travels, Lissa, and have much to discuss with you. I trust I find you well?"

Melissa rose from the couch politely. "I hope your journey was fruitful. You do indeed find us all very well this morning and most pleased that you have returned to us safely, Rebecca especially. She has happy news that she wishes to share." Melissa was full of smiles as she spoke. She turned to Rebecca who was shaking her head, not wanting to tell Antony in this way. "Go on," Melissa insisted in English. "Let's see who's right – you or me."

Rebecca took a deep breath as she moved closer to Antony and began to explain in her broken Latin. "We have baby."

Antony and Vitruvius both looked confused and looked to Melissa for an explanation, but she gave them nothing except another empty smile.

Rebecca tried again, reciting the words in the same way a child learns its verbs. "I have baby, you have baby, we have baby." She reached out and took Antony's hand placing it on her belly, smiling at him as she did so.

Vitruvius gasped and sat down on the nearest chair. The shock on his face said it all. He understood what Rebecca meant, but he could not process the emotions her revelation was generating within him. He knew she had been attracted to Antony at one point, but had thought it nothing more than a passing fancy. Antony had never shown any particular interest in Rebecca and Vitruvius had always thought his commander's attentions were firmly focused on Melissa. His thoughts turned to what Caesar would do when he learnt that he had proved incompetent, unable to prevent the defilement of one of the women in his charge. He had never failed in his duty before, but with Rebecca having Antony's child, Vitruvius' entire world was unravelling.

Antony pulled his hand away from Rebecca's stomach as quickly as if he had just put it into a fire. He stormed over to Melissa. "What is this she accuses me of? Does she dare to suggest I have fathered a child with her?"

Melissa nodded. "She is most insistent that you have." Rebecca had followed Antony and was trying to get his attention by grabbing his arm, but he continually pushed her hand away.

"Why me? Why not him?" Antony pointed at Vitruvius, who was too shocked to respond to the allegation now levelled at him. "He lives here with you. He has more chance than I do to give her a good poke."

"I agree that he does, but Vitruvius does not visit Rebecca's bed in secret when I am out, nor would he dare to misuse the property of Caesar in such a blatant manner. Do not play games with me, Antony. You gave me your word that you would not touch her and still you have been with her. You and Curio both have." Melissa made the last statement very deliberately and then waited to see what Antony would do.

"I said I would not touch you, Lissa. I never agreed to the same for that one." Antony pointed over his shoulder at the poor wretch standing behind him and then paused as he considered what Melissa had just said.

"But Curio, you say ... hmmm ... that is a fair point." Antony took the bait Melissa had so generously dangled. "I am not the only one your friend has been pleasuring. The child could well be his, yet I do not see you accusing him of this act." He turned on Rebecca and grabbed her shoulders. "Curio did this to you?" he kept repeating the words as if he was trying to convince her it was the truth. Melissa could hear the desperation growing in his voice.

"No," Rebecca said and shook her head. Antony began to shake her by the shoulders, still repeating Curio's name until

Rebecca began to cry. It was a pitiful sight to watch, but the truth of how Antony felt was finally beginning to register in Rebecca's shell of a brain. She pulled away from him and ran from the room, tears streaming down her face.

Melissa tried again to get Antony to admit his guilt. "Curio has not been accused, because Curio is not to blame. Rebecca knows when her last monthly cycle was. Her current situation happened here, in this very house, a place that Curio has never visited. This mess is of your doing and yours alone. Tell me, Antony, does your good friend Curio place the blame on you for his mistakes?"

"Now who is playing games with whom? Take care now, Lissa. I will not fall into another of your traps so easily," Antony retaliated. He realised he had been tricked into blaming Curio and he was annoyed by his own recklessness. He was desperate to think of a way to turn the tables on this infuriating woman who was able to outwit him so easily, and smiled suddenly as a way came into his mind. "This has nothing to do with her, does it? This is about you. You are jealous that she has been where you dared not go. I should have seen it before. Your continual flattery of me on our journey to Corfinium, the way you cared for my injuries at Brundisium, even persuading Caesar to let you remain here in Rome was all to be near me. You have wanted to feel me between your thighs all this time! You merely have to ask Lissa, and I will gladly oblige you."

"You flatter yourself. I would not have you if you were the last man alive," Melissa snapped back. She was blushing, but she had no idea why. Her best defence was to attack him again. "I am disappointed in you, Antony. I believed you to be a better man than this, but you are no more than a savage brute that is prepared to take advantage of a pitiful girl to satisfy his lust. What will Caesar have to say when he returns and discovers how well you have been following his orders?" Melissa's sarcasm was cutting and pushed Antony's patience to the limit. He grabbed Melissa's wrist and pulled her towards him, twisting her arm painfully behind her back as he did so.

"And what do you intend to tell him? I doubt it will resemble the truth," he sneered. "Will you tell him how your slutty little companion came to me whilst I slept in my bed. How she excited and mounted me before I was fully awake, making it impossible for me to prevent it. Or perhaps you will tell him how she willingly entertained both Curio and me on several occasions, first one, then the other? No, you will not tell him any of this, nor will you tell him how you failed to see any of it happen. This situation is wholly of her making and it is hers to deal with. It cannot be laid at my feet."

Antony was bursting with rage, but rage and passion are two emotions similar in intensity, and easily confused. The proximity of Melissa's body next to his, mixed with her apparent embarrassment at his suggestion that she was attracted to him, had already given Antony the wrong idea. This idea was merging with his intense passions and awakening something primal in him. He wanted to silence Melissa once and for all, to teach her some respect and bring her to heel. He could no longer resist, and gave into temptation. He moved to kiss her and, to his surprise, she made no effort to resist him. In fact, she began to respond to him, encouraging him to pull her closer.

Unfortunately Antony had forgotten there was another person in the room. "Get out," Vitruvius finally said, coming to his senses in the nick of time. His initial shock was slowly turning to rage, but he was speaking as calmly as he could manage. He could not believe Rebecca guilty of the behaviour Antony was implying; he would not believe it. She was a goddess to be worshipped, not some cheap whore from the backstreets of the Subura. He would not allow these lies about her to continue.

Antony pulled back slightly and both he and Melissa looked at Vitruvius, but Vitruvius did not return their gaze. He sat perfectly still, back straight with his hands on his knees, staring into space and repeated his request to Antony. "I am asking you, sir, to let go of Lissa and leave. Please, do so. NOW!"

"You dare to give me an order in my own house? Remember who you are talking to." Antony barked. He was astonished at such behaviour from a subordinate and he was not prepared to let it go.

Vitruvius exploded. "THIS IS NOT YOUR HOUSE. IT IS CAESAR'S!" He stood up and threw the chair across the room at Antony, who instinctively turned Melissa away from the missile, covering her body with his to protect her from harm. It narrowly missed his head, breaking in two as it hit the floor. "GET OUT NOW OR I WILL KILL YOU WHERE YOU STAND."

Antony released Melissa and pushed her behind him, still protecting her without consciously realising what he was doing. Melissa was shaking, but she was unsure whether it was from fear of what had she had nearly allowed to happen, or from Vitruvius' uncharacteristic display of rage.

Vitruvius took a deep breath to help control his temper, and then began again. "I have always been loyal to you. I have carried out every order you have given me to the best of my ability. I respected and admired you as the kind of man I wanted to be one day, but you are not worthy of that respect. In this act you have betrayed me as much as you have betrayed these women who were in your care. How can I ever trust in you again after this?"

"Those are strong words, my friend." Antony eyed Vitruvius suspiciously. "Be very sure of yourself before you say anything more."

Antony's eyes darted around the room looking for a weapon and began to move slowly towards the broken chair. Melissa knew they were going to fight unless she intervened.

"STOP IT BOTH OF YOU!" she screamed, making both of them turn their attentions towards her. She pointed at the door. "Go, Antony, please, before one of you does something you will both regret. I do not want to have to explain either of your deaths to Caesar." She forced herself to turn her back on Antony and moved towards Vitruvius, placing her hand on his arm, making it plain whose side she was taking.

For a moment Antony stared at Melissa's back in amazement. She was the one responsible for this. She had goaded him, lit the fire beneath his passions and now she expected him to leave, despite the challenge to his authority that had just been made. Backing down was not in his nature and he wanted to retaliate, but not against Vitruvius. That poor sap was only following the orders that Antony himself had given. It was Melissa he really wanted to fight with, but he could not decide whether he wanted to kill her, or kiss her again. She was slowly driving him mad with her hot and cold attitude. He kicked the remains of the chair in frustration and stormed from the room.

As the full realisation of what had happened hit him, Vitruvius collapsed against the wall, his face full of pain as he looked desperately to Melissa for an answer to the question uppermost in his mind. "What have I done?" he whispered as he began to think about the possible consequences of facing down his commanding officer, and the career he had most likely thrown away.

Melissa did not see or hear from Antony again for months. He resumed his tour of Italy with Cytheris in tow. Desperate to forget the woman who infuriated him, Antony deliberately avoided all contact with his charges, choosing instead to spend every available moment with his mistress, a woman who was guaranteed to indulge his whims. The problem was, every time he closed his eyes, it was Melissa's face he saw and not hers.

Rebecca hardly spoke to Melissa after she announced her pregnancy. Antony had stopped his secret visits as Melissa knew he would, but Rebecca chose to believe Melissa had deliberately driven him away. No matter how hard Melissa tried to explain the truth of the situation, it made no difference. As far as Rebecca understood it, Melissa was jealous of her for having stolen Antony's interest. All of this behaviour formed part of the revenge Rebecca so desperately wanted. She had a romantic idea that Antony would come back before the baby was born and support her, leaving both his wife and other mistresses in the process. When he did, she would become mistress of their household and she relished the day she could put Melissa in her place once and for all.

Rebecca now preferred to spend her free time with Vitruvius. He had been a little cold with her to begin with, but had soon forgiven her indiscretions. Vitruvius still loved her regardless of what she had done. He was more disappointed that the man he looked up to had made no attempt whatsoever to help. He was well aware that Antony could not take responsibility publicly for the child of a foreign prisoner, but privately he had hoped Antony would have made some provision. Vitruvius had always believed Antony to be a man of the people. Antony's father had been descended from plebeians, the ordinary residents of Rome, even if his mother was one of the Julii, the same noble patrician family as Caesar's. On campaign Antony certainly did his utmost to be one of the men and this was why he was so well thought of, but now the fighting was over, he displayed the same superior nature of any member of the upper classes. Rebecca was beneath him, and he was treating her with less respect than he would a slave.

Vitruvius continued to teach Rebecca Latin and helped her make plans for the baby's arrival. He even purchased some basic things she would need from his own money. Items such as a cot were far too expensive to come from the limited funds Caesar provided and Vitruvius was more than willing to help. He knew Rebecca would never love him, but equally he knew she needed him, and that was enough. Secretly he hoped that if he was always there to support her, one day her feelings for him might change. He hoped she would to grow to care for him, if she could only find it in her heart to let him in.

As Rebecca and Vitruvius spent more and more time together, Melissa became increasingly isolated. Being alone did not worry her particularly, or so she thought to begin with. She had never had many friends and while she had some scrolls to read she was quite content to sit alone in the courtyard, or occasionally to wander around the crowded streets of Rome on her own. Now that Vitruvius was so disheartened by Antony's actions, he was more willing to ignore his orders and allow Melissa to go out unescorted.

Melissa had always loved the city from the first time she had visited on a school trip, and she made the same trip whenever she could afford it, but the Rome she was trapped in bore no resemblance to the one she knew so well. There were no markets built by Trajan and no trace of the Domus Aurea, Nero's extravagant palace, as neither emperor had been born. Equally, the Arches of Constantine, Titus and Septimius Severus would not be built for centuries. The mighty Colosseum of Vespasian, which so dominated the Forum complex in Melissa's time, was not even imagined in an architect's wildest dream. Instead there was a jumble of narrow, dirty streets lined with inns, shop fronts and multi-storey tenement blocks. People thronged in every direction, going about their business with little concern for anyone else, a sea of bobbing heads that washed past Melissa as she wandered through them, totally alone.

Gradually, Melissa found she was missing Vitruvius' company, but, worse still, she knew she was missing Antony. He drove her to distraction at times, but he was so interesting to be with. He stimulated her mind in ways that she could never hope for from either of the people she lived with, and she secretly enjoyed the constant battle of wills that they were engaged in. She found his sheer presence exciting in more ways than she dared to admit, even to herself.

Chapter 14

Everything changed in November when a victorious Caesar retuned from Spain, sending word ahead to Melissa to thank her for her helpful insights for his campaign. He also sent copies of his Commentaries – journals he was writing about his exploits. He felt she might find them interesting, and encouraged her to comment on them.

Caesar also sent word of two other less than happy events that he hoped Melissa would have been wrong in predicting. Antony's brother, Caius, had surrendered to Pompey's forces in Illyricum and was now held prisoner. Worse still was the news from Africa. Curio and Pollio had been enjoying many successes against the Pompeian allies until they were lured into an ambush by King Juba and his Numidian army. Pollio and a handful of others escaped, but Curio died fighting alongside his men. Antony had reacted badly to the loss of his closest friend, but had nonetheless volunteered to take the news of his death to Curio's widow, Fulvia. That had been two days ago and no one had seen or heard from Antony since.

Caesar was deeply concerned for the well-being of his favourite protégé and asked whether Melissa could provide some insight into Antony's whereabouts. Whilst she could take an educated guess at what he was doing, history had not recorded the specifics of Antony ever disappearing on a drunken binge at this time. She simply replied to Caesar that Antony was grieving for a man who meant more to him than any brother by blood. He needed time to mourn the loss, but would resurface before the week was out. All she could do was pray it was true.

Melissa found she too was worried about Antony. She was still waiting on tenterhooks for an historical bombshell to hit, caused by their presence in the past. So far, nothing appeared to have changed, but she still worried. Yes, Antony was a total bastard at times, and she believed she could cheerfully run him through herself, but she had witnessed another side to him. There were times when he could be so affable that she could not help having intense feelings for him. That was why she had stupidly allowed him to kiss her. She was certain she did not love him, but she did care for him and hated the thought of him suffering alone.

Melissa begged Vitruvius to visit a few of Antony's known haunts to try to track him down and bring him to his senses. Vitruvius was less than certain whether this was advisable, believing that the best way to treat a man in a foul mood was to leave him be. In his opinion, trying to reason with Antony would be impossible, saying he would find it easier and safer to hold onto the tail of a tiger, but, despite his misgivings, he agreed to try. He searched the most likely places that evening, but Caesar was correct: Antony had not been seen in any of them. The next evening Vitruvius went out to tour the inns and whorehouses in the Aventine district by the river. It was not the most salubrious of areas and he could not imagine Antony would ever frequent it under normal circumstances, nor that Caesar would think to look for him there, so it was as good a place as any to try next.

It was late when Melissa heard a knock on the door. Rebecca was asleep and Vitruvius had not yet returned. She considered ignoring it, but feared another knock would wake Rebecca, who would then use the disruption as an excuse to whinge. Melissa went to the door and cautiously slid back the peephole. From what she could see there was no one outside. She began to think she had imagined it when a set of fingers gripped the rim of the opening, making her jump. Then she heard Antony's drunken voice.

"In the name of every god that exists, let me in. I am cold and wet – and in need of a drink!"

Without thinking about what she was doing, Melissa opened the door and Antony fell through it onto the floor. He looked a mess. Wherever he had been for the past three days it had been dirty and disgusting. His clothes were covered in filth and the traces of vomit. His hair was unkempt and he had not shaved. Above all else, he stank of a mixture of wine, vomit and urine. Melissa checked the street, but there was no sign of Vitruvius. She kicked Antony's feet out of the way and closed the door. She was going to have to deal with him alone.

Dragging Antony to his feet, she staggered with him into the main room and dumped him on a couch, where he promptly vomited again. In her youth Melissa had seen Anthony Marcus in a similar state too many times to mention, and she knew what to do. She left him while she went to get water, towels and a clean tunic from Vitruvius' room. She had stupidly left a glass of wine she had been drinking on the table and when she returned he was about to down it. She took it away from him, putting it well out of his reach. Then she closed the doors to keep the noise down. She dreaded the thought of having to answer Rebecca's questions if the girl woke up and saw Antony in such a state.

"Take off your clothes," she said in a matter of fact way.

Antony smiled the happy, stupid smile of a drunk. "Madam, I am deeply honoured that you would ask, but I fear that on this occasion I must decline. I am afraid my performance would be somewhat lacking."

Melissa sighed. "I am not asking you for sex. I want you to get out of those disgusting things so I can clean you up. Then I will put you to bed where you can go to sleep, *alone*. Understand?"

Antony looked sheepish. He nodded and dutifully removed his soiled tunic and loincloth with Melissa's help until he sat before her naked. Melissa poured some of the water into another wine glass and made him drink it. When he had finished, she made him drink another and then set to washing him down. The water was icy cold and he protested to begin with, but eventually he lay back and let her wash the worst of the stench from his skin. When she had finished, she rubbed him briskly with the towel and helped him into Vitruvius' tunic. It was too tight for him, but he was clean and decent, which was all that mattered. Melissa took the dirty clothing and the towels away, returning with a fresh pitcher of water for Antony to drink. She knew she had to keep him hydrated, or face his massive hangover in the morning.

The coldness of the water had a sobering effect. As Melissa poured him another glassful, Antony grabbed her wrist. "I am sorry to come to you like this. I should not have done so," he said sadly.

"Well, you are here now and you are safe. That is all that matters. We have all been worried about you." Melissa's reply was soothing. She knew what it was like to lose someone important. She had felt that all-consuming pain more than once and she was not about to judge him for his behaviour. What he needed was sympathy, not criticism. She sat next to him, taking his hand off her arm to hold it in hers. "Where have you been?" she asked, showing genuine concern.

"I cannot tell you. I do not honestly remember. I went to see Fulvia. I thought it only proper that I be the one to tell her he ..." Antony broke off mid-sentence. Melissa squeezed his hand gently and began rubbing the back of it.

Antony took a deep breath and continued. "I had to be the one to tell her Curio was gone. He was closer to me than either of my brothers. It was the honourable thing to do." Melissa nodded, but said nothing, letting him continue. "I left Fulvia and came here, but it appears I may have become a little lost along the way. How long has it been?"

"Four days," Melissa replied

"Four days," Antony repeated. "That is a long time even by my standards. Caesar will be angry, no doubt."

"Caesar is concerned, but he does not blame you for your reaction. He understands you are in pain, as do I. Curio was a good friend and you must feel his loss keenly."

Antony stared at Melissa for the longest time without speaking. As they looked at each other, Melissa felt the need to reach out and hold him as she would have done for anyone suffering so badly. Curio had played a significant part in Antony's life and his sudden loss appeared to have broken the man now sitting in front of her. Antony looked so alone and vulnerable, which was not something she had expected to see in a soldier with his considerable reputation. She desperately wanted to console him, but she did not dare. She had no idea what he would read into an action that she believed she meant only from kindness. Instead, she let go of his hand and poured him another glass of water.

"Tell me you knew nothing of this. Tell me you did not see his death," he said as he took the glass from her hands.

"I wish that I could tell you that, but it would not be true. I knew he was destined to die."

"Was it out of revenge that you did not tell me? Did you hold your tongue because of what we did to your friend? If that is the case, what terrible justice do you have planned for me?" Antony's mood swung from disbelief to all-consuming grief as he spoke. He dropped his head and began hitting his temple with his hand to try and blot out the graphic images of Curio's death that were filling his mind.

Melissa could no longer bear to watch him suffer such agony. She put her arm around his back and began rubbing his shoulder as she tried to convince him he was not to blame.

"Oh, Antony, it was not from revenge. Rebecca was just as responsible for her actions as you were, perhaps more so. I did not tell you of Curio's demise because there was nothing you could do to prevent it, but I know you would have tried to save him and most likely caused your own death. You may annoy me at times, but I have no wish to see you die. Your future is too important for that to happen."

Antony turned his head to face Melissa. He seemed touched by her sudden admission of concern. He reached out to touch her face and she allowed him to. His hand gently rubbed her cheek and she closed her eyes at the tenderness of his touch, wanting him to continue. For the briefest moment she was in another time with another man, but as he slipped his hand onto her neck and began to pull her head towards his, she panicked and pulled away. She stood up, blushing at how easily she had let him get to her yet again. Antony moved forward on the couch as if to follow her, but stopped himself as another question crossed his mind. He had to ask it before pursuing his quarry.

"Why did you not say something to Caesar of Curio's fate? If he had known of this, he would have sent another officer to Africa in his place."

Melissa turned to face him. "Caesar did know. It was originally his intention to send you to Africa until I told him of all the officers sent only Pollio would return. It is why he chose to keep you in Italy. You are too important to Caesar's plans to be sacrificed at this time. He knew that you would never walk away from a lost cause in order to save yourself. If you had been there, you would have gone to Curio's aid and died as needlessly as he did."

"You lie!" Antony's pent-up frustrations suddenly erupted as anger. He stood up and threw the wine glass at the opposite wall, making Melissa flinch as it smashed and fell to the floor. Then he rounded on her, pushing her against the nearest wall, his hand to her throat.

"Caesar would never have knowingly sent Curio to die. He was a good officer and loyal to the cause. Caesar would never give him up so easily. You must have deliberately misled him into agreeing to such a course of action. There is no other explanation."

Antony paused in his tirade, glancing away to the water as it continued to trickle down the wall. When he looked back, Melissa could see pure hatred in his eyes, and all of it directed at her. "I have suffered enough of your meddling, woman. I will make you remember this day. If not for the loss of Curio, then for the loss of something as dear to you as he was to me."

Antony pushed his body against Melissa's and kissed her forcefully. She struggled against him, which only made him tighten his grip on her throat, making it difficult for her to breathe. She tried to slide a leg between his, with every intention of bring her knee up hard into his groin, but Antony was ready for her attack and prevented her movement by pinning her legs to the wall with his. He pulled his mouth away from hers and shook his head as if warning her not to try it again.

"Caesar will kill me if I let you do this" Melissa croaked. She stared into his eyes, which were wild with a mixture of grief and hatred. In that moment he looked capable of anything.

"And I will kill you if you do not." Antony's grip tightened around Melissa's throat until she could hardly breathe at all. Pain was searing through her chest from the lack of air. The room began to spin and she knew she was going to pass out. If that happened she had no idea what he would do to her. Every instinct told her to fight, but she knew she could not do so for much longer. Melissa allowed her body to go limp and, as she relaxed, Antony responded by lessening his hold on her neck, giving her chance to breathe again. He turned her head away from him and began to kiss her neck, pulling her dress up with his free hand.

Melissa closed her eyes. *Any minute now*, she thought, *and this will all be over*.

And then it was. Antony had released her. For a split second she had no idea why, but she soon appreciated it was nothing to do with him having a change of heart. Her eyes shot open at the sound of Vitruvius voice.

"Caesar said no one was to touch her and that includes you. I will not tell you again." Vitruvius was glaring at Antony whom he had pulled off Melissa and thrown to the floor. He now stood between the two of them, with his back to Melissa and one arm stretched out towards Antony ready to put him down again if he tried to rise.

Melissa had never been so grateful to see someone in her whole life. She glanced across at the door where Rebecca stood, bleary-eyed. The noise had woken her and she had come to see what was going on. She shot Melissa an evil look, then turned and walked out of the room. It looked as if she was blaming Melissa for what had happened. No matter what he did, Rebecca still thought the world of Antony.

Antony stared up at Vitruvius with the same murderous look he had given Melissa as he lay on the floor considering his options. Suddenly his expression changed again. He began to laugh and sat up.

"Have no fear," he slurred, "you may keep her and her damned virtue. I would not want her if she were the last woman alive." Antony deliberately used the same turn of phrase in referring to Melissa as she had used the last time they had met, giving her good reason to doubt his sudden return to his drunken demeanour. He rolled over onto his front and slowly pushed himself up onto his knees. He looked up at Vitruvius pitifully and extended his hand. Vitruvius took it suspiciously, pulling Antony to his feet. Antony fell forward as he stood and hugged Vitruvius as he steadied himself.

"If I were not so drunk, I would take all three ... no, four of you on ... and win," Antony slurred. He was laughing again and still holding on to Vitruvius who assumed Antony was seeing double. Only Melissa saw the cold, sobering stare he was giving her over Vitruvius' shoulder. He was not so drunk that he was beyond reasoned thought, and she could tell he was only withdrawing because his reactions were just a little too dulled by the alcohol he had consumed for him to successfully subdue the sober Vitruvius. Melissa also knew he would be back to try again, and the next time she might not be so lucky.

Antony let go of Vitruvius and staggered to the door, repeating profuse apologies to Melissa as he went. He meant none of it. They were platitudes for Vitruvius' ears. As soon as he had left, Vitruvius shut the door and turned to Melissa.

"How far did he get? Are you still ... intact?" Vitruvius could see the marks on Melissa's throat where Antony had tried to strangle her, so there was no point in asking whether she was hurt. Instead he had asked the only question that really mattered as delicately as he knew how.

Melissa was still unable to speak and simply nodded in reply. Antony had failed in his objective, and Vitruvius looked relieved. Melissa could no longer keep her emotions under control and began to sob, sliding down the wall until she was sitting on the floor. Even though Vitruvius had saved her, her mind was filled with thoughts of what could have happened if he had not returned when he did. She tried to close her eyes, but each time she did she could see Antony's hate-filled face glaring at her. Not ten minutes earlier she had been considering giving in to him. *What a fool she had been!*

Vitruvius had no idea what to do for the best. He was blaming himself for ever having gone out. He wanted Melissa to tell him how to help her, but she could not speak. He decided his best option was to hold her for as long as she needed to cry: that was the sort of thing women expected. Slowly he walked over to her and sat down. He reached his arm over her head and gently pulled her towards him in as unthreatening a manner as he could manage.

Antony meanwhile was not as drunk as he had made Vitruvius believe. He waited outside the room for a few moments while he calmed down. He had been stupid to come to the house in this way. Yes, Melissa could have warned him that Curio would die, but what could he have done? If he had deserted his post and gone to the aid of his friend, he may have suffered the same fate. If he had done so and survived, Curio might still have died, and Caesar would have ostracized him for his poor judgement. Melissa was right once again, and that annoyed him more than anything else.

What Antony had really come looking for was solace. He could get none from his annoying wife, and the delectable Cytheris was out of town. That wretched woman in the other room was too above herself to recognise his pain and to give him any words of comfort. All she had to do was to lie to him and tell him what he wanted to hear, but she would not. Instead she gave him false hope that she cared for him, inflaming further his growing desire for her. He had never met a woman that could make him so angry, yet at the same time so desperate to be with. He wanted to possess her more every time he met her and vowed that one day he would.

He was about to leave when he spotted Rebecca standing in the doorway to her room, arms crossed above her now extended belly. She glared at him as he looked at her, angry because she had seen him kissing Melissa. Antony shot her one of his most disarming smiles and approached her. He bent over and kissed her stomach, rubbing his hand over her bump in pretence of caring for his unborn child. He stood up and gently ran one hand into her hair while the other slid around her waist, pulling her towards him. He kissed her as tenderly as he could and although she resisted him momentarily, she soon slid her arms around his neck and allowed him to push her backwards into her room. As he closed the door behind him, Antony knew that the evening would not be a total loss after all.

The next day Melissa could not face an onslaught of abuse from Rebecca and refused to leave her bedroom. Vitruvius went out late in the morning to find out what news there was of Antony. Neither of them had any idea that he had been in the house with them for most of the night.

Melissa dozed for most of the morning until she was woken by Rebecca shaking her. As she came round from her dazed slumbering, she could see the girl looked distressed.

"Caesar is here. He wants to see you, right now," Rebecca whispered the words as if their patron were present in the room. Melissa nodded and slowly got out of bed. She grabbed a shawl and wrapped it around herself as there was no time to dress properly, but completely forgot about the marks on her neck. She entered the main room alone, as Rebecca refused to follow her.

Caesar was sitting on one of the couches, but rose to greet her. He stared in horror at the finger marks on her throat before he spoke.

"Greetings, Lissa, I hope I find you well?" Caesar's tone was questioning as opposed to a pure greeting.

"As well as can be expected," Melissa croaked in reply. Her throat still stung from Antony's grip. "You honour me with your presence. May I offer you some refreshment?"

"No, thank you. I cannot stay long. I only wished to offer you my thanks. I believe you found Antony and restored him to us, before he did anything untoward?" Again a statement asked as a question.

"Antony came to me last night. He was drunk, distressed and in a sorry state. I took the decision to clean him up before sending him home. His behaviour towards me was uncouth, though no serious harm was done. However, I will think twice before I extend the hand of friendship again." She pulled her hair across her throat, suddenly aware of the marks left there the night before.

"I apologise, Lissa. I should have known he would blame you for Curio's unfortunate demise. I have no need of foresight to have anticipated his need for vengeance. It was a misjudgement on my part, which I sincerely hope you can forgive."

"There is nothing to forgive. Antony's pain led him to act irrationally. I am sure we have all felt such a loss at some time in our lives," Melissa replied with a slight smile to acknowledge the apology.

"You are too gracious, but I find I cannot argue with your logic. Antony means a great deal to me, despite his somewhat common manners." Caesar paused, looking thoughtfully towards the door. "Before I leave, there is another matter we must speak of. Your friend is with child. Tell me, why did you not mention this?"

"It is a trivial matter, not worthy of Caesar's concern. I did not wish to burden you with our problems."

"Ah, but it is my problem. If someone has disobeyed my orders, I should be told. I must know who I can trust and who I cannot. Which of them was it? Antony or Vitruvius? I understand the latter is very fond of her." Caesar tensed as he waited for the answer.

"It was Antony, though he has denied it and takes no responsibility for his actions." Melissa's voice was hardly a whisper as she said the words. She was horrified that suspicion had fallen on Vitruvius and wondered if Antony had placed that seed of doubt in Caesar's mind to deflect attention from himself.

Caesar looked more relaxed. "I am relieved. Had it been Vitruvius, I would have been forced to remove him, leaving me with a new problem of finding someone else to care for you. As for Antony, he has done the right thing in his denial. We have no need to mention it again."

Melissa sat down in shock. "Is that it? Antony can do as he pleases regardless of who else suffers? Rebecca carries his unborn child. He tries to kill me, and that is all you have to say?"

"What would you have me do? Your friend is of little value to me now. I did urge caution on Antony's part, but I cannot undo the deed that is done. Antony is too important to my plans to punish him for such a triviality as fathering the child of a slave. Under normal circumstances I would have her removed from this house. Surely you know this? And yet I will not do so as I know you would not thank me for it. She will remain in your care purely as a gesture of my appreciation of your good service to me. I am more relieved that Vitruvius is still loyal to me and to his orders. I could not leave him to guard you if he were ever tempted, by either of you."

Caesar paused, pressing his fingers together as he pondered the situation. "How close to term is she?" he finally asked.

"She will deliver at the beginning of February." Melissa croaked. She was still reeling from what she had just heard.

"Then you will not thank me for asking you to join me in Greece. I suppose I must leave you here yet again. You will need to provide me with as much information as you can, if I am to grant you this liberty. I will make provision for a midwife to be on hand when the time comes and I will instruct Antony to temper his behaviour towards you, before he makes another unfortunate mistake which would be less easy to forgive." Caesar's eyes flitted towards Melissa's throat again and he wondered how much longer it would be before Antony took his most valuable asset. He toyed briefly with the idea of sending Antony far away from Rome, and from temptation, but his plans relied too heavily on Antony's considerable abilities on the battlefield. He would need his reckless cousin at his side if he were to defeat Pompey in Greece.

Caesar sighed sadly, knowing that one day Antony would eventually succeed in bedding Melissa, and that he would be powerless to stop it, and instead focused on the matter at hand. "That is the best compromise I can offer you, Lissa. I suggest you take it. Now, I must bid you good day. I have more pressing matters to attend to in the Senate." He nodded curtly and left the room just as Vitruvius returned from the town.

Melissa's shock was nothing compared to the horror on Vitruvius' face when she recounted what had occurred. He had believed Caesar would take action once he knew of Antony's failings, but it appeared Antony was being watched over by the goddess Fortuna herself. It planted the first seed of doubt in Vitruvius' mind as to whether Caesar was the man he had always believed him to be.

Chapter 15

Caesar stayed in Rome long enough to oversee the elections for the following year and to make plans for his renewed pursuit of Pompey. He was elected consul, but left long before taking up his office, leaving Antony to tie up any loose ends before joining Caesar with the extra troops he was tasked to recruit. Melissa told Caesar there was no need for haste as the weather would prevent his departure, but he did not heed her words and headed south only to cool his heels in port whilst the winter winds blew their worst over the Adriatic. He eventually set sail from Brundisium in January 48 B.C., proving her right once again.

About the same time as Caesar set sail, Rebecca went into labour. It was too early, if her calculations were correct, and she seemed to sense something was wrong. Rebecca appeared to be in far too much pain for normal contractions. Melissa had no idea what to do other than to send Vitruvius for the midwife, whose help Caesar had promised.

The midwife came immediately and confirmed Melissa's fears. It was too early and the baby had not turned; it was in the breach position. She hardly rated its chances for survival, but worse still, it was going to be agonising for Rebecca to endure the labour.

The midwife refused to let Vitruvius help, slamming the bedroom door in his face. Melissa had appeared shortly after, asking him to boil water and to gather as much clean linen as he could. He willingly headed into the kitchen, where the sound of Rebecca's wailing was reduced by the extra walls that now separated him from her. When Melissa came for the water, he asked what else he could do, but she had simply shaken her head and left as quickly as she had come. Vitruvius was left to sit alone in the kitchen staring at the wall as he allowed a feeling of utter helplessness to wash over him. He closed his eyes and tried to shut out the noise of Rebecca's wails as they turned into screams of agony.

For the first time in years he began to think of his home and of the sisters he had not seen for over fifteen years. They would be fully grown by now and most likely married to some local boys from the neighbouring farms, probably with children of their own. He thought about the times he used to tease them and pull their hair. He recalled one particular day when they went missing. He was supposed to have been watching the girls and his mother had scolded him for not taking better care of them. He had been paralysed with fear for their safety and hid in a barn until they had been found. His father beat him severely, calling him a worthless piece of humanity before sending his son far from his sight. Vitruvius still bore the scars on his backside where the whip had cut through his clothing.

Not long afterwards, Vitruvius had run away to join the legions, determined to prove his father wrong. Thinking back to that past event made him realise that he had been looking on Melissa and Rebecca as surrogates for the sisters he had walked away from. Once again his fear was preventing him from functioning. It was as if he was still hiding in that barn, praying to the gods for the safety of two helpless girls, except now his prayers were for the two women in the other room. He did not even notice as the light of the day slowly faded and left the room in darkness.

Vitruvius woke the next morning slumped across the kitchen table. Every muscle ached from where he had been sleeping across the hard wooden surface. He lifted his head and listened, but could hear nothing. He rose, leaving the kitchen and walked across the courtyard with some trepidation. The silence was far worse to bear than the screaming had been. He paused and listened again. He could hear voices coming from Rebecca's room, but he was unsure whose they were or what they were saying.

Suddenly the door opened and the midwife bustled into the hall. She looked at Vitruvius and shook her head. "It is a boy.

He may live, but the mother will not. The strain was too much for her. Pay me and I will leave you to say your goodbyes," she said, holding out her hand.

Vitruvius was stunned at the news. Rebecca was dying. He heard the words, but he did not want to believe it was true. He could still hear her talking to Melissa, so there had to be some mistake. Rebecca had to be well. He put a small pouch into the midwife's outstretched palm, but made no movement towards the bedroom.

The midwife felt the weight of the pouch and nodded her approval. As she looked at Vitruvius staring blankly into space, she felt sorry for him. "Do not linger here, she has little enough time. I will see myself out," she said and gently guided him towards the open bedroom door.

Vitruvius entered the room cautiously. As he stared at Rebecca lying on the bed holding the sleeping baby, he knew the midwife had not been mistaken. She looked so pale. She was hardly able to raise her arm to welcome him as he approached the bed and sat on a chair to the side. He took Rebecca's hand in his, holding it to his face as the tears began to flood down his cheeks. Her hand felt so cold, as if the life had already drained from it.

Rebecca turned her head and whispered to the tearful Vitruvius, "This is Antonius. Care for him as you have me. Swear it."

"I swear it." Vitruvius almost choked on the words as they left his mouth. He fought to summon the words to tell Rebecca how he felt about her, but they remained stuck in his throat and would not come, no matter how hard he tried to say them aloud.

"I'm tired, I think I'll sleep for a while," Rebecca mumbled to herself in English, but Vitruvius had no idea what she said. He could only watch as she turned her head back towards the baby before closing her eyes for the final time. After a moment, her hand went limp within his. He kissed the back of it tenderly before laying her arm back across her body and around the baby. Then he laid his own head on the bed next to her, and wept.

Melissa stood on the opposite side of the bed. She felt numb. She had lost people in her life before and she had been struck with the grief immediately, but this time she felt no emotion. She and Rebecca had always had their differences, but she had never wished her dead. Now she began to wonder what it was she had failed to do to keep this poor girl safe. All along Melissa had been so concerned with minimising the effect they were having on history that she had failed to consider the impact they were having on their own futures. Could she have stopped this from happening if she had only kept a closer eye on Rebecca's wellbeing? She felt she should have taken more time to explain to Rebecca what Antony was like, convincing her that she would be stupid to get involved with him. Or perhaps she should have insisted Rebecca try a termination when there had still been time, regardless of how dangerous to her health it would have been. It could not have been any worse an outcome than this.

The activities of the day and night before had taken their toll, leaving Melissa mentally and physically exhausted. Rebecca had been terrified when she was told the baby was breach and had said she could not go through with the labour. Melissa had comforted her through every painful contraction. Rebecca had screamed obscenities at her most of the time, but in between the outbursts had been tears and heartfelt regret for not having made more of an effort to be Melissa's friend. Rebecca had longed for Antony to arrive and Melissa had lied continually, telling Rebecca he was on his way, but eventually even Rebecca had admitted that he would never come. This final acceptance of his disinterest had broken Rebecca's will to go on. Melissa had been forced to bully her into every last push to force the baby from her weakened body.

Melissa had relaxed when the baby took its first breath, letting loose its first cry, but then she noticed there was far more blood than she was expecting. The midwife too looked horrified and Melissa knew instinctively that something was wrong. No matter what the midwife tried, she could not stop Rebecca from bleeding. As Melissa cleaned and wrapped the baby in a blanket, the midwife told them that Rebecca was going to die. Oddly, Rebecca had remained calm when Melissa had explained what was happening, asking only to hold her son. Rebecca named him after the father who did not care for him; she named him in Latin, Antonius. Finally she made Melissa promise never to let any harm come to her son and to make sure he had the best chance at life that Melissa could give him, so long as she was alive to provide for him.

Melissa stared down at the tiny infant still cradled in Rebecca's lifeless arms. He was her responsibility now. He was alive and needed the love of someone to replace the mother he would never know, although Melissa had no idea where to begin or whether she was up to the task. Of course, little Antonius still had one parent left alive, and he was a man who could give his son the best chances in life that any child could hope for in Ancient Rome.

It was as if Melissa were guided by some unseen hand. Gathering the baby in her arms, she wrapped him in another blanket before she left the room and then the house, leaving the front door wide open. She had not thought to change her own clothes that were smeared with blood and birthing fluids, or even to cover herself with a cloak to keep out the bitter January winds.

As the icy blast that entered the house through the open door swept into the bedroom, Vitruvius finally raised his head. He realised immediately that Melissa and the baby had gone. He went into the hall and ran to the door where he saw the back of Melissa as she wandered down the hill towards the Forum, wearing only her indoor dress. The few people out on the road stared at her in disbelief as she passed them by. Vitruvius grabbed his sword and cloak, and another cloak for Melissa, and ran after her.

As he reached her, he threw the cloak around her shoulders and pulled her towards him. She was shaking because she was so cold, but he made no effort to try to stop her walking. "Where are you going?" he asked, falling in step beside her. "You will freeze to death like this."

"This baby needs a father," Melissa replied as she took a right turn, heading towards Antony's home. "Without one he will have no rights to a free life in this city. His real father still lives, even if his mother does not."

"You are insane. Antony will not acknowledge the child unless my sword is at his throat." Vitruvius stopped walking as his own words sank in. *What if he were to challenge Antony, for the sake of the child? Could he win? Could he force an admission of guilt from his mentor's lips, and would it have legality if he did?* He redoubled his pace to catch up with Melissa who was still walking at the same steady speed.

"I do not want you to intervene," she said, as he drew level. "This fight is between him and me. Antony began this when he took Rebecca to his bed and he will take responsibility. Without a Roman father, the child has no future of any worth. I do not want you to do anything except get me into his audience chamber. Do you understand me, Vitruvius?"

"Of course I understand, but I can help you force him to concede if you will only let me. I loved her and I will do whatever you ask of me to protect her son."

"No, you must not get involved. If I fail, Antony's revenge will be swift upon me and you will then be this boy's only hope. I have a great deal of respect for you, Quintus Vitruvius, and I know only too well that you would lay your life down for me, but I am asking you to stand aside this one time. You have to do this for me, for Rebecca and, more importantly, for him." Melissa looked down at the small boy asleep in her arms and stopped walking. She had reached her destination. Only one more door and a small queue of people, also waiting for an audience, stood between her and the man whom she sought. There was no going back. Antonius' life depended on what would happen in the next few minutes.

Melissa looked up into Vitruvius' eyes, her own pleading with him silently. He was torn between doing what was right for himself, and what was best for the child. Antony had deprived him of the woman he loved and now that she was dead, he had lost his chance to tell her how he felt. He wanted to run Mark Antony through for that alone, but Melissa was holding the small, defenceless infant who was all that was left of the most beautiful person who had ever been a part of his life. Melissa had been right about so much up until now. Caesar trusted her: he had to trust her.

Vitruvius ran one arm around Melissa and then pushed through the line of people towards the front door. One began to object, but he soon went quiet as Vitruvius pulled the cloak from Melissa's shoulders allowing her sodden, blood-stained clothing back into view. The onlookers spoke to each other in whispers as the pair passed by, but no one made any further attempt to stop them until they reached the door to the atrium where Antony was conducting business for the day. True to form, Antony had stationed two guards outside, overstating his own importance. The guards at the door had seen Melissa before on one of her many trips to Caesar's home, and recognised her immediately. One of them checked the bundle in Melissa's arms and smiled to himself. He had always assumed her to be one of Antony's many mistresses and it looked as if Antony had got a little more than he had bargained for this time around. He nodded to the other guard to take a look and then whispered to him to let her and Vitruvius pass. They kept them back until the man Antony was speaking with had finished, and then let them enter without further question. Secretly they were just as interested in what was going to happen as the rest of the people gathering at the door. Neither of them bothered to search Vitruvius, who could not believe his luck to be entering the chamber armed. He was still considering the possibility of forcing Antony into an admission of fatherhood at the point of his sword, regardless of Melissa's pleas to the contrary.

Vitruvius entered the room first and positioned himself in front of Antony, who was lounging in his chair at the top of a platform raised from the main floor by two steps. To one side of him stood a secretary, who was on hand to remind Antony who it was he was speaking to and to make notes of the day's proceedings.

Antony looked bored senseless. Vitruvius adjusted his cloak slightly to show that he was armed. Antony looked at him quizzically, wondering why he was carrying his sword and then spotted Melissa as she stepped out from behind him. The state of her made him start forward in his chair. He was horrified at her dress and was about to ask how she had been injured when he heard a gurgling noise coming from the blanket in her arms. He knew that noise all too well from when his daughter had been born and presented to him in a similar fashion. He sat back in surprise. Melissa was holding a baby and she was bringing it to him.

Melissa placed the child on the floor below Antony's feet. It was the Roman custom for a baby to be placed at the feet of its father and for him to pick it up, thereby acknowledging it as his. She was determined to make him take responsibility for the child he had fathered.

As she stood up, the two of them stared at each other just as they had the very first day they had met, their eyes locked together in a silent battle of wills, but this time Melissa had no intention of looking away. She made no effort to hide the contempt on her face. At that moment, Mark Antony was nothing to her and she wanted him to know how little she thought of him. Lying on the cold tiles, the child began to cry.

Antony had no intention of picking up the baby. To do so was political suicide. He was in charge of the country in Caesar's absence and could not be seen to give in to the demands of some foreign woman. Antony stared back at Melissa, but the lack of respect she displayed was beginning to anger him. If one of his slaves were to challenge him in such a way, he would beat them, and he was definitely feeling the urge to take a whip to this arrogant woman. His eye twitched involuntarily and it made him shift his glance for a fraction of a second. It was enough though for Melissa to notice. She smiled at him, cruelly.

That was the final straw for Antony. He shot out of the chair and stood on the edge of the raised platform. "WHAT IS IT YOU WANT HERE, WOMAN?" He shouted so loudly that everyone in the room flinched, except Melissa.

She continued to stare at Antony as she delivered her reply in the loudest voice she could manage. "This child is the son of the woman with whom I came to Caesar one year ago. Caesar gave me his word she would not be defiled, yet this boy is proof that some men do not place any importance in the word of Caesar. The mother has died giving him life. The child will die without the love and support of his father. That man stands before me and I demand he honour his responsibilities."

Behind her, Melissa could hear the onlookers in the room outside muttering to each other as they fought to get a better look at what was going on. They could hear every word she was saying. Whatever happened next, she had succeeded in embarrassing Antony, who looked ready to explode. He stepped down off the platform and stood in front of her, his foot menacingly close to the baby's head. With one move of that foot, he could crush the delicate skull and end the child's life. Still the baby cried. Melissa closed her eyes. She could not bear to watch if he decided to murder Antonius; hearing the sickening crunching noises would be bad enough.

The baby's pitiful cries pierced the silence that had descended in the room. They were as agonising for Vitruvius to hear as Rebecca's screams had been just a few hours earlier. He watched the continuing stalemate between Antony and Melissa until it became too much for him to bear. He dived forward and picked up the baby, pulling it into his arms and began gently rocking the boy. As the child's sobs began to subside, he spoke, choking back his emotions. "I take responsibility for this child. I claim him and I will care for him."

Melissa and Antony both stared at Vitruvius in disbelief. Antony recovered his composure first and returned his gaze to Melissa. "It appears you have achieved your objective, woman. The boy has been claimed by a Roman father and so has the right to be a Roman citizen himself."

Antony turned to Vitruvius and slapped him on the back. "Congratulations, Vitruvius. I hope he will make you very proud one day. Now get him out of here before he starts that infernal noise again. I shall join you later in your celebrations." Antony returned to his seat, gloating in his victory over Melissa. He could live with the minor embarrassment she had caused, but she really had gone too far this time and his patience had run out. He would make her pay for her disrespectful attitude later, and enjoy hearing her beg for leniency.

Vitruvius placed the child back in Melissa's arms. "Take the boy home. *Please!!*" There was a hint of desperation in his voice. Melissa nodded and left the room. She knew there was nothing to be gained from staying. Vitruvius' intervention made it impossible to make Antony admit to his parentage of Antonius.

Once Melissa had gone, Vitruvius turned his attention back to Antony, who sat looking at a scroll, ignoring him. Vitruvius coughed. Antony looked up at him and sighed. "What is it?" he asked.

Vitruvius' mouth went suddenly dry. He wanted to challenge Antony and make him pay for everything that had happened, but he could not bring himself to do so in such a public setting. He swallowed his pride and instead asked for help. "I cannot feed the child, sir. He needs a woman who can give him milk. I do not know where to find such a woman."

Antony stood up and walked down to the main floor. He walked round Vitruvius, looking at the guards on the door. He clapped his hands together and dismissed them, ensuring they closed the doors to the chamber behind them. Only his secretary remained.

Then he spoke openly to Vitruvius. "Must I do everything for you? I might just as well have taken the brat myself." He shook his head in disbelief, knowing he was going to have to provide for the boy whether he wanted to or not. "There is a slave in my household who gave birth to a stillborn child not two days ago. As I intended to get rid of her anyway, I will have her sent to you. She can nurse him. Good enough?" Vitruvius nodded and Antony continued. "When it is done, you can keep her for all I care, but I will not provide anything further. You took that baby knowing full well he was not yours and as foolish as it was, you are the one who has to live with that decision, not me."

Antony began pacing to and fro. Melissa had annoyed him and the more he thought about her, the more frustrated he became. He stopped again in front of Vitruvius and pointed towards the door. "And as for that blasted woman, I will deal with her in my own time and in my own way and you ..." he poked Vitruvius in the chest with his finger "... will not intervene when I do. You tell her she may not leave the house again without my permission. I am watching her and she had better start showing me some damned respect or she will end up in the same state as the other one, whether Caesar permits it or not." He waited for a response, but Vitruvius did not speak. He was unable to. He was too angry to do anything but punch his commanding officer.

Antony could see the conflict in his former comrade's face. The two men stared at each other, until Antony broke the deadlock between then. "Is there something more you wish to say to me *legionary* Vitruvius?" The emphasis he placed on the word legionary was meant as a clear reminder of who was in charge. Vitruvius went to raise his arm, but thought better of it and controlled himself by putting his hand on the hilt of his sword.

Antony had seen the initial reaction and knew Vitruvius was near to breaking. He stepped back a little, spreading his hands wide and lifting his arms away from his body slightly. He had adopted the most unthreatening pose he could. He was unarmed and made a very tempting target.

Vitruvius' hand tightened on the hilt of his sword. In one move he could take his revenge for the defilement of the woman he had grown to love. All he had to do was thrust his sword deep into Antony's chest, and, if he were facing any other man, he might have done so, but this was not just any man. He had seen Antony take this exact stance with prisoners after a battle. Antony enjoyed tormenting his enemies, offering them an opportunity to kill an apparently easy target. It was a form of sport he would perform for the men who served under him. A sword would be given to a prisoner and Antony would parade in front of them, daring them to kill him. He would get closer and closer, taunting them, insulting them, even making promises of freedom if they could best him, until the urge simply became too great and they lunged. It never ended well for the challenger. And here he was, taunting Vitruvius, daring the soldier to believe he could bring the great Mark Antony down. Vitruvius knew only too well that he would be on the ground before his sword had left its sheath. When it came to battle, Antony's reactions were lightning fast and his judgement second only to Caesar's. Antony had never got into a fight he could not win, and today was going to be no exception.

Vitruvius relaxed his hand on his sword and raised his eyes to stare at the wall, somewhere just above Antony's head. "No sir," he said, fighting the waves of hatred goading him to react.

Antony moved closer until they were only a fraction apart. He moved his head to the right and spoke so softly that only Vitruvius could hear him. "I see you have remembered your place. It would be best for everyone that you do not need reminding of it again." He turned his head and placed a kiss on Vitruvius' cheek, making it plain that he had been merciful in his actions. Standing back, he placed his hands firmly on Vitruvius's shoulders in an open gesture of friendship, but he exerted far more force than was necessary until Vitruvius' knees buckled slightly under the strain. Antony smiled as he spoke aloud. "There – we are friends again. I would not want it any other way." He addressed his secretary. "I am done for the day. Any other business will have to wait until tomorrow."

Antony stormed from the room, pushing his way through the people still waiting to see him. He was angry with Melissa for her behaviour, but at the back of his mind another thought plagued him, making him angrier still. Despite his attempts to push it aside, the thought kept coming back to him, making him smile. He had a son, and against his better judgement, he was overjoyed at the news.

Antony had no chance to take his revenge on Melissa. A few days later word arrived that Caesar's fleet had returned to allow Antony and the reinforcements to embark for Greece. Caesar's messenger insisted Antony come at once with all the troops he had mustered.

As soon as Vitruvius told Melissa what was happening, she sent word to Antony that she must speak with him. He had no intention of seeing her before he left, but Caesar had also sent specific instructions regarding any further information she could provide, so he was forced to call on her.

Melissa knew Caesar would be expecting word on the outcome of his forthcoming engagements with Pompey, but she also knew that he would not be returning to Rome for a very long time. There was far too much to tell Antony, and so she set about writing as much down as she dared.

Firstly, she had to deal with the impending battle. Caesar's forces' first encounter with Pompey would be at Dyrrachium, but this would prove indecisive. The final battle would be at Pharsalus. Caesar would emerge victorious and Pompey would be forced to flee to Egypt where he had good connections and would hope to receive aid. This much she had already told Caesar, including information on Pompey's tactics, but she had not told him what would happen beyond the battle. She wrote that Caesar would follow his quarry and would be reunited with Pompey in Alexandria, but that he would never see his old friend in the same way again. Melissa had no intention of telling Caesar outright that Pompey would be murdered as soon as he landed in Egypt and that Caesar would be presented with his severed head in a basket. That was a fact Caesar would have to find out for himself.

Melissa knew that Egypt was suffering from its own problems. Queen Cleopatra VII and her brother-consort King Ptolemy XIII were at loggerheads over the rule of the country. Unrest in Egypt was bad for Rome for two reasons. Firstly, the old king, Ptolemy Auletes, had bribed Rome to not annex Egypt even though his uncle, Ptolemy X had bequeathed the country to the Republic in his will. Auletes taxed his people excessively to raise the money, which resulted in revolution and his expulsion. He then fled to Rome and promised even more money to a number of prominent Romans if they helped to restore him to his throne. Troops were sent, including the young Mark Antony, and Auletes was returned to power. His debts were never paid in full, and, as a result, Egypt still owed the Roman people an immense sum of money.

Secondly, the fertile banks of the Nile produced most of the grain that fed the people of Rome and to lose that supply would lead to starvation and rebellion back home. Melissa explained to Caesar that he would need to mediate a resolution to the problems of Egypt to ensure Rome received its annual supply of grain. In short, Civil War in the East meant starvation in Rome and that would turn the populace against Caesar. She told him that she knew he would aim for a peaceful solution, but that in the end he would be forced to choose between the warring siblings and shore up one regime. She did not tell him which side to choose, or that he would lose himself to Cleopatra's charms and remain in Egypt far longer than he should. To have done so would have been too risky. Caesar's future had to unfold as it had already done in the past.

Melissa prepared a second scroll for Antony. She told him he would struggle to reach Caesar until April, mainly because of adverse tides, but also because he would have to dodge Pompey's fleet, which would be intent on blockading him in

Brundisium. He would eventually land north of his intended destination, and Pompey would try to intercept him, cutting him off from Caesar's army. Melissa wrote down every detail she knew to help him avoid capture; far more detail than she had ever given to Caesar. She explained that Pompey would begin a night attack at Dyrrachium and Antony would face the worst of the fighting. He would be greatly outnumbered, but he could lead his men to victory against the odds, if he just believed it possible.

When the final battle commenced at Pharsalus, Caesar would appear to sideline Antony and he would play only a minor part in the battle, but this was all part of Caesar's plan. Antony's reputation had grown over the years and Pompey would be expecting him to be in the thick of the fighting. His actions in the battle for Dyrrachium would only strengthen Pompey's belief in Antony's importance. By keeping him on the periphery, Caesar hoped to convince Pompey that his forces were weaker elsewhere and lull him into making a mistake in where he chose to attack. Caesar would also be tasking Antony with the final rout and round-up of Pompey's fleeing forces, a task that required both him and his troops to be fresh and not battle-weary. Caesar wanted as many of the senators who were supporting Pompey as possible to be kept alive, and he trusted Antony more than any other officer to be able to keep control of the men, ensuring clemency was shown to the right people. Above all else, Antony had to find a young man called Marcus Brutus and return him to Caesar alive. This man was the son of Caesar's lover, and Caesar had a particular fondness for him. If he achieved all the tasks Melissa had spoken of, Antony would return a hero and become master of Rome in Caesar's absence.

Antony arrived on the day he was due to leave Rome. He had deliberately left his visit until the last minute to spend as little time as possible with Melissa. He was still smarting over her attempt to embarrass him with the baby, and made no attempt at the usual pleasantries when he entered her home.

"Well, woman, do you have a message for Caesar or not?" he barked on entering the room.

Melissa was adding a final note to the second scroll. "I do," she replied as she began to roll the document up. "It is over there on the couch in the carry case. I have not sealed it as I expect you will wish to read it."

Antony went to the couch and grabbed the scroll case. He was preparing to leave when Melissa called him back. "Wait. There is another scroll. This one is for you." She rose from her chair beside the window and walked over to where Antony stood. "It tells of your future alone and not Caesar's." She held the scroll out for him to take.

He kept his back turned, not wanting to look at her. He was totally thrown by this gesture. Melissa had never given any details about his future before, so why start now? She had to be up to something and he began to regret not having the time to challenge her over it. He took the scroll without speaking and started towards the door again.

Even though she despised Antony at times, Melissa could not let him leave in such a way. "I know we are not friends, but is there nothing you have to say to me, Antony?" she called after him, making him pause at the door. She continued quickly. "So much relies on your safe return. Whether you believe it or not, I have no desire to see you dead, and, if you are injured this time, I will not be there to tend your wounds."

Antony remained poised on the threshold and Melissa was not ready to give up while he was still in the room. "I must thank you for sending the slave, Renna, to act as wet nurse for the child. Without her, Antonius would surely have died. Do you wish to see your son before you leave?"

Antony finally turned round, but still he did not look at Melissa. This was the first time he had heard the baby's name. Even though he did not regret his decision to disown the child, he was touched that the baby had been given his name. He fought his desire to admit to wanting to see his son, shaking his head in response to the question. After a moment, he reached inside his armour and retrieved a metal locket. He leant towards Melissa and put it into her hand. "For the boy. He has a Roman father and so should observe the traditions of my people as well as yours. Do you know what this is?" Melissa nodded, amazed at the gift. Antony had given Melissa a bulla, a metal amulet that hung around a boy's neck to protect him from evil spirits from his ninth day of life until the day he became a man and donned his first toga. From the look of it, this one was made of gold.

"Good, then you will know when to give it to him," he added gruffly.

Anthony was conflicted in what he should do. He had no idea what it was Melissa wanted from him. To him she was a total enigma. A few months earlier he had tried to kill her, but still she showed concern for him. He longed to know where she got her strength from and what forces drove her to forgive his many shortcomings. Half of him still wanted to tell her how much he hated her, while the other half wanted to take her in his arms and show her how much he wanted to stay by her side, if she would only have him. Unable to speak again for fear he would reveal his true feelings, he simply waved goodbye to her by raising the hand holding his scroll.

Chapter 16

News came in the middle of summer that Caesar had been victorious. The battle went according to the historical accounts Melissa had read, and she breathed another sigh of relief. There had still been no changes to history worthy of note.

Antony would soon be back in Rome, and, to the dismay of the returning senators, he would be in complete charge. Antony's escapades during this time would form the basis for Cicero's later attacks on him, presenting him as a drunken lout who was incapable of leading the Republic. Melissa began to wonder if she should try to temper Antony's behaviour on his return, but to do so would mean breaking her self-imposed rule of not interfering in the past.

The problem was that she knew she had feelings for Antony, despite his abhorrent behaviour towards her. Antony's biggest failing was that he was far too passionate for his own good. He threw his heart and soul into everything he did, be it on the battlefield or in the bedroom, and took every rejection as a personal attack. This he had adequately demonstrated through his earlier correspondence with Cicero. His letters had moved Melissa in ways she had not intended, leaving a part of her desperate to get to know the man that seemed determined to stay hidden behind the boisterous front he preferred to display to the masses. She was sure that inside this shell was a different man, with far greater depth than the frivolity suggested. Yes, she had suffered the misfortune of witnessing his darker, vindictive side on more than one occasion, but there were hints of another man buried somewhere in between these two extremes. This was the man she had first met in the surgeon's tent at Brundisium and then again briefly in the moments before he tried to strangle her. This was the genuine Mark Antony, bereft of his ego, with his true self laid bare. It was this man she really wanted to know and it was for this man that she now considered risking a great many things, including Caesar's displeasure. She wondered if she was blurring the dividing line between the two Antonys, just as Rebecca had done. As much as she hated herself for it, the answer was yes. Her relationship with Mark Antony reminded her of that of Benedick and Beatrice in Shakespeare's 'Much Ado about Nothing': on the surface they feigned dislike of each other, but secretly their feelings were far more complex.

Regardless of how he behaved, Antony had so much promise and could be so much more, given the right guidance. Melissa found herself in an unenviable situation. Now she understood the turmoil Caesar must have felt in the hours before she met him as he stood on the banks of the Rubicon all those months ago, deciding whether to cross. She imagined herself standing on the banks of her very own Rubicon and found her decision was proving just as difficult: should she turn aside and let history run its course, or should she step into the flowing waters of uncertainty and help Antony towards a better future? She decided to try to help him become all he could be, no matter what it did to history as she had known it. His potential was worth the risk, provided he did not drown her along the way.

Antony returned in the autumn. Melissa had been preparing for his return for months, having taken to writing the events of history as she knew it down on scrolls and hiding them in her room. She did this because caring for Antonius was taking up so much of her time that she found she was forgetting things from a mixture of sleep deprivation and simple exhaustion. She could hardly afford to slip up now and give Antony a reason to doubt her.

However, Antony did not visit. He had been intercepted at Brundisium by Cytheris and an entourage of followers intent on welcoming the glorious hero home. The actress had been keeping him occupied ever since. They had moved into Pompey's former home and Antony was spending little time with his own wife, who had begun an affair with Cicero's son-in-law, Dolabella. The gossip in the Forum reached new levels, and each day Vitruvius would bring home some new tale of Antony's appalling behaviour. The day he returned with a tale of Antony pausing a debate in the Senate to vomit and then continuing the discussion as if nothing had happened, was the day Melissa begged him to tell her no more. The old Antony was back, and the secretive, genuine man she had glimpsed was once again hidden well beneath the surface.

Melissa was still fighting with her conscience over whether to tell Antony of the disasters that were about to befall him, but her requests for an audience were continually denied. She was not the only person he refused to see. Cicero had returned to Italy looking to be pardoned for his abandonment of Caesar, but Antony would not allow him to enter the city. Melissa knew this was as much out of spite as anything else. He and Cicero may not have liked each other, but having the elder statesman onside would prove the more prudent approach, if only she could get to tell Antony so.

If his outlandish behaviour was not enough to anger Caesar, then his mishandling of the public soon would be. After Pharsalus, the Ninth and Tenth legions had come back to Italy, but had nothing to keep them occupied. They waited for their discharge orders, but none came. Eventually, the men had had enough and they rebelled. Word was sent to Antony and he decided to quell the rebellion by leaving the city to speak to the men directly. Melissa knew that, for the first time in his life, he would fail in his attempt to resolve a dispute in the ranks, which would be a new and uncomfortable experience for him.

More important than this, was her desire to warn him of what would be waiting for him upon his return to Rome. Most of the population were in debt and prices of the most basic items were becoming higher every day. Whilst Antony was away, his wife's lover, Dolabella, intended to pass a law abolishing all debt. The Senate were not prepared to allow Dolabella to stir up more trouble and so they sent an urgent request to Antony to return and resolve the matter, giving him complete authority to take whatever action was necessary to do so. Melissa knew Antony would return with the troops that had not mutinied and attempt to prevent any rioting before it started, but she also knew it would go horribly wrong and many innocent people would die needlessly. The Senate would then deny any involvement, leaving Antony to take full responsibility for the deaths upon Caesar's return.

If Antony was not cautious, history would repeat itself and he would experience a spectacular fall from grace. She sent Vitruvius to deliver a scroll to Antony, but the scroll and its courier both returned that night. Melissa sent him to try again the next day, which he did grudgingly, with the same result. Melissa pleaded with Vitruvius to try one more time on the morning Antony was due to leave to resolve the problems with the legions, but he flatly refused. "Let him rot in his own stupidity," was all he would say.

Melissa persisted in her attempts to send the scroll in the hope of intercepting Antony before he entered the city on his return. She paid the young boy who worked in the bakery to deliver it, but this proved to be just as pointless. The scroll was returned within the hour by one of Antony's men, along with a note of his own. The letter told her in no uncertain terms where she could stick her advice, including making some less than pleasant suggestions of how she should go about it.

Melissa finally agreed that Vitruvius was right. She had been willing to risk changing history to warn Antony of the mistakes he was about to make, but he would not listen. She could no longer be bothered wasting time on him: Antony was on his own.

Antonius meanwhile was approaching nine months old and crawling, as his father returned from Pharsalus. He was a happy child, who hardly seemed to sleep, but he hated being left alone and would cry if he was not receiving attention from at least one member of the household.

Melissa was amused by Vitruvius' reactions to the baby. When he first took responsibility for Antony's son he was unsure of himself. He was a soldier and not used to being as gentle as he needed to be with such a tiny baby. Watching him try to put a nappy on the wriggling infant was one of the funniest things that Melissa had ever witnessed. First he tried to explain what he was going to do and instructed Antonius to lie still, which seemed briefly to work as the baby responded to the sound of his voice. As soon as he touched the child, Antonius began to squirm and Vitruvius became increasingly impatient. He eventually held him down with one arm and removed the soiled material with the other. Unfortunately, Vitruvius was applying a little too much pressure to the baby's stomach and Antonius responded by releasing his bladder, which he did before the new nappy was safely in place, leaving Vitruvius in need of a bath, and a change of clothing. The veteran of the Thirteenth legion had been defeated by a few pounds of chubby infant. He said he would rather have faced a hundred angry Gauls than ever have to deal with the contents of a soiled nappy again. Despite these initial difficulties, Vitruvius quickly rose to the challenge of caring for his newest charge and soon made any excuse to be the one to deal with the baby, no matter what time of day or night it was.

Antonius took his first steps just before his birthday. Keeping up with him was becoming harder every day. Melissa knew that he would be as unstoppable as a tiny whirlwind blowing through their home, and she was right. He was into everything he could be, seemingly gaining more energy with every pound in weight he put on.

Life now revolved around the little boy who grew more like his father day by day. Anyone seeing him and Antony together would instantly see the resemblance. Antonius had the same colouring and attitude. Every attempt that either Melissa or Vitruvius made to temper his enthusiasm failed dismally. He was becoming as precocious as his father was arrogant.

Melissa spoke to him in English when Vitruvius was out, so it was no surprise to her when his first word was an emphatic "No!" It did not go down too well with the proud soldier, who had no idea what the boy was learning. He demanded that Melissa stop filling the child's head with nonsense. She refused and the pair did not speak for days. Eventually a compromise was reached. Vitruvius agreed to let Melissa teach Antonius her language provided she also taught him what she was saying to the child. Of course, Melissa knew that this would only work when the soldier was in the room, but she was not going to point out the rather obvious flaw in Vitruvius' plan when it was to her advantage. Whilst she understood teaching Antonius a language that would never be used in his lifetime was pointless, it did give her something special that only they would share.

Chapter 17

Caesar returned from Egypt in the autumn of 47 B.C., fully informed of the goings-on in Rome. He met Cicero at Brundisium and Caesar welcomed him with open arms, explaining the senator's prolonged exile from Rome as a mere misunderstanding. On his return to the city in October, Caesar took Dolabella's side over the dispute with Antony and made Lepidus co-consul for the following year. Antony was left with no office, no position in the army and no prospects of obtaining either.

Melissa warned Vitruvius to expect a visit from a displeased Antony at some point, as she suspected he would choose to blame her for his misfortune. Vitruvius simply laughed, suggesting he refuse Antony entry, but Melissa said no. She wanted to see Antony and if he was spoiling for a fight, she was more than willing to oblige. This amused Vitruvius further. He liked the idea of Melissa getting the better of Antony yet again. It gave him a warm feeling deep inside.

Antony arrived the morning after his disgrace was made public. He had assumed Caesar would have given orders to keep him away from Melissa and so forced his way inside unnecessarily. He stormed into the dining room, with Vitruvius following hard on his heels, and straight over to Melissa who was sitting on the couch telling Antonius a story. Antony glowered over her as she pulled the little boy towards her, burying his head against her side to protect him as best she could from the onslaught she knew was coming.

"Caesar has disowned me. He has stripped me of all responsibility and has cast me adrift. He says I need a lesson in humility, but I hear your words in his. I suppose this was your doing?" Antony demanded with more than a hint of menace in his voice.

Melissa raised her hand to Vitruvius, signalling for him to leave. He backed off, but stayed at the door. He had no intention of leaving them alone with Antony in such a black mood.

She spoke calmly. "No, Antony, this is all your own doing. I asked to see you to give you counsel, but you refused me. I wrote to you countless times, but the scrolls were all returned with your less than courteous notes. You were quite clear that you neither sought nor required my help."

Antony was still annoyed with Melissa, but now he was also annoyed with himself. He knew she was right. He had been angry with Melissa when he first left to join Caesar in Greece because she had tried to embarrass him over the baby. As a result, he had ignored the scroll she had given him, but as the weeks of failure to break the blockade of Brundisium rolled by he found the temptation too great. He eventually opened it and used its information to his advantage in the weeks that followed. Every event unrolled as Melissa described, but as time marched swiftly by, Antony became less grateful and more disgruntled at her predictions. They made him feel like a puppet whose strings were being pulled by an unseen hand according to Melissa's direction and he did not like it. It meant she could take credit for his actions and this made the victories seem shallow and meaningless. He had been doing well enough before she had turned up, or so he thought, and so chose to ignore her upon his return. He knew it was his own fault that things had gone so horribly wrong. If he had not allowed his pride and pig-headedness to get in the way, he could have made a success of Caesar's absence with Melissa's assistance, instead of a dismal failure without it.

He backed over to the other couch and sat down in defeat. For a few minutes, he stared at the little boy clinging to Melissa. Antonius had not cried when he had shouted at her, and now the boy stared at his father inquisitively. Antony could not fail to notice his own features reflected in the face of his child and his heart lifted. For a brief moment, his desire to walk back over and hold the boy was strong, but his pride would not allow it.

"How do I repair the damage I have done?" he asked Melissa sullenly, shaking all thoughts of claiming his son from his mind.

As Melissa looked at him, a wry smile crept across her face. Now he actually wanted her help, she was tempted not to give it. As she smiled, his face became a picture of remorse. She wondered how long it would take him to say please. She sat back and waited. They were back on familiar territory, sparring with each other, with neither one wanting to admit defeat. The question once again was who would blink first.

Antony shifted awkwardly on the couch and slouched backwards. "Well, do you intend to give counsel or simply to make a fool of me?" he said.

Melissa bit her lip. She did not mean to gloat over him, but she could not resist the temptation. "I will give you counsel when you give me the respect I deserve. If you will not, Vitruvius has permission to eject you."

Antony sat upright. "You would not dare. I will have you both flogged to within an inch of your lives if you try it."

Vitruvius stepped forwards. He was more than willing to put Antony out on the street whether it led to a flogging or not, but Melissa raised her hand once more and he reluctantly backed off.

"Caesar has given me permission to treat you in the same way as you treat me, and he will not intercede unless in my defence. You no longer have any authority here, unless I allow you to have it." Melissa was lying. Caesar had not discussed Antony with her in any way, but Antony had no way of knowing it. For the first time, she had the upper hand and she was intent on enjoying every minute that it lasted.

"What do you want me to do?" Antony was so desperate to regain Caesar's favour he capitulated immediately.

"An apology is all I ask. I want to hear you say you are sorry for ever having doubted me. I want to hear you admit to being wrong in ignoring my advice and, more than anything, I want you to beg my forgiveness for trying to kill me. For this I will give you the only advice I can. Become a respectable member of society. Ditch that actress slut you have installed in Pompey's home and clear your debts. Divorce your wife. Find a woman who will not cheat on you for the first rake who pays her more attention than you do, and marry her instead. Then do your penance in a quiet, humble manner and Caesar will forgive you in time, provided you have the patience and wit to wait."

Antony sat for a moment not moving. He was completely embarrassed. He hated having to concede any point to Melissa and had no intention of apologising for anything. He stood up suddenly and stormed out of the room without another word.

Melissa looked at Vitruvius who was grinning wildly. He had finally watched Antony being put in firmly his place, and by a woman. He loved the feeling of sheer joy it gave him.

"He will be back, I dare say," he said emphatically, knowing Antony could not let this rebuff go.

"One day, but we may have to wait a while," Melissa replied laughing.

The next day a small chest arrived. Inside was a beautiful necklace. Thirteen oblong drops of lapis lazuli, each separated by a single pearl, hung from a string of elongated lapis beads. It was Egyptian in style, with the drops becoming smaller as they radiated from the centre. A pair of earrings set with the same two stones, and five silver bangles were also in the chest. Underneath it all was a scrap of papyrus. It said:

> *This is an Akila necklace. It represents*
> *intelligence or clarity of mind. The lapis is*
> *for luck and the pearls for purity. All of these*
> *qualities you have in abundance. I should*
> *learn from your wisdom and will endeavour*
> *to treat you with the same respect you show*
> *me – until your luck runs out. M.A.*

Melissa was stunned. All she had asked for was one solitary word uttered in earnest, and instead she had been sent this beautiful gift that must have cost a considerable amount. The apology would have meant more had it been spoken, but Melissa knew Antony's pride would never allow him to give her the satisfaction of hearing it. This was the best apology she could ever expect to receive, even if it was tinged with the slightest hint of a threat.

Chapter 18

Melissa was summoned to see Caesar a few days later and the planning for his African campaign began in earnest. The remainder of the Pompeian forces now looked to Scipio and Cato for leadership. They had joined forces with King Juba of Numidia – the same man who had been responsible for the massacre of Curio and his army. Caesar needed to act decisively to crush the remaining opposition, but did not intend to fall into the same trap as Curio. Juba was likely to use the same battle tactics, so Melissa and Caesar spent hours discussing his options.

Caesar had changed since his return from Egypt. Whereas he had previously been willing to take advice from Melissa without question, he now queried every suggestion she made. She had once enjoyed her conversations with Caesar, but now every session was fraught with difficulties. She had never yet steered him in a wrong direction, but he seemed suspicious of her. She could only guess at the reason and suspected that on some level Caesar laid the blame for Antony's failures at her feet. She thought that, if he only knew how hard she had tried to intercede, it would improve their relationship, but Caesar would not even allow her to mention Antony's name.

The only duty it appeared Antony still had was to administer Melissa's living allowance, which had reduced by half since Rebecca's death. It appeared Caesar's generosity only extended to Melissa, and he would not pay for one of Antony's mistakes. Every quarter Vitruvius would go to collect the money, but Antony never asked after Melissa, or his son, nor did he make any further attempts to visit.

Life continued peacefully for Melissa and her adopted family. Winter rolled slowly into the spring of 46 and then spring began its relentless march into summer.

Renna stayed on to work in the kitchen after Antonius was weaned. She liked the generosity of her new mistress and enjoyed being given more freedom and responsibility than she had experienced in Antony's household.

Antonius continued to grow and became more of a handful every day. He was always getting into some mischief or other, either driving Renna mad in the kitchen, or begging Vitruvius to play with him.

Vitruvius himself became more relaxed. Caesar was out of the country and, with a visit from Antony being unlikely, he allowed Melissa to come and go as she pleased, so long as he could do the same.

Only Melissa felt uneasy at the respite they had been granted. She did not need to see the future to know that this easy life could not continue indefinitely. She knew a storm was coming and it would break over their household like a great wave crashing against the shore. The only question was how long it would take to hit.

September brought excitement for all of Rome. Caesar had been granted four triumphs to celebrate his victories in Gaul, Asia, Egypt and Africa. Each celebration would run one after the other. There would be processions, feasts and entertainments to eclipse any that had gone before. Each morning, Melissa and her 'family' would leave the house early to get a good vantage point to watch the parades, and in the evening they would return home completely exhausted. Antonius would recount his favourite moments over and over until he fell asleep, only to begin again the next morning, until there was something new to fill his head. His favourite day of all was when Vitruvius took him to see the naval battle in the big lake that had been specially dug beside the Tiber. He came home asking for a boat that would be big enough to carry an elephant, which had been his favourite animal from the day before. Vitruvius built a model boat in the courtyard for Antonius to play with, while Renna made him an elephant out of some of his old clothes that no longer fitted and stuffed it with dried grain. Melissa grumbled that he was being spoilt by both of them!

On a few occasions, Melissa caught sight of Antony in the seats reserved for the most respected members of society. He was still out of favour and Caesar had forbidden him to take part in the spectacles, despite his having had a major involvement in two of the campaigns. Every time she saw him, he was accompanied by a respectable Roman matron, who was beautiful, if a little rude in her manners. Although Melissa had never been introduced, she knew this woman to be Fulvia, Curio's widow, and soon to be Antony's third wife.

Caesar's final act of the celebrations was one of generosity. He gave each of his soldiers five thousand denarii, more than Vitruvius could ever have hoped to earn in his entire career in the legions. Every citizen was given one hundred denarii each, Melissa included. She was also given one hundred for Antonius and a further hundred as recompense for the death of the boy's mother. Caesar's generosity particularly surprised Melissa as she was not a citizen of Rome. For the first time in nearly four years she had funds of her own. She treated herself to a scroll that she had been eyeing in the bookstore for some time and then put the rest away. She knew she had to be careful with every last sesterce of what remained.

After his triumphs, Caesar left for Spain again to quell a rebellion. The governor of the region had drowned after fleeing from an angry mob, leaving the region at the mercy of Pompey's sons, who were trying to rally support for their cause. The final decisive battle would be at Munda where the rebellion would be crushed, but Melissa never had the opportunity to speak to Caesar about it as he merely sent a messenger to gather any information she had on a scroll.

Caesar seemed to believe he was indestructible and it appeared he no longer valued her counsel in the same way he had before. Melissa knew that this was partly to do with Caesar having a new counsellor, who was far more persuasive and manipulative than she herself could ever be. Cleopatra had come to Rome at the time of the triumphs. She now held court in Caesar's beautiful villa across the Tiber. Publicly, senators fell over themselves for an invitation to wait on the Queen, though privately most hated and despised her, and deeply resented her presence in their city. The hold she had over Caesar had been apparent from the very first day. It was not that Melissa minded her sudden fall from favour, but she was concerned about what could happen if Caesar decided he no longer needed her services at all. Adding to this fear was the fact that it was now the summer of 45 and Melissa knew that Caesar would be assassinated in a little over six months, on the Ides of March of the following year, although she made no mention of it in any correspondence with him. Antony still made no attempt at contact, preferring to spend his newly-found respectability with his new wife. Quite where this left Melissa and Antonius was a future she had no knowledge of.

During his absence, Caesar made sweeping changes to Roman life through a group of newly-appointed officers operating in his name. Veterans were settled on land that had been promised to them. A programme of civic improvements began, covering large works such as the building of new temples, but also more mundane daily tasks such as keeping the streets clean. A new calendar was introduced by the newly-arrived astronomers from Alexandria, a gift from the Egyptian Queen. In general, Caesar's reforms were meant for the good of the people but, while the plebs loved him for every effort he made on their behalf, the patricians became ever more suspicious of his tendencies towards outright rule.

Antony went to meet Caesar as he returned from Spain at the end of the summer. He was determined to get back in favour, having followed to the letter Melissa's advice regarding divorcing Antonia and living a quiet, exemplary life for many months until he married Curio's widow. Fulvia was an ambitious woman who worked tirelessly to make Antony a respectable member of Roman society.

Even though he was doing very well in his newly-styled life, Antony still harboured a strong desire to get even with Melissa. Now he felt his time had come, both for forgiveness from Caesar, and for revenge on the woman who frustrated him more than any other. He felt he had been patient for long enough.

Melissa wondered how long it would be before she was summoned to see Caesar after his return, if only for him to gloat that he had coped very well with little information from her, and was unsurprised when a letter arrived just two days after his troops made camp beyond the city walls. What she was not expecting was for the letter to be from Antony, or for it to bring such dire news for her.

> *Mistress Lissa.*
>
> *It appears our fortunes are again reversed. Caesar and I are reconciled and I shall be named consul with him for the coming year. As his time is far too precious to be concerned with trivial matters, he has granted me full control over you. As such, you are to remain within the confines of your home at all times, unless you beg my personal permission to leave it. Failure to comply will result in further punishment for you, which I will take great pleasure in overseeing. I look forward to our next meeting.*
>
> *M.A.*

Melissa had long feared the loss of Caesar's patronage, but had not expected it to happen like this. Antony had a long memory and, it appeared, an unforgiving heart. She had spent her early years in Rome rejecting his advances and embarrassing him at every turn. This was his revenge, leaving her under no illusion about what he intended to happen. She thought back to those first days at the Rubicon and remembered the words Antony had said in Curio's tent – *All the while Caesar wishes it to be so, I will not touch you. Should that situation change, Caesar will give you to me anyway.*

Whether Caesar had forsaken her or not, she could not tell, but it certainly appeared he had been ambiguous enough to give Antony an opportunity to seize control of her. She shuddered, knowing Antony had finally outmanoeuvred her.

For weeks Melissa considered her predicament. She could not ask Caesar for help as he was still outside the city, where he would remain until the triumph for his victory in Spain had been celebrated. Even if she were able to gain an audience without Antony's knowledge, he had lost interest in everything except for Cleopatra and her vision of their combined rule. All he would expect to discuss with Melissa would be insights into his planned mission to Parthia — a mission he would never begin as he would die two days before he was due to leave for the east. He would not care less how she was being treated provided she still proved useful. She had a simple choice: either accept her imprisonment for as long as it pleased Antony to enforce it, or risk everything to maintain the freedoms she had become so used to.

If she chose to wait and see how her new 'master' would behave, she would lose everything and far sooner than Antony could ever have dreamed of. He had demonstrated that he was capable of patience, having waited years for this moment. Melissa knew he would be more than willing to keep her here for many more years without relenting, but she did not have more than a few months before Caesar's life would end. After he was gone, Antony would have total control over the city and every person within it. He could send Vitruvius back to the legion, leaving her completely at his mercy, to do with as he pleased.

If she chose freedom, she knew Vitruvius would help her escape, but Antony was one of the best-informed men in the country with a network of spies that was almost as wide as Caesar's. Her mind raced at the thought of the horrible end that would await them when they were discovered. Antony would drag them all back to Rome where he would flay the skin from Vitruvius' back, whilst she was forced to watch, before condemning him to death in the arena. Finally, he would reap his rewards from her flesh in ways that it tormented her to think of.

Of course, if she offered herself to Antony willingly, she might be able to negotiate far more than she already had. At one time she had considered this a possibility, but no longer. The sincere, genuine man she hoped Antony was appeared to be too well buried under Fulvia's ambitions ever to resurface.

Whatever her decision, she would end up as Antony's plaything. It was a promise he had made on the first day they met and she knew he would never relent now he sensed victory was within his grasp. Melissa was doomed, but she was determined to find a way to keep Antonius safe. That meant she would have to entrust the little boy's future to Vitruvius alone, and she could think of no one better to care for him.

Melissa chose not to witness Caesar's final triumph as she had no intention of begging Antony for permission. As she sat alone in the silence of her little house, she realised there was another option — one she had so far failed to consider. Caesar was destined to die and she could help it happen. Offering her services to the conspirators could give her the opportunity she was looking for. If she could strike a deal with Marcus Brutus for assistance, she might be able to get both Antonius and Vitruvius safely out of the city without the fear of Antony hunting them down. If she remained behind, she could most likely guarantee their continued safety by bargaining with Antony for the one thing she still had left to give freely. She was the prize he sought above all else, and she would let him have anything if it meant securing a future for Vitruvius and the little boy she loved so dearly. Melissa had made an oath on Rebecca's deathbed to do whatever it took to keep Antonius safe and she intended to honour it. He was all that mattered now, and to give her life to secure his was a price she was more than willing to pay.

To make contact with Brutus meant leaving the house. This would mean running the risk of incurring Antony's wrath if he found her gone, but it was still the best choice on a list of seemingly appalling options. One way or the other, she was going to end up begging for Antony's mercy, so to do it on her terms would be far preferable to having to do so on his. Going to Brutus was well worth the risk of that happening sooner rather than later.

Chapter 19

It took almost another week for Melissa to persuade Vitruvius to let her out of the house, and even then he refused to let her leave alone. She told him she had had a vision and needed to speak with the man she had seen. She said the man's life depended on it and asked Vitruvius to take her to the home of Marcus Brutus without Antony's knowledge. Quite how they were going to get in to see Brutus was another problem, but Melissa had given the matter plenty of thought. She wanted Vitruvius to announce them as messengers from Antony. She knew his name instilled enough fear in every member of society to get her across the threshold, as to refuse Antony's messenger entry would be a personal insult that he would not leave unanswered.

Vitruvius was surprised by Melissa's request because it was so out of character. She had never mentioned any visions that did not concern either Caesar or Antony before, so this was a new development. As Brutus was a friend of Caesar's, Vitruvius assumed there was some connection, but Melissa refused to tell him any details. She just kept asking him to trust her that what she was doing was in the best interests of the Republic.

Trusting Melissa was not an issue for Vitruvius, he had done for many years. He did everything he could to make her life as comfortable as possible, especially if it meant defying Antony, and leaving the house was an easy way to do that. Antony had first forbidden Melissa from going out without his permission as a punishment for trying to embarrass him into acknowledging his son. His refusal to do the right thing by his child only made Vitruvius more willing to break the rules whenever he felt it was safe to do so. After Antony's spectacular fall from grace, he had stopped worrying what Melissa did, but since the renewed threat that Antony had made just a few weeks earlier, Vitruvius was justifiably concerned for her safety. He had watched her like a hawk ever since. Melissa had never tried to escape from him, and he had never felt a reason to doubt her honesty, but something about this latest request made him worry. They had not seen or heard from Antony since he had sent the note, which made an unexpected visit more likely. Perhaps it was the thought of being caught that put him on edge. He had no concerns regarding what Antony would do to him if their absence were discovered, but Melissa, Antonius, and even Renna, were far more vulnerable to the types of wicked revenge he knew Antony to be capable of.

In the time they had spent together, Vitruvius had grown fond of his charge. He liked being in Melissa's company: she was as intelligent as any of the Roman upper classes, but did not adopt the same superior attitude towards him as they did, and treated him as her equal. With her encouragement, he had expanded his taste in reading material from the bawdy plays and poems popular with the lower classes to the works of the Greek philosophers, which she had purchased one at a time, as and when she could. These were not cheap items and, even though he would scold her for wasting what little money she had, her gifts meant the world to him. It was Melissa's belief that every person had a right to the same opportunities in life regardless of their social status. It was a radical idea for the time, but secretly Vitruvius thought it was a good one. More than anything, he enjoyed watching her get the better of Antony. It gave him an odd sense of fulfilment and, in the end, it was this reason alone that made him throw caution to the wind and agree to take her to meet with Brutus. He hoped that in some way this trip would help to put Antony firmly back in his place.

Melissa put on her best stola and the jewellery that Antony had given her. She wanted to appear to have some decorum and she felt more able to pull off her act as a self-assured seer when she was well-dressed. Vitruvius was unusually tense and insisted they both wore heavy hooded cloaks in the hope of hiding their identities if they were spotted. Rumours about Melissa's identity had circulated for years. Most people assumed she was one of Antony's many whores, but of late Vitruvius had begun to hear tales far closer to the truth. There were rumours that Caesar had engaged the services of a witch to guide him. It made him painfully aware that their movements might come under closer scrutiny and could easily be reported back to Antony. He had told Melissa about the rumours, but she had only laughed at the thought of being considered a witch, and he had dropped the matter.

Melissa felt sure the disguises were unnecessary, especially as Vitruvius took the longest way round to reach their destination. He completely avoided going through the Forum, which was the most direct route to the Palatine hill and Brutus' home, but she knew he had his reasons. At times she could swear they had doubled back and were walking down the same filthy backstreet as before, but she did not question him. Vitruvius had never let her down before, and she knew he was only doing what he believed to be best.

Vitruvius visibly relaxed when they finally arrived at their destination. He kicked the door with his foot and a slave slid open a peephole, revealing only his face.

"You are too late. The master is no longer conducting business. Come back tomorrow," the slave said tersely. He went to shut the hole again, but Vitruvius rammed his arm through it to stop him.

"We are not here for business," he replied. "This woman brings a message from Mark Antony for your master. It is of great importance and must be delivered immediately and in person. We have no time to waste with you."

The slave looked uncertain. As Melissa had suspected, the sheer mention of Antony's name was enough to make him think twice about his actions. He slid back the bolts on the door and allowed them to enter the hall. "Wait here," he growled and disappeared into the depths of the house.

He was gone for some time, giving Melissa the opportunity to study the death masks of Brutus' ancestors that were prominently displayed in niches along the walls of the dimly-lit hall. There were plenty of them to look at. Marcus Brutus was descended from one of the oldest and noblest families in Rome. One of his ancestors had removed the last king from the throne, thus creating the beginnings of the Roman Republic. This was why the conspirators chose him to be their leader. They knew his good name alone was worth more to their cause than any military commander would ever be.

The slave returned and motioned to Melissa to follow him. "You wait here," he repeated to Vitruvius. Melissa put her hand on Vitruvius' arm and nodded to let him know she was willing to go on alone. She had no intention of allowing Vitruvius to hear her conversation with Brutus. She had no doubt he would help her to betray Antony, but to betray Caesar might be a step too far for him to consider, and she did not want to place him in a difficult position unnecessarily.

Melissa was led into a large reception room where an older woman sat on the only available chair. She was well-groomed and obviously someone of great importance in the house. She was too old to be Brutus' wife, meaning she was more than likely Servilia, Brutus' mother and a former lover of Caesar's. Melissa stood in front of the woman and waited in silence, her head bowed in respect. She did not remove her hood.

"Well, woman, speak! What message does Antony send to this household?" the woman said impatiently.

"Madam, I apologise, but I am here to speak to Marcus Iunius Brutus and no one else," Melissa replied.

"Insolent wretch, he does not have time to waste on the likes of you! You will give the message to me or you will speak to no one." The woman's reply, and its tone, was short and scathing.

Melissa decided to go with her instincts. This had to be Servilia. She would address her as such and hint at her reasons for being there. "Madam, I mean no disrespect to you. I must speak with your son regarding the plans he makes with your son-in-law, Gaius Cassius Longinus."

Servilia hesitated. "He has no plans," she said calmly. "Your master is misinformed and he disrespects me by sending one of his sluts to do his bidding."

"Antony has no knowledge of my presence in this house or of my purpose for being here, but your son does have plans to remove Caesar from office and I must speak with him about them." Melissa paused briefly and then continued. "Forgive me for my rudeness. I realise I have failed to introduce myself. I am no servant to Antony, I am Caesar's witch." With that, Melissa dropped her hood and stared at Servilia, who looked astonished.

"Then it is true, you do exist!" Servilia gasped in awe. She quickly recovered her demeanour, but she no longer made any effort to hide her son's intentions. "Caesar mentioned you once, but I did not believe it. So he does have knowledge of his future, through you." Melissa nodded briefly and Servilia responded in kind. "Tell me, if he knows of the plans made to depose him, why has he not moved against my son?"

"Caesar does nothing because Caesar knows nothing. I have chosen to withhold this information thus far. Caesar must go and it is my wish to be of assistance to your son in any way I can, if it will help him to achieve that aim." Melissa was being totally honest, but Servilia still appeared doubtful.

"And why would you do this? With Caesar gone, you have nothing. What do you stand to gain from an alliance with this house?"

A man replied on Melissa's behalf. "Why, her freedom of course." Melissa looked around her in surprise, in search of the owner of the voice. He entered the room from a door behind Servilia.

Marcus Brutus was tall and handsome. His features were pleasing and he had a presence about him that demanded the respect his name generated. He crossed the room and stood beside his mother.

"You said you wanted my attention – well, it appears you have it. Your name is Lissa, I believe. Caesar has spoken of you to me also and I am honoured that you have found the time to call." Melissa smiled graciously as Brutus continued. "I am aware that although your living arrangements are far more than adequate, you are his slave the same as any other in his household. I wager that you want to be free of him and of Antony, at whose mercy you more recently find yourself. You fear what he will do to you when Caesar is gone and justifiably so. What I need to know is whether what you can offer is worth my helping you in return." Brutus spoke calmly and gave no hint of any concern at Melissa's presence in his house.

Brutus was known to be an intelligent man, and Melissa had no intention of toying with him. She went for the direct answer. "I know every detail of your plans to depose Caesar. I know who is involved and whether or not you will succeed. If I choose to tell Caesar, you and your colleagues will be rounded up and either exiled or killed. I do not intend to let that happen because I am in agreement with you – Caesar needs to be removed for the good of the Republic. I am willing to give you information that will ensure you achieve your goal."

"How do I know you can be trusted?" Brutus was right to be cautious. He had known Melissa less than five minutes and she was asking him to take a lot on faith.

"You cannot." Again she was frighteningly direct. "But then you did not know whether or not you could trust Antony and you chose to see if he would be receptive to your plans. I am well aware that Trebonius approached him months ago and I can tell you he has not mentioned any of this to Caesar either."

"You have Antony's confidence?" Brutus asked.

Melissa laughed slightly. "No, I do not. Once I would have said yes, but Antony tells me little of consequence these days. I rarely see him, nor do I expect to until Caesar wishes to speak with me, but all that can change if I ally myself with your household. I have the power to control Antony, and I will use it if an agreement can be struck here today.

"As difficult as this must be for you, you must either have faith in me at this time, or kill me and remove the risk I pose. Be warned, should you choose the latter, you will have to deal with Antony. He may not share Caesar's sympathies for me, but he would kill for me. Caesar placed me under his protection many years ago. If Antony was to lose something of such value, our dictator would not be best pleased, and Antony would again be out of favour. This time he risks the loss of a consulship."

Brutus' eyebrow rose in surprise at the news that Antony was intended to be consul. Melissa carried on with her explanation of the facts. "He will hunt down every last man among you to redeem himself once more and, I must confess, it will be easy for him to do this as I have left a list of your names. It will be delivered to him if I do not return to my home this night; Brutus, Cassius, Trebonius, Cimber, Galba, Casca, Petronius, Spurius. Need I continue? I think not. I am afraid I have been a little vague in my writings, so Antony will no doubt kill the entire family of each man to make sure he finds the right conspirator. His vengeance will be worse than the proscriptions Rome suffered under Sulla."

Brutus whispered something to his mother, who shook her head. They were both aware of Antony's network of spies in the city, but there was no way he could already know the names of the people who had been approached. If their guest was being honest, provoking Antony would be a mistake that could unleash the worst beast that he could be, and both Brutus and Servilia knew it. Servilia remembered all too well the proscriptions Melissa had spoken of, which had taken place when she was a young girl, and had no desire ever to witness similar events again. Thousands had been slaughtered, their possessions becoming forfeit to the state.

Brutus' attention returned to Melissa "Your offer of assistance is ... most interesting, but it is not my decision alone. Come! Some of those you refer to are here. We could present your proposals to them together."

Melissa was thoughtful for a moment. "I agree to your request, but first I must send my bodyguard home. There are matters he needs to attend to in my absence. He may return for me as soon as it is dark, if that is acceptable to you."

"It is," Brutus said with a slight nod.

"I hope you appreciate that I am taking a great risk in remaining here alone." Melissa had no idea yet how she would persuade Vitruvius to do this.

"No greater than the risk I am taking in trusting you, but I assure you no harm will befall you underneath my roof." Brutus was correct. He was taking a very big risk on very little information. "Come with me now, my slave will instruct your man to leave."

Melissa followed Brutus deeper into the house to a larger and more opulent dining room. The room went silent as she entered, and she was very aware that every pair of eyes present was upon her. She knew each man in that room was one of the conspirators, but could only place one name to a face. Sitting alone on a couch to the side of where Brutus now stood was Gaius Trebonius. She had met him many times when she had travelled with Caesar's army. The last time she had seen him, he was building the pontoons at Brundisium.

There were eight people in the room, including Melissa and one slave. She was the only woman. The six men sat on three couches positioned in a u-shape surrounding low tables that held bowls of stuffed olives, dates and figs, along with glasses of wine. Melissa was shown to a solitary chair that had been placed opposite the middle couch, where she was isolated in her lone position. It felt as if she were at a job interview, and, in a way, she supposed she was. When she had been offered some wine, Brutus introduced her to the rest of his guests.

"My friends this woman comes to us with the most interesting of offers. She claims to be a seer who has the ear of Caesar and the protection of Mark Antony. She is unhappy with her current arrangements and proposes a change of allegiance to us. We must decide whether or not to accept her assistance."

Brutus had been looking at Trebonius as if waiting for confirmation of Melissa's identity. Trebonius now spoke, firstly to Brutus, "I know her. She is who she claims to be," and then to Melissa, "I have not seen you for many years, Lissa, but I recognise you. I remember when Antony took you and your pretty friend in. Tell me, is Vitruvius still with you? I never met a more loyal man. He would throw himself off the Tarpeian Rock if Antony asked him to."

"The friend to whom you refer has been dead more than three years, but Vitruvius is still my protector. He felt her death even more keenly than I and still holds in his heart the guilt that he could do nothing to save her. He blames Antony for her demise and as a result, he no longer holds our consul-elect in such high esteem. You see, even he has reason to question his loyalties in such times as these."

"I am sorry to hear of her loss," Trebonius said with sincerity. "Please pass on my best wishes to Vitruvius. He is an excellent soldier. I owe him my life."

Melissa nodded once in acknowledgement of Trebonius' comment. "He will be pleased to know you speak well of him, and you should know that he still has great admiration for you, if not for others he has served with." Melissa smiled and waited while Brutus introduced the remaining guests. They were his cousin Decimus Brutus, Gaius Cassius Longinus and his brother Lucius, and a man Melissa was not familiar with beyond his name, one Quintus Ligarius. She paid particular attention to Cassius, who was lounging on the couch opposite her and appeared totally disinterested in her presence. She estimated him to be as tall as Brutus, though leaner and not as handsome. His face was thin, with sharp features, including particularly narrow lips that made him look a little cruel.

Brutus retook his seat next to Trebonius. "Well, Lissa. I think it is time you tell these men what we have already discussed."

Melissa took a deep breath and began. "Caesar is changed. His intentions were once honourable and when he first marched on Rome he fully intended to restore the Republic, but his agenda is now aimed at personal gain. His association with the Egyptian Queen helps cloud his judgement. She panders to his vanity, filling his head with notions of power and glory beyond that which Roman law finds acceptable. The majority of the Senate blindly follows his lead from fear of reprisal. Many of these men owe everything to Caesar and many call themselves his close friends, including some of those in this room." She looked at Trebonius and then Brutus, who both nodded in agreement. Caesar had made Trebonius the man he now was and he regarded Brutus as he would a son, because of his former closeness to Servilia.

Melissa continued. "Yet many of you cannot condone his actions, despite your loyalties. Caesar goes too far and must be brought to heel before the damage to the state is irreversible. You know he will never go willingly and so you have decided he must be removed by force. It is your only hope to save your Republic."

Decimus Brutus was also indebted to Caesar, having served with him in Spain. He asked the question that many of the others had been thinking since Trebonius had first mentioned Mark Antony. "And what is your relationship to Antony? Trebonius said he 'took you in'. We are all well aware of Antony's penchant for pretty women. He has them installed in many places around this city and some do far more for him than purely opening their legs. Are you another of his voluptuous spies, sent to seduce us with your charms?"

Melissa looked at Decimus. "No, sir, I am not. I have no love for Antony and he has little for me beyond ensuring I remain safe from harm. He has no knowledge that I am absent from my home without permission and will no doubt punish me severely if he discovers I am gone. I have taken this chance willingly, as your need of my assistance is far greater than my wish to avoid a beating at his hands."

Melissa turned her attention to the rest of the room. "I know each of your names and those of many others involved, some sixty in total I believe." Cassius and Brutus exchanged a bewildered look. Melissa spotted it and realised she was ahead of herself. "I speak of the total number who will join you, of course. I can furnish you with a list of the names of those who will be most sympathetic to your cause, but that you have not yet approached." Melissa was on thin ice. She only knew about twenty names, but she could not afford to worry about that for now.

Cassius spoke for the first time. "Will Cicero join us?"

"No," Melissa replied, "nor should he be approached. He will whine later that he would have been honoured to join your number, but he must not be taken into your confidence. He has been exiled from this city twice; once as a result of his own failings and once out of loyalty to Pompey. He will not chance his luck again. In addition, Antony loathes him and watches him like a hawk. He knows every move Cicero makes and that alone makes Cicero too much of a risk to include in your plans. He would snap under pressure if questioned, and give all of you up to save his own skin." Cassius looked away in disgust at her answer. He obviously wanted Cicero involved as he knew only too well that there were many men in the Senate who would not blindly follow Brutus, but would willingly take their lead from Cicero.

Melissa pressed on. "Your best opportunity is in March. Caesar will be leaving for Parthia shortly after the Ides, making this date your last chance. You cannot force him to stand down and so you must kill him when the Senate meets. You will be successful if you act on that day."

Trebonius and Brutus both looked uncomfortable at the mention of murder and Melissa supposed they had not yet agreed to that as the solution. She looked directly at them. "Believe me, the thought of murder does not sit comfortably with me either, but Caesar's actions will become far worse before you act. Arrangements will be made for Antony to lead the runners at the Lupercalia festival. He will be expected to offer Caesar a crown as he passes by, which Caesar will take if the crowd encourage him to."

The entire room looked horrified. Cassius sat forward, suddenly paying attention whilst Decimus and Ligarius began to mutter to each other. Romans hated and feared kingship more than anything else.

Melissa moved quickly to calm the situation. "You have no need to fear, he will not be able to accept it. The plebs are not so stupid as to agree to make him king, despite what you may believe." Cassius was eyeing her with suspicion, but said nothing.

The time had come for Melissa to play her final card. "To assure your success, I am prepared to keep Antony in check until the day you act. I will ensure his eye is diverted elsewhere. You will have nothing to fear from him. He will provide no opposition to your plans."

"No! We must remove Caesar and his lapdog if we are to ensure the security of the Republic." Cassius slammed his hand down on the couch. He was adamant. He had no love for Antony, whom he saw as Caesar's man and not to be trusted, and he wanted him also out of the way.

"The death of Caesar alone will not save your Republic, but the death of Antony will seal its fate forever." Melissa was just as entrenched in her view. She knew Mark Antony had to live if history was to be preserved.

"Ridiculous! What can possibly be so important about that drunken fool that we should let him live?" Cassius had no intention of backing down.

"Antony is no fool and whether you like him or not, you need him. Caesar is not the first man to seek total control of your Republic and he will not be the last. Another will come. His methods will be far worse than Caesar's, for he is more devious. The Senate will not see his betrayal until it is too late. Even Cicero will be fooled by his easy manner and guile. Antony is the only man capable of mustering a force great enough to stand up to this new threat. You should ally yourselves with Antony, not fight him."

"We have other generals capable of leading an army, generals we can trust not to slit our throats as we sleep." Cassius was petulant. He looked at Trebonius for support, but the man shook his head.

"They are not Antony. His men love him and will follow him into the arms of Dis if he asked it of them. You will need him to exercise control over the army following the assassination." As she spoke, Melissa too looked at Trebonius who was nodding in agreement with her assessment.

Cassius smiled victoriously. "Ah, but there is a flaw in your argument. Antony will not be in control of the army, Lepidus will. He is Master of the Horse and as such, he becomes head of the army on the death of the Dictator. That is our law."

Cassius had made a good point, but it was easy to counter. According to every source she had ever read and from her own brief experiences, Melissa knew that Lepidus was loyal to Caesar, but he was not the most impulsive of men. He could not be relied upon to make any hasty decisions either way, even in order to avenge the death of a friend.

"Lepidus may hold the title, but he will not use its power. He will wait and consider his options, during which time the mob will rip you to shreds. Antony will still be consul following Caesar's death and, as such, Lepidus will defer to him when asked to. If you want to live, then you must leave Antony alive. It is part of the bargain you strike with me now. If you are unwilling to heed my advice, then you are obviously incapable of looking beyond your personal differences in order to do what is best for the Republic. I may need to reconsider my change of allegiance." Melissa remained calm, but was losing patience. She did not want Cassius to see how frustrated she was with his attitude.

"You have the nerve to threaten *us*? I can have you killed before you reach your front door." Cassius was incensed. He threw his arms in the air in an expression of his frustrations, glaring at Melissa as he waited for her answer.

"I make no threat, Cassius, I make you a promise. If Antony's life is in question, I will not help you. As for your threat against me, you will not try to remove me for fear of the reprisals Antony will unleash if I do not return safely home. He may not like me, but I am Caesar's property and under his protection. He cannot afford to lose Caesar's patronage and he would, therefore, avenge my loss with frightening speed."

Silence fell as Melissa and Cassius glared at each other. This debate was getting her nowhere, so Melissa calmed herself and tried another tack. "Consider this, Antony knows of your plans already because you asked him to join you. He has not betrayed your confidence to Caesar, nor will he, unless backed into a corner. He can still be persuaded to act in the best interests of the majority to avoid further bloodshed. I can assure you of that."

"How so? What influence do you think you have over a man you say detests you?" Despite appreciating Melissa's point, Cassius intended to be difficult. He did not like being told what to do by a woman, especially a foreign one.

"Antony is a man the same as any other. You must simply learn what his weakness is and have the wits to exploit it when the time is right." Melissa raised an eyebrow slightly as a subtle hint at what she really meant and waited to see if Cassius was bright enough to take her lead.

Cassius laughed immediately at the innuendo. "Well, that is simple then. All we need to do is get an unending supply of whores to service Antony's cock and he will be ours! Fulvia will kill the poor bastard long before he is of no use to us, but I dare say it will be a memorable death!" The others fell about laughing at the prospect of Antony screwing himself to death and the tone of the conversation became more debased.

Melissa eyes had fallen to the floor at the mention of the word whore. She had known for some time that the only way she could control Antony was to give him what he wanted, but something in the way Cassius had made his joke repulsed her and she shuddered at the thought. Mark Antony still reminded her far too much of Anthony Marcus – her Anthony. She had

spent so very long fending off the former's advances, not
wanting to taint the memory of the latter's touch. Her decision
to do so had allowed Rebecca a chance for revenge. The girl
had stupidly welcomed Mark Antony to her bed as a way of
fulfilling her own fantasies of Anthony Marcus. Rebecca had
never wanted to see the difference between the two men and
her infatuation with one had led to her death because of the
actions of the other. Now Melissa faced a similar prospect.
She had to try to keep the man she loved separate from the
man she knew she had to sleep with, but for her the stakes
were far higher. At least her eyes were wide open to the risk
she had to take.

Brutus had said nothing since introducing Melissa to
the group. He preferred to listen and weigh the merits of
both sides of the argument objectively before coming to a
decision. Much of what Melissa said made sense. Lepidus
was his brother-in-law, but he had not been approached to
join their plot as he was known to be both loyal to Caesar
and prone to hesitancy. Antony was a man of action and had
been approached by Trebonius whilst he was out of Caesar's
favour. Antony had refused to join them, but had so far done
nothing to betray them even though there had been plenty of
opportunities for him to act.

Brutus had been watching Melissa closely throughout her
exchange with Cassius. He had spotted the sudden change in her
demeanour and believed it confirmed what he already thought
she was planning. He knew as well as Cassius that there was
only one way to control Mark Antony. As much as the thought
of allowing Antony to touch her obviously disgusted his female
guest, she was offering to do so for their cause. She had to be
truly desperate to give up such a prize under the circumstances.

Brutus rose from his reclined position, but remained seated
on his couch. He spoke suddenly and with more authority than
any of his compatriots could have managed, instantly silencing
the room. "Whilst I am sure we can all draw much amusement
from speculating how Antony could be brought to heel, I feel it
would be better for all of us if the exact details remain beyond
our knowledge. I trust that our guest will illuminate that
particular path at the appropriate time." He stood and raised

his glass "I have heard enough. I believe I speak for us all when I say we accept your offer of assistance and will heed all of your advice. Antony will not die by our hands. You have my word on it." He smiled at Melissa briefly. "I propose a toast to Lissa. For without her change of loyalties, we would surely be dead already."

The others in the room raised their glasses and echoed Brutus' toast. Cassius looked less than pleased to have been outmanoeuvred by a woman, but he made no further argument. Trebonius looked relieved. The thought of killing a man who had been his close friend for many years did not sit well with him. He owed Antony a great deal and liked him, despite Antony's many failings. He nodded in appreciation to Melissa who smiled in return.

The gathering continued for another hour, discussing the finer details of the plan before Melissa noticed the light was fading. As much as she wanted to stay to find out every last fact, she knew Vitruvius would be returning shortly and he would be anxious to leave. She attracted the slave's attention as he was refilling the glasses and sent him to Brutus to tell him she had to leave. Ever the congenial host, he rose and made excuses on her behalf.

Melissa said farewell to those in the room and followed Brutus into the hall. She had one last request to make of him in private and asked him to send the slave away so she could speak.

"Brutus, you must understand that if the totality of my betrayal is realised, I will be as good as dead. I have no concern for myself, but I am responsible for the child of the friend Trebonius spoke of. I swore to his mother on her deathbed that no harm would ever come to him. So this is the true price for my assistance. I want you to arrange for a small parcel of land with a dwelling large enough to support the boy and his remaining guardian. I want it to be purchased in the name of Quintus Vitruvius. I believe somewhere near Ariminum would be acceptable, as that is where Vitruvius calls home. He and the boy may also need safe passage out of the city if anything should happen to me before you and your colleagues can act. If that should be the case, I will instruct Vitruvius to throw himself upon your mercy. In return, I will uphold my end of our bargain regardless of the personal cost. I shall give Caesar reason to doubt my information, keep Antony off-guard and ensure he is delayed on the Ides. I will entertain him as long as I am able, but I urge you not to delay on any account."

Brutus looked thoughtful for a moment then nodded. "I agree to your terms as they are far less than I had anticipated. Vitruvius and the child will have my protection, so long as I am master of this house. I fear, Lissa, it is you who are making the greatest sacrifice of all, and I sincerely hope it does not prove too great a decision for you to live with." Brutus leant forward and politely kissed Melissa's cheek. "Farewell, Lissa. It is inadvisable for us to meet so openly again. It could leave you far more exposed than is necessary. I will send word to you when the arrangements you have requested have been made." Brutus turned and re-joined his other guests, leaving Melissa to wait for Vitruvius in the hall.

Chapter 20

It was late when Vitruvius returned to the house of Brutus to collect Melissa. He was deeply concerned when Brutus' slave had insisted he leave and return after dark, but he was given little choice and reluctantly did as he was asked. On returning home, he gave Antonius and Renna the lamest of excuses for Melissa's absence that afternoon. It had taken an age to get Antonius to sleep in the evening without hearing his usual lullaby that Melissa always sang in her strange language.

Before he left the house, Vitruvius checked in on Antonius. Vitruvius looked down at him sleeping peacefully, and a sense of pride filled his chest. He may not have been Antonius' real father, but to him the boy was as good as a son. He gently stroked the child's hair and then left the house to resume his mission to retrieve Melissa.

Vitruvius had become increasingly annoyed with Melissa over the afternoon for failing to explain her actions properly. She was playing a dangerous game in being away from the house without permission and it would mean the end of them all if she were found to be missing. Vitruvius knew that she was still wary of him despite everything that had happened over the years, but he failed to see how he was supposed to protect her and little Antonius if she insisted on keeping secrets. His greatest fear was that she still doubted his loyalties, but she had no need: Vitruvius' loyalties to Antony, such as they were, had died with Rebecca, and he could no longer bear to be in the presence of the man he had once looked up to, but now loathed.

Antony was not the only man to have dropped in Vitruvius' estimation. He had fought for Caesar loyally for many years, believing him to be a defender of the common people, but Caesar no longer seemed to have the interests of the people at heart. Caesar's return from Egypt with Cleopatra and her bastard son was the final straw. The whore queen, as Vitruvius preferred to refer to her, seemed to have a compelling influence over Caesar. The principles of the Republic were dying at Caesar's own hand, making Vitruvius realise that Caesar was the same as every other senator – interested only in his own gains. Secretly Vitruvius wanted to see Caesar's reign ended by any means. It was treason to think in such a way and he never spoke openly of his feelings, even to Melissa, who was still reliant on Caesar for her safety. The only thing that truly mattered to Vitruvius was Antonius, and he would rather die than let any harm come to the child.

Melissa and Vitruvius hardly spoke on the journey back to the house. He asked her about her afternoon, but she side-stepped his questions, as he knew she would. She did seem unusually quiet though. Melissa knew that the best protection there could be for her surrogate family was for them to know as little as possible. She might well be able to control Antony for a time, but she could never really trust him. She knew Antony was aware of a move to dispose of Caesar and that he had chosen to do nothing, at least not yet. For the first time in his life Antony was exercising caution, preferring to be sure of his facts before acting on the rumours that had reached him. Despite this newly-developed control he was demonstrating, Melissa knew that Antony would kill them all without a second thought if he believed they were complicit in any plot to kill Caesar. She had needed to make sure that she had a back-up plan to secure Antonius' safety and tonight she felt certain all the pieces were finally in place. Arrangements had been made to get the rest of her family out of the city when the time came. Brutus was an honourable man and she knew that he would keep his word all the while he had power. Now the final arrangements were in place for his new life, Melissa intended to tell Vitruvius everything once they were safely back home, but not in the street where they ran the risk of being overheard.

Melissa liked Brutus and she was certain that he could restore the Republic, given the chance, but not alone nor with the men who followed in his wake. They were little more than sheep following a family name. To truly succeed, he needed

Antony. Both men had qualities the other did not possess. With Caesar gone, Brutus would have the allegiance of the ruling classes in the Senate, but Antony would control the army. Apart, they were destined to battle with each other for supremacy, but together they had the potential to restore the Republic to its former glory. It was an interesting prospect and worthy of consideration.

Melissa had again reached a crossroads and, for the second time, she was unsure what to do. She had always tried so hard not to change the past for fear of what it could do to her future, but to change the outcome of this event could make the world a better place for so many millions of people across the centuries. The Egyptians may have believed Cleopatra to be a god, but in that brief moment, Melissa actually *had* the power of one. The possibilities both frightened and excited her. She had an opportunity to change history, but would life be better or worse if she did? The decision loomed before her as if she once again stood on the banks of her own personal Rubicon: should she cross the tempestuous waters into the realm of the unknown, or remain safe on the shores of certainty?

When they arrived at the house, they were both shocked to find the front door slightly ajar. Vitruvius placed his fingers on his lips, signalling Melissa to remain silent and pushed her behind him. He drew his sword slowly to make as little noise as he could and moved forward to the door. He stopped and listened. There were the muffled sounds of voices coming from within. He could not tell who they belonged to, but reasoned that they would be engrossed in their conversation and might not hear him approach. He pushed the door open slowly, and stepped inside. The hallway was lit by the oil lamps he had left burning, but there was no sign of Renna, who was supposed to be taking care of Antonius.

Vitruvius motioned for Melissa to enter and then closed the door as quietly as he could. "Is that a good idea?" Melissa asked in a whisper. "Are we not blocking our own escape route?"

Vitruvius shrugged. "You are the one blessed with foresight – you tell me!" he replied in a hushed tone.

At that moment he heard someone squealing. He knew it had to be Antonius. "Stay here!" he ordered, pushing Melissa against the wall. He broke into a run and followed the sound towards Melissa's sleeping quarters, dreading what he might see. His heart was pounding from fear. He sped into the room sword raised, ready to strike, but he pulled up short at the sight that met his eyes. Lying across Melissa's bed were Antonius and Mark Antony. The boy was squealing from delight because Antony was wrestling with him. They both looked towards Vitruvius in surprise at his entrance.

"Vittores!" Antonius shouted. He wriggled free of Antony's grasp and ran to Vitruvius, hugging his legs tightly. "This man played with me! Look at it!" He thrust his tiny hand upwards proudly showing off a small carved wooden boat that Antony must have given him.

Antony had rolled onto his back. He appeared to be fairly drunk and was laughing at Vitruvius, who was still holding his sword above his head. He reached for a flask of wine that was standing beside the bed and addressed Vitruvius, still laughing as he did so. "I would put that away if I were you. You may hurt someone." He drained the flask and dropped it carelessly on the floor.

Melissa had failed to obey Vitruvius' instruction to remain in the hall. She was sickened by the thought of finding Antonius being tortured in some way by their intruder, but she had to go to him. She entered the room a moment later and was equally shocked at what she saw. She stared at Antonius who had released Vitruvius and was now running back to the bed, onto which he dived, and began to attack Antony, trying to resume their play-fight. Antony lay back initially, still laughing, allowing the boy to jump on him and pinch him with his tiny hands, until his eyes met Melissa's. Instantaneously his mood changed. He lifted Antonius with one hand under the boy's chest, dangling him over the edge of the bed. His expression was deadly serious. Both Melissa and Vitruvius froze in fear.

Vitruvius lowered his sword. He swallowed hard to force away the lump that had formed in his throat and spoke. "Please do not hurt him, consul. He is just a child."

For a moment, Antony did not respond. His mouth had twisted tightly and his face was turning red either from rage or from the exertion of holding the boy in mid-air. Then in a flash, his mood changed back. Antony grinned and lowered the boy until his feet were on the floor. "Enough," he said to Antonius. "You must go to sleep now," he leaned closer to the boy and added quietly, "and I am in trouble with the lady of the house for keeping you up so late."

Antonius looked despondent. Antony put his hands on Antonius' shoulders turning him to face Vitruvius. He playfully smacked the boy on the bottom. "Go! We will play again another day. You have my word on it," he said, and pushed Antonius away.

Vitruvius had put his sword back into its hilt. He bent and gathered Antonius into his arms, lifting him up. Without even realising he had done it, he half-turned his body so that he was now forming a physical barrier between Antony and Antonius. He never took his eyes off Antony as he backed towards the door to stand next to Melissa.

Melissa kissed Antonius gently on the cheek. "You are in big trouble, young man," she said gently. She looked at Antony, who resumed his casual pose on the bed, reclining on one arm. It was obvious he was in no hurry to go anywhere. "Where is Renna?" she said quietly, hoping only Vitruvius would hear her, but she failed.

It was Antony who answered her question. "Locked in her room, where she should be. You allow her far too much freedom for a slave."

"If you have hurt her in any way ..." Melissa began.

"You will do what?" Antony replied coldly. "She is still mine to do with as I please, and it pleases me to lock her up." Antony and Melissa glared at each other for a moment before Antony's face relaxed again. "Have no fear, I have not touched her. She was unwilling to allow me entry to *my* house and so I found it necessary to teach her some manners. That is all I have done." He waved his hand, motioning for them to leave, but turned his attention to Vitruvius. "You may go and release her if you wish," he said in a condescending tone. As they all turned to leave Antony spoke again. "She stays," he said casually.

Melissa and Vitruvius exchanged a look that betrayed the renewed fear that each of them was suddenly feeling. Vitruvius whispered to Melissa "I will not leave you alone with him. Not like this."

Melissa closed her eyes briefly. She shivered with revulsion at the thoughts flooding her mind. She had not anticipated that this would happen so soon. In her plan, she intended to sleep with Antony much later, say around the Kalends of March. That way she would limit her exposure to him and maximise any influence she gained. If she gave in to him now, tonight, she would be forced to do so again and again for the next four months. He would be the one in control, not her. Worse still, Caesar might discover their affair before Brutus could fulfil his end of their bargain and get both Vitruvius and Antonius to safety. The die was once again cast, but this time for her. She had no choice but to go through with it and try to retrieve the situation later.

Melissa placed her hand on Vitruvius' arm and opened her eyes. "I will be fine, you go to Renna," she said weakly, then added, "I have foreseen this. He will not hurt me." She hoped she had said the words with enough conviction for Vitruvius to believe her even though she was having trouble believing them herself.

Vitruvius' face was filled with desperation. He could tell she was lying to make him leave. She had no idea what was going to happen and she looked terrified. He was torn between his need to get Antonius away to safety and his urge to run Antony through to prevent the defilement of another woman he had grown to care about. Antony was alone and drunk, after all. He must have dismissed any guards he had brought when he arrived at the house and without them hovering in earshot he made too tempting a target to resist. It was probably the best chance Vitruvius would ever have. He turned to look at Antony, considering his move one more time.

The two men stared at each other briefly and then, as if Antony had read Vitruvius' mind, he rose from the bed with far more speed and agility than a drunken man should have been capable of. As he moved towards them, he reminded Melissa of a cat stalking its prey – every move deliberate, cold and calculated. Antony reached out slowly and took Melissa's hand. He raised it to his lips, kissing the back of it.

"I must speak with your ..." Antony paused, smiling cruelly at Vitruvius. He began to back away still holding Melissa by the hand, pulling her with him, and continued in a heavily sarcastic tone "... your virtuous mistress. What we have to say to each other is not for the ears of a *common* soldier!"

That insult was the final straw for Vitruvius. Anger erupted in him like a volcano. He threw Antonius at Melissa and stepped forward. Grabbing the front of Antony's tunic with his left hand, Vitruvius pushed him back towards the wall. His free hand was already on his sword and, as he began to pull the blade from its sheath, he could hear Melissa shouting something at him, but paid no attention to her. Antony had not fought him thus far. This was going to be easier than he had thought.

As the two men slammed into the wall, Vitruvius was filled with a surge of ecstasy at the thought of the revenge he was about to exact for Rebecca's death. For more than three years he had waited for this moment and now Antony's life was finally his to take. He leered at his victim who simply stood still with a look of surprise on his face. Vitruvius slid his hand upwards from Antony's chest to his throat. He pressed closer to Antony, fully intending to tell him how much he hated him before dealing the final blow, but he stopped as he felt a sharp stabbing pain in his groin. He moved back slightly from Antony, looking down between their bodies. Antony had a dagger Vitruvius had not seen. It was pressed against the main blood vessel that ran through the groin and down the leg. The knife had not yet pierced the skin, but the pressure Antony was applying was increasing. The two men's expressions had reversed: Antony's look of surprise now been replaced by a sadistic leer, as Vitruvius' expression changed to one of total disbelief.

Vitruvius could still hear Melissa shouting, but could not focus on her words, since he was too busy concentrating on the dagger that could tear his artery in an instant. She put Antonius on the bed and came to their side. She grabbed each man roughly by the shoulder and forced them apart, shoving Vitruvius away to safety, but keeping her hand on Antony, holding him against the wall. She knew she could not hold him for more than a second, but it would be long enough to defuse the situation. She blocked Antony with her body, pressing herself against him as suggestively as she could, hoping to remind him of his original intentions. She stared up at his face pleadingly as she ran her hand down his chest. She was fully aware that Antony had been in total control of the situation from the first moment. Whether he was drunk or not, he was still dangerous and unpredictable. Could he also be merciful? She believed he could.

Vitruvius could not believe his own stupidity. He was ashamed at himself for allowing his bloodlust to control him instead of rational thought. He had no choice but to yield. He fell to his knees, still drawing his sword but now placing it in on the floor, the hilt towards Antony. He stared at his opponent's feet, not daring to make eye contact. He hoped Antony would make his death quick. He could hear Antonius crying. The little boy wriggled off the bed and ran to him, throwing his arms around Vitruvius' neck. As much as he hoped Antonius did not understand what was going on, Vitruvius knew he was scared; he always ran to Vitruvius when he was scared. He was filled with remorse at his thoughtless actions and clutched Antonius tightly to him, wondering what would become of the boy once he was gone.

Antony meanwhile was amused at the havoc he had caused. He looked first at the scene on the floor. Vitruvius was pathetic to him. The man had obviously spent too long in the comfort of a warm bed and had lost his fighting edge. Killing such a fool was hardly worthy of his effort. Then Antony turned his eyes to Melissa. She was moving her body against him, deliberate in her efforts to excite him. A knowing smile spread across his face. He knew she would do whatever he wanted to save the pitiful wretch on the floor. He nodded to her and stroked her face before gently pushing her aside. He crossed to Vitruvius, picking up the sword.

Vitruvius gasped and held Antonius tighter as tears began to trickle down his cheeks. He raised his eyes to Melissa who moved to take Antonius, but the little boy would not let go. She finally wrenched the boy away, screaming, and turned him towards her. She buried his head into her chest not wanting him to see what was about to happen, fighting him all the time. The adrenalin pumping through her body made her feel sick. She wanted to run from the room without looking back, but instead stood her ground, staring defiantly at Antony.

Antony placed his free hand on Vitruvius' head and twisted it to one side, exposing the area above the collar bone where he could drive the sword through until it pierced his victims' heart. Antony bent over, placing his mouth against Vitruvius' ear. The smell of stale wine on his breath only emphasised just how close Vitruvius thought he had been to success.

Antony spoke with menace. "Too many times now, you have challenged my authority. Twice I withdrew and did not engage you, but twice now you have lost and I have been forgiving. Know this. I will not make either mistake again." He thrust the flat of the blade against Vitruvius' chest so hard that he forced the air from the man's body. "Get out of my sight before I change my mind," he growled, pushing Vitruvius' head backwards. Antony straightened up and walked back to the bed. He resumed his reclining pose, propped on one arm to watch everyone's reactions.

Vitruvius collapsed backwards and sat on his ankles, shaking. Antonius freed himself from Melissa's grasp and dropped on to the bed, still screaming. He punched Antony in the leg surprisingly hard for such a tiny boy and then ran back to Vitruvius.

Antony laughed. "The child has guts! He must inherit them from his real father! I am so proud of him." It was the first time he had ever acknowledged his son and his words were designed to cut at Vitruvius' heart as deeply as the sword could have.

Vitruvius rose and looked at Melissa sheepishly. Back in Vitruvius' arms, the boy's screams had subsided to sobs. Melissa reached to stroke his face, but Antonius turned away from her, gripping Vitruvius with every ounce of strength he had.

"Take him to bed with you," she said finally. "Do not let him out of your sight." Vitruvius nodded. He made no attempt to argue with her. He was lucky to be alive and he knew it. Slowly, he retreated from the room trying not to think about what Melissa would have to endure as payment for his survival.

Chapter 21

A s Melissa watched Vitruvius depart, a feeling of utter resignation swept over her. There was no escaping what she had to do.

As she turned and faced Antony, she spotted the empty flask next to the bed. "Would you like me to get us some more wine?" she said airily.

"I would like you to come here and sit on my cock," Antony replied. His bluntness appalled her and she shuddered slightly. Antony rolled onto his back and sighed. His hand moved to cover his eyes and he gripped his temple as if he were in pain. "Fine, get the wine," he said with a tone of resignation. "Do not try to trick me though, or I will gut the boy … and his guard dog!"

Melissa ran to the kitchen and grabbed another flask of wine and two glasses. She returned to the bedroom slowly, gathering her thoughts as she went. Antony had wasted no time waiting for her. He had removed his clothes and now lay under the sheet, all of the pillows pushed under his head and back, propping him up so that he could see the door. He had doused most of the lamps leaving only one alight on the table next to the bed. It gave off a warm glow in that part of the room, but nothing more. Melissa put the glasses on the same table. She poured wine into both of them before offering one to Antony. He took it but did not drink. *He thinks I've poisoned it!* she thought. She rolled her eyes to the ceiling and grabbed the glass back from his hand. She took a large mouthful and swallowed.

"Happy?" she said handing him back the glass.

"Deliriously!" he replied. "Now be a good girl and take your clothes off. Take as long as you like. I am in no rush." He settled back against the pillows watching every move she made as he sipped his wine.

Melissa downed her own glass of wine in one go. She walked to her dressing table and sat on the stool in front of it with her back to Antony. She was unable to see his clear reflection in the mirror and she had no idea what he was doing. She slowly removed each earring and returned them to the box in which she kept her few pieces of jewellery. She took each of the bangles off of her wrist one at a time, deliberately placing each one on top of the last, forming a perfect stack of rings. Next, she reached behind her neck to remove her necklace. Her nerves were stretched to their limit and she fumbled with the clasp, struggling to release it, before placing it alongside the earrings in the box. She moved onto her hair, slowly removing the combs that held it in place, allowing it to tumble around her shoulders. Behind her, she heard Antony moving, making the sheets rustle. He uttered a long, deep sigh and, despite his explicit instruction to take her time, she knew she was trying his patience. She bent over and removed each of her sandals as slowly as possible, placing each one under the dressing table.

Behind her Antony groaned in frustration. "Come here, woman – now!" he demanded. She rose slowly and walked over to the bed, sitting down on the edge, her back straight, hands clasped tightly together in her lap. She could not stop a tear from falling down her face and turned her head away so he would not see it. She heard him moving behind her until he sat with one leg on either side of her body. He ran his hand up her arm to her neck and into her hair, running his fingers through it. He undid the pins that held her stola in place and the fabric dropped loosely around her waist. He resumed stroking her hair, pulling it to one side and began kissing her neck. She flinched and moved away slightly, but he grasped her neck and held her firm. She closed her eyes, fighting back a fresh wave of nausea that washed over her. He resumed kissing her neck, moving down onto her shoulder. His free hand slid first around her waist, then upwards, tenderly cupping one breast. He brushed his thumb to and fro across her nipple until it became erect and then he gently tweaked it, forcing her to gasp involuntarily. The skin on his hands was roughened from years of fighting, but the gentleness he displayed surprised her. Maybe this experience was not going to be as bad as she had initially thought. She relaxed backwards slightly pressing her body against his warm, muscular chest.

"That's better," he murmured. "Now, tell me ..." he continued to kiss her neck between each phrase he spoke, "... where were you tonight? I do not recall you asking for my permission to leave the house." Melissa's body went rigid. She had been expecting an interrogation at some point, but the timing surprised her. She opened her mouth to speak but could not think of anything to say. To tell the truth would be disastrous, but she was lost for an excuse that Antony would find plausible. She closed her mouth and said nothing.

Antony stopped kissing her and moved his head next to hers, pressing their cheeks together. His stubble scratched at her cheek, but it was not unpleasant. Antony spoke again quietly, still continuing to rub her breast gently. "We can do one of two things, Lissa. You can answer my questions honestly and in return, I promise you I will be the most gentle lover you could ever imagine, or ..." his hold on her breast tightened sharply and the hand that was still in her hair clutched a handful, using it to wrench her head backwards until she yelped from pain. He continued, "... I can squeeze you until you bleed." He twisted the fingers holding her breast and dug his nails into the soft flesh. Tears ran down Melissa's cheeks and she yelped again. "Then I will tie you to this bed and fuck you to within an inch of your life. Either way you will tell me what I want to know," he concluded, with such menace that Melissa had no reason to doubt he meant every word.

"Please," she begged, "please stop and I will tell you."

"Tell me first." The hand on her breast twisted again. One of her arms was pinned tightly to her body by Antony's. She moved her other hand over his in a desperate attempt to pry his fingers back.

"I was visiting a friend," she cried, wanting the pain to stop.

"The only friend you have that is not in this house is Caesar and you were not with him. Try again." Antony released Melissa's hair and brought his arm around her. He lay back on the bed so that she was on top of him looking up at the ceiling. He began to push her dress down below her hips. She tried to twist her body away from his to prevent him from removing the last of her clothing, but it had the opposite effect. Antony's grip on the cloth was too tight and as she moved, it ripped and he easily pulled it away.

"It is the truth, I went this afternoon, but I stayed too late." Melissa began crying openly. Antony rolled them both over, using his full weight to crush Melissa into the bed. He forced his legs between hers, pushing them apart. She could feel him pressing against her buttocks. He pulled one arm out from under her belly and gripped himself, preparing to enter her, but stopped short of the actual act.

"I am losing patience with you. This is your last chance. Who were you with?" he demanded, pressing himself a fraction closer to his destination, but still not penetrating her.

Melissa could no longer take the pain. The fear of being raped was so strong she was desperate to stop him, regardless of whose life she was risking, and gave in to his demands. "Marcus Brutus," she gasped.

Antony paused for a second, stunned by the name he had heard. He moved to continue and, as Melissa once again begged him to stop, he suddenly did. His curiosity at her revelation was too great not to hear more. He reasoned that showing clemency at this point might pay more dividends than further torture. In any case, he could still have her later, when she had told him all he needed to know. He relaxed his grip on her breast and, to Melissa's relief, rolled onto the bed beside her.

Antony lay motionless while he considered his next question. Melissa lay sobbing next to him, shivering from both fear and cold. Her breast stung and she wanted to look at it to see how badly she was hurt, but she was too afraid to move.

"Get into bed," Antony ordered. Melissa slowly lifted herself off the bed and slipped under the covers, dreading what was coming next. She took the opportunity to look at her sore breast. Even in the dim light she could see two places where his nails had cut into the skin and knew the bruising would be painful. She lay on her back and took deep breaths, trying to control her sobbing. She could not afford to make Antony any angrier than he already was. What was coming would be bad enough without any further violence on his part.

Antony followed her under the sheets and slid a pillow beneath her head, but made no further attempt to touch her. He propped himself up on one arm, his head resting in his hand, having decided to interrogate her before making any more sexual advances. He knew she would talk rather than face a further assault.

He was calm when he spoke. "So there is a plot to dispose of Caesar? Tell me who else was with you tonight?"

"If I tell you that you will have them killed. I cannot betray their trust so easily," Melissa replied as she stared at the ceiling. She could not bring herself to look at him.

"Lissa, I do not think you understand the seriousness of your predicament. What I will do to you if you do not tell me is far worse than what I will do if you speak. I can use you for my pleasure until I tire of you, which will not be for some while after all these years that you have made me wait. I will keep you here beneath me for many days, until you cannot bear the pain and the humiliation any longer. At some point in the not-too-distant future, you will beg for me to listen to what you know."

Antony ran his finger down her body, making her shudder in terror. He sighed at her reaction. Threats were getting him nowhere, so he decided to change tack. "Shall I start by telling you what I already know?" he offered. Melissa gulped and nodded, knowing every minute he was talking was another minute he was not forcing himself on her.

"I am prepared to wager that you already know I have been approached on the matter of Caesar and his more outlandish proposals; you would not be much of a seer if you did not. Trebonius spoke to me months ago, long before Caesar's return from Spain, to sound out my feelings on the matter. I know it was Cassius that approached him, at which point I should have realised Brutus was involved because the sheep in the Senate would only follow a banner raised in his name or Cicero's, but the latter is far less likely. Cicero is too much of an old woman ever to get caught in such a scheme and would give his fellow conspirators up in an instant to save his own flabby neck. There is also the fact that he detests me, so, if he were involved, I would never have been approached as he would want me disposed of too. That leaves Brutus as the only logical option to be planning a coup, which your actions tonight confirm. How am I doing so far?" Melissa nodded again.

Antony grunted. "I will assume that means quite well." He picked up a strand of her hair beneath his fingers and began toying with it. "This may come as a surprise to you, but I have no intention of killing any of my distinguished colleagues in the Senate, unless it becomes absolutely necessary. If I wanted to I would already have done so, but what benefit would that be to me? Yes, I would relish an opportunity to get rid of that old goat Cicero, but we both know he is not involved and I cannot simply kill him without a good reason. As for the rest of them, I cannot be expected to know what to do until I know what my options are. I want you to fill in the gaps and help me decide whether to support the action against Caesar, or to turn your friends in."

Melissa turned her head to look at man beside her. She was completely confused. Mark Antony was closer to Caesar than any other man. Yes, they had had their differences, but he was Caesar's second-in-command and would share the consulship with him the following year. Surely he could not mean what he had just said? *Was he just trying to play her?*

Antony sensed her confusion. "You think I have too much to lose by betraying Caesar. Have you considered I may lose more by supporting him?"

Melissa rolled on to her side. "Explain your meaning," she said, unable to hide her growing curiosity.

Antony obligingly continued. "Caesar has not been the same since his return from Egypt, and for that we have only one person to credit. The more time he spends in Cleopatra's company, the more Egyptian he becomes. Do not misunderstand me, I too have spent time in that country and I grant that there is much of their culture that would be good for us to assimilate into Roman life, but their system of rule is as corrupt as ours. It is my belief that Caesar wants to be king and he expects the people to want it too. He knows the patricians will not go along with such an idea, but the plebs just might if he bribes them enough. To begin with, it will seem like a brave new world, but eventually we will all become his slaves. Having a semi-divine ruler as head of state is a step too far for our Republic, and, it appears, for me. I like my life well enough as it is, thank you, and I will only go so far in helping Caesar to achieve his goals. I will not become his slave, no matter how well he chooses to reward me for my pains. But before I choose which side to support, I want to know what the alternative is and what your new friends are prepared to offer. So you tell me Lissa, who lives and who dies? If you truly see the future, why don't you tell me what I am to do?"

Melissa considered Antony's words. Perhaps he was sincere and perhaps not. She had never believed him good at politics because history had taught her he was not. Of course, history is written by the victors and Antony had not been shown in a positive light by any of the sources she had read. During her years in Rome, she had learnt history had been wrong about so much of Antony's character, why not this also? When he was sober and lucid, he seemed to have a pretty good idea what was going on. She decided to test out just how far he would be prepared to go.

"If I told you the intention was to remove Caesar from office peacefully and to allow him to continue life as a private citizen, what would you do?"

Antony nodded as he responded. "I would want to know whether I can still take up my position as consul. If so, I could not be seen to assist any plot to depose him, but I may be content to remain blind to one developing around me. Far be it from me to stand in the way of progress. I would, however, suggest immediate exile would be safer than leaving him in the city to cause havoc by stirring up the masses, but not to Egypt. Cleopatra would place him at the head of an army so great even I would not fancy my chances against it. I would suggest house arrest on a nice little island just off the coast where he can live well, and be watched at all times."

"And if Caesar were to die?" Melissa held her breath waiting for his response.

Antony shook his head. "No, I cannot condone that. Caesar has done more for me than any man. If his time is up, then so be it, but I will not play any part in his murder, not even indirectly. He is family after all, however distant."

Melissa had only a moment to make the most important decision of her life. Antony as an enemy was a prospect too frightening to consider, but as an ally perhaps she could still control the situation at least for a while. Earlier on the journey home, she had toyed with the idea of changing history. Now she knew Antony would never go along with any plan that involved murder, and although Brutus and Trebonius would consider a less drastic solution, she knew most of the other conspirators would not. Antony had also been right in the comment he had made about the masses. Caesar would always be a danger so long as he could count on the support of the people and of Cleopatra. There was only one option: he had to go. Her hands were tied and her imagined Rubicon had faded from view. History had to be allowed to run its course with as little interference from her as possible, but now she knew for certain Antony could never know the entire truth.

"Then it is good that Caesar's death was not under discussion. I am sure we would all prefer to be friends rather than enemies," she replied, hoping he would not spot the blatant lie she had just told.

"I find it hard to believe Cassius would regard me a friend!" Antony grunted again at the thought.

"Cassius wants you dead." Melissa was deliberately sharp in her initial reply, which was designed to shock Antony and distract his thoughts away from Caesar. She knew it had worked as she watched Antony raise an eyebrow, so she quickly continued. "He feels you are far too dangerous to be trusted. Brutus, however, is a man of reason. I have argued that a Republic without Caesar needs a strong man with the respect of the army at its head, until the situation settles. Brutus agrees with me and has given his word that you will not be harmed. I am content that he will honour his decision."

"And why would you do that for me?" Antony stroked Melissa's arm tenderly, as if suggesting her reasons were sexually motivated.

"I know what lies ahead. Nothing lasts forever and whilst the Republic will indeed end one day, your premature death will only hasten its demise. You are Rome's future, Antony, not Caesar. I have always known this." Melissa was trying to keep his mind away from sex, but she knew she was running out of luck.

"Well then, it appears I win either way. I can see advantages in waiting a little longer to see which way the wind will eventually blow. Be assured your friends will remain untouched for the time being, though you will not." He raised her hand to his lips and kissed her fingers tenderly before placing her hand against his chest. "We made a bargain earlier. I spared the life of that shit Vitruvius in return for the promise of having you. I expect you to honour it, and willingly at that."

Melissa looked down at the mattress between them. "I will do as you ask, if you will promise to leave him alone always."

Antony reached out and lifted her head until she was looking at him once again. "He really means that much to you that you would give yourself to me to save his pathetic life." Antony looked genuinely surprised at her offer.

"He means that much to your son." Melissa stared straight into Antony's eyes so he knew she was telling the truth. Antonius had fought her when she tried to separate him from Vitruvius. The soldier meant far more to him than she did.

"But surely you will lose your gift and with it Caesar's patronage the moment my body joins with yours. He will cast you aside for such a betrayal of his trust." Antony was smirking. He had the look of a man who already knew all the answers, but he wanted to hear her admit it.

Melissa sighed deeply. Perhaps more honesty now would gain her a little more leniency. "I am no virgin. You are correct in your belief that I only said I was to avoid being taken by you and half the legion."

"Cunning mare!" Antony declared as he reached down and slapped her on the backside. "Well, well, this changes things. You appear to have nothing left to bargain with."

Antony lay looking at Melissa for a few moments. His expression was not one of victory, but one of admiration for a woman who had successfully pulled the wool over Caesar's eyes for a very long time. He knew he had her at his mercy, and was not about to let a chance like this get away from him, but he wanted something more. Melissa was an amazing woman and he wanted her to welcome his attentions, but he knew that would most probably take time and a substantial amount of control on his part. Only in that way would his victory over her be complete.

"I will make you another bargain," he said as he began stroking her arm again. "This one is to the advantage of us both. Caesar will not hear of your indiscretions from me, meaning you will retain his patronage and the money he provides. I will also agree to stop goading Vitruvius and so will not need to kill him. My reward for granting these two favours will be to come to you as often as I like and you will willingly comply with whatever I ask of you."

Melissa breathed in deeply. If she said yes, she would be Antony's plaything for as long as he wanted. If she said no, he would rape her anyway and probably kill the others in their beds. She gulped and simply nodded again, unable to speak.

"Good. You will find I can be the most generous lover, given the right encouragement." He ran his hand across her breast and she shrank away from his touch. Antony sighed, the impatience showing again in his voice. "I know I hurt you earlier, but that was your own fault. You have to trust me. Tell me the truth always and I will reward you with tenderness. Lie to me again, and the consequences will be very different." He ran his hand back across her breast and this time Melissa was ready for him; she did not move.

"Better," Antony smiled, his tone softening. "We are going to try this again, and I promise you it will do anything but hurt."

Antony pulled Melissa towards him. She was shaking, more from fear than anything and no matter how hard she tried, she could not control it. He tried to kiss her, but her shaking put him off.

"What is it now?" The impatience was back in his voice.

"C-cold," Melissa stammered. Antony looked at her. Instinct told him she was lying again, but she suddenly looked so small and frightened next to him. She reminded him of a sacrificial lamb being herded in its pen, evading capture as long as it could before eventually being pinned against a wall, its eyes wide open, frozen in terror. Despite his desperate urge to make love to her, he found he could not bring himself to do so. If he pursued her now it would have to be by force and any further attempts he made to bed her would always end in violence. Melissa had once called him a savage brute, and he was determined to make her retract that statement one day.

"Turn over," he said quietly.

Melissa panicked. She could not face him taking her from behind. She knew he could hurt her too much. "P-please, I ..." she began, but Antony put his fingers over her lips.

"Shhh," he murmured kissing her forehead. "Not another word. Keep to your promise and do as you are told."

Melissa gulped. She could feel the tears welling up again and she complied as much to hide her face as anything else. She slipped her arm under the pillow and gripped the bed with her hidden hand. She shut her eyes so hard that she could see an imaginary kaleidoscope of reds and yellows moving inside her eyelids.

Antony rolled onto his back and reached for the lamp, extinguishing it. He turned back towards Melissa and moved behind her, spooning her body with his. Inadvertently, she moved away. He reached one arm over her waist and pulled her as close to him as he could. His other arm slid under the pillow and found her hand. Peeling her fingers gently away from the sheet, he wrapped his hand around them, before he spoke softly one final time. "If you are cold I will warm you. I do not want you to fear me – I want you to welcome my touch. Go to sleep. I will ask nothing more of you tonight."

Melissa's eyes shot open, trying to focus in the darkness. She could not believe her luck again. This was the second time Antony had backed away from a sexual encounter with far too much ease. There had to be a catch. It had to be a trick of some sort, but she could not think how. She stared into the dark for what seemed like an age, willing herself to stay awake, until Antony's rhythmical breathing eventually lulled her into a deep, comforting sleep.

Melissa dreamed that night, so many dreams all rolling together into one long confusing memory. Her final thoughts were of a hilltop in Somerset a few miles from her home. It was a dream she had had so many times since she had been trapped in the past – a dream of the most beautiful place she knew and a place where she had always felt safe. Melissa was lying on the slopes beneath the solitary sycamore tree that crowned the hill. Someone was there with her. She could never see his face, but she knew it was Anthony. Anthony Marcus that was, not his evil doppelganger. They were lying together looking up at the stars, watching as the deep murky blues of night slowly paled into the glorious yellows and oranges of dawn.

They were naked, despite the coolness of the air. Anthony was kissing her stomach, slowly moving downwards onto first one thigh and then the other. He gently pushed her legs apart and began kissing between them. At the first touch of his warm, wet tongue against her, she sighed, filled with anticipation at his next move. As his tongue continued to deftly flick across her, she groaned with desire, pushing her hips upwards, moving closer to his kiss. She ran her fingers through his hair and as he began to move away, she pulled his head back down, desperate for him to continue. He obliged her a little longer, before moving back up across her stomach, kissing every inch of flesh. Her hands slid down over his back trying to pull him up quicker, but he did not alter his slow pace. As he reached her breasts, his kisses seemed to sting, but she was beyond caring. He was teasing her now and she wanted him all the more for it. As his lips reached her neck, she moved one hand under his taught, muscular stomach and slipped it downward to stroke his erection. Wrapping her legs around his waist, she guided him inside her, raising her body to meet every one of his thrusts. As their movements became more intense, she could feel her control slipping away. His hands moved under her buttocks, pulling her ever closer to him. The feelings were all too much. She was so close now to giving in to him that her breath came in short pants. She dragged her nails down his back making him groan with ecstasy. She heard him whispering to her, "Lissa, Lissa."

Melissa's eyes shot open. Anthony never called her that and she had never dreamed it before; something was wrong. She looked around her. There was no hilltop and no tree; she was in the bedroom of the house in Rome. She stopped moving instantly, but the realisation had hit her far too late to stop Mark Antony. Still thrusting deep inside her, his body tensed and convulsed as he climaxed. He collapsed on top of her, laughing as he pinned her to the sheets. She made no attempt to move. She was too disgusted with herself. Despite their uncanny similarities, she had succeeded in keeping the two men apart in her mind, until now. Even on the few occasions she had confused the two men, she had always pulled herself back to reality in the nick of time, but no longer. Whilst she had been dreaming of Anthony Marcus, she had inadvertently given Mark Antony a way to get to her. She felt the same wave of nausea rising up from the pit of her stomach as she had the night before.

Pushing against his shoulder, she managed to force Mark Antony to move off her body. He lay on his side next to her, making sure he left one leg over her to keep her in the bed. She turned her head away to the side, so she no longer had to look at him. He stroked her face and gripped her chin, turning her head back towards him. He was grinning at her, enjoying his victory. "I told you I would not hurt you, but this was far beyond my expectations!" The laughter was still in his voice, taunting her as he moved his head forward to kiss her.

Melissa pulled her head free from his grip. Without stopping to think what she was saying she blurted out what was in her mind. "You tricked me! I was dreaming of someone else!" As soon as the words left her lips she regretted them, suddenly fearing that Antony would not be pleased at such a damning revelation, but oddly he was laughing even more.

"Provided you continue to respond like that you can dream of whoever you want, for the time being at least." He slid his body half on top of her and grabbed her face again. "One day I promise you, Lissa, I will make you want me and only me. There will come a time when you will beg for me to make love to you, and I will hear you say you want me and no other. His mouth closed over hers, smothering her. She wriggled against him, eventually slipping out from underneath him, but Antony caught her arm, preventing her from leaving the bed. He was still laughing at her and she began to blush. She glared at him, pulling the sheet up tightly under her chin to hide her nakedness.

"A little late for that I think," he said, still laughing as he let go of her and got out of bed. Antony made no attempt to wash. He pulled on his clothes and sat back on the edge of the mattress. Melissa had rolled into a ball facing away from him, pulling the sheet with her to cover herself, but exposing most of her back. Antony leant over and ran his forefinger down her spine. As he kissed her shoulder, Melissa pulled away from him, yanking the sheet even further and slamming her arm on the bed in a gesture of defiance.

Antony laughed again "Good day to you, my stunning temptress," he said. "I trust you will perform as admirably on my return." With that he left, his laughter echoing as he walked down the hall.

Vitruvius entered the room almost as soon as Antony left the house. Melissa lay so still, he was afraid that Antony may have gone too far and strangled or stabbed her. Part of him did not want to look, but he had to know if she were alive or dead. He approached the bed and spoke her name quietly. Melissa did not speak or move. Vitruvius reached out his hand and touched her shoulder and she pulled away from him giving the slightest whimper as she did so. Vitruvius' relief was instant. At least she was alive. He sat on the bed and tried again to get her to talk, but she shook her head. Melissa felt totally humiliated by Antony. She could not bear to let Vitruvius see her like this. Eventually he withdrew, allowing her some peace.

Chapter 22

Antony did not return that night, or the next. He came back on the third and took Melissa directly into the bedroom, allowing her no rest until dawn. Their encounters became a fight for supremacy, Melissa doing her best to resist every advance, while Antony experimented with new ways to make her respond to him. Some nights, she could not be bothered to play his games and just lay there. On these occasions, sex became perfunctory and he would deliberately hurt her in his frustration. She tried hard to hide the bruises she received from Vitruvius' watchful eyes, but it was not always possible and the more injuries she sustained, the more Vitruvius' patience wore thin with his former mentor. Melissa's fear that he would confront Antony once again grew more each day. She knew only too well that Antony would kill Vitruvius if the latter ever dared to challenge him again, regardless of any promise made to her to the contrary and she had to prevent that from happening, whatever the cost to herself. She began to fake enjoyment and it did the trick. Antony experienced less frustration and so became far less violent, meaning there were no more bruises for Vitruvius to see.

Every morning when he left, Antony would leave a gift of jewellery, perfume or a new stola and often another little boat for Antonius. Vitruvius regarded the gifts given to Melissa as payment for services rendered, but he could not understand the reason for the toys. Antonius loved them though, so Vitruvius made no comment about Antony giving them.

This pattern continued until Saturnalia. Antony spent the week-long festival with his wife, Fulvia and their new-born son, leaving Melissa to enjoy the time with her own surrogate family. She helped Antonius to make gifts for Vitruvius and Renna, and insisted on carrying out the tradition of preparing a meal for her slave. After two disastrous attempts at the dishes for the feast, Renna could no longer endure the disruption in her kitchen and insisted that Melissa left the cooking to her. She prepared all the food, but did allow Melissa to serve it. Antony even sent them a gift. On the first day of the festival, two amphorae of the finest Falernian wine arrived with a simple note – *Enjoy*.

At the beginning of January, Antony and Caesar took up their posts as consuls. A few days after the inauguration, Antony's wife left for their country estates. Two days later, Melissa was woken early by the sound of pounding on the front door. She dragged herself out of bed and hurriedly threw on a dress so she could go and find out who was visiting at such an early hour. When she got to the hall she found Vitruvius arguing with a pair of rather burly slaves. As she approached, Vitruvius turned towards her, giving the slaves the opportunity to run off. Although Vitruvius gave chase, they proved to be decidedly fleet of foot for such large men and he could not catch them as they twisted and dived through the narrow streets and alleys that they obviously knew far better than he did. He lost them at a busy intersection and returned to the house to find Melissa examining the two large chests that they had deposited in the hall.

"From Antony," he said, gasping for breath as he came in the door. He closed it behind him and collapsed against it.

"What is in them?" Melissa enquired.

"No idea," was his response as he shrugged his shoulders. "They are locked so I imagine this means we will be seeing *him* tonight!" Vitruvius' voice was laced with hatred. Relationships with Antony were still as strained as ever.

Melissa put her hand on Vitruvius' arm. "I know this has been difficult for you. I am not exactly best pleased how things have turned out, but I have to think of your safety. Surely you do not think I enjoy him coming here?"

"You could have fooled me with the noises you make of late when he is in there!" Vitruvius gestured towards Melissa's room and shot her a look full of distrust as he wrenched his arm from her grip. She was so shocked, she stepped backwards. She could tell he thought she was starting to care for Antony and that hurt her. *If he only knew how many lives were at stake, he would understand,* she thought.

Her thoughts were interrupted by another knock on the door. Vitruvius answered it to find another slave there, this one a young boy clutching a letter and a small casket. He allowed the slave to enter and the boy went straight up to Melissa.

"Mistress Lissa," he began, "I bring greetings to you from my master, Marcus Iunius Brutus. He wishes me to convey this message to you and to wait for a response." He thrust a pair of wax tablets at Melissa, along with a small wooden writing implement. She took the tablets from him, undid the cord from around their wooden backing and flipped them open. The message on the first tablet was what she was expecting:

> *I trust you are in good health and are not too troubled by the developments in your situation. The box this boy carries contains the papers you requested, thus formalising our agreement. My apologies for the delay, but it took a little time to find a fitting setting to meet your requirements.*

Good, she thought. The box contained the ownership documents for the land and home she had asked Brutus to provide. "Give him the box," she said to the slave boy, pointing at Vitruvius without looking at either of them. She continued to the second tablet, raising an eyebrow in surprise as she read it:

> *My sources tell me that A mutual acquaintance has been seen leaving their home with two large gifts. Whether you were aware of this development or not I must advise caution. A tiger is always more dangerous if the lamb shares the same cage.*

From the emphasis on the 'A', Melissa knew Brutus was referring to Antony and from the rest of the message, she guessed what was contained in the trunks. She took the wooden stylus from the boy and used its flat length to wipe both tablets clean. Then she used the point to write her reply to each message on the side that had contained the original:

> *Greetings to you, sir. You find me well and coping with the strain of running such an interesting household. I deeply appreciate your concern for the matter at hand. Please know that you have greatly eased my mind.*

> *As for the other news, I can tell you the gifts have been received, though not necessarily welcomed, or encouraged. I thank you again for your Assistance and wish you well.*

Melissa followed Brutus' writing style so that he would know that she understood his message. She handed the tablets back to the boy and ushered him out of the door.

Once he had left she turned to speak to Vitruvius, who looked utterly confused. "I know I have given you reason to distrust me, but I swear to you I have no love for Antony. I only do what he asks to keep you alive. That is the agreement I made with him on the first night he ..." She tailed off, shuddering at the memory of Vitruvius kneeling on the floor waiting for death to come to him. She recovered herself and continued. "Please take that casket and hide it in your room. Antony must *never* find it. Should anything ever happen to me, you and you alone must open it and follow the instructions within. I neither want nor need to see what it contains."

Vitruvius went to speak, but Melissa silenced him with a gesture of her hand. "Please do not ask me what this is all about. I promise you I will tell you what is going on when the time is right, but for now your safety, and that of Antonius, depend on your remaining completely ignorant of my dealings with Marcus Brutus."

Vitruvius realised Melissa looked genuinely scared. She grabbed hold of his hands and continued talking. "Vitruvius, I hate saying this, but relations between us will become far worse in the coming weeks and I can do nothing to prevent that from happening. I know I have already lost your trust and I will most probably lose your friendship. That pains me deeply, but what you think of me will soon be irrelevant. You only have to believe that everything I am doing is to secure your future and that of Antonius. Search your heart, deep down you know as well as I do that Antony will kill you both if I do not please him. The two of you are all that matter to me and I will do anything he wants to prevent him from hurting either of you, regardless of how degrading it may be. Do you understand me? *Anything!*"

Vitruvius did not fully understand, but he knew Melissa well enough to know she would not explain. Something in the message from Brutus had scared her. He needed to know what that was at least. "What did Brutus have to say?" he asked as casually as he could.

Melissa sat on the trunk nearest her. "Brutus has sent us word on the purpose of these," she replied resolutely. "It appears Antony intends to move in!"

In an instant Vitruvius understood what had scared Melissa. With Antony in the house, he would be able do what he wanted to her and there was nothing Vitruvius could do to stop him without risking all their lives. They would all be at his mercy every moment of every day. He nodded to show he understood what she had been saying. He did not like it, but he understood.

Antony did indeed move in later that day. He did not arrive quietly as Melissa hoped, but instead he came directly from the Senate, accompanied by his lictors, men who acted as guards to a serving consul. He dismissed them at the door, telling them to return for him the next day. His behaviour would be the talk of the Forum in the morning, but he had no concerns. Antony's nocturnal habits had been the subject of scandalous rumour for years – one more was nothing for him to worry about.

Melissa had insisted Renna prepare a meal far in excess of their usual standards in the hope of impressing their new houseguest. She had even raided the money Caesar had given her after his triumphs to have Vitruvius fetch some of the same expensive Falernian wine Antony had sent them for Saturnalia. This pleased Antony, who was in celebratory mood. He even offered to refund the cost of the wine after Vitruvius complained about the added expense, and subsequently agreed to double the amounts he handed over to support them for the duration of his stay. The standard of living was going to be considerably higher now that Antony was under the same roof.

Melissa knew all this generosity would come at a personal cost to her. Whatever Antony gave them in cash, he would expect her to pay back in the bedroom. It was still only mid-January and a full two months until Caesar was due to die. She was going to have to put up with a lot to keep his eye off the ball for that long.

She had been watching Antony all evening, waiting for a hint that he wanted to go to bed, but he seemed content to lie on the couch telling Antonius tales of his past exploits in the army, until Melissa insisted the little boy went to sleep. Still Antony did not move. He lay drinking his wine and was even laughing with Vitruvius about one particular incident at which both had been present.

Vitruvius seemed to have relaxed for the first time in Antony's presence, probably due to the copious amounts of wine with which Antony was plying him. When Antony did finally take Melissa to bed, he passed out immediately, pleasing her no end. All in all, the evening was quite enjoyable. If this was a taste of things to come, life with Antony might well be bearable after all.

As the days dragged on, it became obvious that Antony had no intention of leaving any time soon. To begin with, he made a conscious effort to get on with Vitruvius and relations between the two men improved. It was too much to ask for it to continue indefinitely and as time wore on, they began to get on each other's nerves once again. After a couple of weeks, Vitruvius could not take the uncertainty any longer and asked Antony outright whether he was staying for good. Antony explained that, as charming an idea as that was, he could only stay until Fulvia returned from the country. Melissa realised Antony had engineered this whole situation so that his wife and child were safely out of the way when Caesar's downfall came. If Brutus' coup failed and Antony was somehow linked to the plot, Fulvia was more than likely under instruction to head for the coast and to board a ship for Massilia as soon as possible. That was the favoured destination of Roman exiles and she would find safety there with Antony's uncle.

Admittedly, being the lover of a consul had its advantages. Melissa had new freedoms, being officially allowed to go out alone for the first time. She found that using Antony's name in the markets got her better prices, which made the housekeeping go much farther. This, combined with the extra funds Antony provided, meant she was able to put a little money aside every week. It was her intention to give the funds to Vitruvius when the time came for him to leave with Antonius. She knew Vitruvius had his own savings from the money Caesar had gifted him following the triumphs, but she was determined to make some contribution to Antonius' upbringing, however small it might be.

The best part of her new relationship with Antony was the baths. Antony did not use the public baths in the town, as his villa had their own suite, installed by Pompey when he had owned the place. With his wife away, Antony would take Melissa to his home to use them. She loved every minute of these private bathing sessions as she had always hated the openness of the public facilities. It became a ritual. She would be collected in a litter carried by four of Antony's slaves and would be taken to meet him at the house. They would enter the changing room together and cover each other with oils. Antony would not let any of his slaves touch his lover and he seemed to enjoy carrying out the somewhat menial task of massaging oil into her body. In the warm room, Antony would teach Melissa Roman dice games, gambling for kisses as opposed to coins. In the hot room they would sit and talk about his day before removing the oils and grime from each other with their metal scrapers, called strigils. A quick dip in each of the hot and cold pools would end their bathing and return them to the changing room, where Antony would insist on drying Melissa very deliberately. There were always far more towels in the room than were needed and he would pile the dry ones on the floor before tenderly making love to her on top of them. Over time cushions began to appear, which made the floor even more comfortable.

Antony became so relaxed and amiable in the baths that Melissa found it easy to forget which man it was she was with. She too could relax here, pretending she was with Anthony Marcus and allowing herself to enjoy Mark Antony's touch without fear of what Vitruvius would say the next morning.

Melissa had long ago given up hope of going home and she had the same needs as any other person: if this was going to be her life, she was damned well going to get some pleasure out of it. Antony was a skilled and generous lover, so why not enjoy him on the odd occasion? Antony too had noticed the difference in Melissa's behaviour when they were away from her home and it pleased him to have her enjoy their encounters. He began to suggest more visits to the baths, until they were going three times a week.

For Melissa, the worst part of their relationship was the fact she was losing the only real friend she had. The closer she allowed Antony to believe he was getting, the further it pushed Vitruvius away. He was always civil, but it was obvious he no longer sought her company, even when Antony was out of the house. To begin with, it had appeared that Vitruvius understood that Melissa was giving Antony what he wanted to make all their lives easier, but his patience with her now ran as thin as it did with Antony. He was by no means stupid. He could see she was beginning to enjoy her new relationship, despite her attempts to hide it. He knew Melissa looked forward to the visits to Antony's bath house and could guess what went on there. He could not understand why they did not simply stay at Antony's house and leave him and Antonius alone, though he supposed Antony had too many feelings for his wife to move another woman into her home so blatantly the minute her back was turned.

Melissa missed talking to Vitruvius so much that she took to spending more time in the kitchen every day with Renna. This was not an easy relationship to foster as Renna had also become suspicious of Melissa for her increasing closeness to Antony. Renna had good reason to hate her former master. When she had worked in his household under his second wife, Antonia, she had been in love with a young male slave. They had a relationship even though it was not permitted for them to do so, and Renna had become pregnant. She had hidden it for as long as possible, but eventually they were discovered. Antony forced her to watch whilst he whipped her lover into unconsciousness, before selling him to the owner of a quarry miles away from Rome. Renna had never seen him again and, when her baby was stillborn, she had been sent to Melissa to be a wet nurse to Antony's bastard child. As much as she had tried not to, Renna had grown to love Antonius, and, as much as she liked her new mistress, she no longer trusted Melissa now that Antony was her lover.

Melissa became increasingly isolated until she had only Antonius for company. No matter how tired she was after her long sleepless nights, she always made time for him. She had already begun to teach him English so she would have someone else to talk to in the future, but this now annoyed Vitruvius even more that it had in the past. Antonius still loved her, but, as he witnessed Vitruvius' behaviour towards Melissa, he too became wary of her and would sometimes run away from her when she called him.

It was a vicious circle. The more her surrogate family isolated her, the more Melissa turned to Antony for comfort; the more she turned to Antony, the more isolated Melissa became from the rest of the household. Antony seemed to be the only one who was enjoying himself. He was getting what he wanted from Melissa and the more time he spent with her the more she seemed to enjoy his company. Initially, he had only intended to use Melissa for his sexual gratification, but he found it increasingly difficult to bury the feelings he had developed for her over so many years. He began to confide in her his concerns regarding some of Caesar's more outlandish proposals. He was particularly worried by a request Caesar had made for him to make the offer of kingship during the Lupercalia, a fertility festival that took place in mid-February. The young men of the city would run through the streets of Rome, dressed only in loincloths, flicking women with goatskin whips in the hope of increasing their fertility. Caesar had arranged for Antony to lead the runners and demanded he make an offer of a crown as the runners passed through the Forum. Caesar felt the mood of the people was with him and intended to accept. Antony was incensed at Caesar's arrogance. He wanted to refuse, but Melissa knew he had to go through with it for history to be maintained. For the first time, Melissa began to believe Antony might be persuaded to go along with the assassination, but she did not trust him enough even to dare to hint at it. When he suggested paying some men to infiltrate the crowd and stir up sentiment against Caesar's plans, she agreed with him wholeheartedly and encouraged him to take the necessary action. She also sent a secret note to Brutus, suggesting he might wish to take similar steps to ensure Antony's plan succeeded.

The more time he spent with Melissa, the more Antony found he craved her conversation and sought to gain her approval for his actions. Caesar had been correct when he had said Melissa was Antony's equal. He enjoyed the time he spent in her presence, whether they were locked in a debate about Roman law, or locked in a passionate embrace. He admired her intellect and her logical approach to every problem that presented itself. He loved that she listened to what he had to say and encouraged him to have belief in his own abilities as a leader. He was in awe of her determination and spirit, which he found he could not break, regardless how hard he tried. He quickly came to understand why Vitruvius had become so willing to lay down his life to protect this odd foreigner from harm, and he too began to share that desire to keep her safe at any cost.

Melissa was becoming the most important part of Mark Antony's life and he began to realise he never wanted to lose her.

Chapter 23

Antony had been in the house for five weeks when Melissa was woken one morning by someone hammering on the front door. The noise continued until Melissa heard Vitruvius answering it, after which she heard voices in the hall which then became muffled as they went into the dining room. Melissa moved Antony's arm from across her body and slid out of bed quietly to avoid disturbing the man lying at her side. Antony grunted and rolled over, but did not wake. She grabbed her shawl and slipped out of the door, closing it quietly behind her.

She met Vitruvius in the hallway. He was coming to get her and looked extremely agitated. "Caesar is here," he said looking over his shoulder. "He is demanding to see you. He has his whore queen with him."

"What?" Melissa was confused by this information. "Why is Cleopatra here?"

"I do not know, but Caesar is annoyed about something. Do you think he knows that Antony is in there?" Vitruvius' voice had dropped to little more than a whisper. Even though Vitruvius hated Antony, he had every reason to hope Caesar was ignorant of the fact he was in Melissa's bed.

Melissa thought for a second before replying. "No. If Caesar had any suspicions whatsoever you would not have been asked to get me, but I do not like this situation in the slightest. Even though he could sleep through a stampede of horses," she nodded her head towards the bedroom, "I would feel happier if Antonius was far from here, just in case."

As Vitruvius nodded in agreement, Melissa decided the time had come to send her family away. "Go to Antonius, dress him and take him, and the box that Brutus sent, away from here. Go to the bookshop in two hours. If I am not there, do not come back to the house. It will no longer be safe for you here. Go to Brutus and tell him what has occurred. He has promised to give you shelter if anything ever happens to me. He will not betray you to Antony or to Caesar, and will help you leave the city undetected." Melissa grabbed his wrist in an open gesture of friendship and hoped he believed her. There was so much she wanted to say to him, but there was no more time. She kissed him gently on the cheek and then prepared to walk into the lion's den.

As she did, Antonius ran past her legs and into the room with her before Vitruvius could catch him. He stopped momentarily when faced with all the strangers and then ran across the room to where one of his little boats was lying on the floor. He turned and presented it to a great hulk of a man standing at Cleopatra's shoulder. "Play?" he asked innocently.

The huge man looked down at his feet. Antonius was tiny next to him. He bent over, picking the boy up under his armpits and stood holding him.

It felt as if Melissa's heart had jumped into her throat. For a moment she was overcome with fear and could not move or speak. Vitruvius pushed past her but was restrained by one of the two lictors who had accompanied Caesar into the house; the others had remained outside.

"Please, sir, let me remove the boy. He will only distract you from your business," Vitruvius pleaded with Caesar, without attempting to hide the fear in his voice. He was desperate to get Antonius as far away from that room as possible.

Caesar appeared not to notice Vitruvius' agitated state, but Cleopatra did. She instinctively knew something was wrong in the house. These two people were attempting to deceive Caesar in some way and she was well aware that the child could prove useful in teasing out the truth. "Nonsense," she said with a disarming smile, "he is most charming. Apollodorus may play with him. I will allow it."

Caesar looked at Cleopatra and nodded. "The boy will stay, but you may leave, Vitruvius. Go now!" His tone was gruff, indicating his displeasure. The lictor grabbed Vitruvius under the arm and threw him out through the door.

Vitruvius did not know what to do. His gut reaction was to force his way back in the room, but he knew he could not hope to take on both Caesar's and Cleopatra's bodyguards and he would most likely get Melissa or Antonius killed in the process. However, if Antony was found in Lissa's bed, they were all as good as dead.

He only had one option. He had to ensure Antony was conscious enough to function, and make him leave Melissa's room. Once that had been achieved he hoped that, between them, they could formulate an excuse for Antony's presence that would not endanger Melissa any further. As much as he hated asking him of all people for help, Vitruvius knew that Antony was his best chance for a peaceful end to the situation, as Antony always functioned best with his back to the wall. He had watched his commander talk his way out of many awkward situations when they had served with Caesar in Gaul, most of which had usually involved some woman or another. Vitruvius could only hope that Antony cared enough about Melissa to help.

Vitruvius stormed into the bedroom and approached the bed. Grabbing Antony roughly by the shoulders he shook him, half-dragging him to the floor.

"Consul! Consul!" he cried. "Wake up. Caesar is here with his whore queen. He has Lissa and Antonius and is not best pleased. If he finds you here, I fear what he may do to them."

Antony was still groggy from sleep, but he had registered Vitruvius' words. He raised his arm, simultaneously acknowledging Vitruvius' sense of urgency and stopping the latter from dragging him any further. He got up off the floor, staggered to the dressing table and poured some water from the jug into the bowl. He submerged his face in the freezing water, clearing his head. He rose and began to dry himself, considering his options.

He knew only too well that there was no way out of the house, except through the front door, and he could not leave unnoticed, as at least some of Caesar's lictors would be outside in the street. Vitruvius had said that Caesar appeared to be displeased. It was logical to assume that he already suspected something was going on. The gossipmongers in the Forum had already spread the news that Antony had shacked up with another 'tart', so it was reasonable to assume Caesar was aware of his philandering. If Caesar suspected that Melissa was the 'tart' referred to, then she was already in grave danger. The unknown quantity was Cleopatra. It was certainly strange that Caesar would bring her here, especially if he had come to confront them over an affair, and perhaps it was her presence that Antony could somehow turn to his advantage. He decided it was best to walk into the room, tell a story close to the truth, and front it out. Now he was an elected consul of Rome, he could bear the brunt of Caesar's wrath with little comeback, and perhaps he could use his position to save his lover. It was not the first time he had been in this sort of situation, and most probably it would not be the last either. His strategy was risky, but there was no other choice.

"I am going in there," he said decisively. Vitruvius looked absolutely dumbstruck. "I intend to reason with Caesar and talk him round. If I am successful, I will send Lissa and the boy out to you." He turned to Vitruvius, giving orders as if they were on the field of battle once more. "Get your sword. If I fail, it could get nasty in there."

Antony put his hand on Vitruvius' shoulder and gripped it tightly. "My old friend, I know that we no longer see eye to eye and that the respect you once had for me is gone, but I must know if you are with me on this and whether you are prepared to do whatever it takes to save them. Whatever it takes, Vitruvius. Do you understand what I am saying?"

Vitruvius swallowed hard. He knew only too well that he had just been asked if he was prepared to dispatch both his dictator and a visiting monarch. Whilst he had no concerns over killing the lictors or Cleopatra, Caesar was a different matter. He was still not sure if he could do that. This course of action was insanity, but he had witnessed Antony do insane things before and get away with it. He also knew Antony believed it was the best chance Lissa and Antonius had. He was the one who had asked for help, and he had to trust Antony's decision. "Yes," he whispered finally.

"Good," Antony replied, patting Vitruvius on the shoulder. "Destiny awaits, then. Either we will be successful in our endeavours for a peaceful outcome or we will have to subdue Caesar and his concubine, though I do not relish that idea."

Antony stopped speaking and looked deep in thought for a moment. "Although that possibility would certainly resolve the Senate's concerns, would it not?" he added with a wide grin on his face, before his mood sobered again. "Be ready for my signal." He grasped Vitruvius' shoulder one last time, then turned and headed towards the door.

"Consul? Do you not intend to dress first?" Vitruvius had to ask. He could not believe that Antony was preparing to leave as he was.

Antony stopped and looked down at his naked body. He turned back to Vitruvius, laughing. "No, I think I will make more of an impression like this!" He turned again to leave.

"Consul?" Vitruvius said again.

Antony spun round again and the look on his face said it all − *what now??*

Vitruvius asked the question that had been plaguing him since Antony had first moved in. "Are you in love with Lissa?"

Antony had not fully considered his real feelings for Melissa before that moment. He had certainly gone a lot further for her than for most of the other women he had relationships with, but was he in love? He honestly had no idea. All he knew for certain was that being with Melissa made him happier than he had ever been. He smiled at Vitruvius and gave an answer that asked as many questions as it answered. "Why? Are you?" He then turned and left the room, still contemplating his feelings as he headed down the hall.

In the main reception room, Melissa was feeling increasingly uncomfortable. Caesar had rarely visited her, in fact she had could only remember it happening once before. She was always summoned to him or messages were passed via Antony. She was even more uncomfortable that the Queen of Egypt was with him.

Cleopatra was reclining on the couch opposite Melissa, watching Caesar speak with a look of utter boredom on her rather plain face. History had recorded that Cleopatra was a great beauty, but Melissa found her features rather ordinary, although her nose was certainly worthy of note. It was a huge, hooked beast that dominated her face despite the attempts she had made with her make up to draw the eye to her other features. She was certainly not a patch on any of the actresses who had immortalised her on film. Her cat-like eyes shifted suddenly to Melissa, who felt like an animal in a zoo being stared at from behind the bars of her cage.

If only Antonius had not run into the room, she would have felt more comfortable. As Caesar would not let him leave with Vitruvius, he had become a most effective form of leverage to gain information from her. He was standing at the far end of the couch occupied by Cleopatra, with the Queen's bodyguard, the giant of a man called Apollodorus. The bodyguard was squatting down performing the old magic trick of making a coin disappear from his hands and reappear from behind the boy's ear. It was making Antonius giggle. Every time the trick was over the little boy would say "again!" and the bodyguard would willingly comply.

Even though she could not take her eyes off Antonius, Melissa's mind was elsewhere. If there was even the slightest suspicion that Antony was in the house then her life as she knew it was over. Of course, if Caesar did already know, then she could understand him wanting to confront Antony, but why bring that woman with him? The only reason Melissa could imagine was to turn her humiliation into some form of public sport.

Caesar was in an appalling mood, mostly because Melissa had kept him waiting, but it appeared there had been some disagreement between him and Cleopatra. He had been talking for some time as he paced up and down, mostly about his plans for his expedition to Parthia, but he had not explained the reason for his visit, and Melissa had not been paying attention. Suddenly, Melissa realised that everyone was looking at her once again. Caesar had stopped next to Cleopatra and was waiting for Melissa to reply to a question that she had not heard. *Shit,* she thought and immediately turned her attention back to the dictator.

Caesar spoke again. "You seem distracted, Lissa. Surely you are not concerned for the boy? He is happy enough with Apollodorus. I see no reason to stop their game. Is it that you have had no visions, or is there some other reason you are out of sorts?"

Melissa gulped. At least she could answer one of those questions and recover the conversation. "No, Caesar, there is no other reason for my distraction. We have so few visitors that I am simply not used to his being with strangers. I apologise for my lack of concentration. It will not happen again. What was it you wanted to know?"

Caesar was not accustomed to having to repeat his commands and looked less than pleased at having to do so. "As I said, I have told Cleopatra of your unusually accurate abilities in seeing the future. She is unconvinced and has spent many hours in earnest debate, trying to change my opinions. I can no longer afford such distractions, regardless of their appeal," he nodded briefly to Cleopatra who acknowledged him with a coy smile. "The debate will be settled today, and I will get some peace. Cleopatra will ask you questions that concern her future. If your answers please her it will be the end of the matter. I trust this is acceptable."

Melissa had no chance to answer as Cleopatra had no intention of waiting. She sat up and turned her attentions fully on Melissa. "Tell me what the future holds for Caesar's son."

Melissa could quite easily lie, but she disliked the woman in front of her. Cleopatra reminded her of Rebecca in a way, with her petulant and impatient manner. She had obviously been poisoning Caesar's mind with regards to Melissa and that was her reason for being here today. Melissa was overcome with an urge to take her down a peg or two and so gave an honest reply. "Caesar's son will be master of a great empire. He will rule over all lands from the cold seas at the north of Gaul to the warm deserts of the East."

"Caesarion will be master of Rome and Egypt!" Cleopatra gushed with excitement, pulling on Caesar's arm as she spoke.

Not bad for a woman who thought I was lying two minutes ago, Melissa thought. She knew she should leave it there, but Caesar looked somewhat appalled at Cleopatra's interpretation and Melissa simply could not bring herself to do so. "I do not speak of Caesarion. He is not Caesar's son," she said coolly.

"Liar!" Cleopatra spat the word at Melissa. "Caesarion *is* our son. Caesar has no other."

"Not today perhaps, but he will. Caesar will have a legal Roman heir. It is that man I speak of." Melissa stared at Caesar. He looked at her quizzically. He had never discussed his will with her, but he knew she was speaking of his intention to adopt his nephew Octavian as his son. He had been considering adding it as a codicil to his will lodged in the Temple of Vesta, but had not yet done so because he was unsure what to do about Antony, who was still his favourite officer and preferred successor, and had long been the main beneficiary of his estate.

"Then what does the future hold for my child?" Cleopatra glared at Melissa. It looked as if she wanted to strike out, but Melissa calculated that she would not dare to do so in front of Caesar.

"Caesar will have him killed," Melissa responded coldly.

Caesar looked all the more horrified at this suggestion. "Never! I may not acknowledge him, but I would never hurt that boy!" he said aghast.

"I agree *you* would not," Melissa nodded in agreement with Caesar's statement, "but as I have said, more than one man will carry the name of Caesar."

Cleopatra rose from the couch. She walked across to stand in front of Melissa and bent slowly as if taking a close look at her victim before passing sentence. She glanced at Melissa's neck and spotted some slight bruising half hidden by Melissa's hair. She smiled knowingly. These were the marks left in the height of passion by a lover and gave Cleopatra a way to retaliate.

As she straightened up again, Cleopatra composed herself. Her face was now a mask, still and serene, with no emotion displayed: the face of a true queen. She addressed Caesar in her most regal tone. "Noble Caesar, did you not tell me that this woman's foresight is linked to her virtue? If so, then she can have no ability, for she has had a man this very night. I can smell the scent of his sex on her. Perhaps it was that man who answered the door? He was not unattractive, for a common man. I would wager he has been making use of Caesar's assets for his own pleasures!"

Caesar looked perplexed. "Vitruvius? I do not believe it! He is loyal to me and an honourable man. It is why he was chosen to guard Lissa."

"Even the most pious man can falter, given enough temptation." Cleopatra appeared to be oozing malevolence from every pore of her body as she returned to the opposite couch. "If he has indeed succumbed to her witchcraft, he must be punished for his betrayal, as she must for her lies. You should question him immediately."

Cleopatra was enjoying herself far too much for Melissa's liking, and now she appeared intent on hurting Vitruvius. She had to be stopped. "Please, Caesar," Melissa begged, "Vitruvius has never touched me. I swear it to you."

Caesar looked doubtful at Cleopatra's accusation, but he was not prepared to let the matter drop. "If not him, then who?" Melissa did not answer and looked away until Caesar turned to one of his lictors and gave the order Melissa dreaded. "Find Vitruvius and bring him to me. If he is responsible for her defilement, you will castrate him as punishment for his disloyalty."

Melissa reached for Caesar's hand to beg him again to believe her. She would say anything to stop him torturing Vitruvius, but she never got the chance. From the door another voice spoke.

"I would prefer it if you did not! It makes such a bloody mess and the poor bastard has done nothing to deserve it!"

Antony walked into the room with so much confidence even Caesar was taken aback. Still naked, he walked round the room slowly, surveying every person there, gauging the strength of the opposition. He paused at a side table and toyed with the fruit in the bowl that sat on it. He eventually picked up an apple and took a bite. Melissa did not dare look at him or move. Of all the stupid things he could have done, this had to be the worst.

Apollodorus stopped playing with Antonius. He gave the boy the coin and rose to his feet, lifting Antonius into his arms. Antonius made no sound of complaint. He was simply fascinated by the magic coin in his hands and turned it over and over, trying to make it vanish.

Caesar recovered himself first. "Consul Antony, do you not think you are inappropriately dressed to receive a Queen?" He walked over to a chair and sat down.

"This is my house and I am dressed as I usually am at this time of day. Had I been advised of your visit, I may have made other arrangements, but as it is ..." Antony yawned and stretched himself, displaying every muscle in his body to good effect, "... I did not have the time. I am sure that I have nothing her majesty has not seen before." His last remark was addressed to Cleopatra alone and he had stopped just in front of her, facing her full on.

Cleopatra had at first been as surprised as anyone at Antony's entrance, but she maintained her air of indifference. She had, nevertheless, made a thorough assessment of him. He was younger than Caesar and in much better physical shape – very well proportioned in fact! She found his behaviour reckless, but it was obvious he was not scared of anything or anyone, including Caesar. She was not used to such arrogance being displayed in her presence, but the sheer nerve of the man fascinated her. He must have known that at the snap of her fingers he would be dead. She was a Queen, to be respected and adored, yet he showed no regard for her position. As much as his apparent lack of respect annoyed her, she was intrigued to know what he would do next.

"No, sir, I agree that you do not," she replied, "though it must be said that since I have been in Rome I have neither seen it in such quantity nor on such prominent display." Cleopatra nodded slightly and gave him a half-smile, signifying her approval of his physique. She raised her hand and Antony bent to kiss it, never taking his eyes off hers.

"Your Royal Highness." He was oozing charm now, every word spoken as if Cleopatra was the only person in the room who mattered. "I welcome you to my home." This was the second time he had made a reference to the ownership of the house and he hoped his point was getting across. "I trust that Lissa here has been a decent hostess in my absence. She is not Roman and her manners can appear sharp, even rude, until you get to know her." Antony had turned and was walking towards Melissa as he spoke. He crossed behind the couch she was sitting on and placed his hand firmly on her shoulder, making her jump.

"Passable!" Cleopatra gave a curt reply, glaring at Melissa. She returned her attention to Antony and continued in a more seductive tone, playing the same game with him that he was playing with her. "Caesar has told me much about you, though I must admit I am surprised to find myself in your house." She looked around the plain room again, obviously surprised that a man of Antony's position would have such a dull residence, but she had acknowledged Antony's comments. *Good,* he thought. This was his house on paper, even if Caesar had paid for it, and he could do what he wished in it.

"Ah, a man of my position has many homes," He began stroking Melissa's hair as he continued, "and I do like to make my presence felt in *all* of them." Cleopatra's eyes returned to Antony and she raised an eyebrow. From the way he said the word *all* she guessed he had been the man in Melissa's bed. This development would make things interesting. Cleopatra's gaze shifted to Caesar, but he seemed either not to have picked up the reference or had chosen to ignore it as he sat in silence, glaring at Antony.

Antony bent over and kissed Melissa on the top of the head. As he did so he whispered to her, "Be ready." She gave the slightest nod she could in response and tensed her body, ready to move on his signal.

Antonius was still being held by Cleopatra's bodyguard. Antony moved towards him. He had to retrieve the boy first or he knew Melissa would kill him herself. The bodyguard was a great hulk of a man, with biceps as thick as Antony's neck. He looked like he could snap Antonius like a twig. Antony reached out and put his hands under Antonius' armpits. He pulled slightly, but the other man did not yield. Antony had already gauged his distance from the nearest weapon and was steeling himself to make his move when he saw something out of the corner of his eye. Cleopatra had gestured to her servant to release Antonius. The man did so without further resistance, and Antony breathed a sigh of relief as he gathered the boy into his arms.

"And what about this one?" he turned back to Cleopatra, ruffling the boy's hair affectionately. "He has not given you any trouble has he?" Antonius wriggled, trying to get free, but thankfully he did not cry out.

"The boy is charming. He reminds me of my son. They are not too dissimilar in age, though this one is perhaps a year older.

His father must be so proud of him." Cleopatra was fishing. She knew only too well that Antony was the boy's father from the striking similarities between them, but from her experience of Caesar, she fully expected Antony to deny it.

"I am," Antony said calmly. His voice displayed no hint of dishonesty and the lack of a denial of his parental status shocked not only Cleopatra, but Caesar and Melissa as well. The latter spun her head to look at him and for a moment she and Antony stared at each other. It seemed that just when she thought she had figured him out, Antony could surprise her yet again.

"And what of his mother?" Cleopatra seemed keen to continue the conversation.

"She died giving birth to him. Lissa takes care of him for me. Someone has to, and my wife will not allow him in her house." That was it! Melissa realised that by declaring feelings for Antonius, Antony had a bona fide reason for being there without implicating her. Caesar would be livid. She stole a quick glance in his direction. His mouth had twisted tightly and he was biting on his bottom lip, definitely livid, but his anger would be directed at Antony alone. Feelings of relief began to spread over her and she relaxed slightly for the first time that morning.

Antony continued talking. "Now it is time for his breakfast, so he must leave us. Lissa, would you mind?" Antony walked over to Melissa who stood up, preparing to take Antonius from him. A look of relief passed between them, but, before the exchange was complete, Caesar spoke in a cold, heartless monotone.

"No, Antony, there is still a matter I need Lissa for. She may not leave us."

Panic welled up inside Melissa again. Antony could see the fear in her eyes and shook his head very slightly. He indicated for her to sit back down, which she did. He took Antonius to the door, put him on his feet and pushed him through it to Vitruvius who was anxiously waiting on the other side. Caesar made no objection. Whatever happened next, at least the child was safe.

Antony returned to the couch. He lay down on it and put his head in Melissa's lap. Melissa threw a cushion across him to provide a little modesty. He looked up at her and winked.

He closed his eyes, sighed and then resumed the conversation. "What is it you need from her at such an early hour?"

"The question of her ability to foretell the future is in doubt. It must be resolved. It has been suggested that her guard may have defiled her, despite your assurances that he was trustworthy." Caesar's annoyance at Antony's continued display of arrogance was now more than clear in his curt tone.

Antony took Melissa's hand in his and gently rubbed it. He placed it on his chest "Doubtful," he replied thoughtfully. "The fool definitely has some feelings for her, that much I grant you, but he has not had the opportunity to enter her, nor will he." Antony turned his head to look at Caesar and then delivered the blow Melissa had dreaded from the outset. "Believe me, there is not enough room in there for both of us."

Melissa's head began to spin and she nearly fainted. It was all she could do to stay sitting upright. Accustomed as she had grown to Roman coarseness in sexual matters, she still cringed at Antony's vulgarity. What was he doing? He had just admitted to having slept with her.

Cleopatra gasped with excitement and sat forward on the couch, eagerly waiting for the next exchange. All eyes fell on Caesar, whose face was becoming redder by the second. His hand gripped the side of his chair so tightly that his knuckles whitened under the strain. Melissa was trembling now, terrified of what Caesar would do. Antony had completely humiliated Caesar in that one sentence. He would not get away with it. She only hoped Vitruvius had already taken Antonius away to a safe location.

"Get out! All of you!" Caesar barked the words while holding on to what little remained of his rapidly disintegrating composure. No one moved. "OUT!" he shouted as he rose to his feet. "GET OUT NOW!" Caesar screamed again and his men finally moved towards the door. At a nod from Cleopatra her bodyguard followed them. The Queen then settled back on her couch. She was enjoying this unexpected entertainment and had no intention of leaving just as it was becoming so interesting.

Caesar had been adjusting his toga whilst the room was emptying; concentrating on something trivial was a way for him to regain his self-control. He turned to Cleopatra and spoke with a familiarity that was unusual for him. "My dear, I would be grateful if you would leave us. What I now have to discuss with my fellow consul is a private matter pertaining to the security of Rome. It would be inappropriate for me to continue in your presence."

Cleopatra pouted like a child. She did not like taking orders from anyone, including Caesar. She stood up, her fists clenched at her sides. For a moment Melissa thought she was going to argue, but then her expression changed. She smiled graciously and replied with equal familiarity, although to Melissa her tone sounded less than sincere. "Of course, my love, what pleases Caesar pleases me also." She turned to Antony and her eyes wandered along the entire length of his body before she spoke. "Farewell, sir. I do hope I will be seeing more of *you*." The way Cleopatra emphasised the word '*you*' left little doubt of her meaning. She offered her hand to Antony once again. He sat up swiftly and obligingly kissed the back of it. Cleopatra turned on her heel and left without a second glance at Melissa.

An uneasy silence descended after Cleopatra's departure. One of them had to speak to end the deadlock. Antony sighed. "Interesting woman," he said and gently slapped Melissa on the thigh.

Caesar stared at him momentarily, then began to pace the room, back and forth from one side to the other. "Here we go," Antony said under his breath, making Caesar stop dead. He was so calm when he spoke that it made the hairs on the back of Melissa's neck stand on end.

"Explain to me, if you will, why it is that each time I give you an opportunity for advancement you choose to abuse my trust? What gives you the right to ignore my express instructions time and time again? I have given you the most important tasks, shared with you my most intimate secrets. I have even regarded you as I would a son at times, favouring you when I should not and forgiving your many shortcomings. You have ruled in my stead and yet to be second to Caesar is not enough for you. It seems you wish to take those things which I value most in an attempt to humiliate me. On the subject of Lissa I was more than clear. I could not keep the two women because to do so would have done untold damage to my reputation, so I entrusted their safety to your keeping. You had no reputation to damage and were paid exceptionally well to act as my agent in this." Melissa looked at Antony, her mouth wide open. All these years she had been living frugally on the little money Antony provided when he had apparently been given a small fortune.

Caesar continued. "When you took the younger one, it was only to be expected. I knew you would not be able to refrain from helping yourself to one or the other, and I told you as much. As her alleged ability had not developed, her loss was of little consequence, although I must say I am surprised that you would so openly confess to fathering her child in front of a woman whom you know to be pressing me to make a similar admission. You know that such an outcome is impossible and so your intention must have been to embarrass me and place doubt in the Queen's mind of my loyalties to her. All of this I can forgive, but what you have done here ..." he gestured at Melissa, "... is beyond contempt. She was not to be touched unless I ordered it. Her gift was of too great a value to me in such uncertain times. For five years I have been blessed with the knowledge of my success in every endeavour. It has allowed me to chance my hand when caution might have been the more logical course. All that time her virginity remained intact. Now I am to embark on the greatest campaign of my life and I am left without the security of her advice. My disappointment in you is complete. I do not know you, Mark Antony. You are a stranger to me."

Antony was grinning. He knew of course that the last five years had been a complete deception on Melissa's part. The worry for her now was how much he would tell Caesar to save his own skin. Melissa held her breath as Antony spoke.

"What if I were to tell you that I had Lissa before the other one? That she came willingly to my bed years ago and I have been enjoying her all this time? What would you say then? She would still have been providing you with valuable insights, but without her precious virginity. Perhaps her kind does not require celibacy to be intuitive."

Caesar looked directly at Melissa. She could feel his eyes burning into the side of her head, but she could not meet his gaze. "Is this true?" he asked, almost whispering.

Antony replied for her. "No it is not, but what if it were the case? We only have her word for it that it is so. Perhaps she can still do it. Maybe she lied out of fear of becoming my sex slave, or yours, come to think of it. Consider the possibilities from her perspective. It is a plausible suggestion that we ourselves discussed the first day we met her." Antony moved closer to Melissa. He took her hand and placed it on his thigh. He left his hand over hers and squeezed gently, as if trying to give her some of his strength.

Caesar was still looking at Melissa. He spoke to her directly, raising his hand to indicate that he expected Antony to be silent. "Lissa, is what Antony suggests true? Have you lied to me about the nature of your gift?"

Melissa still could not look at Caesar and she was no longer sure whether Antony was trying to save her or get her thrown into the arena. She had also heard Caesar use the word 'ruled' when he spoke of governing Rome. A slip of the tongue perhaps, or was it a warning of his real intentions? He had refused the crown Antony had offered him the previous week at the Lupercalia festival, but only because the people had mercifully booed the gesture, thanks in part to the paid dissenters that both Antony and Brutus had spread throughout the crowd. Melissa was now certain Caesar was intent on absolute power, and that made him more dangerous than she had ever imagined him to be.

She could not hide the fear in her voice as she finally spoke. "I have always been Caesar's faithful servant and will continue to be so as long …"

"When did he take you? Did you go to him willingly? Did you choose to do this?" Caesar cut her off. Melissa gasped for breath. She was sure she was about to be condemned to death and she could think of no way out. There was so much she still needed to tell Vitruvius and she would never get the chance. She was wracked with guilt at the thought that she had failed him and the little boy she loved so dearly.

"Last night." Antony butted in ignoring Caesar's instruction for silence. "I was a little drunk when I got here. I threatened Vitruvius' life and forced him from the room before I forced her into bed. Do you really need all the details? I know I penetrated her, but it really is a bit of a blur after that. I would suggest anything you got from her up until last night is reliable, but as of this morning? I suggest you make your own judgement on that." This was at least partly true. Every event Antony described had happened, just not on the timescales that he had implied.

Caesar looked at the floor. His shoulders had dropped and he was shaking his head. "I am saddened by this news, Lissa. I had always known that one day you might choose to end your service to me and I would be powerless to prevent it, but I believed your dislike of Antony to be so strong that you would sooner die than allow him to be the one to take your gift from me. Entrusting you to him was a mistake that I should never have made and I apologise for his brutish behaviour towards you. That said, what is done cannot be undone. You are of no further use to me, and I cannot continue to support you. From the surprise you displayed earlier, and from the state of your living arrangements ..." Caesar paused and looked around the room, noticing how tired the house looked, "... it is apparent that you have not received all of the money I have provided for you to date. It was not an inconsiderable sum and there must be a significant proportion of it remaining. I will ensure it is passed from Antony's estate to you along with a sum of ten thousand denarii from his own money to provide for the son he has acknowledged. It should provide enough for you to live on for some time."

"Just a minute!" Antony began to protest, but Caesar silenced him with a withering look.

"Caesar is most gracious," Melissa found her voice at last, "but I cannot accept the money because I have done nothing to deserve it. I knew that Antony was coming to the house last night, but I did nothing to prevent his advances – I welcomed them." She was following Antony's line of half-truth about their liaisons. He had lied for her, it was the least she could do in return. "I ask that you give the money to Vitruvius for the provision of an education and a good future for Antonius. He is more of a parent to the boy than I will ever be."

"Your gesture is truly noble, Lissa, but without money you will not survive long in this city." Caesar had made a point that needed a response.

"I still have options open to me." Melissa turned her face towards Antony so that Caesar could not see her expression. Mouthing the words "play along", she ran her hand up his thigh and under the cushion. Antony groaned and leant back against the couch. She returned her gaze to Caesar. "I do not feel I will be without means just yet."

Caesar nodded, agreeing with Melissa's assessment of her situation; mistresses of the Roman elite lived exceptionally well. "I see your logic, though I am uncertain which of you will benefit from the arrangement more. Make sure you charge him the going rate, mind, as he will no doubt try to fleece you if you give him the opportunity."

Melissa knew this was her last chance to fulfil her obligations to Brutus. She had to warn Caesar about the assassination and make him doubt her words at the same time. "Noble Caesar, there is one last piece of information I must give you. Last night as Antony … whilst he was …" she lowered her head, then raised it again taking an over-exaggerated gasp as she did so, "… After he had taken me, I saw your end. I cannot be sure of the exact date, but you will not have power in this city beyond the Ides of March. You must take great care, Caesar."

Caesar looked thoughtful for a moment. "After he took you, you say … hmmm … it appears on this matter we will have to wait and see." He turned and walked to the door, pausing on the threshold "Lissa, I wish you well as you embark on your new career! Antony, I will decide how to deal with you later. It would be best if you remain absent from my presence for the time being." And with that he left, passing an anxious Vitruvius who was still standing in the hallway, having sent Antonius into the kitchen to wait with Renna.

Back in the main room, Antony and Melissa both slumped on the couch in relief. Melissa began to sob quietly. Antony pulled her towards him and held her head to his chest, whispering gently to her. Vitruvius entered the room and stopped, fearing the worst. Antony looked at him and shook his head, requesting silence. He needed time himself to gather his own feelings under control. Vitruvius walked to the chair that Caesar had vacated and sat down. Melissa was glad to be alive, but was still stunned that they had survived. Her fear and relief flowed from her like the fast-running waters of the Tiber and her sobs turned into wails. Gradually the crying subsided, leaving her feeling utterly drained. She lay against Antony's body unable to move, allowing him to stroke her arm and back in a clear display of genuine affection.

Vitruvius was desperate to know what had happened, and looked at Antony beseechingly. Antony cleared his throat and displayed his usual bravado as he spoke.

"Well, I thought that went rather well. We are all still alive and reasonably unscathed. You, Vitruvius, are now quite a wealthy man, or soon will be, once Caesar has reallocated a considerable proportion of my personal wealth. And as for this one," he rocked Melissa slightly as he spoke, "she proved to be an exceptional little actress, playing Caesar until the very last." He bent his head closer to Melissa's so that only she could hear his words. "Of course you realise that you have cost me a great deal of money and I expect an opportunity to recover at least some of that expenditure in other ways."

Melissa knew what he was hinting at, but she no longer cared. He had walked into a room where he could easily have met his death. He had faced down unenviable odds and survived. He had lied for her at great personal cost to himself. She had not expected any of this from the man she thought had only wanted her out of revenge. She raised her head from his chest and stared into his dark eyes. His pupils had dilated, showing that his passions were running far closer to his outwardly calm exterior than he was displaying. She pushed herself up his body until her head was level with his. "Whatever you want from me is yours," she said and kissed him passionately, her tongue sliding sensuously between his lips.

As she began to pull back he grabbed her and held her to him, returning her kiss. Her unexpected show of willingness excited him physically to the point where it was showing far more prominently than even he would have liked as the cushion slid to the floor. He released her and stared back into her eyes.

"Why not take the boy out somewhere?" Antony was speaking to Vitruvius, but could not take his eyes off Melissa. "All day would be best. And take that slave with you. I do not want any more interruptions."

Whether her reaction was from relief or genuine emotion, Antony had no idea, but, for the first time he could remember, Melissa had kissed him willingly. He had no intention of letting the moment pass and resumed their kiss, slowly turning her onto the couch behind him, oblivious to whether Vitruvius had followed his instructions or not.

In her litter on the return journey to the villa across the Tiber, Cleopatra was considering the events of the morning carefully. The woman who supposedly saw the future was obviously a fraud and the Queen was pleased with herself for exposing that drain on Caesar's resources.

Mark Antony was not what she had expected. She knew he was rumoured to be an amazing tactician, who was more than able to rival Caesar in battle and today she had watched as he had used those skills to outmanoeuvre, and then embarrass his mentor. She had also heard of his alleged charms, equally on display, along with his total lack of regard for authority. The real surprise was his acceptance of the child. She had heard that Antony was in some ways as much a typical Roman as the next man, despite his more liberal attitudes to other traditions. As such, she had never expected him to acknowledge a foreign child that he had fathered. This was not the act of a normal Roman citizen.

Cleopatra began to wonder if she had chosen the wrong Roman commander with whom to ally herself. She decided it might be prudent to keep one eye firmly fixed on Antony in the future, and watch for any opportunity that could prove advantageous to them both.

Chapter 24

That evening at dinner, tensions between Vitruvius and Antony were higher than ever. Vitruvius had taken Antonius out as instructed and then put him to bed as soon as they had returned. He had no intention of allowing the poor, innocent child to be scarred by what was going on in the house. As he saw it, Melissa was a changed woman. Where she had always professed to have seen Antony for what he was, she now seemed to have warmed to him. Whether it was as a result of the events of that morning or whether spending so much time in his presence had de-sensitised her, Vitruvius could not tell, but she was no longer the woman she had once been. He was no longer certain where her allegiances lay.

Antony, on the other hand, was ecstatic. The rush of adrenalin associated with his brush with disaster and possible death had given him a renewed energy that had not dampened, despite his hectic day. Melissa had not only been willing to spend the entire day in bed with him, she had initiated much of their lovemaking, which had only excited him further. It seemed she finally wanted him as much as he wanted her. That evening, as they had reclined to eat, she had remained close rather than moving to the opposite end of the couch. Their bodies were still touching as they had been all day. It was as if she could not bear to be apart from him for even a second. Antony felt on top of the world. The victory he had sought for so many years now had no meaning: all he wanted was to keep this new, accommodating Melissa happy and contented in his arms and, most importantly, in his bed.

Over the course of the meal the exact details of Vitruvius' new-found wealth were explained. In this much at least, Vitruvius believed the others had been honest with him, but he was not sure how much further he could trust either of them. Even though the man had probably saved all their lives, Vitruvius still struggled to be civil to Antony and would have no doubt failed dismally had he not drunk an entire flask of wine. He was working on an excuse to leave when Antony mentioned Melissa's final prophecy to Caesar.

"So, the Ides then? Is that when the deed will be done? Is that when your good friend Brutus will remove Caesar from power?" Antony's mood was upbeat. His questions were direct, but implied he already knew more than he was letting on. Melissa looked awkward and became suddenly withdrawn and silent. "Will one of you please answer me, or do I really have to work everything out for myself?" Antony looked alternately between Melissa and Vitruvius as he waited for a response.

"Consul, I swear I have no idea what it is you speak of. Lissa has never spoken to me of her dealings with Marcus Brutus. If I have ever asked, she has insisted it is none of my business." Vitruvius' answer was the truth.

Antony surveyed him with suspicion, then, realising that Vitruvius' expression was truly one of honesty, he began to laugh so hard he nearly choked. "I would not have believed it if I had not seen it with my own eyes," he said, tears running down his face. "She tells *you* even less than she tells *me!*" Once his laughter had subsided, he rephrased his question. "Time you told us both the plan. Truth please, Lissa. We both know what happens when you lie to me." There was a hint of menace in his voice that betrayed the fact that the old Antony was not buried far beneath the surface of this new one.

Initially Melissa remained silent, pushing the two remaining olives around her plate as if she were trying to ignore the question. Antony sat up suddenly, reaching across Melissa for his wine, ensuring he brushed his hand across her breast as he did so. His action made her flinch away from him at the memory of the last time she had resisted his questioning. She spoke softly to the room in general. "At the Senate meeting on the Ides, Brutus will table a motion proposing Caesar willingly puts his powers aside in the best interest of the Republic, just as Sulla did before him. He has the support of enough of the senators to carry the motion through. Caesar will be exiled, but he will be allowed to retain his wealth, his status and the office of Pontifex Maximus. As we all know, that post remains with him until death." She placed her hand over Antony's and spoke to him directly. "Antony, if you truly do not wish to be part of his downfall, you would be advised not to go to the Senate that day."

Vitruvius had begun to pay closer attention, despite his somewhat inebriated state. Antony's movement was obviously intended to loosen Melissa's tongue and it had worked. He wondered what the beast had done to her in the past to get that kind of a reaction. Perhaps he had been too quick to judge her? Perhaps there was more here than he could fathom, but he still did not understand why she had not told him what she had been planning with Brutus and, more importantly, why she had told Antony any of it. It was suicide to trust him of all people – she had said so herself.

Vitruvius needed clarification. He looked at Melissa. "Lissa, are you saying that all these months you have been working with Brutus to dislodge Caesar from power?" She nodded. He turned to Antony. "And you knew of this and did nothing?"

Antony shrugged. "What can I say? She can be very persuasive when she wants to be." He settled back on the couch. "The truth of the matter is this. Trebonius approached me to join the plot many months before her involvement and she knows it," he pointed at Melissa, who nodded again. "What neither of you know is the night you collected Lissa from Brutus' little gathering, I was here far earlier than you thought. I had this house under watch from the day Caesar and I reconciled our differences. I was told that Lissa had left against my orders and I was waiting outside for her return, but only you came back. I waited until I saw you leave again and tried to follow, but you were too good for me and I lost you. As I did not know where you had gone I came back here and let myself in. On your return you assumed, wrongly, that I was drunk. You see, I have spent more than enough time with actresses to have picked up a thing or two on the art of misdirection. You never had a chance really, either of you. I had witnessed your temper many times before, Vitruvius, and knew it to be your weakness. You have wanted revenge on me since the death of the other one and tricking you into challenging me was easy. Your hatred for me played right into my hands, leaving Lissa with little choice but to offer me a trade: your life for sex and information. And a more pleasing bargain I could never have hoped to strike."

Antony was silent for a moment, allowing his words to sink in He was obviously pleased with himself, smiling as he continued. "The question you should be asking is not why I have done nothing as of yet, but whether I will do anything now I know the date. I have pondered this question for some time, but this morning's display has only helped to make my path clear. Caesar has been a different man since he returned from Egypt with that harpy in tow. Lissa, you must have heard him this morning? He said he ruled Rome! How dare he speak such treachery? No, Caesar pushes too hard for too much change and he must be brought to heel. That much is obvious even to me, but I cannot afford to be seen to be involved in any way if I am to retain enough power to ensure the continued protection of both my families. Caesar no longer believes anything Lissa says, thanks to my actions today and, whilst that may yet prove to be a significant factor, I cannot be implicated by it alone. The fact she so openly shared the date of his departure leads me to believe that it was her intention to do so all along, once Caesar had a reason to doubt her. I am now considering the possibility that I too have been used, but life has been so pleasurable of late that I am prepared to forgive any such indiscretion and choose to believe it was done with my best interests at heart." Antony leaned over and kissed Melissa's cheek, then settled back on the couch again. "Lissa assures me that no harm will come to Caesar, so I choose to do nothing. I will not attend the Senate on the Ides. I will instead spend the day in bed with my new mistress, which will not be seen as out of the ordinary and so clear me from any suspicion. I will then take over from Brutus and that upstart Cassius in restoring the Republic and become a hero to the people. The best part is …" he reached up to Melissa and pulled her towards him, "… I get my reward in advance. Too many people's lives now rely on my silence for it to be any other way. It is an interesting position to be in."

Antony lay smiling, waiting for a reaction from Vitruvius, who could only stare at him open-mouthed. Vitruvius had always assumed Antony was simply a lucky bastard who often happened to be in the right place at the right time, but this revelation showed the man in front of him to be fully in control of his own destiny. It unnerved him that he had misjudged Antony all these years.

Vitruvius looked from Antony to Melissa, who seemed suddenly uncomfortable. "Is this all true?" he asked, still in shock. She nodded. "And you trusted him over me with this?"

The shock was beginning to pass, turning instead to anger. Vitruvius agreed with Antony's statement that Caesar had to go, but the sheer depth of this betrayal was too much for him to cope with. Caesar had looked on Brutus as a son. Antony was Caesar's closest friend. How either of them could plan such treachery was beyond him.

Vitruvius stared at Melissa as he waited for an answer. Her betrayal was the worst of all – not of Caesar, but of himself. Melissa had deliberately kept secrets from him and confided in her lover instead. For a brief moment he wondered if she had ever trusted him in all the years he had protected her. Finally Melissa turned her head away from his unwavering stare, burying her face in Antony's side.

Vitruvius stood up and threw his plate across the room. He rounded on Melissa, filled with a sudden hatred of the woman he had sworn to protect and whom he had long regarded as a friend. "SLUT! WHORE!" he shouted. He pointed at Antony. "You sold yourself for a ride on his cock! And you!" He looked at Antony. "Caesar is your friend. How could you sell him out for a cheap fuck? I do not know either of you." He stormed to the door, shouting back as he went, "And stay away from Antonius, both of you!"

Antony waited a moment until the sound of Vitruvius' footsteps had faded, then pulled Melissa's head up to face him. "It appears I am the only friend you have left, Lissa. You had better make sure you continue to keep me happy." He smiled wickedly as he said the words and pushed Melissa's head down towards his groin.

Chapter 25

The next morning Antony was in no hurry to leave and stayed in the house all day, giving Melissa no chance to speak to Vitruvius. She was desperate to explain the truth of what was really happening, but knew she had to get him alone to do so. This pattern continued for the entire week. When Antony did eventually decide it was safe to face Caesar, she breathed a huge sigh of relief.

Speaking to Vitruvius would still not be easy. He had taken to rising late and going straight out with Antonius. He would come back only briefly in the evening to put the boy to bed, then he would go out again and not return until late into the night, so that he could spend as little time in the house as possible. Melissa knew he was drunk when he did come home, but she made no comment. She could not afford to fight with him whilst Antony was about, for fear of his reaction if Vitruvius lashed out against her.

On the morning Antony decided to resume his duties as consul, Melissa persuaded him to leave early by promising him all sorts of favours when he returned. Cassius had been right when he had intimated that the way to Antony's heart was through his penis; it seemed the happier she kept him in bed, the more pliant he was.

As soon as Antony had left, she rushed into Antonius' bedroom and got him up. She had made Renna agree to take him to the market for the morning and was soon hurrying them out of the house. Once they had gone, she sat in the hall by the front door waiting for Vitruvius to surface. This confrontation would not be easy or pleasant, but she wanted to get him back on her side.

The sun had risen quite high before Vitruvius finally dragged himself out of bed. Once he had prided himself on his drive to get up and make the most of each new day, but lately there did not seem any point. He had lost his faith in Melissa now that she had become Antony's latest plaything. She would no doubt have the consul punish him for his insolent behaviour one day, by removing Antonius from his care. It was only a question of when it would happen and until then, every day with the child he regarded as his son was precious. He would have left and taken Antonius with him, but he believed there was nowhere he could go where Antony could not hunt him down like a dog in order to retrieve the child.

The house seemed so quiet to him today, but he hardly gave it a second thought as he dressed. He staggered out into the hall to find Melissa dozing on the floor beside the door. He wrongly assumed Antony must have kicked her out for refusing one of his more absurd requests. He would have to wake her to get past, but he would fetch Antonius first. She would cause less of a scene in front of him.

He went into the boy's room and stopped short. Antonius was gone. He knew instantly that he was not in the house, as it was far too quiet. Desperation filled him. Antony must have left and taken the boy with him. He had not even had the chance to say goodbye. The feeling of desperation slowly changed to sheer rage and he stormed into the hall. He grabbed Melissa roughly, pulling her to her feet as he began shaking her. "Where is Antonius? Where has that bastard taken him?" He screamed the words at her as his anger began to turn to panic again.

"H-he-e is fi-ine" Melissa struggled to get the words out between the shakes. Realising he could not understand a word she was saying, Vitruvius stopped his shaking to let her speak clearly. She continued, "Antony left early this morning, alone. Antonius has gone to the market with Renna. They will all return by tonight, but we must talk before they do."

Vitruvius let go of Melissa and backed away from her. He went back to his room, collected his sword and cloak and returned to the hall. He headed straight for the door, but Melissa still blocked his path.

"I have no desire to hear any more of your lies, woman," he said tersely. "I am going to Antonius. Get out of my way."

He tried to pull her away from the door, but she stubbornly held tight to the handle with both hands.

"You have to listen. There is not much time for me to explain everything that is going on." Melissa remained calm, despite fighting to keep hold of the door.

"I do not need to hear any more details. I hear quite enough through the walls of your room as it is, and what I do hear sickens me." He wrenched one of Melissa's hands away from the handle, keeping it away by holding her wrist with his hand.

"Do you think I wanted any of this? I had no choice other than to let him use me. Everything depends on my keeping him occupied and off-guard, but I cannot do this without you."

"Oh he is well occupied from what I hear. Every night you manage that! What could you possibly want me for?" He succeeded in wrenching her other hand away and pushed her back from the door.

As he grabbed the handle, Melissa cried out in desperation, "I need you to hide Antonius from him when Caesar is dead."

Vitruvius paused. His hand still gripped the already turned handle, but he did not pull the door open. "What did you say?" he asked. He had heard her clearly but he could not believe what she had said.

Melissa took a deep breath. "Caesar will die before the month is out. He will be murdered on the Ides, not deposed. Antony does not know and must not find out, else we are all dead. Please, come back into the house. I will tell you everything that has happened and the plans I have made with Brutus for your escape from this life you hate so much. I always intended to tell you all of it, Vitruvius, but Antony's continued presence here made it impossible. Your innocence has kept you safe from any possible recriminations on his part, and it may continue, as long as he believes you and I are at odds with one another. Your outburst of the other night has placed you beyond his suspicion."

Vitruvius was in two minds about his best course of action, but decided it might be better to hear her out. He put his sword down and followed her into the courtyard, taking a seat on the bench opposite her.

Melissa told Vitruvius every detail from her meeting with Brutus to the events of a week earlier, when Antony had paraded naked in front of Cleopatra. She omitted nothing, and gave him every detail of the forthcoming assassination including the names of all the conspirators she knew. Finally, she told him about the smallholding Brutus had acquired on her behalf and her plans for him and Antonius to go there.

Vitruvius could not believe what he was hearing. He knew Melissa had been keeping things from him, but the sheer amount shocked him. Deep down he knew she had been right to do so. Vitruvius was loyal and stubborn and would not have succumbed to torture easily, but he did have one weakness and Antony knew only too well what that was. If anyone were to threaten to injure Antonius and not him, he would give up everything he knew to save the boy he looked on as his own. He sat in silence, considering what she had said.

"Vitruvius," Melissa was still speaking, "you have a choice. You can leave now if you want to and I will make some excuse to Antony for your absence, or you can stay and help me. Two weeks is all I am asking. After that you and Antonius are free to leave and never look back. Antony will not be able to force your whereabouts out of me as I have not seen the documents in the chest Brutus sent."

"And what of Brutus? He can reveal our whereabouts." Vitruvius did not trust Brutus any more than Antony. Both had been Caesar's friends and both intended to betray him, though the betrayal Brutus was planning was far worse than Antony's.

"Brutus will not get the opportunity. Antony will make a deal with him and it will appear in the best interests of all, but he will betray him on the day of Caesar's funeral and he will be forced to leave Rome forever."

"And you? What happens to you?" Vitruvius was not sure if he cared, but he needed to know.

Melissa looked at her feet. She was not meant to be in the past, so what would it matter what became of her? She knew only too well that to stay was suicide, but it was the best chance Vitruvius and Antonius had of survival. Once Antony knew she had lied to him, her death would be assured, though she imagined it would be far from quick or painless. Still she could not bring herself to say the words out loud. She simply shook her head in response.

Vitruvius said nothing for some time as he considered Melissa's fate. Finally he asked the question that had been eating away at him for weeks. Her answer would help him decide his course of action. "Tell me honestly, Lissa – do you love Antony?"

Melissa did not look up, but she did answer. "To begin with I hated him. That first night, I was prepared to let him have me to save your life. He would have killed you and Antonius, and forced himself on me if I had not relented. I have let him do everything he wanted, purely because of the threat of what he could do to you if I ever said no. I will admit my feelings towards him have softened lately, especially since the day Caesar came." She laughed a little at the thought of that day, "Antony risked his life to save us all and he has earned my respect. It no longer disgusts me to let him touch me in the way it once did, which certainly makes living with him easier. These past few days I have done everything I could to make him believe I care for him deeply and, from your reactions, I believe I have played my part well. It was all necessary to keep his attentions on me and away from the business of this city, just as I promised Brutus I would do. But do I love him? No, I do not. I am in love with a man I will never see again; a man who would never hurt me or force himself on me. Rebecca was infatuated with him too, and hated me because he felt nothing for her. Unfortunately he is very like Antony in many ways, especially in his looks and stature. Rebecca could not separate the man from our past with the one here. That is why she gave herself to Antony so easily. She thought it would hurt me to know she was his, but she did not realise until it was too late what he was really like. I have found that if I pretend he is the man from my past, having Mark Antony near me is quite bearable. It is how I get through each night with him and why I now seem to enjoy his touch. I have found it is far more pleasurable to do so than suffer the painful alternative that the back of his hand can so readily inflict."

Vitruvius was suddenly filled with pity for the woman in front of him. She was not the same person he had first met so many years before. Back then, she had been proud and strong-willed and he had admired her for standing up to the brute he knew Antony to be. Now, partly because of his stupidity, she had endured continual sexual abuse and it had taken its toll on her. He felt guilty for ever having doubted her motives. As he moved to sit on the bench next to her, he put his hand over hers and spoke quietly. "You could come with us. If you stay here he can hurt you in ways I cannot even begin to imagine. I can protect you as well as Antonius, if you will let me."

Melissa looked at Vitruvius, her eyes full of despair. She looked utterly defeated. He had never seen her looking so lost. Even when Rebecca died and he had been overcome by grief and anger, she had remained strong and in control, but no longer.

She shook her head frantically and began to sob as she revealed her final secret. "I cannot ask you to do that. Vitruvius, I was not sent here to assist Caesar, I came here by accident from another time, one so different to this that I cannot ever begin to explain it to you. You have done so much for me and made my time here quite tolerable, but I was never meant to be here and so my death will not matter. If I stay behind, only I will suffer and I may be able to buy you more time to get away. Antony will have his revenge on me and be done. Please believe me when I say it is for the best. I never expected you to take responsibility for one of his bastard children, but you did and Antonius loves you like a father. I could never ask you to take on another." Her hand moved across her stomach and she turned her head away.

Vitruvius was not surprised that Melissa was pregnant. He had always known it would only be a matter of time before this happened. Antony had hardly left her alone since he had arrived. There had been no time for her usual monthly cycle. This outcome had been inevitable.

Vitruvius felt a need to comfort her, but did not want to overstep his boundaries by being too intimate. He put his hand on Melissa's shoulder, gripping it lightly. "What is one more mouth to feed? Antonius needs a family and he needs you."

Vitruvius paused. Less than a week before, Antony had joked with him about being in love with Melissa. He knew he was, but it was the love a man felt for a sister, not a lover. All the hate he had felt building towards her in the past few weeks was not real, just frustration that he could do nothing to prevent the man he truly did hate from abusing someone he cared for. He had been too scared to tell Rebecca how he had felt about her and he had regretted it every day since her death. He was unsure how his next words to Melissa would be taken, but this would be his only chance to say them and he would not make that mistake again.

"I need you too, Lissa. I have feelings for you, but as I would for my own sisters and I have long hoped you would look on me as a brother. I will never expect anything from you beyond that, but you must understand that I do care what becomes of you. I will not stand by and watch you sacrifice yourself, when I can offer you some sort of life. We can put all this behind us in time, if not for each other, then for the sake of the children – both of them."

Melissa leant against Vitruvius' side. He dared to put his arm around her and to his surprise she did not pull away. "You know he will kill us all if he ever finds us?" she said in a half-whisper.

Vitruvius knew she was right. Antony had an army loyal to him. They would be hunted for the rest of their lives. Many years before he had sworn to protect Melissa and the thought of death at Antony's hand did not change his feelings, or his continued need to fulfil that oath.

"Then it would be best that he does not," was the only response he was prepared to give.

Antony returned late that evening in a foul mood. Caesar had sent word to Fulvia, requesting her early return to Rome, forcing Antony to go back to his marital home that night. Vitruvius made himself scarce as Antony stormed around throwing his possessions back into the two chests he had arrived with. He was almost emotional when the time came to say goodbye to Melissa, vowing to be back at her side as soon as he could. He hugged Antonius, giving him yet another little boat, and was even polite to Vitruvius, telling him to care for the family in his absence. His final gift was the most shocking of all. When the slaves came for his luggage, they brought with them yet more chests. As per Caesar's instructions, Antony handed over the ten thousand denarii for Antonius' upbringing in cash, as well as the balance of Caesar's payments he had received for Melissa's keep. In total, they had a sum just short of fourteen thousand denarii. Added to the money Vitruvius had acquired after Caesar's triumphs, it was a substantial sum. Quite how they were going to get that amount of coinage safely out of the city was a new problem to consider.

The next morning, Melissa sent word of the previous night's events to Brutus. She knew he would already know what had taken place, but she had more she needed to tell him. She needed to explain how Trebonius and Decimus should be prepared to prevent Antony from entering the Senate with Caesar on the Ides. This was the way it had happened in history as she remembered it, and this was how it would happen again. She did not dare risk any correspondence being intercepted, and so sent Vitruvius to deliver the message personally.

It was late in the afternoon before Vitruvius returned. He had to wait most of the day for Brutus to receive him, but it had been worth it. Brutus now knew all that had occurred and he was as prepared as he could be. Brutus also sent a message by return. If Melissa felt they were in danger, Vitruvius was to take her and Antonius to Servilia, who would hide them until she could arrange for safe passage out of the city. All they could do now was to wait.

There was no word from Antony from that day forward. Melissa and Vitruvius made plans for their escape. Melissa insisted that they had to wait until the Ides before leaving, just in case Antony did return. She had to keep up the pretence of being his caring lover until the last moment.

They could not risk telling Renna what they were planning, and sent her on daily shopping trips to keep her out of the house. They decided they would tell her at the last minute and offer her a choice of risking death in coming with them and being free, or of remaining behind in slavery in Antony's household.

Vitruvius had a friend in the horse trade and he made arrangements for a wagon and horses to come to the house before daybreak on the Ides. He and Melissa would pose as husband and wife until they were far away from Rome.

Vitruvius purchased more storage chests and they packed as many of their belongings as they dared, storing everything in Vitruvius' room for fear of Antony's return. They split the money between each case, putting it at the very bottom beneath false bottoms that Vitruvius constructed whilst Renna was out.

If Antony did visit before the Ides, they would be in terrible danger. He would see items had been removed and would become suspicious if he was left to his own devices for more than a few minutes. Melissa and Vitruvius agreed that she was to stop at nothing to keep Antony off his game, even though the thought of it sickened Vitruvius. Melissa would have to make love to Antony in such a way that he had never before experienced with her, ensuring he never wanted to set foot out of the bedroom. Whatever he wanted she was going to have to do, no matter what he asked. There was no other way, although Vitruvius hoped more than anything that it would not come to this.

By the evening of the fourteenth they were ready. Melissa explained everything to Renna in the evening, especially the danger they could be facing if Antony decided to hunt them down. Renna chose to join them. She had no loyalty to Antony, who had been responsible for the loss of her lover. Melissa had always been kind to her, giving her freedoms far beyond what a slave could have expected, and she was more than willing to take the risk. She dragged Vitruvius off to the kitchen to help her pack as many provisions as she thought they could safely carry.

It was nearly midnight when there was a knock on the front door. Melissa felt a familiar sinking feeling in the pit of her stomach. She knew it was Antony and knew he would notice that the contents of the house had been packed away. Her best chance was still to distract him. She sent Vitruvius to put out every lamp and then told him to go to bed with Antonius, and his sword. She went to the door herself, opening it a crack and once she was certain it was Antony, she let him inside.

There was no real need to worry about distracting Antony. As soon as the door was bolted he pushed her against it, pressing himself into her body as he kissed her passionately.

His mouth moved down her neck and he began to lift her dress. She pulled his head up to face her. "I did not think you would come tonight," she cooed lovingly, kissing him again.

"Oh I always intended to *come* tonight." Antony grinned at her. The double entendre was not lost on her. One hand moved around her waist. "The only question is whether you intend to make me work hard or not?" Antony's eyes twinkled wickedly in the dim light from the single lamp at the door. Without waiting for her to answer him, he slid his other arm behind her knees, lifting Melissa off her feet and carried her to their room.

The remaining lamps in the house had all been successfully extinguished, leaving only moonlight shining through the chinks in the shutters of the window. Antony paused at the door, taking a moment to adjust his eyes to the darkness and then moved towards the bed. He lowered Melissa gently onto the covers before standing back to rip off his toga, casting it carelessly on the floor as if it were a useless rag. Then he began raising Melissa's dress up her legs, kissing every piece of flesh as it became exposed.

Chapter 26

Melissa was woken early by the sound of birdsong. She reached for Antony, but the bed was empty. It was too early for him to have left, and if it was truly his intention to use her as his alibi for not being in the Senate, he would not be going anywhere all day. She looked around the room and saw him sitting on the stool in front of her dressing table. He was staring at her thoughtfully as he squeezed one hand with the other, making his knuckles crack. She glanced at the trunk beside him. It was open and he had obviously been through it.

"Going somewhere?" Antony's question was direct. She could tell he was in no mood for games.

"Yes, actually," she replied casually, sitting up and stretching so the sheet fell away from her body. "We are going next door."

Antony seemed doubtful of this answer, but Melissa decided to press on with telling the lie she had been rehearsing before she had gone to sleep. "The other room gets less light in the mornings. You are not an early riser, not in the sense of actually getting out of bed at least, and I thought you would prefer that room, assuming you are intending to continue to visit. Vitruvius flatly refused to move the furniture unless it was empty so I have packed all of my things and those of Antonius into boxes and I intend for us to swap rooms with him. I plan to decorate at the same time, now we have a few sesterces spare. But if you prefer things as they are, I will unpack and cancel the painter." Melissa lay back on the bed seductively, praying he would fall for the excuse she had given.

Antony made no move. He sat perfectly still, mulling over her words. Melissa needed to get him back in the bed and thinking of other things. "Come back here. I want you to do

what you did last night again, or I may have to do it myself."
She tried to sound as inviting as she could. She lifted the knee
that was furthest from him, raising the sheet slightly with her
actions and slid her hand underneath it giving the impression
she intended to satisfy herself if he was not going to join her.

Antony rose and walked over to the bed. He still looked
suspicious, but his curiosity was getting the better of him. He
pulled the sheet away and sat on the edge of bed. "I do not seem
to remember what you are referring to," he said, playfully.
"Show me what it is you want and I am sure at some point
it will come to me." He lay across the leg that was closest to
him calling her bluff and leaving Melissa little option but to go
through with what she had intimated she was prepared to do.

Less than an hour later, Melissa was staring at the ceiling,
waiting for Antony to climax, when she became aware of raised
voices in the hallway. Vitruvius was arguing with someone. She
heard him shouting the word "*Consul*" and thought initially that
he must be trying to get Antony's attention, but then she heard
him shout "*Caesar*" and realised to her horror that Caesar was
in the house. She began to thump Antony on the back, trying to
get him to move off her, but he had no intention of stopping. As
the door opened she tried to reason with him, but he was lost in
the moment. Even the sound of Caesar's own voice did nothing
to lessen his resolve. Instead he simply grunted two words in
response, "Busy now."

"Get out of that bed!" Caesar demanded. He was
unimpressed at Antony's behaviour. As the latter continued
with his energetic display of stamina, the former was forced
to shout over the noise Antony had decided to make. "If you
refuse me, I will summon my lictors and your whore can
pleasure each of them in turn while you are made to watch."

Antony took immediate exception to Melissa being called
a whore. He stopped his thrusting and rose onto his elbows,
looking straight at the wall. "I will not be given an order in this
house. I will not leave this bed until such time as I choose to
and if any man so much as touches this woman, he will find his
balls removed and thrust down his throat." His voice was full
of anger and his face was turning red.

Melissa wanted the bed to open up and swallow her. This was not supposed to be happening. Everything was going horribly wrong. If Antony lost control of his temper now, she did not know what the end result would be. She was truly frightened. She put her hands around Antony's face and tried to pull his head down to look at her, whispering soothing phrases to try to bring him back to her and away from the dark mood that was descending on him.

Caesar sat on the stool Antony had earlier vacated. He was barely able to hide the disgust in his voice as he continued to speak. "Who do you think you are speaking to? I am not one of your drunken gambling comrades. I am Caesar and you have me to thank for your position and privilege." Caesar paused, drawing breath. He stood and began to pace the room. *Oh great*, Melissa thought, *he's going to deliver an oration!* She was still pinned under Antony, who looked as if he would explode at any minute.

Caesar began his speech. "You and I have not fought together for so long and for so much to allow our acquaintance to end in such a way. Over a mere woman? Surely not? Mark Antony, you are a consul of Rome and the people need you to fulfil your duties to them. All I ask is for a few hours of your time spent in earnest debate on the issues that are of concern to the multitude of your people. I wager she will wait ..." he gestured at Melissa "... as she is now, her legs apart in preparation for your return. She has your patronage and will do nothing to chance it to loss." He paused as he turned to cross the room again and his tone changed to one of concern.

"Antony, I have no intention of limiting your time here, for here is obviously where you wish to be. I only ask you to set aside the time that is necessary for you to discharge your obligations. I have no doubt that your need of this woman is great, but think of the needs of your people, your family and your wife. Think of Fulvia and the pain you must be causing her. Has she not already suffered the loss of two husbands? My sympathies go out to her as I watch her lose a third."

Caesar paused again. The final part of his speech he delivered softly and with genuine understanding. "My friend, I understand your mind. I too have been tested by the attentions of a woman I should not have wanted, but I understand that I must put her aside when the people's needs are greater than my own. You have the opportunity for greatness before you, if you do not lose yourself to lust. I will wait for you in the hall while you make your choice, whatever it may be." And with that, he left.

Vitruvius had been watching the whole scene from just inside the door. He found it difficult to look at the bed, but he hoped that his presence there would be enough to stop the situation getting out of hand. When Caesar left, he remained where he was, staring at the wall.

Antony looked down at Melissa. There was concern for her in his face, but there was also a deep sadness in his eyes, as if something in Caesar's words had hit a nerve.

"I have not hurt you, have I?" he asked with genuine sincerity. Melissa shook her head and he bent his head, kissing her gently. Vitruvius shuffled awkwardly at the door causing Antony to whisper, "Are we not alone?" Melissa shook her head again and a look of embarrassment crossed her face.

Antony turned his head and glared at Vitruvius. The latter's gaze shifted. He returned Antony's glare without moving. "Caesar waits," he said simply.

Antony groaned in frustration and rolled off Melissa and onto the bed. "Fine, tell him I will dress and join him presently. Make it known that I am not best pleased about doing so. Go on," he waved his hand towards the door, "I do not need you to watch me dress."

Vitruvius left and pulled the door to behind him. There was silence in the room and for a moment neither of them moved. When Antony finally rose from the bed, his mood was significantly more sombre. He recovered his crumpled toga from the floor and did his best to dress himself as Melissa too scrambled into her discarded clothing.

When he finished, Antony turned to Melissa, arms spread wide and said, "Tell me honestly, how do I look?"

Melissa was unable to stop herself laughing. Antony's toga was in a sorry state from the night it had spent in a heap on the floor. There were so many creases in it that it looked as if he had slept in it.

Antony looked at himself and joined in her laughter. "A toga fit for the most debauched consul Rome has ever seen!" He sat on the bed and took Melissa's hands in his, pulling her to stand in front of him as he looked up at her. His laughter had subsided and he looked more serious than she had ever seen him before.

As Antony spoke, Melissa could hear the sadness in his voice. "Caesar was right in many of the things he said – you do know that?" Melissa nodded and he continued, "I enjoy my time here with you, but I have others dependent on me. I cannot leave Fulvia. Our son is but a few months old. It would not go well with the people for me to leave my Roman wife for a foreigner. They would exile us and send us far from this city. The best I can ever offer you is what you have now and that is a life as my mistress. If you had only given in to me sooner, you could have had so much more. Once I would have given everything I owned to have you care for me, but now there is too much at stake for me to walk away from my responsibilities." Antony sighed as he stood up, pulling Melissa into his arms. He held her tightly and it felt that he knew as well as she did that it would be the last time they would ever see each other. Melissa felt a lump forming in her throat. Antony had made reference to his own future, although he did not know it. He was destined to abandon his pregnant fourth wife Octavia, and Rome, for Cleopatra and exile. It would set in motion a chain of events that would lead to both his and Cleopatra's death, and the death of the Republic that he was trying so hard to maintain.

Antony was in love with Melissa and he knew it. Perhaps he always had been, but fate had prevented him from ever expressing his true feelings in the ways he would have liked. He regretted so much of his behaviour towards the woman in his arms. He was desperate to lay his heart open to her and beg her to stay with him, but there was no time left to say the words whose meaning could never be fully explained in the fleeting seconds that remained. He had to force himself to walk away from the woman who gave him so much happiness. It was the only action he could take that was fair on Melissa, even though it broke his heart to do it.

As they separated and Antony walked to the door, his final words came as a complete surprise to Melissa. "My sources tell me Vitruvius has acquired property in the north. Perhaps you should go there with my son. He is an honourable man who will keep you both safe in the dark days that will no doubt haunt us for many months. I will not look for you, Lissa, if you ask for it to be so. You have my word on it." He waited at the door for an answer, closing his eyes in preparation for the rejection he fully expected to hear. Melissa said nothing and he left, slightly relieved that she had chosen not to tear his heart out with a reply.

Melissa just stood there, legs frozen to the spot, unable to move. It was as if Antony knew everything they had planned, but Melissa could not fathom how he could without a spy in Brutus' house. She finally found her legs and ran through the door and across the hall after him. As she entered the street, she nearly ran into Caesar. One of his lictors grabbed her and pushed her backwards, but Caesar waved him away.

For the first time that morning Caesar acknowledged her. "Well, Lissa, as you see, the Ides are upon us and I am still here."

Melissa replied without thinking. "Yes, Caesar, the day is here, but not yet passed." She gasped, horrified that the words she remembered from Shakespeare had come from her lips. Her gaze drifted to Antony, looking to see if he had any inkling of what was going to happen, but he had taken up the stance of a man too hung over to care, staring at his feet, barely registering where he was. She knew Antony's behaviour was merely an act, but if that was how he chose to get through the day, Melissa would not betray his secret. By the end of it he would have many reasons to wish he was drunk. He stood next to Decimus Brutus, who looked away, not wishing to acknowledge Melissa. She nodded curtly to Caesar as he climbed into his litter, then turned and went back inside the house.

Chapter 27

Vitruvius could make no sense out of what Melissa was trying to say. Whatever had happened outside had obviously shocked her, but she was unwilling to speak about it. All she kept saying was she had to leave Antony with enough information to save him. Vitruvius left her with Renna and continued on with their escape plan.

The wagon had arrived just before dawn and he had already packed as many of their belongings as he dared, sending it back to the stables to wait for him. Now he ran as fast as he could to retrieve it. By his estimation they would have little more than an hour to get to the city gates before the news of Caesar's death spread panic. Even if the assassination failed, they would only have the same amount of time before Antony shut the city down in order to search for conspirators, and, once he knew Melissa had lied, Vitruvius imagined their house would be the first Antony would target. Speed was of the essence, but Melissa now chose to lose control of her mind.

By the time he had returned to the house, Melissa was calmer and able to function, but she was not herself. She was still writing her letter to Antony, just as she had been when he left. He loaded the last remaining chest from Melissa's room into the back of the wagon before dragging Melissa from the house. He put her and Antonius in the back and climbed up in the front alongside Renna. In his absence, their former slave had realised that Melissa was a risk to the safety of them all in her current state. Renna exchanged their clothing and now it was she who would pose as Vitruvius' wife, while Melissa sat in silence in the back, as any good slave would do. Melissa seemed content to comply and sat in the wagon, hugging Antonius as if her life depended on it, whilst tears poured down her face.

They met no resistance at the gate and left the city without incident. It had all gone so smoothly, Vitruvius found himself saying a silent prayer to the goddess Fortuna to thank her and to ask for her continued protection. All day he kept expecting to hear the sound of hooves thundering along the road behind them, chasing after them in order to punish them for their treachery, but no horses ever came.

They heard no news of events in Rome that evening when they stopped at a small inn on the road. It was not until the next night that they overheard people talking of Caesar's murder. There were many rumours, it seemed. Some said he was dead, others that he was merely wounded. One even suggested he and Antony had fought off their attackers and had both fled into hiding. No one was really certain what had happened, but it seemed nobody was searching for Melissa or her friends. They were safe, for a while at least.

It was not difficult to follow Brutus' instructions and two days later they found the smallholding located a few miles from a small village just south of the Rubicon. Vitruvius was not overly impressed with Melissa's choice of location. She had thought he would like to go home, whereas he had hoped never to set foot in the area again. Despite his misgivings, the land seemed reasonable enough for growing food. To one side of the house was a small grazing paddock with four olive trees. This was a definite advantage as olives were a highly- prized commodity. Vitruvius had to admit that Brutus had chosen well.

The house itself was small, and had only the most basic furniture. It needed work and a good clean, but it was nothing that could not be managed between them. There were only two beds and they had to share: Melissa with Renna to begin with, and Vitruvius with Antonius. Renna was now an equal partner in their odd little family, and took to every task with vigour and determination. In the days that followed, Vitruvius began to notice their former slave in ways he never had before and it was not too long before the sleeping arrangements changed. Melissa was happy for them both. At least something good was coming out of all the terrible things that had happened.

It was not safe to keep all the money in the house. Melissa and Vitruvius took a joint decision to hide most of it in various locations around the farm and nearby woodland that formed part of their property. Melissa chose to hide the pieces of jewellery Antony had given her along with it. She could have sold the gems, but to do so might draw unnecessary attention to the new arrivals, and they needed to keep a low profile. Vitruvius always kept a coded map of every location on his person which only he and Melissa knew how to read. Despite his growing feelings for Renna, he was unwilling to trust her with too much information just yet.

As they searched out new hiding-places, Melissa had a feeling of déjà vu. It was as if she had been to this place before. She soon realised that their new home was right next to the point that Caesar's army had used to ford the Rubicon, bringing her and Rebecca with them into Rome so many years before. This had to be the same place where she had passed through time, or very close to it. For the first time in years, she began to wonder if there was a chance she could return home.

Each week passed without incident, and then another after that. The farm was coming on well. Vitruvius turned out to be a reasonable carpenter and made more furniture as they needed it, including a chair with a back to it that Melissa had designed. He thought it an odd piece, but Melissa loved it because it supported her back.

Melissa was not much help around the farm, due to her condition. She became increasingly sick in the mornings which made it difficult for her to perform physical labour, so instead she schooled Antonius. She taught him Latin, mathematics, Roman history and, much to Vitruvius' annoyance, she continued to teach him English. She knew he might never have any use for the language, but it did give her something special that only she and the boy shared. Antonius was a poor student, despite his finding learning easy: he had very little concentration and was always looking for some way to avoid his lessons.

As the weeks passed, Melissa became closer to Antonius than she had ever been before, although Vitruvius was still his favourite. Every afternoon in good weather she would give into Antonius' pleading and take him for a walk down to the Rubicon. They would take some of his little boats to play with and she began to watch for any sign of a way home. Every night, she would tell him wild stories of ships that could sail through the stars to other worlds, adapted from episodes of TV shows she had seen. She would sing him lullabies taken from her favourite songs by James Reyne and Bruce Springsteen. Who cared whether it was appropriate – no one would ever know or understand. Antonius had no part to play in history to her knowledge, and these tiny links to Melissa's world kept her dreams of home alive. Antonius' favourite song was one that referred to living in the future, though of course Melissa was the only one who understood the irony.

Over the weeks they heard more of the events in Rome from travellers passing through the nearby village. Melissa knew what was happening, of course, but had chosen to have no more visions in order to stop Vitruvius from asking too many questions about their futures. Antony first made, and then retracted, a deal with the conspirators, leaving Brutus and Cassius exposed and forced to go into voluntary exile. Caesar had cut Antony out of his will in favour of his nephew, Octavian, who tried to execute the provisions Caesar had made to give money to the ordinary people, only to be blocked by Antony at every opportunity. Each new piece of information made Melissa smile. It seemed history had not been affected by her presence in the least. Antony, it appeared, also intended to keep his promise: no one came looking for them and Melissa felt safer in her new home every day.

As May began and the days became warmer, Melissa spent more and more time at the river with Antonius. She was becoming obsessed with the idea of going home and took ever greater risks wandering its banks, searching for a way back and paying little attention to her surroundings. It was on one such day that she was spotted by two riders. They made no attempt to approach her, but watched carefully from the tree line as she played with Antonius on the river bank. When the heat of the day became too great, they followed her back to the farm at a safe distance. These men had been in the region for a few days, searching for a family from the south. They were looking for a man, a woman and a child of about four years of age. It appeared they had found their quarry.

Melissa and Antonius walked along the track from the river, over a small rise and down towards the gate that led into the yard. As Melissa undid the latch, Antonius charged on ahead into the kitchen and then came running out again with a huge piece of bread in his hands. Renna followed, shouting at him in mock annoyance. As Melissa came closer, Renna turned to speak to her, raising her hand to shield her eyes from the sun. As she did so, the former slave spotted the two riders appearing over the brow of the hill. Renna did not at all like the look of them. Both men were wearing riding cloaks that were too heavy for such a warm day, and both seemed far too interested in their surroundings for her liking. She could tell they were looking for something, or someone. She pointed over Melissa's shoulder. "Who are they?" she asked.

Melissa turned and looked "I do not know. I have never seen them before."

A flash from under one of the men's cloaks caught Renna's eye. Sunlight was glinting off of something metal he had hidden beneath it. It had to be a sword. She was alarmed at the thought of two armed strangers being so close to the house when Vitruvius was working in the fields. She put her hand on Melissa's shoulder. "Go and find Antonius and take him away from the house. If I go, he may think I am chasing him because he took the bread, and run further away. I will find out what they want here."

Despite her attempts to remain calm, Renna's voice shook and Melissa picked up on the fear her friend felt. She gripped Renna's hand. "I should face them, Renna, not you," she replied.

Renna's eyes never left the men. "You think I would leave you alone with their sort in your condition? You may be a clever woman, but you have no talent for self-defence and words will not help you today. Anyway, Vitruvius would kill me for even thinking of it. Find Antonius and take him to Vitruvius. I will be fine until your return."

"I will go. Where is Vitruvius?" Melissa asked.

"In the fields beyond the paddock," Renna's eyes still followed the strangers who were coming very close. "Go around behind the house and do not run." Melissa nodded and walked away towards the building as Renna crossed the yard to meet the men who were dismounting at the wall. Renna knew they were soldiers by trade. Both were stocky in stature, with muscular arms, and one had a nasty scar down the side of his face.

"Greetings to you," she said calmly. "It is a warm day for travelling. You must be tired. Have you come far?"

"Far enough," said the first man. "Will you let us water our horses at your trough before we go on?"

"Of course," Renna said airily in the hope of appearing friendly and not suspicious. She had the distinct feeling they were coming in whether she agreed or not, so she decided to try to buy Melissa as much time as she could to find Vitruvius. "Can I offer you some refreshment? We have bread and cheese. It is not much, but I would willingly share it with you. Please come into the shade, my husband will be returning for lunch very soon."

The men looked at each other and nodded. "That is most kind of you," the first man replied. He opened the gate and led the horses through, tethering them to the post on the inside by the water trough. They followed Renna into the kitchen where she felt a little safer. Although she could not run far inside the house, she had plenty of weapons with which to defend herself.

The table was already laden with bread, cheese, olives and a jug of water. Renna put a flask of wine and two cups on the table and motioned for the men to sit. Neither man removed his cloak, making Renna even more certain that their intentions were not good. She backed up against the side table where a large kitchen knife was lying. Her body hid it from the men's view. She put her hands on the table top, feeling for the handle and gripped it, ready to use it if necessary.

The first man took the flask of wine and poured some into a cup. He did not dilute it, but drank it straight down. "Not joining us?" he said, eying her carefully.

"I will wait for my husband. It would not be proper for a Roman matron to drink with two strangers unless he is present." As soon as the words left her lips she cursed herself. *Why did she say Roman?* She knew they had not missed it.

"Been here long?" the man asked.

"Only a few months," she replied. There was no point in her lying, not after her slip.

"Who was your friend?" Renna pretended she did not know who he meant, so he rephrased the question. "Outside – you sent her after the brat."

"Oh her. She is just our slave. She can read and so teaches the child his letters, which is a good use for her, since she is useless at most other things." Renna's hand tightened on the knife she was holding behind her back.

"So there's you, your husband, a boy and one slave? All moved here from Rome. When? About the same time as Caesar's death?

"Yes," Renna whispered the answer, her terror suddenly rising.

"Well then, that is good news for us." The first man looked at his companion. "Looks like we found them," he muttered, before returning his attentions to Renna. "And if you are the *wife*, we have a special message for you. Our mistress Servilia sends heartfelt wishes for your slow and painful death. She wants revenge for the betrayal of her son that you and your pet, Mark Antony, arranged. Good job that *husband* is not here as I would rather deal with him later." The man stood, throwing off his cloak and drawing his sword "First I intend to enjoy you. I have never fucked a consul's whore before. You must be very talented to have kept his interest for so long." He ran the blade down Renna's dress from her groin, tearing it in two. He pushed the flat of the blade against one of her thighs, trying to separate her legs. "Going to need to open those a bit, my dear. When I want a tight fit, I will look to the boy!"

Renna obligingly moved her legs apart and the man lowered his sword to raise his own tunic. In the split second he was distracted by his clothing, she pulled the knife round from behind her and drove it hard into his stomach, screaming as loudly as she could. The man stumbled backwards towards the table and Renna bolted for the door.

His colleague rose, drawing his blade. He managed to grab Renna by the hair and pulled her backwards. Throwing her across the table, he gripped her tightly round the throat. He had been completely taken off-guard by the sudden change of this woman from timid victim to wailing banshee. He looked at his associate writhing on the floor. Blood was now pouring from his wound and his mouth. Knowing his comrade was as good as dead, his eyes returned to Renna, who was frantically pulling at the hands round her throat, trying to draw breath. He pushed the tip of his sword against her stomach. He would not waste his time with her, she was too much trouble. He slowly drove the blade upwards under her ribs, piercing her lungs. He took pleasure from watching the expression of excruciating pain on her face as she fought to breathe while her life ebbed away from her. He held Renna's throat for a few more seconds until her body went limp beneath him.

A thudding noise from outside made him realise he would soon have company. He reached for the water jug and slipped behind the door to wait for the next victim.

Melissa found Antonius sitting at the back of the house, in the shade of the building. She pulled him up, telling him that she had a surprise for Vitruvius and they had to find him. She headed across the paddock towards the fields beyond, Antonius running happily in front of her.

Vitruvius saw them coming and waved. He guessed it was time for lunch and put down his tools. He drew his arm across his brow to wipe away the sweat that was dripping down his face and then crouched down, preparing to grab Antonius. As the little boy ran at him he swept him up, throwing him in the air, then catching him. Antonius squealed with delight.

As Melissa drew nearer he could see from her face that something was wrong. "What is it?" he said, as lightly as he could manage, ruffling Antonius' hair as he put him down again.

"We have visitors," Melissa replied with the same false lightness. "Two men. I believe they have brought a personal message from our consul. Renna is at the house with them."

Vitruvius knew what Melissa meant. If Antony had sent men, the only message they carried was a violent one. His thoughts turned immediately to Renna. She was alone in the house with two of Antony's thugs, where all manner of horrible things could be happening to her. He reached down and grabbed the shovel he had earlier discarded.

As he stood up, he gripped Melissa's shoulder. "Take Antonius away from here." He pulled his hand away and pointed to the far side of the field. "Go down to the river, then double back to the crossing in the woods. On the other side, turn upstream away from where we were camped with Caesar on the day we met. There is another farmhouse one mile over the hill on that side. They are good people, and will hide you. Do not return to this house unless I come for you."

Melissa and Vitruvius exchanged a final look, but there was no need for words. They had been through so much together that neither needed to voice their fears for the other's safety. Melissa grabbed Antonius tightly by the hand and watched as Vitruvius ran back across the field.

As Vitruvius entered the paddock, he heard Renna's scream. It stopped him momentarily, filling him with terror mixed with panic. He shook the feeling off and then redoubled his pace, vaulting the fence at the far side and landing with a heavy thud. He ran straight round to the front of the house, no longer thinking of the danger he was facing. He burst through the door into the kitchen and came to a halt in front of the table where Renna lay, covered in blood, her eyes staring blankly at the ceiling, drained of all life. He was too late. He had failed yet another woman he had grown to love.

Vitruvius' thoughts were interrupted by a searing pain in his head. The room began to spin and he staggered forward and fell to the floor. The last sight he had was of two feet moving beside him.

Chapter 28

Blackness. Total, consuming blackness was all Vitruvius could see. The air was hot and stuffy and made it hard for him to breathe. His limbs were heavy and he was unable to move them, no matter how hard he tried. His head pounded as if it was being used as a drum by some unknown musician. *Was he dead? Was this what the afterlife was like? Was he destined to spend eternity without movement or sight, but with conscious thought?* He heard a rustling noise to the side of him and turned his head towards it even though he could not see where it was coming from. Fear surged through his body as he strained to listen for the noise again.

There was a sudden rush of air, and then blinding light. The searing pain in his head exploded as the glare filled his eyes. He closed them and turned his head away from the brightness until the pain subsided to its previous dull drumming. Slowly he re-opened his eyes and looked around. He was not dead after all. He was in the main room of the farmhouse.

He looked down at his body, which was tied to Melissa's chair from the kitchen. The kitchen! The sight of Renna's lifeless body lying across the table flew into his mind. He closed his eyes again as his body was wracked by a painful new sensation, but this pain was not a physical one. This time it was caused from an overwhelming sensation of grief tinged with guilt. He had promised to protect every member of his adopted family and now one of them was dead. What of the others? Would he see the bodies of Melissa and Antonius lying limply before him when he opened his eyes again? He screwed up his face, closing his eyes tighter as he tried to shut the image of Renna's body out of his thoughts.

The rustling noise returned, this time behind him, accompanied by a sudden jerking on his arms. Vitruvius realised his bonds were being adjusted. His eyes shot open and he strained to move his arms again, hoping to break free, but it was pointless, since the knots were too tight.

An unfamiliar voice spoke to him. "Awake already? I thought you would be out for much longer. You have a hard head, my friend, but you Thirteenth boys always were tough bastards." A man Vitruvius had never seen before walked into view. He was holding a thick black sack, which he had used to cover Vitruvius' head; he was older than Vitruvius, but he had the look of a soldier about him – stocky, with well-defined arms that had once swung a sword for a living. He was most likely a veteran turned assassin, one of many who had been forced to find other ways to survive after their time in the legions had ended.

Vitruvius' situation was hopeless. The assassin had tied him to the ridiculous chair he had made for Melissa, his arms bound behind him to the bars that formed the back. He cursed himself for ever making the wretched thing. The man had been extremely thorough, binding his ankles to the chair legs as well. This meant that he had lost his best opportunity to extricate himself. He had hoped that when the assassin left, he would be able to stand up, enabling him to smash the accursed chair against the wall. His only option now was to try to tip backwards, but, in doing this, he would land on his arms and might break those instead of the chair. He strained against the ropes holding him, until they burnt into his flesh. He could loosen them eventually, but it would take too much time – time that Antonius and Melissa did not have. Brute force was not going to help him. He had to think his way out of this. He began by asking the obvious question.

"Why have you come here? Antony gave his word he would leave us alone."

"Did he now?" The assassin began walking around the chair in slow, endless circles with the intention of disorientating his victim. "Well, our consul is not so good at keeping his promises, is he? My employer knew that, but her son was taken in by your slut back there," the man nodded at the kitchen behind Vitruvius. "Now he is gone and she is the one calling the shots. She cannot take revenge on Antony for his betrayal, but she can get to you. The witch is dead, Vitruvius, and you will join her soon enough. First though, I want to get the boy back here. My instructions were that you were both to feel the pain of his loss, same as the mistress felt the pain of losing her son. That one ..." the man nodded towards the kitchen again "... feels nothing, so now you alone will listen to his squeaking as I cut off his limbs."

Vitruvius felt oddly relieved that Antony was not to blame and that these were Servilia's men. Vitruvius knew Antony had spies everywhere and perhaps he already knew of this development. If so, then help could already be on the way to them. He knew the depth of Antony's feelings for Melissa, and reasoned he might even come himself to rescue her. Of course, there was always the possibility that Antony was letting Servilia do his dirty work for him, thus erasing the only living link between him and Caesar's conspirators. Whichever was the case, Vitruvius needed to buy more time.

"I have money." he blurted out. "Let the boy live, and it is yours."

He had said enough to rouse the assassin's interest. The man stopped circling the chair. "How much?" he asked.

Vitruvius started low, expecting to barter. "A thousand denarii."

The stranger barked a callous laugh. "She will pay more for his head than that!"

"Five thousand. Please! I will show you where it is, just swear you will let the boy go."

The assassin began his circuit again. "What if I take the money and kill him anyway?"

As the assassin believed Melissa was already dead, Vitruvius decided to use this inaccuracy to his advantage. "Because the slave can get you double the amount back in Rome. The child is worth far more to Antony alive than he is to Servilia dead."

The assassin stopped in front of Vitruvius and folded his arms. He was definitely interested in the offer. "Go on, I am listening," he said.

"He is the consul's son and the woman is his nurse. That is why I thought Antony had sent you. Lissa knew he would betray Brutus, so we stole Antony's money and the boy, and came here. We wanted him for insurance, to stop Antony coming for us. The slave is the only one the boy trusts. He is a mischievous child, but she can control him. Return them to Antony and receive the reward you truly deserve." Vitruvius said these words aloud, whilst thinking to himself, *and you will, when Antony rips out your throat with his bare hands!*

"Interesting." The assassin rubbed his chin with his hand. He was considering what he had heard. Alive, it seemed the boy could be worth more. He could take the cash on offer now, kill the man and get more money in Rome. Things were looking up, but he was not ready to commit just yet. "Servilia never mentioned any of this. Maybe you speak the truth and maybe not. I will think on it while I look for the others. Does the woman know where this money is?

"No. I am the only one who does," Vitruvius lied.

"Well then, you just sit tight until I return with your friends. If she confirms your story about the brat's father, and you up your offer to ten, we may have a deal." The assassin leant over Vitruvius and began to laugh. "If not, you can watch me screw her until she begs to die. Then I will bugger the boy before I slit your throat!" He walked out of the house leaving the sound of his laughter ringing in Vitruvius' ears.

Melissa followed Vitruvius' directions. She and Antonius crossed the field and doubled back on themselves when they reached the river. The open fields gave little camouflage, but Melissa knew she had to reach the crossing upstream and the farm beyond, as it was the only place for miles where she could get help.

She tried to make a game of their escape so as not to frighten Antonius, but he knew something was wrong. He continually asked her questions, all of which Melissa avoided answering, until he fell silent and walked at her side, holding onto her hand as tightly as he could.

As the river narrowed, the banks became more wooded. Melissa spotted an old path that left the side of the river and headed deeper into the trees. Following this would make it easier to hide, so she took it.

It was far darker in the wood and their presence made the animals and birds occupying the undergrowth run from them. The noises frightened Antonius even more and he clung to Melissa. She picked him up to comfort him, even though his weight was really too much for her. There were noises coming from behind her that seemed too loud to be made by the wildlife. It had to be that the men were in the woods and catching up with them. Suddenly, she heard one of them calling out. Melissa moved forward to the thickest group of bushes she could find and pushed herself backwards into them. The twigs and branches scratched at her arms and face as she did so. She sat on the ground, holding Antonius. "We have to be quiet," she whispered, "can you do that for me until I say you can speak?" Antonius nodded and clung to her even more tightly.

Melissa could hear a man approaching, searching the wood as he went, but in a very haphazard fashion. With any luck he would go straight past. He was close enough for Melissa to hear his words clearly. "I know you are here, girl. Bring me the boy and I will let you go. I have no quarrel with you," the man was yelling.

Melissa knew he was lying. If Antony had gone back on his word, then they were all targets. She was not surprised he had sent men after her: she was a conspirator in Caesar's assassination, after all, but she found it hard to believe that he would kill his own child. Unless of course, these men were meant to take them back to Antony and not to kill them, but that seemed unlikely. No, she decided, they were assassins sent to remove the one woman who could ruin Antony's career.

Antonius was by far the most vulnerable. He was totally defenceless against the unimaginable torments these evil men might have planned for him. Melissa knew she could not hide for long. What she did not know was whether she had one or two men to deal with. If the other man was dead, Vitruvius would be coming after them, unless he too was dead. No, she could not think that. He was a skilled soldier who would triumph and come to their rescue. Melissa convinced herself that Vitruvius had been held up fighting the other man and was coming for them. She just had to wait a little longer.

Their assailant was getting closer by the minute and he was now being very thorough in his search. He continued to call to them. "I was only paid for the witch, the boy and the man, so why not do us both a favour? I have the other two, I just need the boy. You can go once we have had a bit of fun."

Melissa shuddered. She knew only too well what fun meant. The rest of his words were a shock. He must have mistaken Renna for her. She had to be the one he referred to as 'the witch' and not the former slave, so he had made a mistake, but the news that his companion had Renna and Vitruvius at the house was heartbreaking. Melissa realised she was alone. It was down to her to save Antonius from this man.

Melissa hugged the little boy sitting beside her tightly and whispered in his ear, "I have to go to the river. Stay here. Do not make a sound and do not come out until the bad man has gone. Understand?" Antonius nodded. Melissa kissed him on the nose. He still looked frightened, but he had not cried, and Melissa was proud of his courage. Reluctantly, she let go of him and moved out from under the bushes as quietly as she could and through the trees towards the river's edge.

As Melissa reached the bank she began to run, making as much noise as possible. She had to put as much distance between her and Antonius as she could before their stalker caught up to her. She prayed he would not decide to ignore her and continue looking for the little boy. As she ran she began to look for any likely weapons – rocks, broken branches, anything she could use. She hardly noticed the mist that was forming over the water.

Suddenly, Melissa stopped. She might have imagined it, but she could have sworn she heard someone calling her name. She looked around her and for the first time realised the river was covered in a thick mist. If she crossed over, she might be able to lose the man following her in it. The river did not appear to be too deep, so it was worth a try.

At that moment, Melissa saw a figure coming towards her out of the mist. She recognised him instantly; it was Antony. *He has come to oversee my torture,* she thought. A familiar wave of nausea hit her. She knew that anything Antony would do to her was far worse than she could expect from the man in the woods behind her. If Antony had his way, it would take her days to die: he had promised her such a fate more than once. A feeling of resignation swept over her. She felt there was no escape for her, but she might still be able to reason with him for the lives of Antonius and the others. Antonius was Antony's son, after all, and she still could not believe he would hurt him. She changed direction and headed down to the water's edge, determined to throw herself upon his mercy, and beg for the lives of the others.

As Antony came nearer, Melissa realised something was wrong with her assessment. He looked like Antony, but his clothes were not those of either a consul or a general, or indeed of any Roman. He was wearing what looked like a t-shirt and shorts. It was all far too ... modern!

Melissa heart leapt. It was not Mark Antony, but Anthony Marcus in front of her. In that moment she forgot everything – where she was, why she was running. She even forgot that the life of a helpless child hung in the balance. All she could think about was getting to Anthony and being swept away by him to her real life.

At that moment, the assassin came out of the bushes and ran straight at her. He caught up to her in seconds, grabbing her dress and tearing it from her shoulder. She slipped on the wet ground and fell into the river, swallowing large mouthfuls of cold water in the process. Choking for air, she pulled herself onto the bank, away from her attacker. There was an odd ringing noise in her ears. It sounded like someone shouting *"NOOOOOO!!!"*

Chapter 29
Present Day

Every day for a month since Melissa's disappearance, Anthony Marcus had come down to the stream to look for clues. Every day Victor told him it was a waste of time, but he did it anyway. It gave him something to do, and distracted him from feeling that he was a helpless bystander, watching the situation from a distance, but completely unable to affect the outcome. He hated the feeling of uselessness that had descended on him, and he had resolved never to give up on Melissa, no matter how long it took him to find her.

The longer he spent at the water's edge, the more time he had to reflect on his own past. Slowly, memories from his childhood began to resurface, memories that had so traumatised him, he had buried them deep in the back of his mind. The more he remembered, the more questions he put to Victor. The old man feigned ignorance to begin with but, as time went on, he had given in to the constant interrogation Anthony put him through. Gradually, Anthony had put together a picture of his past that was both shocking and surreal.

From what he remembered, or forced Victor to recount, he knew that he had indeed been on that river bank as a child. The water had been much higher back then and that was why initially he had been confused. He had been hiding there, playing with his aunt, when she was attacked. He was unsure of the exact details, but he vaguely remembered a man rescuing her, whom he believed to be his father because this man was very similar in looks to Anthony as he was now. He knew he had run away, because the river turned red and it terrified him. He had run to Victor, but they never found his aunt or the mystery man. There was one more thing: there had been an unusual mist that day and that mist had a smell about it he would always remember. It was a musty, earthy smell similar to the smell he associated with an earth floor in an old cellar. He had hated that smell for years and as a result he had always loathed having to work in the musty, damp basements of old buildings, which was a distinct disadvantage for an archaeologist. He also knew that he had been in that mist more than once. As a child, he spent hours searching for it, desperate to find it once again, despite the nightmares he suffered as a result. He had never before made the links to explain his behaviour, but now he knew the answer.

Victor told Anthony how he had first met Melissa before Anthony was born and long before people called him Victor. His real name was Quintus Vitruvius, a native of the area and a distinguished soldier who had served under Caesar in Gaul. He explained how, on the day Mark Antony returned to the legion following his ejection from the Senate, he arrived with two foreign women he had stumbled upon beside the Rubicon. Victor told a tale of one of the women convincing Caesar she could see the future, offering her services in return for his protection. That woman was Melissa, and the other Rebecca. Caesar had appointed legionary Vitruvius to watch over them, which he had done for five years. Anthony had been born during that time and Melissa and Vitruvius had assumed joint responsibility for him after his real mother, Rebecca, had died giving him life. Anthony still did not know who his father was, other than it was not Vitruvius, but he did know that Melissa was the aunt he had lost. The surreal nature of his relationship with her was difficult to comprehend. The love of his life turned out to be the woman who had effectively brought him up, even though he could not remember her clearly from that time.

He and Vitruvius also passed through the mist after Melissa had vanished and ended up in the 1970s. They were taken in by a kindly widow, who did not think it odd to find a man and child who spoke fluent Latin wandering on her land. It felt as if she knew more about their appearance than she let on, but she had never said a word about it. When he was a little boy Anthony was unable to say Vitruvius and had called him Vittores. This was how Vitruvius' name changed in translation to Victor Reyes.

Everything Anthony had learnt gave him reason to hope that Melissa could find her way back to him. This mist was a doorway to the past, but also to the future; the problem was there was no way to predict where you would end up if you used it. He and Victor had been lost in the mist and ended up in the future. Melissa, his lover, had disappeared into the past. As a boy he had watched Melissa, his aunt, vanish in the same circumstances, though he had no idea where she had gone.

He could not explain why, but he had a really good feeling about today. This morning felt different to every other one so far. For a start it was unusually cold, which Anthony noticed on his way down to the stream. The air felt damp, as if it had been raining, but the ground was parched. It was also eerily quiet. The usual sound of birds singing their morning chorus was absent and the woods were far too still. Usually he would notice movements in the undergrowth as small animals tried to flee when disturbed by his approach. The only noise today was made by his own footsteps as he walked, and the only movement, from the wisps of ground mist that were coming off the fields, twisting as they rose into the light breeze.

As Anthony exited the tree line and approached the water's edge, he became more aware of just how thick the morning mist had become. It hung like a curtain in front of him, so thick that it separated the area into two distinct zones. He felt his pulse quicken and he paused to take a deep breath. He was unsure, but he thought he could smell something. He tried again, closing his eyes in order to concentrate only on his breathing. It was definitely there – that same earthy smell. It was faint, but getting stronger. His pulse began to race, urged on by a sudden rush of adrenalin pulsing through his body. He felt an urge to run, but fought it, knowing he had to remain calm. All the while he believed there was nothing there that could hurt him, he could master his fear. His vision was limited by the mist, but every other sense in his body felt heightened, as if trying to compensate. He could hear the water in the stream, but its gentle trickling had been replaced by the much more forceful sound of water gurgling as it ran across the rocks and pebbles in the river bed. He edged forward slowly into the mist and accidentally stepped into the river up to his calf. He had found the water's edge, which was far higher than it should have been.

Anthony knew where he was, but he was no longer certain of when it was. His heart pounded in his chest, screaming its urgent need to move him forwards, but he remained still, scanning the mist for any hint of movement on the far bank. He had to wait for some kind of sign that he was in the right time before he continued. At the moment he was still close enough to the present to turn and walk back to the clear air behind him. He could not afford to be sucked into the right place at the wrong time, because, if he did, he would never find Melissa. He had to be patient.

A few moments passed that seemed like an age. There was nothing. Moments turned to minutes and still nothing. Just as he was about to give up, he saw a movement to his left. The mist had cleared slightly and he could see a person running on the other bank. He felt sure it was a woman and he shouted at the top of his voice, "MELISSA!" The woman stopped and looked towards him, but the mist re-formed and obscured his view. He stepped forward, despite knowing that it could be the wrong thing to do, but rational thought had long since left him.

The mist cleared again and he could see the woman coming towards him. She had seen him too. His heart leapt as he waded deeper into the water that now reached his knees. He knew it was Melissa – it had to be.

He was almost across when another man appeared from out of nowhere, armed with a sword, and chased after Melissa. He grabbed at her dress from the rear, succeeding in gripping a section of cloth at her shoulder. As she struggled to free herself, the material ripped and she fell sideways into the water. Anthony heard himself bellowing again.

"*NOOOOOO!!!*" he yelled, as he forced his way through the water and hurled himself at the other man, knocking the stranger off his feet and sending the sword flying across the ground. The two men came to rest on the muddy edge of the bank, where Anthony pressed his advantage by punching the man repeatedly in the face.

Anthony's initial attack had caught the other man off-guard, but he was quick to recover himself. A well-aimed punch to the solar plexus, and Anthony was winded long enough for the assassin to throw him off. The man looked around desperately for his sword and lunged for it as soon as he saw it lying on the ground, but fell well short of retrieving it as Anthony grabbed at his leg and pulled him backwards across the wet, sticky ground.

The assassin twisted his body to focus on his opponent and kicked Anthony hard in the jaw with his free leg, forcing him to let go as he slid backwards into the river. Melissa screamed, fearing he had been knocked out.

After she had dragged herself out of the river, Melissa had become a spectator to the fight. The sight of Anthony sliding into the water horrified her. Despite knowing how fit and capable he was, Anthony was facing a hired killer and she could not stand by and do nothing, especially when it looked like he was losing. She looked for a weapon and saw a fallen branch about the size of a baseball bat lying on ground, light enough for her to lift. Failing to spot the sword, it appeared the best thing to hand.

The assassin, on the other hand, had not failed to spot the sword. He scrambled to his feet, heading straight towards the blade, but was sent sprawling once again before he could reach it, this time by Melissa. She swung the branch and made contact with the assassin's head, knocking him over. She dropped the branch and stumbled forward, grabbing the sword herself.

Despite being dazed from the blow to his head, the assassin was not about to withdraw. He had learnt his skills under Pompey and had fought for him on his right flank at Pharsalus. He recognised the man he was fighting, or at least thought he did, and wanted to settle an old score. The idea of murdering Mark Antony was fuelling him with thoughts of revenge for so many comrades who had fallen to Antony's sword on that day, and a surge of pure adrenaline now spurred him to continue. He hauled himself to his feet and looked again for the sword, which had vanished. Confused, he spun round in time to see Melissa throwing the sword to Anthony standing in the shallow water.

Anthony caught the sword easily, but he did not intend to use it. Whilst he was more than prepared to beat the man unconscious, his moral compass was not going to swing to murder. Instead he intended to reason with him.

The assassin stopped in his tracks. He was unarmed and believed himself to be facing one of the most fearsome warriors he had ever known. He fully expected to be dead in moments, but to his surprise Mark Antony was lowering the sword and trying to talk to him. He assumed his opponent had gone soft, having spent too much time in a warm bed enjoying the comforts of a woman like the one on the riverbank. The assassin stepped forward, yet Mark Antony made no attempt to raise the sword. Again the assassin paused, pretending to listen and raised his hand to check his skull for blood. His fingertips made contact with a sticky mass at the back of his head which confirmed the severity of his wound.

"No one need die here," Anthony was saying in Latin. "I just want Melissa. I will take her away from here and you will never see either of us again."

The assassin shook his head in disbelief. Either he was mishearing what was being said, or the situation was becoming farcical. It appeared Lissa was not the dead woman in the house, but the woman here at the river. His opponent was implying he would walk away and never return, if he could take the woman with him. Did she really mean that much to him? Was the great Mark Antony about to give up his consular responsibilities for some foreign slut? It seemed unlikely, but perhaps his understanding was becoming as blurred as his vision. Whatever the truth of the situation, he had one remaining chance for success.

"As you like, Consul," the assassin said, as he feigned turning away and giving up. As Anthony dropped the sword to his side, the assassin turned again and threw himself at his opponent, screaming at the top of his lungs, intent on terrorising him. As he reached the edge of the bank, his foot slipped on the muddy surface and he skidded into the water.

More by instinct than by intention, Anthony raised the sword and impaled his attacker on the point. Both men looked down in surprise. Anthony had never meant to harm this man, even though he had been threatening Melissa's life, but now, watching the blood oozing over his hands, Anthony was overtaken by an urge to end the man's life. His mind filled with horrifying images of a room with a dead woman lying in a pool of her own blood, and of Victor, tied and bound to a chair. These were painful memories from his past that he had buried so deeply until this moment: the nightmares of his youth. Reliving these past terrors filled Anthony with a desperate need for revenge. He gave one final push on the sword, thrusting it deep into his opponent's body. The assassin fell forward into the water, blood now pouring from his wounds to join the flow of the river as it headed downstream, turning the water red.

The realisation that you have taken another man's life is enough to send a person into shock. Anthony stood over the body of the assassin staring down at him in bewilderment. He looked down at the blood on his own hands and arms, slowly turning them over, first one way and then the other. His whole body felt numb. Melissa was pulling on his arm and saying something, but he could not hear her. He raised his head to look at her. Her mouth was moving, but he still could not make out her words. She slapped him round the face, but he did not react. It was as if he was incapable of hearing or feeling anything anymore. She slapped him again. Still he felt nothing.

Melissa was equally horrified at what she had witnessed, but it seemed her experiences of life in the past had made her face many unpleasant situations and had taught her how to react to death. Now was not the time to fall apart. They had to get to safety first and deal with their emotions later. *One more time for luck,* she thought and she went for the third slap.

This time Anthony definitely felt it. He grabbed her wrist, smearing her with the blood from his hands. "Stop doing that!" he demanded, glaring at her momentarily before pulling her into his arms. He hugged her so tightly that she could hardly breathe, smearing more blood over her back and arms as he held her.

"I thought I'd lost you!" he gasped, his voice full of relief. Despite her lack of breath, Melissa held onto Anthony as tightly as he held her and for the first time in years she felt completely safe.

As they clung to each other, Anthony noticed the mist was shifting. He had no idea how long it would last. He moved away from Melissa slightly and began to move towards the other bank. "We have to go," he said.

Melissa shook her head, pulling away from his grasp. "No, I can't. There are people here relying on me to bring them help, but first ..." She turned and stepped back to dry land, her eyes searching the trees until she spotted what she was looking for. She pointed towards a particularly large tree. "There!" she said.

Anthony followed her gaze and watched a small boy of around four or five clamber down the bank and walk towards them. He was obviously frightened by what he had witnessed and seemed unsure whether to come out or not. He seemed familiar to Anthony, but he could not think how he knew the boy.

Melissa was relieved that Antonius was alive and uninjured. As she stepped towards him, the boy backed away in terror. Melissa looked down at herself, covered in smears of blood, and understood his fear. "It's OK," Melissa said gently, "everything is going to be fine, but you have to come with us." She took another step forward and held out her hand, encouraging the boy to move forward and take it. "Please come, Antonius, there is no time for this."

The sound of his former name put the last piece in the puzzle for Anthony. He had always thought that his aunt had left with his father, but in that second Anthony understood he had been looking not at his father, but at an older version of himself. He also knew he had to force Melissa to leave his younger self behind or it would obliterate his life as he had lived it. He grabbed Melissa's arm and pulled on it harshly, making her turn back to face him. "No, Lissa, he can't come with us. He has to go back to free Vitruvius."

"How do you know about Vitruvius? Is he still alive? We need to get him and Renna and take them all with us. What did you just call me?" Melissa was babbling. Anthony tried to calm her by telling her Vitruvius was alive and well back at the house, but she would not listen. She had failed to make the connection between the man at her side and the frightened boy standing on the bank.

"I can't leave him here! He's so tiny, he needs me." Melissa was becoming hysterical and tears poured down her cheeks as she struggled to escape Anthony's grasp. She bent her head and bit his hand hoping to force him to release her, but he anticipated her move; he had watched her do it once before, after all. He wrapped his free arm around her waist and dragged her towards him, lifting her feet off the ground. She struggled vigorously, punching his shoulders and kicking at his legs determined to make him drop her. Anthony threw Melissa over his shoulder and started back across the river. Still fighting him, she stared in desperation at Antonius, screaming at him to follow them, but the little boy was too terrified to come any further. As the mist began to thicken around her, Melissa watched Antonius turn and run into the trees. Then both he and the Rubicon disappeared from her view.

By the time Anthony and Melissa had reached the other bank, the river had been replaced by the trickling stream once again. The mist had vanished completely and with it any chance of Melissa ever finding Antonius.

Anthony put Melissa down on the ground and collapsed beside her. Every muscle in his body ached from fighting with two different people. He would be covered in bruises later and many of them were probably caused by Melissa. He lay on his back staring at the sky, trying to blot out the face of the man he had just murdered, a face that haunted him every time he closed his eyes.

Melissa sat hugging her knees. She was overcome by the grief of losing Antonius. She knew she would never see him again or know what had happened to any of the people she had just left behind. Her thoughts turned to Vitruvius and Renna. They could be badly wounded and in need of some help, if they were not already dead.

But they were dead! They had all died centuries ago even though she had been with them only moments earlier. Finally she spoke. "How could you be so cruel? I'll never forgive you if anything bad happened to that boy." Her words tailed off, knowing it was nothing more than an empty threat.

Anthony began to laugh. He pulled himself up to sit beside her. "Haven't you worked it out yet?" he asked. Melissa did not reply, but the angry look that she shot him from behind the streaming tears on her face gave him his answer.

Anthony continued. "We left him there because he has to go and free Vittores." Anthony deliberately used the mispronunciation of Vitruvius' name to give a clue to his identity, but he was unsure if she had picked up on the reference. He raised his hand and gently pushed Melissa's hair behind her ear. "You don't have to worry – that wily old goat has no serious injuries, other than to his pride, and he's going to be fine. They both are."

"What makes you so sure?" Melissa was confused and tired and her heart was breaking at the very moment she should have been happiest. She needed to know why Anthony was so confident, but she had no idea what words he could possibly have that could take her pain away. She leant towards him, resting her head on his shoulder and wrapping her arms around his waist, desperate for some comfort.

Anthony wrapped his arms around Melissa and gently kissed the top of her head. They were both soaking wet and covered in the blood of a dead Roman assassin, but in contrast to Melissa, Anthony was the happiest he had been in years. He had achieved the impossible in rescuing the love of his life from the past, and he was determined he would never let her go again. He stared into her hair, not wanting the moment to end. Then he lifted her chin so that he could look into her eyes as he gave her the answer she so desperately craved.

"That little boy is going to get to fall in love with you all over again, and you're going to spend the rest of your life with him. That's if you still want to. He's me, Liss. I'm Antonius!"

Chapter 30

Melissa sat on the veranda staring down the drive towards the road. It had been two weeks since her return and she was finding it difficult to settle. Anthony had hardly let her out of his sight, terrified that he might lose her again. He had reluctantly gone into town alone that morning only because Victor needed more medication, and even then he only went after she had promised not to leave the safety of the house.

Melissa felt trapped by all the attention; what she needed was to be alone, with enough time to make sense of all that had happened. Now she finally had that opportunity, her memories had become too painful to bear and she found herself longing for Anthony to return.

Melissa's thoughts were interrupted by the noise of a walking stick tapping on the terracotta floor tiles. She had been wondering how long it would be before Victor decided to speak to her. It looked like her wait was over.

"May I join you, Lissa?" he asked. Melissa nodded and Victor settled into a chair beside her. He sat in silence for some time, his laboured breath the only noise disturbing the tranquillity. He looked so old and withered in comparison with the strong soldier he had been the last time she had seen him. There were so many answers she wanted from him, but she did not know where to start and so she waited until Victor reopened the conversation.

"How are you feeling? Any sickness or headaches? I had headaches for a time, but they pass."

"No headaches. I do feel sick in the mornings, but we both know that's nothing to do with moving through time by two thousand years." Melissa looked away down the drive again.

"You have not told him about the baby?" Victor meant, had she told Anthony that she was carrying his father's child.

She shook her head. This was another problem that she did not know how to begin to explain.

"He will know soon enough. You cannot hide it for much longer. Lie. Say Antony raped you. I will not say any different. Antonius loves you and he will understand. You will stay here and he will look after you both."

"He shouldn't have to. This is not his responsibility."

"He was not my responsibility, but I took him on because I loved his mother as much as he loves you. He has loved you all his life and he needs you to care for him because he does not cope well on his own. When you disappeared from his life he was distraught – both times. He waited for you at that river every day, as a little boy and as a man. If you leave him again, it will destroy him and I am too sick to piece him back together this time. Anyway, you promised his mother you would not let any harm come to him as long as you live."

"Why did you do it? Why take him away from me? What happened to you, Quintus Vitruvius? Was it because you felt I had abandoned you? Did you really hate me that much that you had to ruin my entire life?" Melissa could no longer control the anger she felt at Victor for all the pain he had caused her.

Victor sighed. His body ached and he was tired, but he had started this conversation and knew he owed Melissa an explanation. He was touched that she had used his real name. He had not heard it for so many years and this gave him strength to continue.

"Yes, I hated you. When Antonius found me all he could tell me was that the boat man took you. I knew he meant Mark Antony because of all those toys. I assumed Antony had discovered Servilia's plot and come to rescue you."

"Servilia?" Melissa cut across him. "She sent the men?"

"Yes. It was Servilia. She wanted revenge on you for Antony's betrayal of her son. I thought Antony had come for you and taken you back to Rome, and that you had gone with him willingly. I believed you lied to me when you said you did not love him because I know he loved you. I only realised just how much on that last morning in Rome. I had left you as he asked, but was listening at the door. I knew his true feelings when he told you to leave with me. Mark Antony had already risked his life for you, so it made sense he would let you go to save you from suspicion. I was angry with you for deserting us to be with him. How could I have known back then that it was a different man who had taken you from the river? How could I know Antonius had seen himself? He begged me to find you, but I refused to go back to the river. He hated me for it and he cried for days. I buried Renna and the assassins and we got on with our lives. A few months later we were down at the river by the crossing and there was a thick mist, unlike any I had ever seen before. Antonius ran away from me into it calling for you. I followed him to bring him back, but the current was too strong for a child and he was washed downstream away from me. I followed and when I finally dragged him out onto the other bank we were in a different time and I could not get us home. We were as trapped in the future as you had been in the past, but it was not your future. Not yet, at least.

"We were lucky in a way. We had stumbled onto the land of an Englishwoman, this land here in fact. Her name was Lenore Marcus. I must admit, I was actually glad you taught Antonius to speak your language because I could not talk to her, but he could. She was the widow of an archaeologist, with no family of her own, and she took us in. I worked on her estate in return for a home and for her schooling Antonius in your ways. I learnt to speak and read Italian and English with her help, by reading the books in her husband's library, those same books in the library today. I found learning easy, I always did. She never questioned that I only spoke Latin at the start. She knew more than she ever said about how we came to be here, but we never discussed it until many years later.

"When Antonius, whom we now called Antonio, was older, Lenore sent him to a boarding school in England, which he hated. He was the one to call himself Anthony because he wanted to fit in with the English boys. That is when he really began to rebel." Victor laughed to himself, obviously remembering some past event. "He was just like his father in so many ways, but all that is for another time. He took Lenore's surname because he found it amusing to make comparisons between himself and Mark Antony. I think you would call it a good chat-up line. I could never bring myself to tell him just how close to the truth he really was.

"Lenore and I became intimate over the years. I suppose I should have married her, but I never considered it a possibility. I still thought in Roman terms and she was from a far better family than I could ever hope to marry into. She sent me to college when Anthony went to England and I studied to be an archaeologist. She knew by then that I was a quick learner and believed my unique understanding of Roman life already made me better qualified than anyone to work in that field.

"Just before she died, she told me why our arrival was no surprise to her. Her husband had disappeared into the mist for many weeks as you did, but more than once. He would return and then go again many times. Research, he called it, but she believed he became addicted to the exhilaration he felt as he cheated time again and again. She said he went slowly mad from his experiences and the constant time shifts, until he had difficulty remembering where he was. Eventually he disappeared for good, but not before he told her to expect us. I do not remember ever meeting him, but he told Lenore that a man and a young boy would come to the farm from the past and that she had to help us because we would be unable to help ourselves. She was worried that if she told me sooner I might have tried to go back. She had no idea where or when I would end up, and did not want to think of me suffering the way her husband did. When she died, she left everything jointly to Anthony and to me. The rest you know."

"Not really. I know you became a tutor on our course and screwed me over. I still don't know why." Melissa was still bitter about Victor's actions on her Master's course.

"Why? Because you were so brilliant and because I knew what would happen to you if you continued down your chosen path. And it was because Anthony adored you. He was prepared to give up everything if it meant being with you and I could not let him be nothing. I was not prepared to let you break his heart again, which I knew you would when you went back to my time." Victor began to cough and took a moment to catch his breath. "And I did it for myself. I believed that if I ruined your career before it started, you would never end up in Rome and we would not end up here. I thought that if I could change your future, perhaps I could change my past. Do not mistake me – it is not that I have had a bad life here, but I did not belong in your world any more than you belonged in mine. I wanted to go home."

"Didn't you realise that if I never went back, then neither would Rebecca? Anthony would not have been born so I couldn't have met him at university. I may not be an expert in the mechanics of time travel, but messing with our history that way could have had repercussions for more people than just the four of us." Melissa was shocked by what she had heard. If Victor had succeeded in changing his future, their lives would have unravelled, along with history as she knew it. She was beginning to feel as if all the time she had spent in the past trying to maintain the future had been irrelevant. She had helped to write that version of the past in the first place, with Victor being the one trying to destroy it by altering the present day.

"To begin with, I did not think of it, but perhaps it would have been better that way for all of us. Rebecca would still be alive if she had stayed here. She was young and beautiful and I loved her. She was much more than the woman you ever knew. She kept herself hidden from you because she hated you so much. I knew she could have had so much more here in this life and instead she suffered at the hands of some of the biggest bastards I ever knew. I wanted to save her. You do not know what could have been changed for the better."

"Or what could have become a lot worse. Rebecca could have ended up there alone without either of us to try and protect her. Curio and Antony would've had her that first night and probably killed her in the process. You are talking about playing God. What gave you that right?" Melissa was incensed at Victor's lack of judgement.

"What gave it to you?" he countered. "You did not know any more of Caesar's future than you read in a book, and that is what you used to save yourself. I cannot blame you for that, but what about me? I have read your books too, Lissa, and I am not in any of them. There is only one Vitruvius in any of those books in that library and he is not me. You knew nothing of me, yet you controlled my life, playing with me just like a god in one of those Greek poems you used to encourage me to read. You tried to control Mark Antony too, because you thought you saw a different man to the one history has portrayed, but Fortuna would not let you change the past concerning him any more than she would let me change your future. No matter what our actions, the end result is the same, Lissa. I began to realise that when Anthony announced his grand plan to get you back. You were the best thing that had ever happened to him in either life. He was lost without you and would have eventually destroyed himself, just as his father had and, I have to admit, I would have been lost without him. I had to help him get you here, so you could go back to the past and we could start this cycle again. Rebecca had to go back so he would be born. You had to go back to keep him and history safe. I always knew you would come back one day, but I did not know when. Fate wants you to be with Anthony. Why else did you come back to him when we came through almost thirty years ago? You are meant to be together here and now! Accept it. I have."

Melissa thought hard for a moment. She knew she loved Anthony, but there was a nagging doubt in her mind whether their life could ever go back to the way it had been. After all, she had been in his father's bed. Would he ever be able to forgive her for that? She changed the subject. "What about Anthony's amazing finds? They were around here, weren't they?"

"It was the money you and I buried along with your jewellery. I knew where it all was, and I steered him to it. There is still some money left, along with your lapis necklace. That too is buried on land that Anthony will own when I am gone. I have left the map of its location to you in my will. It is your property, Lissa, to do with as you please."

Melissa sat in silence remembering that beautiful necklace and the circumstances in which she had come to own it. It only confused her more, knowing that the man who had given it to her may have come to love her as much as his son did. Had her feelings for the son transferred to the father? Was he the one she really loved?

She changed the subject again and asked Victor another question. "Did you know that when you are gone, Anthony intends to tell the world the truth about his life and about what you did to me?"

"If you have ever loved him, you will not allow that to happen. More questions will be asked than either of you can answer. Then you will both be disgraced. Anthony has already proved he is his father's son in so many ways. Would you want him to be destroyed over the love of a woman, just as his father was?"

"Now who thinks he can tell the future?" Melissa tutted and shook her head.

"DO NOT BE SO STUPID!" Victor slammed his stick against the tiled floor in annoyance. "Think, Lissa! Someone will ask questions about your lives before this dig. Someone *will* ask about Rebecca and how will you explain her disappearance? It is only luck that she has no one who cares for her in this life. If she had any family it would be different, but luckily for you she does not. Who would believe that she died in the past, long before she was ever born? What is done is done. It cannot be changed. You have an exceptional brain, Lissa. Use it to keep yourself as safe now as you did two millennia ago. You promised Antonius' mother you would not let any harm come to him as long as you lived. Her lemur, or ghost as you call it, is always watching. She will hold you to that oath."

Melissa sat in silence, thinking about Rebecca. Victor was right. They could never explain her disappearance. If Rebecca's ghost was watching she would no doubt haunt Melissa for eternity if anything ever happened to her son. Victor was right about Anthony too. Victor may have stolen Melissa's work for his Master's, but the Doctorate was Anthony's own work. It was him she loved, not his father, and she loved him exactly the way he was.

It had always been Anthony she loved. Every day she had spent in Rome, it was the thought of him waiting for her that had kept her going. Every night, it had been him she had pretended was holding her. She could not bear to think of his reputation being ruined and all his past achievements becoming barely more than footnotes in modern texts. He had plenty of faults, but he was a better man than his father and he deserved a far better fate.

Somehow she and Victor had created a paradox. She was not sure whose actions had started it, but they were caught in a loop in time that seemed destined to repeat itself no matter what actions were taken to stop it. She too felt that fate had decided the outcome long before either of them had played their part. She only regretted that two innocent people had died as a result.

Melissa was distracted by a jeep turning into the drive and heading to the house. Anthony was back and she still had no idea what she was going to do. There was one final question she had time to ask. "How much does Anthony know?"

"He knows Rebecca was his mother. Beyond that he only knows that which directly concerns your disappearance." Victor rose out of the chair with some difficulty and steadied himself with his stick. "He knows nothing of who his father was or of your relationship with him. That is not my story to tell, Lissa. How much you tell him, is for you alone to decide."

Victor slowly walked along the veranda and back into the house as Anthony bounded up the steps and straight over to Melissa. He bent over and planted a kiss firmly on her lips. "Miss me?" he asked, smiling at her.

"More than you could ever know," she replied, returning his smile. She took his hand, pulling him down to sit next to her. Her demeanour became more serious. A relationship built on lies and deception was not worth having – Melissa knew that from her love-hate relationship with Mark Antony. His son deserved to hear the truth and all of it, no matter how much it might hurt both of them. Only then would they be able to move on with whatever direction their lives took.

She had made her decision and spoke out with a calmness she did not feel.

"Anthony," she said, "we really need to talk."

Authors Note: *The Mists of Time: Rubicon*

Mark Antony has fascinated me for many years. He is the stuff of legend: a fearsome warrior, an infamous lover, a loyal friend. His history was written, in the main, by men intent on belittling his achievements and emphasising his faults. That is something with which I can personally empathise, and is perhaps why I find him so interesting.

I have tried to keep to the historical facts as closely as possible in terms of events and timelines, though on occasion I admit I have used a little artistic licence to fit the events to my story. For example, it is a fact that Antony knew of the conspiracy to assassinate Caesar, but it is entirely my idea to take his involvement further than this. However, there is no record of him tormenting captives in the way described.

Until recently, finding books on Antony was not easy. However, in the past few years a number have been published. My particular favourites are those by Adrian Goldsworthy and Patricia Southern, which are both informative and eminently readable.

Over the years many people have played Mark Antony on stage and screen and for most people I dare say Richard Burton's portrayal in the 1963 movie CLEOPATRA is the epitome of Antony. Burton was undeniably one of the greatest actors ever to have lived and his performance was excellent, but I do not believe it accurately represents the man. In my personal opinion, the closest portrayal of what the real Antony may have been like was given by James Purefoy in the HBO series ROME. Purefoy's Antony displayed a cunning and vindictive side that we do not see in Shakespeare's interpretation of the facts. He gave us a man who was as intelligent as he was devious, with a good understanding of the politics necessary for his survival. His Antony had a delicious wickedness, making him the perfect bad boy we can all choose to love or hate. I have tried to replicate his fine portrayal in my Antony.

A number of people have given me support in writing this book and I would like to thank them all for their patience, assistance and advice. Suffice to say, they all know who they are, and know I could not have done this without any of them. Some people do deserve a special mention. Firstly, thanks to my agent, Owen Burnham, for never giving up even when I tried to; secondly, to Maria Smith at The Booksmith, for liking my work enough to offer me a publishing deal; and then to Sheila Mackie, my editor, who has far more faith in me than I have ever had; to Giacomo, for proofing the same chapters over and over (you can read the whole book now!); to Caroline and Sonia, for much needed moral support; to my husband, Richard, for ignoring the continual typing and the general lack of housework (you are a man who deserves better); and to my best friend, Mark, for everything else.

Lastly, I must say a personal word of thanks to James Purefoy. I doubt he remembers it, but he took the time to show an interest in the work of a complete stranger. I felt extremely honoured to speak to him, and that he agreed to let me mention him in this book. He gave me the inspiration to write, and that is why I have dedicated this work to him.

About the Author

Linda Coleman is an author of historical fiction novels. Born in Chatham in Kent, her interest in the Roman period was sparked by a school trip to Lullingstone Roman Villa. This interest was fostered during her time at Chatham Grammar School, where she studied the Classics. After joining the Civil Service at seventeen, she has since carved out a successful career in administration in both the public and private sectors. Writing is her hobby. She now lives in Wiltshire with her husband.

Made in the USA
Charleston, SC
19 March 2016